The Prote<

Patriarcn

A vampire sworn to protect the secret existence of his people risks everything to save a human child — and love a mortal woman.

Tracking him to a Paducah bar, Protector Aiden Marschant must stop the rogue vampire's mayhem before he betrays the secret of the Shanrak people. When the rogue strikes again, Aiden finds the victim's infant daughter in her car. Unable to expose his identity to surrender the child to human authorities, and unwilling to let her fend for herself, he makes the ultimate mistake of taking the baby home with him.

Questioning witnesses at the bar, rookie county sheriff's deputy Shanna Preston learns of two men, possible suspects in the young woman's murder. When the FBI takes over the case, Shanna's determined to help bring down this vicious killer.

Aiden must find someone to care for the human child before she awakens in him a fatherly instinct that could bring on the forbidden *bloodlust* mating urge. He sets his sights on lovely redheaded Deputy Shanna Preston. But Shanna suspects he's guilty of kidnapping and fears he may be involved in murder. Can Aiden keep his cool around Deputy Preston long enough to stop the dangerous killer? Can Shanna survive the affections of Protector Aiden Marschant and live to tell about it?

The Protectorate

Patriarch

Licensed and Produced through
Penumbra Publishing
www.PenumbraPublishing.com

Previously published electronically Sept. 2006 by New Concepts Publishing ISBN 1586089536

~Author Preface/Acknowledgement~

This vampire romance is the first installment in a planned series. I've taken license with the usual vampire lore (no reflection in mirrors, incineration in sunlight, etc.) to fit the needs of this storyline. Due to sexual and violent content, this book is intended for adult readers.

I must express gratitude to friends, family, and fellow authors too numerous to name, for their time and effort in helping with the development and promotion of this story. You know who you are — thank you!

In particular I'd like to thank C. Fern Cook for her continued camaraderie, and my husband, whose support and understanding help make my writing possible. Any errors are strictly my own.

Happy reading...

Dana Warryck

The Protectorate

Patriarch

Paranormal Vampire Romance

by

Dana Warryck

CHAPTER 1

Aiden Marschant sat motionless in a darkened corner booth at Smokey Joe's Roadhouse, trying to ignore the stench of stale beer and burnt barbeque. The dirty wood plank floor beneath his boots vibrated with karaoke country music. He glowered at the stage twenty feet away as the crowd howled and booed at a fat drunk in slouching jeans slobbering on the mike while wailing off-tune like a bobcat caught in a bear trap. Aiden tuned out the noise and focused his attention on a young woman seated at the bar.

Pretty, with cascading brown curls and a ready smile, she wore a low-cut stretchy pink shirt and skin-tight jeans. She flirted skillfully, but Aiden knew she was out of her element, seated next to Cameron Ryben doing his best imitation of a smooth one-night stand. She had no idea what Cam Ryben *really* wanted.

Aiden scowled at the handsome blond man of medium build. Ryben fancied himself a slick predator above the laws of their people. A gifted amateur, he had received some training within the Protectorate until he'd dropped out of the program. Later he had gone rogue. Now he was nothing more than a rutting animal letting his bloodlust run rampant as he mauled his way through humanity, leaving a trail of dead bodies like a crazed grizzly. Aiden had tracked him across four states, catching up to him in this grungy backwoods roadhouse outside Paducah, Kentucky.

Ryben glanced around, as if sensing he was being watched. Aiden eased out of sight until Ryben relaxed and turned back to his mark to whisper something in her ear. She squirmed on her barstool and giggled, then stood unsteadily. Ryben took her by the arm and guided her to the door.

Aiden followed at a discreet distance until a huge mound of a woman with stringy brown hair stumbled up from her chair and blocked his path. Poured into jeans and a tee shirt big enough to make a circus tent, she yelled obscenities at a beefy, red-bearded man seated at her table. Aiden dodged the woman as she staggered against a nearby table, raising protests from patrons whose drinks threatened to tip over. Her equally inebriated companion lunged at Aiden and roared, "Watch it, asshole!" Aiden shoved past the couple and barged outside.

Leaping off the wooden front porch into the cool spring night, he let the heavy plank door slammed shut behind him, muffling the music still reverberating inside. Frogs chirped in the foggy distance as he darted along haphazard rows of beat-up cars and pickups parked out front. He couldn't see Ryben or the girl anywhere. Stopping, he stilled his anxiousness and opened his mind to get a fix on Ryben. Immediately a sickening wave of hunger and lust washed over him like a blast of hot water. The scent of warm blood saturated the air, and the amphibian concert stopped. *He'd screwed up. He was too late!*

Running to the parking lot at the back of the building, he spotted a car with the dome light on. He found the girl sprawled on the gravel like a discarded rag doll, her head twisted aside, and a jagged hole torn in her throat. Her pink top glistened dark red as blood gushed and pooled around her. Aiden snorted at the cloying smell of death, careful not to inhale deeply.

The keys still dangled from the driver's door of the car. Aiden assumed the car belonged to the murdered girl. With the front and rear doors hanging open, the car's dome light glowed like a macabre nightlight on the bloodshed. Ryben, in his usual fashion, had ripped open his victim's throat. But he must have sensed he was being tracked — he'd fled without fulfilling his sexual urges and feasting on the spoils. Aiden knew he'd kill again before the night was done. Cursing, he opened his mind and scanned the area, but sensed Ryben was gone.

Hearing voices, Aiden glanced back at the roadhouse and saw two men approaching in the neon-illuminated fog. He couldn't afford to be seen near this body. Wrapping himself in calm, he assumed the mental cloak of near invisibility that allowed him to move unnoticed among humans. The men didn't look his way.

He turned to leave, but stopped when a faint sound like a kitten's mew came from the rear seat of the car. He glanced at the two men coming closer, then ducked down to peer inside, avoiding the bloody handprints smeared across the top edge of the door opening.

He froze and sucked in a swift breath. *Sweet Mother Earth!* The bundle strapped in a car seat, a silken-haired cherub wearing a pink sleeper, yawned with her plump arms askew.

Straightening in shock, Aiden glanced at the two men opening the doors of a pickup five cars down. They didn't seem to notice anything amiss but, with his concentration shaken, he couldn't be sure they hadn't spotted him.

He wanted to turn and walk away, but the baby inside the car whined. How could he leave? If he'd been more attentive, he might have prevented her mother's murder. Still, he couldn't stick around and get involved unless Ryben was lurking in the area with his urges dampened, waiting for the opportunity to strike again. Could the child be in danger from him? The bloody handprints smudging the roof and doorframe suggested Ryben had noticed her. Perhaps he would have drained her blood too, if he'd had the time.

Aiden grimaced and dared another look inside the car. The baby sat alone, defenseless, strapped in her car seat, with no one to protect her.

I am a Protector.

He shook his head and straightened. Humans had their own government agencies to handle these situations and would place the child with relatives or other proper guardians. He had no business taking responsibility for this tiny human. He wasn't equipped for such things. His life had no room for a baby.

He turned to the sound of an engine starting. The men in the truck drove out of the parking lot. The roadhouse's neon sign blinked like a beacon in the mist. He glanced down at the body lying in the pool of blood spreading near his feet. He couldn't afford to be caught standing over a dead woman, or stick around to answer questions from the police and destroy the anonymity required for his work.

He looked at the building again, figuring someone would find the victim and report her murder. But how long before they did? In the meantime, what would become of the baby? He couldn't very well leave her sitting in the car, unattended for hours.

Yes, you can. It's not your responsibility or your duty.

He shook his head again. *But I'm a Protector!*

The frogs resumed their rhythmic song. A coyote yipped in

the distance, and a chorus joined in, seeming to surround him. Aiden swiped a hand across his mouth. The child cried out, and the sound tugged at something inside him he hadn't realized was there — something he'd worked all his life to ensure would never be there. Obviously his efforts had gone unrewarded. He felt that twinge of compassion twisting in his chest. He knew what he must do.

Oh, hell.

He took a handkerchief from his leather jacket and, careful to avoid brushing against the bloodied doorframe, leaned inside the back of the car. Wrestling with the seat belt strung through the baby's carrier, he tried not to leave fingerprints as a clue that might link him with this murder-kidnapping.

Murder? Kidnapping?

He hadn't murdered the woman, and this wasn't kidnapping. He was just taking the baby for safekeeping. As soon as he could, he'd make sure she was placed with the proper human authorities.

The baby fidgeted and looked up at him, running her chubby fingers across his hair dangling in front of her. He glanced at her wide blue eyes full of curious, trusting innocence, then reached for the car seat. His hands froze mid-motion. If this wasn't kidnapping, what was it? Who was he trying to fool?

When he withdrew, the child screwed up her rosy face and whimpered. Was she hungry? Wet? He touched her cheek and found her hot, almost feverish. Was she sick? Good grief, he didn't know anything about taking care of a baby! And Noel and Marta wouldn't appreciate having the responsibility dumped on them. That would be like asking two Rottweilers to baby-sit. What was he thinking?

As he reached to refasten the seat belt and leave the child just as he found her, she grabbed his index finger. His insides melted, and he let himself smile. "You're in a lot of trouble, little one, but you have no idea, do you?" His smile turned to a frown when he wondered what would happen to this baby inside Kentucky's state child welfare system, assuming she survived long enough to be shunted into it. He didn't want to think about that.

The waif cried louder. He looked over his shoulder, hoping the music filtering outside the roadhouse would drown out her caterwauling. If only he could go back to the bar and report the murder without getting himself involved ... but he couldn't. *Damn it!*

You're a Protector. You do what must be done.

In a blinding flash, he grabbed the car seat, the diaper bag, and a stuffed pink rabbit no bigger than his fist. With the baby in her seat tucked securely under his arm, and her bag straps draped over his wrist, he backed out of the car. Catching sight of the bloody wallet lying near the woman's body, he ducked down and used his handkerchief to retrieve it. Maybe later he could find some information inside to help him locate the baby's nearest relatives.

Hugging his newfound charge close to his chest, he paced toward the line of trees glistening in the misty darkness beyond the parking lot. At the edge of the trees his dark blue rental sedan waited. He unlocked the doors, stowed the baby in the back seat and secured her, then dived for the driver's seat. Starting the car, he resisted the urge to peel out of the parking lot in a fast getaway.

The baby wailed, and he met her anguished gaze in the rearview mirror. "Hush, little one. You'll be all right." She calmed at the sound of his voice — an effect he could induce at will. He smiled, shook his head, then frowned. "You'll be all right, but will I? Right now, I'm having serious doubts."

* * * * *

At 2:17 a.m., County Sheriff's Deputy Shanna Preston eyed Darryl Goggins, the bartender on duty at Smokey Joe's Roadhouse when the murder had occurred. Skinny and scruffy, he wore a sleeveless black tee shirt with a Goth band emblem emblazoned across the chest — a skull and scythe. She wondered about his drug of choice. Meth? Judging by the way his eyes had sunk into their sockets and his teeth had turned askew, she figured that was it. A damned semi-rural epidemic.

Despite his suspected drugged-out state, he'd given a solid description of the man who'd left with nineteen-year-old Melody Jean Hanks just before she'd been killed. Medium build, height about six feet tall. Wavy, shoulder-length, honey-blond hair. Dark eyes, maybe brown. No visible scars. Good looking, "if you're into guys," which the bartender assured her he was not.

She snapped her report pad shut. "Okay, Mr. Goggins. If you remember anything else, be sure to give me a call." She handed him a business card, a precious commodity she'd fought hard to get ... like the respect of her peers. She stifled a sneer.

Back at the station the men treated her as a joke — too new to know anything about *real* police work, and too young and pretty to be a deputy for the McCracken County Sheriff's Department. They judged her by her petite package, but they didn't know her at all. She wagered she could outshoot any of them, and she knew some special moves that would help her kick their strutting, good-ol'-boy asses in a fair fight. She would change her situation one step at a time, and doing her job well was part of that plan.

But sometimes doing a good job was more difficult than she expected, especially when she felt like gagging. It wasn't that she'd never seen a dead body before. Having to identify her parents after their car accident was the worst nightmare she could possibly imagine. But when she and Deputy Jake Fenshaw took a look at Miss Hanks' body, she was lucky not to toss her cookies. She suspected a coyote had wandered over to the body and eaten away part of the throat before the two customers leaving the bar had discovered it. But Jake had insisted with a gleam in his eyes that this was the work of the infamous serial killer dubbed by the media as the *Bloodsucker*, wanted in four states for the gruesome murders of over forty women in the past two months.

She couldn't deny Melody Hanks' murder bore garish similarities to the MO of the Bloodsucker. The possibility that the murderer had relocated his operation to Paducah made Shanna a teensy bit leery of stepping outside alone in the dark.

"Well, there was somethin' else," Goggins volunteered after a moment, bringing Shanna back from her musing. "I mean, somebody else who kinda caught my attention."

Shanna flipped open her report pad and prepared to jot down additional notes. No telling what tiny detail might become important later. "Go on, Mr. Goggins," she urged in a friendly tone, chastising herself for letting Jake pull her chain about some insane serial killer. Why would he come to Paducah? She winced inwardly when the answer echoed in her mind ... why wouldn't he? There were plenty of potential victims available here, just like any other small city embedded in a rural area. Maybe he thought the police force wouldn't be prepared to handle his antics. And he maybe he was right.

"Well, it was probably nothin'," Goggins mumbled. "But there was this other guy..."

Shanna zeroed her eyes on him. "At the bar?"

Goggins shook his head of drab, scraggly dishwater-blond hair. "Nope. He just sort of appeared all of a sudden, out on the floor, in the middle of the tables. I didn't remember seein' him until that blond dude was walkin' out the door with the girl that got killed."

"Why did this second man catch your attention?"

"He looked like he was in a hurry. You know, like he was followin' the guy and the girl." Goggins shrugged his bony shoulders. "At least that's what it seemed like. He bumped into some folks at a table, and they raised a ruckus. Then he rushed out."

Shanna warmed with excitement. Another possible lead. "Could you describe this man?"

Goggins shrugged again. "It was kinda dark, and I didn't get a good look at him. But he was tall. Like over six feet. He had really long, dark hair, and a black leather jacket."

"Motorcycle jacket?"

"Longer. More like an overcoat. About knee-length."

Shanna smiled. A better description than she'd expected. "Anything else?"

Goggins shook his head.

"Okay. Thanks for your cooperation, Mr. Goggins. We may want to contact you again later."

He grinned. "Sure thing — if it's you doin' the contactin'."

Smiling evenly, Shanna ignored the heavy hint and closed her pad. She turned to Deputy Fenshaw interviewing a couple sitting at a nearby table. He towered over them, big and imposing with his shaved head and holstered sidearm. Everybody in the bar seemed very cooperative — probably hoping they wouldn't get tagged with a DUI on the way home.

Jake closed his pad and strolled toward her. "All done here, Preston?"

Shanna nodded. "The bartender gave me the names of two regulars who left just after the victim and her escort. He also mentioned another possible suspect and gave me a description."

"Okay," Jake said. "We'll question the regulars later. I think the meat truck just left, so I guess the coroner's finished. Let's go back outside and see how they're wrapping things up."

When Shanna followed Jake out the door, he said, "Whoa, looks like we got company." She looked around him, annoyed to see a dark-colored, late-model government-issue sedan parked askew in the lot near the victim's car. When she spied the suits swarming around like locusts, she figured the Department of Criminal Investigations was on the job. Her enthusiasm for the case faded.

She knew the drill. DCI, created by Attorney General Jack Conway through executive order to replace the Kentucky Bureau of Investigation, the commonwealth's counterpart of the FBI, would take over from here. DCI officers were supposed to provide investigative support for local authorities, but they wouldn't appreciate the help of lowly sheriff's deputies. They'd take the information she and Jake had gathered and then dismiss them as bumbling amateurs.

Damn! This was their case, their turf, and she had as much right as anyone else to help catch the bastard who did this. But she knew she'd never get the chance. Single and permanently relegated to the night shift, all she'd ever handle were domestic-disturbance interventions, Saturday night DUI roadblocks, and emergency traffic calls. She knew she was capable of more — so much more.

"I'll go see what's going on," Jake announced. "You might as well go on home, Preston. Your shift was over an hours ago. We'll touch base tomorrow."

Jake had several years of seniority on her, and she knew arguing with him to stay put wouldn't accomplish anything. "Yeah, whatever. 'Night." She sighed, shaking her head as she walked to her patrol car.

She felt for the victim's family, knowing what it meant to lose loved ones to violent death. She wanted to be more than just a shadow doing cleanup work in the background. But what else could she do? No one could change what had happened here tonight. The only way she'd be of service to herself, the victim's family, and the community was to help take down this vicious animal and make sure he didn't kill again. Somehow she had to stay on this case, whether DCI liked it or not.

As far as she knew the Sheriff's Department was entitled to provide a representative to interface with DCI on this case. She just hoped she could convince Sheriff Grainger she was worthy of the job.

And maybe, for once, he'd give her a break and let her choose her own assignment — one that could actually mean something for a change.

Yeah, right. Fat chance. She'd have a better luck getting hit by lightning in a snowstorm. Still, she had to try.

She unlocked her patrol car, then stopped to look around at the trees towering in the damp mist. Shaking off the edginess tightening her shoulders, she slid in behind the wheel and shut the door. She'd talk to Grainger tomorrow, as soon as the morning shift started.

CHAPTER 2

"Oh, bloody hell, Aiden! Why'd ye have to go and do a fool thing like bringin' a human's baby home with ye? Nothin' good'll come of it, I'll tell ye that right now."

Leaning against the granite counter in the kitchen, Aiden eyed Noel, his vassal for more years than he cared to count. Noel swiped a gnarled hand through his wild shock of white hair and shook his head in obvious disgust. Aiden took a deep breath and glanced aside at the child sitting attentively in her car seat on the counter. "I didn't have a choice."

"Of course ye had a choice, man! Ye could've left the little bugger right where she was! It's not for us to be takin' in human strays. Ye can't tame 'em, ye can't train 'em, and ye sure as hell can't keep 'em. They're neither fit pets nor good companions, and ye know that!"

Aiden slid a hand beneath his curtain of hair to rub the back of his taut neck. Noel was right. He knew he was right. When he held the baby or just looked at her, he felt a frightening warm, soft twinge in his chest. It was an unfamiliar sensation he didn't know how to handle.

The stringy old man rambled across the tiled kitchen floor and faced him. "I could understand if ye had a touch of the bloodlust, and it was a woman ye was bringin' to the house. But a baby? What in bloody hell are we to do with a baby?"

Aiden folded his arms across his chest and shook his head. He had no answer for Noel's legitimate concern.

"Mayhap ye wasn't thinkin' straight. And, by the way, what the hell *was* ye thinkin'?"

Shrugging, Aiden swiped a hand over his face. He knew he had to protect the child. That was the only urgent thought in his mind, and it alone had spurred him to take her away from the scene of her mother's murder.

"Mayhap it was the bloodlust workin' its neediness on ye. The lure of fatherhood can be very strong when there's a little one around. Get's a fella thinkin' what he might be missin', not havin' a wife 'n' all."

Aiden scowled. "I have no desire for fatherhood, and I have completely sublimated all urges of bloodlust."

"But if the bloodlust took hold of ye, would ye even recognize the signs, seein' how it's been so long since ye last trained for it?"

"I know the signs and have experienced none of them."

Noel grunted. "Still, it's an urge most of us suffer, and Masters have it the worst. To ignore it goes against the grain. Considerin' all ye've given up, surely the Enclave would overlook one time of backslidin' —"

"I am a *Protector*," Aiden growled, shoving away from the counter. "As such, I've sworn never to take a mate. I have never yielded to the bloodlust and don't intend to start now."

"Well, mayhap ye don't intend to, but ye've had to fight the urge a long time without a proper outlet. Excuse me for speakin' ill of the Enclave's rules, for they surely do think they know better, but I still say it's not natural."

Noel rubbed his chin, scruffy with white stubbles, and narrowed his eyes. "Supposin' ye did have a wee slip-up? Once ye was done with yer mark, one glance from ye, and she'd forget all that happened."

Perking one eyebrow, Aiden gave his vassal a sharp warning glare. "I hope you're not suggesting I find some hapless human woman and *relieve* myself." The release of control even once could open a floodgate he might never be able to close. After going so long without appeasing the urge, he could end up worse off than rabid Cameron Ryben. Then who would put *him* down?

Noel gave him a sideways glance and shrugged. "I wasn't suggestin' anythin'. But supposin' somethin' unforeseen happened, and ye was overcome by the urge? Takin' a human woman would be one way to curb it for a time. All I'm sayin' is, perhaps ye should ... make arrangements. Just in case. Find yerself a likely —"

"No."

"But —"

"The subject is not open for further discussion."

"Well, I just thought..."

When Noel's objections sputtered to a halt, Aiden turned his attention to the baby. "The only concern now is the child's safety. Cam Ryben might have killed her too if I hadn't been there."

"Ye would've been better off lettin' him have her," Noel mumbled.

Aiden turned on his faithful servant and scowled at that appalling statement.

"I'm just sayin' a Protector hidin' a human baby won't go well with the Enclave. She'll bring nothin' but trouble down on us if they discover—"

"The Enclave doesn't need to know. Just take care of her."

"Like bloody hell I'll take care of her! Are ye daft? We should cart the waif off to the nearest church doorstep straight away and be rid of her!"

"We'll do nothing of the sort, Noel Eugene Montgomery," Marta announced as she breezed into the kitchen with her usual commanding scowl, board-stiff posture, and sleek gray hair pulled back in a tight bun at her nape. "And you'll cease that yelling right now. You're frightening the child."

When she shot Aiden a scorching glare, he stepped out of her way. She took the baby in her arms and turned on him, ordering, "And you, Master Aiden, will not pass off this duty to us. We are your sworn servants and will aid you in whatever tasks you deem necessary. But you brought the child here, and you must take charge of her care for the short time she'll be here." She thrust the baby at him. "She needs a bath and a fresh diaper."

Aiden backed away. "I know nothing about—"

"You will learn."

Stumbling against the table behind him, Aiden couldn't escape as Marta pressed the baby into his arms. He dangled the child, keeping her at a distance when he got a whiff of the unpleasant odor emanating from her. She whined with uncertainty.

"Bring her over to the sink," Marta ordered. "I've laid out towels and cloths. You'll need some disposable wipes to clean her up before you put her in the bathwater. I saw a packet in the diaper bag. Fetch it, Noel."

Noel hopped to attention as Aiden followed Marta's instructions. Still holding the child at arm's length, Aiden eyed her with wariness. In the line of duty he had been forced to bring down many a rogue in bloody battles, but this chore, he feared, would make his previous deadly exploits seem tame in comparison. "I'll see about making alternate arrangements for the child as soon as possible," he mumbled.

Marta frowned. "Yes, I trust you will, Master Aiden."

* * * * *

Ensconced naked in his plush king-size bed under the soft glow of the bedside lamp, Aiden propped himself up on an elbow and glanced at his closed door. The baby's squalling protests still echoed in his mind, making him cringe. Finally, after the fiasco of the dirty diaper and the slick-as-a-greased-piglet bath in the kitchen sink, the two-story house stood quiet. Across the hall in a room he used for storage, the baby slept in a makeshift crib fashioned from a large, open-top cardboard box filled with extra pillows and bedding.

The baby. Her name was Jewel Ann Hanks, and she was nine months old. He knew that after searching her dead mother's wallet and finding various pictures with her name and photo dates written on the back. Her birthdate handwritten on the back of the earliest picture showing Jewel Ann as a newborn gave him the clue he needed to calculate her age.

He also knew Melody Jean Hanks' legal address, according to her driver's license, which might come in handy if the address was still valid. Jewel Ann needed fresh clothes and food, and any other useful supplies they might find. They could of course purchase what they needed, but Aiden wondered if Jewel Ann might be attached to specific toys at home.

He lay back against his pillows and stared up at the soft shadows cast about the trey ceiling. Marta and Noel had retired for the remainder of the night, of which there wasn't much left. In another few hours, daylight would break the somber peace of darkness, and the human world would come alive with its usual hustle and bustle. This he knew without consulting a clock. Subtle signs from his body told him.

But his body didn't warn him that he would rest little with a baby in the house. That news came in the form of a piercing shriek. He tossed back the covers and lurched from bed, stepping into his discarded silk boxers as he raced for the door.

Bursting into the baby's temporary quarters, he rushed to the box crib and peered down, afraid he'd find little Jewel Ann smothering or otherwise suffering.

When she saw him, she whimpered and reached for him. He lifted her out of the box and held her sleeper-clad little body against his naked chest. "This is not a fit bed for you, is it, my princess?" She wrapped her chubby arms around his neck, crushing his dark tresses in her tiny fingers. He hugged her and bounced her gently, breathing in her soft, powdery scent — a definite improvement over her pre-bath state. "I suppose you'll just have to stay in my room until we can find you more suitable sleeping accommodations."

Still jostling her in his arms, he turned to find Marta and Noel in their robes, standing in the doorway, glowering at him. He held up a hand. "Everything's fine. Go back to bed."

As he walked toward his bedroom, they parted to let him pass. Laying Jewel Ann down in his bed, he tucked the comforter up to her plump chin. "There. How's that? Comfy now?"

He looked up to find Marta and Noel standing in his doorway, watching him with keen interest. Not liking the puzzled frowns they wore, he shooed them off with a swish of his hand. "To bed with you. I'm handling this."

Finally Noel turned with a snort and grumbled under his breath, "Blasted baby'll wreck everything. Best get rid of her now. Make a stew of her. There's the ticket."

Marta gave her mate a parting smack on the back, then scowled at Aiden from the doorway. "He's right, you know. That baby's going to turn everything topsy-turvy. You, your emotions, your duties as a Protector. There's a killer on the loose, and look at you, doting like a proud father. You don't have time for this. And who knows what other emotions her presence will awaken in you? You can't afford to lose your focus and your self-control, Aiden. She has to go. As sweet as she is, you can't keep her."

Aiden grimaced and climbed into bed beside the baby, who turned and smiled at him. He warmed with an unsettling giddy feeling and tweaked her cheek. When he looked up, he found Marta still staring him down. He reached for the bedside lamp. "I said I'd take care of it."

"See that you do, Aiden. And quickly."

With the light off, he heard Marta shuffle away. Taking the baby in his arms, he felt the cozy heat of her tiny body permeate his skin and warm his chest, making him aware of the emptiness there. He'd felt that cold hollowness for so long, he hadn't realized it was a space waiting to be filled. *Filled with what?*

He sighed and closed his eyes. He didn't want to think about it right now. He just wanted to rest. When morning came, he'd deal with what had to be done.

* * * * *

At 9:15 a.m., Deputy Shanna Preston stood in the hallway outside the county's basement morgue. Turns out, DCI didn't get to handle the Bloodsucker murder at Smokey Joe's for long. The FBI was quick to step in and take over. They'd wasted no time setting up a task force to include liaisons from DCI and local law enforcement, including the sheriff's department. Apparently they wanted to catch that bastard serial killer bad enough that they went against the normal grain to include others in their efforts, and presumably share their information. Perhaps their 'need to know' approach would be taking a back seat in this investigation.

She should have been ecstatic that, at her adamant request, Sheriff Grainger had assigned her as a liaison to the FBI's task force — like Grainger actually believed they'd let her help. She knew the real reason she'd been given this assignment. Grainger, the fat bastard, had already assigned a detective from the department, in the same breath stating the task force was a waste of time. If they hadn't caught the killer after forty-some murders, he'd grumbled, they never would. He just wanted her to get up early and run around as the FBI's lackey after spending half the night investigating the murder of Melody Hanks. What did Grainger care if she was used to sleeping during the day and would have to change her schedule? As long as she was out of the office and off his duty roster, he was tickled pink. With a grimace, she reminded herself she'd asked for it, and he'd gladly given her the assignment. She had no one to blame but herself.

Scowling over her own arrogant stupidity, Shanna looked up when she heard the clacking of FBI Agent Victoria Reissenor's sensible dress pumps accompanied by the listless shuffle of house slippers. Tall, and thin, Agent Reissenor wore a business-like frown on a narrow face framed by straight blonde hair pulled back with a barrette at her nape. Attired in a smart pinstripe jacket and matching skirt, she escorted Crystal Hanks to identify the body of her daughter Melody.

According to the records Shanna had been allowed to review, Mrs. Hanks was forty-five, but she looked seventy with her gray, frazzled hair and dumpy, overweight body devoid of any detectible muscle tone. Her suspected affiliation with known drug dealers, including one who was currently listed as her live-in boyfriend, could possibly explain her lackluster appearance.

Mrs. Hanks cringed with a sob and staggered, letting Agent Reissenor support her by grabbing her arm. "Why would anybody wanna hurt my sweet Melody?" she wailed. "And my grandbaby! Why would they take an innocent little child?"

Shanna stared at the floor, wondering the same thing. She didn't want to think of the child's fate after seeing the condition of the mother's body. She'd learned from Agent Reissenor's brief review of the FBI's ongoing investigation that Melody Hanks' murder was the second most recent in a string of killings spanning four states from Minnesota to Kentucky over a two-month period.

Forty-three deaths so far, with the same MO. The victims were all women in their early twenties to late forties, sexually molested before, during, or sometimes after the throat was torn open. Evidence of teeth marks showed a bite pattern identifiable as human, but the canines were unnaturally oversized. Most of the bodies were left drained of blood. With a jugular wound, the body would pump itself dry, but the estimated volume of blood left at the murder scenes rarely matched what would be expected. At each scene, several pints remained unaccounted for. Consumed, carried off, who could be sure? With bite marks, it was easy to assume the killer ingested a certain amount of his victims' blood — and the unfortunate leak of that information to the media prompted his highly publicized nickname, the Bloodsucker.

Semen, saliva, and hair samples — even some skin and blood found under some victims' fingernails — should have made DNA typing of the killer easy. But the crime lab still had difficulty detailing the culprit beyond his blond hair and Caucasian skin. From insufficient blood samples they deduced the killer possibly had a problem with his hemoglobin. A preliminary analysis suggested his blood suffered a mutation that made him chronically anemic. More precise genetic data was needed to confirm the hypothesis. That information was kept from the media. It was bad enough they were slinging the name Bloodsucker around. Nicknaming the killer with that ridiculous moniker gave him a comic-book aura that cheapened the devastation of the murders he'd committed.

Shanna looked up as Agent Reissenor passed in front of her with Mrs. Hanks. What had made Melody Hanks a target for murder? Maybe she was just at the wrong place at the wrong time. At first pass it could have seemed like a random incident, or the result of a copycat killer. Melody hadn't been molested. The blood at the crime scene matched the expected volume, so presumably the killer hadn't consumed or carried off any, like in previous murders. But everything else added up — the sighting of a blond-haired suspect combing the sleazy bar for his next mark, the jugular wound, the teeth marks. Shanna bet it was the same killer, and apparently so did the FBI. The only difference in this and previous murders, according to Agent Reissenor, was the killer apparently had been interrupted — perhaps by the unidentified dark-haired man in the leather coat. The bartender at Smokey Joe's Roadhouse said the dark-haired man had rushed out after Melody and her escort. Had he somehow guessed what was going to happen and tried to stop it? Or was he an accomplice?

The metal door to the morgue clanged shut, and Shanna cringed, forbidding herself to recall the details of her own trip to the morgue to identify her parents more than a year ago. She knew what Mrs. Hanks was going through, but she didn't want to empathize too much and lose her detached professionalism. She couldn't afford to appear too emotional in front of peers. Shaking off her defeatist fears, she almost reached a state of calm until she heard Mrs. Hanks scream in despair. A second later, Agent Reissenor ducked her head out the door and waved a dollar bill. "Get a soda. She's collapsed."

Shanna rushed down the hall to a small cantina of vending

machines she'd scoped out earlier. The dollar changer was empty, so she fished in her pockets for enough loose change to buy a soft drink.

Hurrying back to the morgue door, she opened it and saw Agent Reissenor crouched on the concrete floor, motioning her inside. She closed the door, ignoring the pungent chemical odor as she glanced at the white sheet draped over the human-shaped form on the metal gurney. She gulped several times and glanced away from the drain under the gurney as she stepped forward with the drink can.

Agent Reissenor and the medical examiner, a plump balding man in a white coat, tried to help Mrs. Hanks stand up. Finally they wrestled her to a nearby straight-back metal chair next to the sickly green metal desk parked against the far wall. Shanna handed over the soda, then stepped back a respectful distance, staring at her black polished shoes while Mrs. Hanks moaned and sobbed to the point of hyperventilating.

Once Agent Reissenor forced the woman to take a few swallows of the soda, her sobbing subsided. Trembling with weakness or rage — Shanna wasn't sure which — Mrs. Hanks demanded, "I don't care what you have to do, get the bastard that did this to my poor Melody. And find my grandbaby."

* * * * *

Shanna thought about having lunch with Agent Reissenor and her partner, Agent Roger Norris, but after spending the morning in the morgue, she decided she needed a little quiet time to herself. Driving her patrol car down Route 62, she arrived at Lady Mae's Café, a mom-and-pop diner she'd discovered on her routine patrols of the area. With its roadside ambience — gravel lot, country floral wallpaper, and Formica tables — the little restaurant offered a good opportunity to hide out unobserved. Shanna just needed some time to herself, to think and unwind a little.

At 11:10, she'd managed to beat the main lunch rush of regulars patronizing Lady Mae's. A slender, smiling, middle-aged woman with the nametag *Nora* came and took her drink order — coffee, black. Shanna couldn't concentrate on the menu enough to consider what food she might be able to keep down. She sighed and rubbed her forehead as Nora left.

"Mind if I join you?"

Shanna frowned, curious about the smooth baritone voice daring to interrupt her solitude. When she glanced up and caught sight of the long black leather coat, she lurched and reached for her gun.

"You're perfectly safe," the male voice assured as the coat — and its owner — slid into the booth seat opposite her. She looked up and met the most amazing green eyes she'd ever seen. She froze, then went limp. Her hand slid harmlessly to her lap.

"You helped investigate the murder at the bar last night," her uninvited guest said. It was a statement, not a question.

Shanna wanted to ask how he knew that, but the tingling numbness cascading through her body as she appraised the gorgeous man before her kept her mouth from forming words. His thick, almost black mane shone with dazzling auburn highlights and billowed about his aristocratic face and broad shoulders as if possessing a life of its own. His light golden skin shimmered with an inner glow, like hand-rubbed marble. Dark lashes rimmed sparkling emerald cat eyes that assessed her with the arrogance of a sheik inspecting a new harem slave. His long, straight nose led to lush, expressive lips that spread in a smile as he whispered, "Like what you see, deputy?"

She scowled, managing to break free of his odd spell. "You were seen leaving the bar moments before the murder. You're wanted for questioning in connection with the death of Melody Hanks, and the kidnapping of her infant daughter. The FBI's put a BOLO out on you."

A sexy quirk to his luscious lips made look as if he were almost smiling. "I saw it on the news. But it's highly unlikely anyone will ID me from that vague description and the terrible likeness the police sketch artist rendered." He huffed and toyed with the bright red-dyed carnation sitting in a bud vase on the table between them. He seemed disappointed his gorgeous likeness hadn't been captured better.

Shanna sat there, staring at him with her mouth open. He didn't act worried, and that worried *her*. "I'm duty-bound to bring you in."

"Yes, I suppose you are." He sat back against the booth seat with a sigh. "But first, could we talk and perhaps have a bite of lunch?"

She glared at him, unable to come up with a suitable retort to his audacity.

He held up an elegant, powerful hand. "I promise not to make trouble or to try to elude you. I simply want to talk."

She shook her head as she eyed him in amazement. "How did you know I was connected with the case?"

He shrugged and clasped his hands together on the tabletop. "I saw you converse with two individuals possessing the general appearance and demeanor of government investigators. It's no secret the FBI is tracking what they believe is a common serial killer. When you left the morgue parking lot in your patrol car, I followed you here." He shrugged again and lifted his hands, as if to suggest the deduction had been mind-numbingly simple.

She leaned forward, bracing herself against the table with her hands. "You were casing the morgue?"

He shrugged again.

She sat back with a huff, thinking she should cuff him right now and drag his handsome ass in for questioning. But something told her she'd find out more about this case if she let him have his way for a while and *talk* as he said he wanted. "What's your connection with this case, Mr. —"

"Marsh. Aiden Marsh. You may call me Aiden."

She smirked. "And I suppose that's your real name?"

"It's close enough. How may I address you, Deputy..." He leaned forward slightly to eye the nametag sewed to her breast pocket. "Deputy Preston," he clarified, letting his gaze linger on her breasts a moment too long before looking up to meet her eyes.

"Deputy Preston is sufficient," she shot back.

He rolled his amazing eyes. "Come now. What possible harm is there in telling me your first name?"

She screwed up her mouth. She didn't like his smarmy attitude, but something in his eyes made her want to tell him every secret she harbored, every dirty little fantasy she enjoyed. And she was having a doozy right now that involved him sans clothing. She cleared her throat and blurted, "Shanna."

"That's better." He bowed his glorious head. "Shanna Preston,

I'm pleased to make your acquaintance."

"Look, I don't know what—"

"Oh," Nora the waitress interrupted, setting Shanna's coffee in front of her. "Will the gentleman be joining you for lunch?"

"No, he's not st—"

"What'll you have, hon?" Nora asked, turning to the mysterious Mr. Marsh. The moment he looked up at her, her face went slack with a drooling, dreamy smile as she waited for his response.

"Same as the deputy. Black coffee, please. Decaf."

Nora loitered for a second with a simpering grin, then gushed, "Right away, sir. I'll be back in a moment to take your order." She left, not giving Shanna a second look.

Shanna frowned. "You seem to have a way with the ladies."

He shrugged yet again, as if his allure were a common and expected occurrence.

"Look, Mr. Marsh—"

"Aiden. Please."

"Aiden." She huffed. "You're a material witness — maybe a suspect — in a federal crime. I can't just sit here and have a friendly chat with you over lunch."

"Why not?"

"Because ... because it's not proper procedure."

He leaned forward, his mesmerizing eyes glittering as he whispered, "Sometimes proper procedure interferes with getting the job done."

Her mouth dropped open again. She couldn't believe this guy. "That may be true, but to get the job done *right*—"

"I didn't murder Melody Hanks," he said in a grim, matter-of-fact tone, "but I do have her daughter."

CHAPTER 3

Before lovely Deputy Preston could say anything, Aiden put up a hand and whispered, "The baby is safe and in good health. No harm has come her, I assure you."

He watched her, not sure how she'd react. When she scowled and reached down for the radio on her utility belt, he leaned forward. "Before you sic the dogs on me, just hear me out. Please."

She stuttered and huffed, then blurted under her breath, "You kidnapped a baby from a murder scene!"

"I didn't kidnap her," Aiden insisted, stiffening his back.

He marveled at the various emotions warring over Shanna Preston's delicate features as she considered his statement. Finally she stilled her expression and glared at him. "Why'd you take her?"

"To protect her."

"From what — whom?"

"Legitimate questions on both counts."

She blanched, her face glowing like an exquisite porcelain mask framed by shimmering copper tresses. He imagined touching her smooth young skin and running his fingers through her hair, crushing it in his fists. The idea startled him — where had it come from? He exhaled carefully to ease away the growing tightness in his chest.

Shanna sat back in her seat and eyed him. "You know the murderer's identity, don't you?"

"Yes."

"Your coffee, sir." Nora, their waitress, set the steaming cup in front of him and grinned. "Ready to order?"

Without a menu, Aiden looked up and asked, "Do you have flapjacks?"

"Pancakes? Yes, we serve them during breakfast hours."

"But not during lunch?"

"No, sorry. But we do have a lot of other tasty choices."

He eyed his lovely companion and smiled. "I like the word *flapjacks*. Don't you? It's an amusing term."

Shanna blinked, then gave him a deadpan smirk. "Yeah, downright hilarious."

"My apologies, Nora," he said, looking back at the waitress. "I realize you're busy. I'll take a chef's salad — no ham, no cheese, no eggs, and no dressing."

"Just ... lettuce and tomatoes and onions?"

"Yes — but leave off the tomatoes and onions too, please."

"Maybe you'd like just a house salad, hon. It doesn't come with many extras."

"Whatever you think, Nora. But leave out everything I mentioned."

"No problem. How about croutons?"

"Why not? What fun is life if you can't splurge once in a while?" Aiden eyed Deputy Preston gawking at him, and smiled.

"What'll you have, ma'am?" Nora said, turning to Shanna.

Finally Shanna looked away from him. "Cheeseburger and fries. No lettuce, no tomato, no mayo."

The instant Nora left, Shanna zeroed her gaze back at him. "What'd you mean, 'legitimate on both counts'? Are we talking about a man — or some kind of animal?"

Leaning forward, he sniffed his coffee — horrible stuff — and considered Shanna across the table. "Both."

She sat back in her seat. He could tell she didn't trust him and didn't believe him, but was nevertheless intrigued as she demanded, "Where is the baby? Why haven't you returned her?"

"She's at my home, being cared for by trusted associates. And to whom would I return her? The grandmother whose live-in boyfriend deals drugs?" He scowled at the thought of Jewel Ann staying in that filthy hellhole. After he'd gone there to check things out, it had taken him all of two minutes to figure out Melody Hanks' mother was not a fit candidate to care for her orphaned grandchild.

"Have you considered why Melody Hanks would choose to take her daughter with her barhopping and leave her unattended in a locked car rather than let her mother watch her? If the child's mother wouldn't trust her safety to the grandmother, I wouldn't dare turn her over to the woman."

He could tell by the frown shadowing Shanna Preston's face that she knew or suspected enough about the grandmother's background and character to agree with his assessment.

"Then why not take her to Family Services?" Shanna challenged.

He rolled his eyes. "And have her shuffled among orphanages and foster homes, never knowing what might happen to her? I don't think so. She deserves a stable family environment, with parents who want to adopt her and raise her as their own. And were I to approach the authorities with the child, I'd have to explain how she came under my guardianship. I'm not prepared to handle the awkwardness of that scenario."

Shanna eased out a breathless laugh. "You can't just *keep* the baby. She doesn't belong to you."

He held out his hands, palm-up. "Now you see my dilemma. I hoped you could help."

She blinked her aqua-blue eyes, and he found himself wanting to delve further to discover what secrets they held. He swallowed the urge and leaned back to avoid another whiff of his rank coffee. "My temperament and lifestyle are ill-suited to caring for a young child, and my associates are dedicated to other duties."

"What do you expect *me* to do? You haven't left many options."

He shrugged. "You're a woman. I assume childcare would come more naturally to you."

She laughed, looked aside, laughed again, then scowled at him. "I don't appreciate sexual stereotyping, Mr. Marsh, or whatever the hell your real name is. And I'm a single woman working nights for the Sheriff's Department. My lifestyle doesn't lend itself to the care and attention a baby requires either."

"But you do plan to have children of your own someday, don't you?" Not knowing why he asked that question, he masked his confusion with a smooth smile.

"What does that have to do with anything?" She leaned forward. "I should haul your ass in right now. I don't even know why I'm sitting here talking with you."

"Because you want to. You enjoy my company as much as you

want to learn specifics about the serial killer the FBI has been tracking for the last two months." She blinked again, and he knew he'd startled her to silence once more.

When she ran a hand over her mouth and stared at the table, her vulnerability hit him square in the gut. She was small but determined. He didn't understand what her life was like, but he could tell by her body language and general demeanor that she spent most of her time on the defensive. He didn't like the idea she had to be tough to make it in her world, but he knew adversity fostered strength. That's how he'd managed to become a successful Protector, by pitting himself against adversity others of his kind shied from. In her own way, the lovely Shanna Preston was trying to be a kind of protector too. He could sense in her the need to do what she felt was right.

"Help me," he whispered. "Help me find a good home for the child, where she will be cared for and loved."

Shanna gaped, then shook her head. "You know I can't do that. It's not proper procedure. By law, the child's grandmother is entitled to legal guardianship. If I helped you circumvent returning the child to her, I'd become an accessory to kidnapping."

He managed a smile, realizing this human woman was in no position to fulfill his request, and he had no right to jeopardize her situation by asking. He'd risked much just contacting her, but instinctively he knew she wouldn't give him up. He could trust her to keep their conversation confidential — at least for a while. To be sure, he would have to wipe her memory of him. He hated to do it. Vainly, he wanted to be remembered by her. But he had no choice.

Nora's imminent approach gave him the exit he needed. He smiled at Shanna and whispered, "I enjoyed our conversation more than you'll ever know." Reaching across the table, he touched her hand. The moment his fingertips made contact with her skin, he felt a charge of excitement course through him, quickening his pulse. That was all the warning he needed. He knew he had to sever all ties with her and never see her again.

With a subtle wave of his hand, he veiled her eyes, then left the booth and walked out of the restaurant unseen.

* * * * *

"What happened to your lunch date, honey?" a twangy feminine voice asked.

Shanna blinked her eyes and rubbed her forehead as she stared at the vacant booth seat across from her. She remembered someone sitting there, talking to her about something, but now everything seemed foggy, like a dream that faded the moment she awoke. Had she fallen asleep? She checked her watch and realized her lunch time was almost over. A greasy cheeseburger and a side of fries sat on the plate in front of her. Finally she looked up at the woman standing next to her. "Uh, I'm sorry. Could I get this to go?"

"Sure." The woman — Nora, yes, now she remembered — took her plate. "You want the gentleman's salad too?"

The gentleman. That luscious, infuriating man who called himself ... Aiden. Yes. Aiden Marsh. The man who admitted taking Melody Hanks' baby.

"Yeah, sure," she answered with a shrug. Maybe she could save all this food and eat it for dinner, because she sure wasn't hungry now. The peculiarities of her strange time spent with the mesmerizing Mr. Marsh had stolen her appetite — as well as the sharpness of her memory about their meeting.

She looked down at her untouched cup of coffee, then grabbed her wallet to lay down a tip and pay the bill. This had to be the weirdest encounter with a man she'd ever experienced. She couldn't wait to cross-reference his name to find information on him — DMV record, criminal record, whatever.

She thought about having the table dusted for fingerprints, then dismissed the idea. Aiden Marsh hadn't touched anything but the red carnation in the bud vase sitting on the table. Every smooth and solid surface that might yield clues to his identity remained free of his trace. And even if she managed to recover a stray fingerprint or a strand of hair, she knew she wouldn't find any matches in the database if he hadn't already been fingerprinted or DNA-typed. As careful as he'd been not to leave any prints, she guessed he wouldn't be registered in any database she could access.

As she glanced at his abandoned coffee cup, she realized he hadn't taken a sip of his beverage or sampled a bite of his salad, but simply treated them as props in a stage scene. Like an actor he'd gone through the motions of ordering a drink and a meal to keep her riveted long enough for him to check her out. But what had he been after?

A twinge in her gut told her she'd lost perhaps her only opportunity to follow a legitimate lead in this case. She'd blinked her eyes and let him walk out on her. But she wasn't going to let him slip away that easily. She *would* track him down somehow. And until she knew more about him, she couldn't mention her strange meeting with him to anyone. Right now, it had all the earmarks of a fantasy-hallucination, and she had no intention of getting herself laughed off this case for mental or procedural incompetence.

* * * * *

"You want a *what*?" Marta demanded as she marched after him from the foyer to the great room.

"Steak. Rare." *Bloody.* Aiden tore off his coat and tossed it on the plush modern couch covered in some boring neutral khaki color. He rolled up the sleeves of his shirt. He didn't want neutral. He didn't want boring. He wanted *red.* *Blood* red.

"You know we don't keep meat on hand. You never eat it."

He plopped down on the bland couch in the dull, colorless room. "I do now — and quick. I'm starved."

He looked up and caught Marta giving a private look to Noel, who'd just entered the room. "Go to the grocery and buy some steaks," she whispered. "Get a good cut."

"Oh, Lord," Noel mumbled. "I knew this would happen."

"Hurry," Marta urged, then turned to face Aiden. "What's going on?"

He lunged off the couch. "Nothing." Pacing aimlessly through the tasteful monochromatic room, he stopped and turned. "Where's the baby?"

"In the kitchen."

He charged in that direction.

"She's fine, Aiden. Don't disturb her. She's napping."

He stopped and looked over his shoulder. "I just want to see her."

Marta crossed her arms. "You were supposed to make

arrangements to take her elsewhere."

He rubbed his forehead. "I tried approaching someone I thought might help, but was unsuccessful."

"Keep trying. For your sake, that baby has to go."

He turned and headed for the kitchen. What was happening to him was not the baby's fault — it was his own. She just reminded him how empty his life was, and she couldn't be blamed for that.

As soon as he spotted her curled in her car seat on the counter, he hurried over to her and touched a hand to her rosy cheek. She stirred, and he unbuckled the strap holding her in the seat. Cradling her in his arms, he felt the soothing warmth of emotion he'd denied himself all his adult life. As she stretched and yawned, he held her against his shoulder to nuzzle her soft baby hair. At that moment, he realized the truth. Despite all sense and reason, his heart told him to keep this baby. He wanted a family — the one thing of vulnerability forbidden to a Protector. He wanted this child and a mate to be her mother. In the darkest recess of his heart, he knew he'd found the one woman he desired — the *human* woman, Shanna Preston.

The dull burning sensation in his chest reminded him how crazy these ideas were. He caressed the baby's head and put her back in the car seat. When she whined, Marta stepped over to calm her. He saw the look on Marta's face as she stole a glance at him, obviously trying to assess how hard he'd fallen from his lonely pedestal as Protector of the Enclave. He exhaled and growled, "Never mind about the steak. I'm going to my room." *So I can try to forget why I want to screw up my life.*

* * * * *

Shanna arrived promptly at 8:00 a.m. at the address of the task force's temporary digs. The spacious office suite in the vacant complex owned by the city had been stripped of divider walls and outfitted with desks, phones, and computers. Tan open-weave drapes concealed the outer wall of large plate-glass windows, hiding the task force's flurry of activity from casual observation by curious citizens and the media. A bulletin board the size of Texas covered one wall. Filled with maps and notations, it detailed the Bloodsucker's circuitous two-month killing spree from Minneapolis to Paducah. A file cabinet full of copies of murder reports from various cities also documented the Bloodsucker's activities along the way here.

Gazing at the collection of law enforcement personnel — agents from the FBI's Louisville field office, an officer from DCI's Frankfort office, a sergeant with the state police, a homicide detective from the Paducah Police Department, and of course the Sheriff's Department's own Gil Becker — Shanna felt under-qualified for this assignment. But as she dutifully reported to Agent Victoria Reissenor's partner, Agent Roger Norris, she quickly realized she was to be just another gopher available to run errands and perform whatever support services might be needed. This, she guessed, would amount mostly to fetching coffee and sandwiches, and performing low-end clerical work.

Norris, a stout, short man who looked to be in his early fifties, with cropped gray hair and bright dark eyes like buttons on a teddy bear's face, was anything but soft and cuddly like the stuffed animal his shape brought to mind. Despite his stubby appearance, Shanna could tell he worked out to stay in shape. He was just one of those guys cursed with the build of a fire hydrant and the charming demeanor of a ravenous pit bull. Without a wayward glance or how-do-you-do, he put her to work following up on crank phone calls and other dead-end leads forwarded to the task force for routine investigation.

After she spent half an hour conversing with a little old lady convinced the Bloodsucker had moved in next door and was planning to devour her peekapoo, Shanna decided to do a little in-depth investigating on her own. With the discovery of a new victim killed in another part of the county a few hours after Melody Hanks, the FBI ramrods on the task force took off on another tangent. But Shanna felt sure Aiden Marsh would be her ticket to glory, if she could just manage to find him.

Pretending to be busy at her assigned tasks, she searched the various databases at her disposal. As she suspected, Marsh was a phantom who didn't exist in any official records she could access. Obviously the name Marsh was an alias. If this man had a valid driver's license, it was under another name.

Assuming Marsh had been shadowing the serial killer's four-state murder spree, Shanna decided he'd either register at hotels or secure other temporary digs as a base of operations. She doubted he slept in his car and washed up in gas-station restrooms. He appeared to be too well groomed for that kind of nomadic lifestyle.

After making the excuse that she was going to follow up on questioning one of the customers at Smokey Joe's Roadhouse, she left the task force office. Nobody there really seemed to care what she did, which was no small relief to her. That left her free to make the rounds and visit every Paducah-area hotel to check the registries for the past two weeks. Coming up empty, she began contacting real estate rental agencies. Marsh struck her as a man accustomed to a level of luxury necessitating high-dollar investment, even for a temporary residence that might be used less than a month. That deduction narrowed her search considerably, and she concentrated on furnished apartments or homes leased short-term. After seven calls, she hit the jackpot. She couldn't believe Aiden Marsh had given her the same name he used to lease an executive home in one of Paducah's newer, posh, upper-class suburbs surrounding a private golf course. He'd freely volunteered his name. Did he actually think she wouldn't have the resources or the tenacity to find him? Or maybe he *wanted* her to chase him. That possibility gave her pause.

Near the end of her duty shift at four o'clock, she reported her fictitious lack of findings to Norris at the task force, then went home to change clothes and pay Mr. Marsh a little surprise visit. A nagging worry warned her she might be inviting danger going alone, but she ignored it. She could just hear the hoots and howls and taunts from Jake Fenshaw, or whatever man in the department she might ask to back her up. "Checking out this guy for a date, Preston?" *Yeah, right.*

All the guys she worked with assumed she was a piece of fluff who didn't have enough sense to tie her own shoelaces every morning. They openly repeated the rumor that fat-ass Grainger had hired her simply to ogle her. And forget the few other women working in the department. Most were just sliding by as clerks and relished their free time too much to bother chasing a suspect off-duty. *Yeah, well, screw them.* She'd completed training at the Chicago Police Academy, and she knew how to handle herself with tough or suspicious characters. To be on the safe side, she slid her personal subcompact Glock into her custom-made shoulder holster, camouflaging it with a lightweight jacket.

* * * * *

Aiden awoke with a start from a fitful nap. Something had put him on alert, but he had no idea what. A sudden noise, perhaps. Of late he'd slept lightly, and any small disturbance roused him.

A sliver of early evening sunlight pierced through a gap in the heavy drapes, reminding him he had work to do. Cameron Ryben was still on the loose, and he couldn't allow himself to be sidetracked any longer with the predicament of Jewel Ann Hanks. He'd have to leave the baby with Marta and Noel, despite their grumbling, and hope a solution to the situation came to him. Otherwise he'd have to start interviewing nannies, and he didn't want to chance having someone report the baby's whereabouts to the authorities. In any case, he couldn't devote any more time right now to that problem. He had to focus on trying to anticipate Cam Ryben's next move. That meant he'd be slumming in roughneck bars frequented by desperate, lonely women — not a chore he relished.

Hearing Marta's footsteps on the stairs, he arose fully dressed from his rumpled bed. Before she could tap on his door, he swung it open.

"There's a young lady here to see you," she said. Her look told him trouble was afoot, and her cryptic announcement confirmed it. The only young lady he knew in the area was Shanna Preston, but he'd wiped her memory of him. Even if he hadn't, she'd have no way of tracking him to this house. Unless...

He barged past Marta, then stopped at the head of the stairs, taking a moment to calm himself. He wanted to greet his guest with some measure of dignity. The instant he reached the landing in the foyer and set eyes on Shanna, his dignity fled. In its place flooded a wild mix of emotion he fought to control. Gasping for air, he swallowed hard and managed to croak, "How did you find me?"

In the light shining through the leaded glass of the entry door, she looked like an angel surrounded by a halo. Her hair shone like fire, and her smile lit him up like a burning building. He gripped the stair newel to keep from staggering forward.

"I'm a law officer," she said in a voice that floated like sweet music to his heart. "It's my job to locate people — even those who don't want to be found."

Shaking his head in confusion, he said, "But I—" He stopped himself before blurting out that he'd erased her memory of him. Something had gone wrong. Had he lost his touch, or was she stronger than he realized? A tingle of excitement made him smile despite his concern. She was much stronger than he realized. A worthy opponent. *A worthy mate.*

No—

"I want to see the baby."

He stepped off the landing, but turned to look back when Marta descended the staircase and said, "She's in the kitchen. Noel's feeding her pureed peas."

Aiden glanced at Shanna still looking like an angel despite her casual faded jeans and loose twill jacket. The burning sensation in his chest grew stronger, and he took several calming breaths to try and stave it off. Luckily Shanna didn't seem to notice his discomfort as she followed Marta into the kitchen. Aiden trailed behind, trying not to look at Shanna's nice round ass swaying invitingly before him.

* * * * *

Shanna stopped when she saw the stringy old man with shocking white hair hovering in front of the baby seat perched on the counter. She noticed the flailing arms of a child and moved forward in time to see Jewel Ann Hanks eagerly gulping another spoonful of green mush.

She sensed Aiden Marsh moving up behind her and turned. He stepped around her and went straight for the baby. Relinquishing the baby-food jar and spoon to him, the old man stepped back. Shanna was amazed to see the glow in Aiden's eyes as he offered the baby another mouthful. The baby's face seemed to light up in his presence. Shanna could easily imagine he was the child's father, but knew from the grandmother's brief summary of her daughter's past that Jewel Ann Hanks had been the product of a brief affair between Melody Hanks and her married boss that ended as soon as Melody announced her pregnancy. She lost her job and had been man-surfing ever since — until her life came to an unexpected end last night.

"All gone," Aiden cooed, scraping the jar with the miniature rubber-clad spoon. "This is the last bite, my little princess."

Shanna gawked at the domestic scene, feeling as if she were intruding. Reminding herself that this child didn't belong here, she moved forward and peered at the baby, who seemed healthy and happy. If any harm had come to her at the hands of these people, she wouldn't be so giddy in their company — in Aiden Marsh's company.

"She seems to have taken to you," Shanna observed, looking up at the wondrous man beside her. His hair shimmered like a dark curtain of silk as he moved his head to face her, and she had to fight the urge to run her fingers through the thick tresses. Normally she didn't think much of men with long hair, but he wore it well — very well, indeed.

"She's a very affectionate and trusting child," he murmured. "It's easy to become attached to her." When Jewel Ann reached out and grabbed a finger of his nearest hand, he laughed softly. The sound burned Shanna's gut with unexpected pleasure. She sucked in a quick breath and turned to him. "You have to give her back."

He stared at the child, then faced Shanna and asked, "Would you like to hold her?"

Shanna wanted to say no. She knew he was trying to work on her emotions and draw her into his fantasy of keeping the child as his own. She wouldn't buy into it. She couldn't. But before she could object, she found the plump bundle of joy being placed in her arms. She laughed nervously and tightened her arms around the wiggling load. "She's heavy. And strong."

Aiden shrugged. "She's a healthy eater and almost a toddler."

Shanna drew her attention away from the overwhelming man long enough to focus on the child. "Can she walk?"

"Not by herself. So far she can't keep her balance long enough to take steps without holding onto something for support."

Shanna bent down and set the baby's feet on the tile floor. Grabbing hold of her hands, she held her erect, and the child shuffled forward like a wind-up toy. Shanna laughed. She'd never been able to spend much time with her sister Julie's kids when they were babies. Julie and Tom had moved to Texas right after they got married, and by the time Shanna was old enough to visit them on her own, Jenny and Mikey were both school-age.

She grabbed Jewel Ann up into her arms and smiled at her.

The child grinned and babbled something she didn't quite understand. It sounded like *Mama* repeated over and over again. The idea that this child was trying to identify her as her mother made her feel odd. She started to hand her back to Aiden, then remembered he wasn't even supposed to have her.

As if he could read her mind, he grimaced and whispered, "Don't take her away. She's safe and happy here. I don't want any harm to come to her, and I can't guarantee it won't if you give her to her grandmother."

Jewel Ann started to fidget and twist, and Shanna feared she'd drop her. When Jewel Ann reached out for Aiden, Shanna let him take her. He hugged the tot, then handed her over to the woman Shanna assumed was his housekeeper. Turning, he extended a hand toward the front of the house and suggested, "Let's sit down and talk about this."

Shanna followed him into the great room. "There's nothing to discuss. You have to give the child to her next of kin. I'm sorry, but it's the law."

He sat down on the couch and looked aside as if in anguish. She sighed and sat down beside him. "Look. You can make an anonymous call from a phone booth and say you've dropped the child off at a local church. That way you can avoid prosecution and leave her in a relatively safe place for retrieval."

"But what about later, when her grandmother goes on another drunk ... or worse?"

He turned to face Shanna, and she felt the flush of something — attraction, embarrassment, she wasn't sure. But the effect he had on her put her in defense mode. She had to keep her wits about her. "Mr. Marsh—"

"Aiden," he purred.

"Aiden." Just saying his name sent a hot flash down to her belly. She fidgeted and edged further away from him. "I appreciate your concern. I really do. But you simply cannot keep this child from her family. It's not legal, and it's not right."

"Is it right to deliberately put her in a situation of potential danger and abuse?"

"You don't know that living with her grandmother will put her in danger."

"I *do* know. I scanned the woman when she left the morgue. She harbors rudimentary feelings for the baby, but doesn't want the responsibility of raising her. She may have made the right noises in front of those FBI agents, but—"

"Wait a minute. What do you mean, you 'scanned' her?"

He frowned and sighed. "You'll just have to trust me when I tell you I know what I know. There are things you don't understand. Things I'm not at liberty to explain to you."

"Don't hold out on me, Mr. Marsh. We've got a maniac loose in town, and he shows no signs of slowing down his killing spree. Some tiny detail you've decided to withhold could prove vital in capturing him."

She thought of the women who'd suffered at the hands of that vicious murderer. Aiden Marsh seemed to know about him, yet held back information. Could he be protecting him? She shuddered inwardly, hoping that wasn't the case. Who would want to shield a horrible creature like the one responsible for all those gruesome deaths? When she tried to picture a blond man of medium build sporting the oversized canines presumably used to rip out his victims' throats, her mind wouldn't let her conjure an image. "You said something to me earlier today about the serial killer who murdered Melody Hanks and over forty other women being part man, part animal. I need to know what you meant by that."

He reared his head back as if she'd insulted him or startled him. She scowled. "Modern forensic science can reveal a lot about crimes and the criminals responsible for them. It's all part of solid police work. Now, why don't you tell me what you think you know, and let me decide whether or not it meshes with what I've learned about this case?"

When Aiden Marsh opened his mouth to speak, Shanna caught a glimpse of his canines. Suddenly they seemed longer than the rest of his large, even, white teeth, and that revelation sent a cold chill of fear down her spine. If she wasn't sitting next to the killer, she was sitting beside someone very similar to him.

Just as she shot off the couch, the old man she'd seen in the kitchen earlier appeared in the entryway. "Sorry, lass. Now that ye've found us and know who we are, we can't let ye leave the house and go tellin' on us. Now, can we?"

CHAPTER 4

Slightly dazed, Aiden was surprised to realize Noel and Marta had entered the room without him noticing. All his senses and attention remained focused on Shanna standing in front of the window. When had he grown so feverish? How much time had passed? He remembered Shanna getting up from the couch and hearing someone speak to her. He guessed it had been Noel, but he couldn't seem to concentrate enough to think straight.

The room shimmered with heat, and the light from the window blurred Shanna like a vision. His chest burned, and breathing came hard as he looked at her, barely able to make out something dark and metallic clutched in her hands. He moved his aching eyes to follow the path of her outstretched arms while Marta and Noel both talked in soft, soothing tones, as if trying to coax a cat from a tree. He touched a hand to his forehead and felt sweat beading on his flaming skin. Something was terribly wrong, and it seemed an hour passed before he figured out what it was. *The bloodlust.*

He looked up in panic, the realization clearing his head a little. When he eyed Shanna, he saw the compact item in her hands was a pistol aimed at Noel and Marta. Her stance said she knew how to handle a firearm. Of course — she was an officer of the law.

"I'm taking the baby and leaving," she said. "And nobody better try to stop me."

Recognizing things had gotten out of hand, Aiden pushed himself up from the couch. His knees threatened to buckle under him, and he had to concentrate hard just to stand up straight.

"Stay where you are, Mr. Marsh. I won't bother reading you your rights. I'm guessing by the time I get back here with reinforcements, you and your associates will be gone. As a courtesy for your cooperation, I'll tell the FBI I followed an anonymous tip and found the baby abandoned unharmed."

"Shanna, please," he growled, his voice hoarse and low. When he saw the startled look of fear on her face, he knew he must be exhibiting overt signs of bloodlust. His mouth ached, and he guessed what that meant. Sliding the tip of his tongue across the edge of his teeth, he confirmed the worst.

Gods, have mercy!

Swallowing down the burning sensation in his parched throat, he tried again. "Please put your gun away. No one here will harm you. I promise." He took a step toward her, hoping he could convince her to stand down and be reasonable. They had to work out something amicable.

"You stay away from me!" She stumbled back and bumped into a chair behind her but didn't lose her balance.

He sucked in a deep breath, trying to draw on his reserves to calm himself. A glow of heat surrounded him like a blast furnace, but the sensation wasn't painful or discomforting. It felt *right*. "You won't harm anyone," he commanded in a soothing tone. He took another step closer.

She stiffened and readjusted her grip on her gun. "I'm warning you..."

"We'll work this out," he whispered, walking nearer.

"Don't think I won't shoot, because I will."

He looked at her quivering arms and forced a smile. "I think you believe you should, but you won't."

With another two steps, he stood directly in front of her. Her wide eyes followed his movement as he raised his hands, but she didn't flinch. He touched his fingers to her hands and felt the charge of need sizzle through his body. His stomach churned, and his loins burned as he placed his hands over hers, forcing the gun barrel against his chest. "If you must shoot, Shanna," he growled, "go ahead. Do it. Put me out of my misery."

Her arms trembled. He willed her to pull the trigger, to end his suffering. The bloodlust had taken him. There was no hope for him now. His life as he knew it was over. *End it, please.*

He locked gazes with her. His heart swelled. Heat poured off his body like the blaze from a roaring fire. She bit her lower lip as tears slid down her cheeks. He leaned in toward her, and her knees quivered. When he felt the tension leave her fingers, he slid the gun from her grasp. Noel and Marta rushed up beside him. He handed the gun to Noel, then reached out to take Shanna by the arm as she faltered on the verge of collapse.

* * * * *

Damn it, damn it, damn it! Shanna shuddered as Aiden Marsh gripped her arm and escorted her to the couch. He helped her sit down, then released her and turned to his two lackeys.

How had he taken her gun from her so easily? One second she had a straight aim on him, and the next, he was handing her gun to that old coot he called Noel. What kind of pansy-ass law officer was she? Nothing like this had ever happened to her before. Had she lost her nerve or her mind? His touch set her on fire and made her forget who she was. Now *he* was in charge, and she was unarmed. She was screwed.

She looked up at her captor's back, instinctively knowing it would be useless attacking him from behind or trying to run. She was outnumbered and didn't see how she'd get out of this alive. Tears burned her eyes, but she blinked and swallowed them back. Why was she letting defeatism get the best of her? There was still a chance she could turn things around. They hadn't harmed her or the baby — yet.

* * * * *

Aiden kept his back turned on Shanna. He'd neutralized her as a threat, and the sensations of her fear and anger and self-reproach ate at him. He couldn't bear to look at her. Every nerve in his body screamed with fire, and the very sight of her drove him closer to that edge he dared not cross. He wondered if he'd already gone too far to come back unscathed, but the possibility frightened him too much to even contemplate it.

"Bloody hell, Aiden," Noel whispered, looking him over. "I knew it. Ye're deep in the bloodlust." He ducked his bushy head around to glance at Shanna, then straightened and murmured, "Remember what we talked of yesterday? Ye best reconsider the option, and be quick about it."

Nauseated and dizzy, Aiden knew he needed to lie down. The

hunger made him too ill to think straight.

"The woman," Noel urged. "Bed her but don't partake of her blood. That won't satisfy ye completely, but it'll help take the edge off."

"No!" Aiden roared. "I will not." He couldn't use and abuse Shanna that way. There was no telling what he'd do to her in the midst of his madness. He could hurt her — maybe even kill her — and not even realize it until too late.

"Sit, lass!" Noel yelled, pointing a crooked finger past Aiden. "Don't ye be tryin' no fool escape attempts. Mind ye, me and the missus might be on the far side of old, but we ain't decrepit and can still move fairly quick. And recall, lass, we got yer gun."

Noel still wore a tinge of his intimidating scowl on his craggy visage as he looked back at Aiden and whispered, "Just wipe her mind so's we can leave her and her car somewhere far away from here. We can't let her go off knowin' —"

"No." Rubbing his forehead, Aiden tried to resist the ideas Noel offered. "I've already tried memory cleansing, and it didn't work. She's too strong for casual mind tricks."

"Bloody hell." Noel took another peek at Shanna, then shook his head. "Ye're gonna have to deal with her somehow, Aiden."

"Don't taunt him," Marta warned as she took the gun from Noel. Turning to Aiden, she ordered, "Go upstairs to your room right now. You're not well. We'll see to things for you."

Aiden glanced at Shanna and instantly regretted the mistake. As soon as he laid eyes on her, he burned for her and ached to have her. His mouth watered at the thought of laying claim to her throat, and he focused on the pounding pulse in her neck. When she looked up at him and cringed, he whirled away. Marta was right. He needed to get the hell away from her, or in another minute he'd do just what Noel suggested — or worse.

He staggered toward the stairs, his legs protesting as he moved farther away from Shanna. Just as he reached the landing, he heard a wail from the kitchen. Jewel Ann needed attention. He turned, but Marta pushed him forward, insisting, "Upstairs, now."

The baby cried out again, and Aiden charged in her direction, ignoring Marta's protests. As soon as he pulled Jewel Ann from her car seat, he felt better, saner, more in control. He held the baby close and patted her back, intuitively knowing what she needed. "Thirsty, little one?" He filled a glass at the sink, feeling suddenly thirsty too. Carefully he held the glass to the baby's mouth and tipped it up. As soon as she stopped taking gasping gulps, he lifted the glass and swallowed the remainder.

Swiping a hand across his mouth, he turned to the kitchen doorway and saw Marta staring at him in disbelief. Noel, holding Shanna by the arm, grumbled, "Blasted baby's gone and wrecked everything! Look at ye, man, dotin' on her like a blitherin' fool one minute, then lustin' after this bonnie lass the next. Ye've done lost yer mind to the bloodlust, all on account of that tot."

"Quiet, Noel!" Marta barked. She marched forward and took the baby from Aiden. "Go upstairs and lie down, Master Aiden. You need to rest."

"Yes, ye have work to do tonight," Noel added.

Marta turned on Noel. "He has no business going out in his condition."

"What better condition than a touch of the bloodlust to give him the edge he needs to find that killin' bastard? His senses'll be heightened, and my guess is Ryben won't be eludin' him so easy anymore. Aiden most definitely should go out tonight."

Marta glowered at Noel. "You old coot! Why can't you keep your mouth shut?"

When Shanna cleared her throat, Aiden locked his gaze on her and felt the shadow of the bloodlust returning. To keep himself reasonably calm, he lowered his head and avoided looking at her as she said, "Excuse me, but what in the hell are you people talking about? Who is Ryben, and what is this bloodlust thing you keep mentioning?"

Aiden lifted his head as the burn crept back into his chest. "None of this concerns you, Deputy Preston. You need to go now."

"I'm not leaving without the baby."

"Baby or no baby, ye ain't goin' nowhere, lass," Noel interjected.

Aiden glared at Noel as Shanna jerked her arm, unable to break the old man's grip. "Ease up, Noel," he warned.

"Aiden, ye can't just let her scurry off and tell—"

"We'll deal with the situation after I've had some time to

think, damn it!" Aiden felt his blood boiling, on the verge of exploding his arteries. He swiped a hand over his sweaty face, trying to calm himself. His mind roiled like a stormy sea. How could he expect himself to come up with a solution when his body was trying to rip his very sanity from him?

In distraction he glanced at Jewel Ann cuddled in Marta's arms, squeezing the stuffed rabbit Marta offered. Another anguished breath escaped him when he thought of the baby no longer in the house. The silent absence of her coos and whines would be deafening. Clenching his fists, he straightened and turned on Shanna. "Do what you think is right for the child." He lunged for the diaper bag and grabbed the car seat off the counter. In three steps he stood before her and shoved the items at her. "Go, and take her with you, before I change my mind."

* * * * *

As Aiden Marsh shoved the baby seat and the diaper bag into her hands, Shanna wondered what had driven this odd turn of events. She never expected him to voluntarily give up the child. She expected a battle royal. When she saw the pained look in his eyes, she suffered a peculiar twinge of guilt deep in her chest.

"I'll bring her out to your car," he mumbled.

She couldn't believe her good fortune. Or was this just a ploy to ease her defenses until he lowered the boom on her? "What about my gun?" she asked, still not ready to believe he'd given up the fight so easily.

"You'll get it back as soon as you have Jewel Ann settled in."

Shanna scowled. She definitely wanted her gun back. It was a personal piece, not police-issue, but still, it had cost a pretty penny, and it was registered in her name. Its loss represented her failure as an effective law officer. Getting it back wouldn't erase the weird and potentially fatal mistake she'd made earlier, but at least she wouldn't be leaving it behind.

More important than her gun, she wanted the child out of here. Obviously these people were not stable, and they appeared to be involved in some shady goings-on, the details of which she decided she did not want to know. This seemed to be her only opportunity to take the child and be free of these strange people, but something in Aiden's eyes tugged hard on her. She didn't want to take the baby from him. *She* didn't want to leave him. When she thought about leaving, she was overwhelmed with the sick feeling that it was the absolute wrong thing to do, and taking the baby would make her one giant heel.

She shook her head in amazement. What in the hell was wrong with her? "Look," she offered in a surge of desperation, "I can see you're attached to the baby, and you seem to genuinely care about her safety and comfort—"

"You need not justify yourself, Deputy Preston. I understand your position. I only hope you will honor your pledge not to involve us in your explanation of how you found the child."

Shanna sighed. Aiden Marsh seemed dependent on the baby for his continued well-being. How could he have developed feelings for little Jewel Ann so fast? It would be a shame to remove the child from his custody — and a crime not to. But she didn't know anything about him, and his erratic behavior made her think twice about leaving the baby with him, or even standing close to him, especially after witnessing the frightening transformation he'd suffered earlier.

Transformation? She had to have imagined what she'd seen. It was physically impossible for his canine teeth to lengthen right before her eyes. Wasn't it? She shook her head as she eyed him. The feverish look in his eyes and the sexual aggression she sensed gave her serious doubts. She watched his chest rise and fall with heavy breaths and feared he was about to undergo another bout of that *bloodlust* thing the old man had mentioned. She took a discreet step back to rethink her position.

"The truth is, I don't want to see the baby end up with her grandmother any more than you do, Mr. Marsh. But that's exactly what will happen if I take her back right now. To turn her over to social services instead, there'd have to be an established complaint against Mrs. Hanks, and a complaint wouldn't be lodged unless someone witnessed something bad happening to Jewel Ann, or had reasonable cause to ask that Mrs. Hanks be investigated as an unfit guardian. I don't see that happening anytime soon, and I don't think either of us wants to wait for a situation to develop."

Aiden raised his brows. "What alternative do we have?"

She handed the baby's accessories back to him. "I'm not equipped to take care of her until I can turn her over to Mrs. Hanks. And I'm not sure she'd be safe in the meantime if her location became known. The man who killed her mother might come after her too, although I can't quote any precedent for that behavior. As far as we know, the serial killer hasn't harmed any children. Since Jewel Ann seems to be reasonably safe and happy and well cared for here, I can't see a good reason to take her away, at least not in the next few days."

Aiden let out a big sigh of relief, but it caught in his throat as she added, "Now I expect something in return."

"Oh?" He tilted his head and his luscious dark auburn hair shimmered around his face.

"I know you're tracking the man you think murdered Melody Hanks. If you're on a vigilante quest, I don't want to hear about it, because then I'd have to haul your ass in. But I want you to tell me everything you know about him."

Noel, standing nearby, shook his head. "Ye don't realize what ye're asking, lass. There's much ye can't know, for reasons we aren't at liberty to explain."

Shanna ignored the old man and focused on Aiden. "I want to go with you to hunt him down. And when the time comes, I want to be in on the collar."

"Out of the question!" Aiden boomed. He whirled away to deposit Jewel Ann's baby accessories on the counter, then turned on Shanna. "I won't expose you to that kind of danger."

"I'm a trained law officer. I can handle myself around some psycho—"

Shanna flinched when grizzly old Noel placed a hand on her shoulder and whispered, "Lass, ye're not understandin' his gist. The rogue ye be huntin' is a danger for sure, but Aiden's more worried about the danger of ye spending time with *him*."

Before Shanna could comment on that revelation, Marta moved toward Noel and handed the baby to him. "Take her upstairs to the new crib you spent all those hours putting together." To Aiden she said, "It'll be dark in a few hours, and the wolf will be out again amongst the sheep. Get yourself upstairs and rest. You'll need your strength and concentration. I'll wake you when dinner's ready." She pushed him out of the kitchen.

Having dispatched both men and the baby, Marta took Shanna by the arm and guided her toward the island counter. "You'll help me prepare dinner while I explain the situation. If you're determined to involve yourself, you can't afford any missteps. And, trust me, going anywhere alone with Aiden right now would be the biggest mistake of your life. Perhaps your last."

* * * * *

Still stewing over Marta's cryptic warning about Aiden, Shanna chopped tomatoes and tossed the pieces into the greens already in the glass salad bowl. Marta had remained quiet all through the preparation of the squash casserole. When she popped the dish in the oven to bake, she dried her hands on a dishtowel, then turned to face Shanna.

"I'm hoping Aiden will sleep until dusk, which will give me perhaps the only opportunity I'll have to speak privately with you about things he would prefer were never discussed."

Shanna wanted to bombard her with the questions fighting in her head, but she remained quiet and let the woman talk at her own pace.

"When I explain our unique situation to you, I won't give many details. I'll tell you as little as I feel you need to know. Questioning me further will do you no good, so don't bother. Understood?"

Shanna shrugged and nodded.

"As long as we are in agreement, this should be fairly painless. Sit at the breakfast table. I've made lemonade." Marta filled two glasses then set them on the tile-top wooden table.

Shanna sat opposite Marta. The woman sipped her lemonade, then said, "Your interference is inconvenient and unwelcome." Shanna opened her mouth to object, but Marta put up a hand to stop her. "I understand you feel it is your duty to investigate the murder that took place in your legal jurisdiction. But your excessive enthusiasm has led you to Aiden's doorstep and embroiled you in a situation you are not prepared to handle."

"Excuse me, but Mr. Marsh led himself to me."

"I'm aware of that." Marta frowned. "And his true name is

Marschant. Aiden Jules Marschant. Marsh is an alias he sometimes uses when he's working."

Shanna filed that information away for later use. Knowing his real name — if this woman wasn't lying — might come in handy. "Look, Mrs.—"

"Marta. There's no need for formalities at this point. And, yes, I admit Aiden made a terrible error in judgment by seeking you out. But he was merely looking for an alternative arrangement for the child. We aren't suited to care for a baby. Nevertheless, your mental strength in resisting his suggestion that you forget you ever met him, and your dogged persistence in locating him, have created an intolerable situation."

"I'm sorry, but it's my job to—"

"What county sheriff's deputy pursues a case with your zeal? I assumed the Sheriff's Department was little more than an auxiliary force dedicated to patrolling donut shops."

Shanna scowled. "That's totally out of line."

Marta shrugged and took another sip of her lemonade. "The point is, you don't belong here. You should never have come here. And it isn't feasible for you to work with Aiden in catching that rogue."

"Why?"

"Because Aiden can't work with you."

"Can't, or won't? It's because I'm a woman, isn't it?"

Marta sat back with a sigh. "Partly."

"I'm as good a police officer as any man, and I—"

"I'm sure you are, but that's not the issue. Your gender is the problem — that, and the fact you've awakened something in Aiden he has worked years to subdue."

Shanna eyed the stodgy woman with her chignon and plain dark gray dress so unstylish it almost looked like a uniform. "What are you talking about?"

With a huff Marta moved her lemonade glass aside and leaned forward. "Aiden has been specially trained to hunt rogues like the man you're after. He's spent many years perfecting his sensibilities to track them and defeat them. The *reaction* you caused in him this afternoon is the very thing he cannot afford to experience if he expects to continue doing his job."

Shanna shook her head, unable to make sense of the woman's vague references. "What *is* Mr. Marsh's — Marschant's — job?"

Marta placed her bony hands flat on the table and examined them for a long moment. Finally she eyed Shanna and whispered, "He is dedicated to protecting the secret existence of our people. And my telling you this negates his efforts. Before I say more, you must swear on your life you will never reveal to anyone what you have seen and heard and may yet learn about us."

Shanna sat back and studied Marta, trying to decide whether she was delusional or just trying to pull one over on her. "Okay, I'll bite. I promise not to divulge any information about you and your people. Unless, of course, my secrecy would put me in opposition with my duty and ability to uphold the law."

Frowning, the old woman folded her arms in front of her chest and leaned back. "All right. I'll allow you that caveat, but let me tell you now that you *will* have to make a choice. At some point our situation will come into conflict with the laws of your people. At that juncture I reserve the right to do whatever I deem necessary to keep our secrets." She smiled briefly. "With that understanding, shall we continue, or cease discussion now?"

Shanna didn't like the tone of that veiled threat, but she knew she'd never find out anything that would help her with this murder investigation if she didn't go along with this strange bunch, at least for the time being. They seemed to know about the serial killer. How deeply they were involved remained to be seen. "Tell me about this reaction Mr. Marschant is so dead-set against experiencing. Is it that bloodlust thing your husband Noel kept referring to?"

Marta nodded. Shanna waited for her to say more, but the woman remained silent. Shanna grabbed her sweating lemonade glass, wondering just how weirdly insane these people really were — and just how stupid she was for coming here without backup. However nutty they might be, she was here, and she had to follow through. She sipped the lemonade — tart with just enough sweetness — then set her glass down and prompted, "The bloodlust. You were saying...?"

"Put simply — very simply — it is a mating urge."

Shanna chuckled in amazement. She'd awakened in Aiden Marschant a *mating urge*? Sitting back, she folded her hands in her lap.

"And he's been avoiding this — um — *urge* for many years because...?"

"Once it is awakened, left unchecked, or insufficiently satisfied, it can become a *killing* urge."

Blinking her eyes, Shanna recalled Marta had said Aiden's job was to protect the secret existence of *their people*. "Who *are* your people?"

Marta tugged at the prim collar of her dress. "Historically, humankind has referred to us as *vampires*."

Shanna got up from her chair and took a few steps around the kitchen. The tasty smell of the cooking casserole lent a warm, homey feel to a house she was supposed to believe was infested with *vampires*? She turned to eye the old woman still sitting stiffly at the table. Suddenly this whole situation made perfect sense — and no sense at all. She coughed out a giggle, then laughed some more until she was on the verge of hysteria.

Marta got up from the table and faced her. Shanna wiped her eyes and tried to choke back the uncontrollable chuckles still threatening to bubble out of her.

"I realize this is difficult for you to accept. By design, the myths surrounding our existence have been ridiculed and blown out of proportion to make the very belief in us seem ludicrous. That is the only way we can protect ourselves and live in relative peace alongside humans."

Shanna caught herself wanting to burst out laughing again, but cleared her throat and took several deep breaths until the urge faded. "Okay. Suppose I actually believe you. What does this have to do with the serial killer the FBI is after?"

"Think about it," Marta said, bending down to open the oven and check the progress of her casserole. She closed the oven door and straightened. "The rogue you seek has sexually assaulted a multitude of women and killed them by ripping out their throats and drinking their blood."

"And you're suggesting this is all an elaborate attempt by the killer to conform to vampire lore? Does he think he's a vampire too?" She snapped her fingers. "That must be why he only kills at night!"

Marta scowled. "Joke if you must, but what I've told you is true. After the bloodlust goes beyond the mating urge, and the rogue drinks enough human blood, he may fall victim to several symptoms, including an increased sensitivity to sunlight, so severe even brief exposure can produce painful burns. With the ingestion of enough human blood over a long period of time, the human hemoglobin interferes with the chemical makeup of his own blood, which is significantly different."

At the mentioning of the difference in hemoglobin, Shanna perked up. The FBI's DNA evidence had suggested a genetic hemoglobin peculiarity in the killer. Maybe these people weren't as crazy as she'd first assumed. "So, how does a vampire become a rogue — a bloodsucking maniac on a murdering rampage? Assuming, of course," she added in a cautious tone, "that all vampires aren't bloodsucking maniacs to begin with."

Marta frowned, then clasped her hands together in front of her white apron. "Contrary to popular belief, we are not all indiscriminate blood-guzzlers. But the urge to share blood during mating is a part of our culture and our physical makeup. The bloodlust is a difficult time, especially for the men of our race. The various hereditary lines each have different levels of reaction. Noel and I are from a line that is as close to human as we can come and still be considered Shanrak."

"*Shanrak?*"

"An ancient name for our kind. Our own racial myth declares us the descendents of angels." Marta's quick, cold smile, in conjunction with the idea that she thought she possessed angelic heritage, sent a sudden chill coursing through Shanna. If they were descended from angels, they must have been fallen ones.

Shanna watched Marta take plates and silverware from the cabinets. "Set the dining table while I bring the food," she instructed, handing Shanna the dishes and flatware.

"So, the Shanrak — vampires — have different levels of ... vampirism?" Shanna prodded, her arms full of dinnerware.

"Yes. As I said, Noel and I are of the line least likely to exhibit the extreme abilities of our kind — extraordinary strength and speed, heightened sensory capabilities, even something similar to what you might call telepathy, with a little mind-control thrown in for good measure. But we are also least likely to suffer the adverse symptoms of bloodlust. Aiden is at the top end of the scale, one of the most powerful of our kind and also most likely to succumb to the madness of bloodlust if he doesn't control the urge."

Shanna raised her brows and entered the formal dining room. Alone in the fading light of sunset, she glanced at the shadows lurking in the corners, half expecting some fanged monster to jump out at her. As she busied herself laying out the plates and silverware on the traditional oval cherry table, her mind churned with more questions. Assuming what Marta told her held a level of truth, she still couldn't believe in vampires. But if an isolated group of people *thought* they were vampires, they'd certainly try to exhibit behavior consistent with the lore surrounding those mythical creatures. Was it safe to leave a nine-month-old baby with them? She shook her head, not sure what to think.

One thing she did know was that she'd have to approach this case with the assumption the killer believed he was not human, instead superior to humans. That would explain his seeming guiltless compunction to kill. If he was one of *them,* she'd have to find out more about what these people in this household believed about themselves, if she hoped to figure out how his mind worked and how to anticipate his next move.

Marta brought in crystal water glasses and filled them from a chilled pitcher. She left for a brief moment and returned with the steaming casserole and the crisp salad. "I hope Aiden will be satisfied with one of his favorite dishes, and forget his earlier request for a bloody rare steak."

Remembering his lunch order of a chef salad with no meat, Shanna asked, "Is he following a vegetarian diet for his health?"

"He avoids ingesting animal flesh or anything with blood traces. He also avoids alcohol, and even goes so far as to ensure his environment is free of bright or vivid hues that might accidentally spark unwanted excitement."

Shanna glanced into the tasteful but bland great room, then spied the stairway landing in the foyer. Making sure no one was within earshot, she said, "Why? So he won't feel any effects of the bloodlust you were talking about?"

"He maintains a very low emotional level in part to remain receptive during his work. But yes, the main reason is to avoid succumbing to bloodlust. As a Protector of our people, he is forbidden to take a mate and produce offspring."

When Shanna gave Marta a surprised look, the woman didn't hesitate to explain. "Because of the built-in vulnerability a family would create, he is not allowed to maintain affiliations with anyone or develop emotional attachments that would interfere with the proper performance of his duty. Noel and I have dedicated the remainder of our lives to his exclusive service, and we are as close to a family as he will ever have."

"But he seemed so wonderful and caring with the baby."

"Yes." Marta undid the apron around her waist and folded it into a neat square. "That's why we are anxious to have the baby taken elsewhere. She has awakened in him a fathering instinct that also unfortunately opened the way for the mating instinct. Once *you* showed up..." She shook her head and grimaced.

Shanna glanced again at the empty stairway bathed in shadowy light, then turned back to Marta. "Are you saying Aiden's *never* had sex with anyone?"

"That is correct."

With her mouth agape, Shanna considered that admission, wondering whether she could accept it as truth. "He's ... what? In his thirties and totally a fox. And he's still a *virgin*? How is that possible?"

"He is much older than he looks. And self-control makes it possible. Something your kind obviously knows little about."

Shanna ignored the offhanded insult. "How much older?"

"That is not your concern. What is of concern is the fact that your very presence threatens his control of his libido and his ability to do his job. If you insist on interfering, it's possible he will fail to bring down the rogue, and the killings will continue unabated."

"Or," said Noel as he crept from the stairs to stand in the dining room doorway, "the lass could bed him and help him get over his bloodlust in jolly good time. Then his head would clear and he could catch that Ryben bastard before he exposes us all."

Shanna turned to find the old man wearing an ornery smile. She'd overheard him whispering to Aiden earlier and didn't care for his repeated suggestion that she engage in sex with his boss, but he seemed stuck on the idea. She shook her head and wondered about her sanity. She should have left with the baby an hour ago and turned these crazy people in to the FBI. But the idea intrigued her ... *a virgin vampire daddy.* How bizarre was that?

The chandelier over the table lit up, seemingly of its own accord. Shanna turned to find the subject of their discussion standing in the dining room doorway. He'd changed into stonewashed black jeans and a tight black tee shirt that showed off every muscled detail of his glorious body. When he met her gaze and smiled, she looked away, realizing she was staring. As he sat at the head of the table and spread his napkin in his lap, she stole a glance at him, wondering how much of their conversation he'd overheard. His chiseled face revealed nothing.

Grinning, he looked up at Marta and said, "Squash casserole. Smells great, but I thought we were having steak. I'm definitely in the mood for *meat* tonight." He shot Shanna a pointed look, as if to clarify just what kind of flesh he had in mind.

CHAPTER 5

"I thought you'd be gone when I awoke," Aiden said, trying to sound casual as Shanna passed him the casserole dish. Seated next to him at the table, opposite Noel and Marta, Shanna avoided looking him in the eyes. He let his gaze cascade quickly over her luscious form. Only the casserole dish occupying his hands stayed his urge to reach out and touch her.

Staring down at her plate, she mumbled, "I still need more information."

He made a humming noise in his throat that felt like a sensual growl. What the hell was wrong with him? He thought getting control of his unexpected bloodlust would be a simple matter of concentration, as he'd been trained. His short rest upstairs seemed to settle his nerves, and peeking into the spare bedroom to see Jewel Ann snoozing peacefully in her new crib helped console the intolerable ache in his chest. But deep down he knew trouble shadowed him. The whole time he was upstairs, he felt Shanna's presence and imagined her light, clean scent in the air around him. As soon as he came downstairs and laid eyes on her again, his hands flexed with the need to touch her fiery hair and every other part of her body.

With the burning renewed in his chest, and his insides churning, he took his fork and stabbed the pile of casserole he'd plopped onto his plate. Putting a bite into his mouth, he hoped he'd be able to swallow without vomiting. It scared him senseless to realize how easily Shanna knocked him off-kilter.

After years of flawless control, he never expected to have a serious problem with bloodlust. But this woman — this *human* woman — proved him wrong. Why did she, of all people, affect him this way? He didn't understand. He'd been approached by many females of his own kind and had resisted them all. Yet Shanna, in her unknowing innocence, had managed to snag his heart with a ferocity that alarmed him. He didn't like being afraid — he wasn't accustomed to it.

"Mayhap it's good the lass is still here. Eh, Aiden?" Noel, seated at his other side, prodded with a leer. "Seems to me, the two of ye have some things to work out, if ye get my drift."

Aiden ignored Noel's bold implication. Taking another bite of his food, he looked Shanna over with deliberate thoroughness, testing his resolve. When he felt his control falter, he returned his focus to his plate and swallowed. "Perhaps if you let us know what information you seek, Deputy Preston, we could attempt to accommodate you and speed your departure."

She set her fork down on her plate and straightened. "I know you're all itching to get rid of me, but let's get one thing straight. I'm not leaving until I figure out how to find this Ryben person you've been talking about — assuming he's the killer we're both after."

Aiden glanced at her, then gazed across the table, over Noel's head, at the darkened sky outside. "You won't find him tonight. He killed twice last night. More than likely he won't kill again for another night or two."

"How do you know?"

Aiden lifted his water glass to his lips and eyed Shanna. "He's satiated, at least for a while." *Unlike me.* He let his gaze rove over her form. She'd shed her jacket, and her empty shoulder holster pinned her arms back so that her luscious round breasts thrust forward under her pastel-pink tee shirt, as if in overt invitation. He clenched his hands, aching to caress them, swallowing when his mouth watered in anticipation of suckling them. He looked back at his plate, and felt the burn spread lower to the core of his lust.

"Then we'll go after him tomorrow night. How do you decide where to look for him?"

Aiden took another bite of food, not even tasting what he chewed. When his mouth was clear, he murmured, "Cameron Ryben seeks emotionally vulnerable women who have no self-confidence or self-respect. They make the easiest targets because they are ready to fall in with any man who pays attention to them. Such women are plentiful in your culture. Your society seems to deliberately set up the circumstances that create those emotional flaws, to ensure a steady supply of victims waiting to be abused."

He glanced at her, but she said nothing, merely watched him. He focused on an indeterminate area beyond the tabletop. "He could search for them in any social setting, but a crowded bar is his location of choice, for the simple reason that he can blend in and hunt unnoticed."

"That won't be the case anymore. The FBI has issued a BOLO with his general description."

Aiden shrugged. "*General* being the key word. A blond man of average height and build describes roughly a third of the men in this county."

Obliquely he watched Shanna huff and cross her arms under her breasts ... those luscious breasts he yearned to fondle, to feel pliant in his hands. Shaking his head, he dismissed the idea. No way could he touch her. She was human, and—

"Are you all right?"

He whipped his head up and stared at her. "Yes, fine."

"So, then, how do you figure out which bar he's going to show up at?"

He opened his mouth to speak, then realized he had no words ready to explain his very private method of sensing his prey. Finally he admitted, "I feel the heat."

She leaned forward. "The heat of what?"

"Of his ... desire. His need."

She sat silent for a moment, then whispered, "How do you feel it?"

He caught her staring intently at him with her big aqua eyes full of innocent eagerness. He shifted in his chair and shrugged as he glanced at the tabletop. How could he explain what he experienced from Cameron Ryben, night after night? That awful essence of hunger, burning — an anger so intense, senseless rutting and killing was the only appeasement, until the hunger returned again, demanding more.

Encased in a cocoon of cold emptiness, Aiden insulated himself from the intensity of those sensations and still remained receptive to any changes in the realm of his sensory plane. On a rogue hunt he had to tune out everything but the most intense emotional projections. And when he felt it strongly enough, he knew where to find his target.

"Aiden?"

He looked at Shanna and found her studying him with something akin to fearful pity. His anger flared. He didn't want her pity or her fear. She didn't understand anything about him or his life. He was a Protector, and that was all that mattered.

"How do you sense him? Is it like ... telepathy?"

He shook his head. It would sicken him to go inside the disturbed mind of that killer — assuming Cam Ryben still had a mind left to touch and explore. Mostly what Aiden sensed from him was on the order of animal instinct. The only time Ryben seemed to use higher reasoning was when convincing his next victim to go off alone with him. "Mental sharing," he explained finally, "would create a bond too personal to endure — and too difficult to break off."

"Mental sharing?" she scoffed with a little snort. "You're not suggesting you actually *can* read people's minds, are you?"

When he saw a hint of fear around her eyes, he recalled the look on her face when she'd pointed her gun at him — the same gun Marta had not yet returned to her. What was it in him that engendered Shanna's revulsion? His fangs had returned to dormancy, and he had contained the burning, at least for now. He forced a smile. "Does the possibility of mind-reading frighten you?"

Her laugh came out sounding breathless. "Well, yeah."

"Because you don't want anyone to know your most personal, secret thoughts and yearnings?"

"It's not anyone else's business what I think and feel."

He raised his brows. "I never said I could read minds. Where did you get that idea?"

Shanna glanced at Marta sitting silently at the table, eating her dinner.

"Ah." Aiden nodded. "That *girl-talk* you and Marta had while I rested upstairs."

Shanna and Marta both glared at him. When Marta stared at the table, Shanna demanded, "How do you know about *that*?"

He didn't say anything, just continued smiling. Finally Marta murmured, "Even when he chooses not to read minds, he still hears like a bat. There are few secrets kept in this house."

Shanna huffed and puffed as she looked from Marta to him,

then back to Marta. "You're joking." When Marta shook her head, Shanna wailed, "Why didn't you warn me?"

Marta shrugged. "I assumed he would be sleeping and wouldn't be listening."

"Son of a—" Shanna lunged up from her chair and threw her napkin on the table beside her plate. "This is too weird. It's just too frigging weird!" She raked her fingers through her hair, then propped her hands on her hips. "Give me my damned gun. I'm going home."

"Leaving so soon?" Aiden taunted as he rose from his chair. "We haven't had dessert yet."

"Screw dessert. I need to get the hell out of here and clear my head. I'm on overload right now."

He smiled with satisfaction tinged with regret. He'd managed to drive her away — his professed goal — but deep inside he didn't want her to go.

When she saw the smile on his face, she flushed and crossed her arms under her breasts. "Don't think you're getting rid of me that easy. I'm not giving up."

"I wouldn't dream of thinking that, Deputy Preston. I can see you are determined to stick with this murder investigation and follow it through to its conclusion."

"Damned right I am."

He lifted his hands in a gesture of appeasement. "If you're ready to leave, may I assume that we've satisfied your curiosity sufficiently this evening?"

"No, you may not."

"What else do you require?"

"I told you, I want to go with you to hunt down that murdering bastard."

He stepped away from the table. "That isn't possible."

"That's not the answer I want to hear," she said, charging toward him.

"Why is it so important to you to break this case?"

She stopped short a few feet from him. "Because ... because I want to stop the murders."

"But there's something else." He tapped his index finger on his chin as if considering possibilities. "Let me think. Yes, I believe it has to do with your feminist sensibilities."

"What?"

"I notice a distinct defensiveness on your part whenever your gender comes up in discussion."

"I never said—"

"Yes, you did. And if I had to guess, I'd say you want to show those backwoods good ol' boys you work with in the Sheriff's Department that you are a better police officer than all of them put together."

She glowered and turned away. "They treat all the women in the department second-rate. Like we're some kind of joke. It's not right." She whirled back to face him. "I am a good officer. I can do this. I know I can."

"Why didn't you stay in Chicago and join the police force there? You would have had plenty of opportunities to prove yourself and move up in the ranks to become a detective."

She blinked at him and took a step back. "How'd you know I came from Chicago?"

He shrugged. "Your accent. You're not from around here. It was a simple matter of deduction."

She tilted her head, considering him as if she didn't quite believe his answer. Finally she said, "Yeah, okay, I went through the police training academy there. But right after I graduated, my parents died in a car accident. And I had a hard time adjusting. I had to sell the house and take care of all the other arrangements." She turned away. "It took a lot out of me."

"So you moved to Paducah."

She faced him. "I saw the job advertised, and I wanted to get away from Chicago and all the memories. I figured Paducah was a nice-sized town to make a new start."

He nodded once, giving his approval of her answer. He knew she was being honest, even though it caused her discomfort to discuss the matter. When he realized he was sensing her emotions, he mentally backed off and withdrew into himself. It was so easy to reach out and touch her mind. He couldn't afford to let his concentration slip and settle into a comfort zone he knew was inappropriate — forbidden.

"So, are you going to let me go with you to hunt this Cameron Ryben, or not?"

"I already told you. No."

"Damn it! If you think I'm giving up just because you say no, you don't know me at all. The more you tell me I can't, the more determined I'm going to be to prove you wrong."

"Let's all of us go to the kitchen," Noel interrupted, rising from his chair. "We can all have a nice friendly chat about it over coffee and tea, while me and the missus clean up the dishes."

* * * * *

Aiden stood in the kitchen dinette area, staring through the French doors at the darkness surrounding the patio outside.

"*Take her*, damn it," Noel whispered beside him, glancing over his shoulder at Marta and Shanna preparing refreshments at the other side of the kitchen. "She's practically beggin' for yer attention. Get it over with, then ye can focus on what's important."

"Good advice, except for one critical point. I might never 'get it over with,' as you put it."

His faithful servant frowned. "Ye've no real worries about losin' yerself in the bloodlust. Ye're nothin' like Ryben."

"We're descended from the same line. When he came of age, he was selected to be a Protector, just as I was."

"He started trainin', but turned down the Enclave's offer, wantin' no part of the responsibility. I tell ye, there's more differences than similarities between the two of ye."

Aiden shook his head. At the moment he wasn't so sure. He stepped away as Marta brought a tray of cups and two carafes to the table.

* * * * *

Seated at the small table near Aiden, Shanna sipped her coffee and accepted a fresh-baked sweet roll from the plate Marta offered. Since they'd retired to the kitchen, Aiden seemed withdrawn, uncomfortable, brooding. He didn't offer to help with the dishes, but stayed near the patio doors, staring out at the darkness.

She knew it was getting late and she should leave, but she couldn't help hoping she would get more information from him. His claim that he could sense Cameron Ryben's lust to kill intrigued her. And the truth was, she still felt that strange, unexplainable yen to stay near him. It didn't faze her so much anymore. She just knew it was there.

Washing down the last bite of her roll with the remainder of her coffee, she tapped her lips with her napkin and eyed him. He refused to meet her gaze as he sat staring at his untouched teacup. "So," she prodded, "this connection you have with the killer. How strong is it?"

"It is not a connection. It is more like ... awareness."

"Is he aware of you too?" She waited for him to look at her, but he wouldn't.

"Perhaps." He shrugged, still staring at his cup. "He is very gifted and powerful."

She glanced at Noel and Marta sitting in silence, both of them watching their fearless leader with an intensity that suggested worry. What did they think he was going to do?

"Is this awareness something just you and he have? Or are you aware of other people in the same way?" She tipped her hands up. "Give me something to work with here. I'm not getting it."

He looked at her then, just for a second. "I can sense emotion from my own kind, from your kind, from animals, from anything living that feels. Generally I screen out all but the most intense feelings such as fear, anger, lust, anguish, pain, and hunger. This allows me to zero in on troublesome sources, particularly a rogue I'm after."

"And that's how you've been tracking Cameron Ryben — by tapping into his urge to kill?"

Aiden nodded without looking up.

"Why haven't you caught him? You were there in the bar just moments before he killed Melody Hanks."

He looked at her then, his eyes narrowing with regret. "I started to follow them outside but was distracted for an instant. I arrived too late to prevent her murder."

"So then what happened? Where'd he go? He couldn't have just vanished into thin air."

"Yes, he could. And did." Aiden stared evenly at her.

She looked away, not liking the implication. Pouring herself more coffee, she sipped slowly and considered what he said. Finally she faced him. "You're saying he can dematerialize at will?"

"Perhaps not at will, but when he is close to desperation. I told you he was gifted."

She put her cup down on the saucer with a clatter. "And you can do that too? Dematerialize?"

"When necessary." He shrugged then looked back down at his cup. "It's a way to change location, not simply disappear."

Noel cleared his throat loudly and got up from the table, making Shanna jump with a start. She looked up and caught the old man giving Aiden a nasty look. "Ye shouldn't be fillin' her head with such nonsense, Aiden." He turned on her and smiled, his big crooked yellow teeth shining garishly. "It's all poppycock, lass. Don't believe a word of it."

When Noel turned to carry his cup across the room to the sink, Marta got up from the table as well. "Listen to him, Aiden. Don't be telling her things she doesn't need to know."

'Need to know' — the FBI's favorite phrase. Shanna turned back to Aiden as his associates retreated. Were they trying to make too much of this silliness to throw her off the track and thereby ensure she believed nothing? Or was it true — all of it? She shook her head, more confused than ever. "Look, all I'm trying to do is understand how to catch this killer."

"You can't catch him," Aiden declared. "He's much too powerful for you."

"But *you* can catch him?"

Aiden shook his head slowly, then looked back at his cooling tea. "I'm beginning to doubt that."

"Why?"

"Because ... because so far he has succeeded in eluding me. I sense him only when he's hungry to kill, when he goes on the prowl for his next victim. And usually, by the time I locate him, he's already done the deed." He put his elbows on the table and covered his face with his hands. "And now I'm so *clouded* in my judgment, I don't know if I can sense him at all above the roar of my own—" Glaring at her, he shoved up from the table. "It's time for you to go home, Deputy Preston."

"And then what?"

"And then you forget about everything. This is not a case I want you involved with."

"I'm not tucking my tail and running." She charged around the table. A mere foot from him, she glared up into his face, then shoved a hand against his chest, expecting him to falter. He stood solid as a boulder, and that startled her. "I'm staying on this case whether you like it or not, Mr. Aiden Marschant. And nothing you do will change my mind."

He raised his brows. *"Nothing?"*

"Nothing. If you're having a problem because you're attracted to me, man up and deal with it. No matter what your lackey over there says, I'm not having sex with you."

His face darkened as he glared down at her. She saw his mouth twitch with the hint of a smile as he purred, "That's a relief to hear, Deputy Preston."

"Can the sarcasm. You and I," she said, poking a finger in his chest covered with solid muscle, "are going to be like two peas in a pod, thick as thieves, joined at the hip—"

When his mouth twitched again, she realized what she'd said and backed up a step. "Whatever cliché you like best, I don't care. Bottom line is, wherever you go, I go. And we're going to stay together until Cameron Ryben is behind bars."

"Or dead."

She let out a sigh. "Or dead. But I'm in on it all the way. You got it? Or I go straight to the FBI right now, and tell them everything I know about you." She crossed her arms. "Deal?"

With his face still flushed with anger — she hoped it was anger and not something else — he smiled and said, "Sounds like I don't have a choice."

* * * * *

"Damn right, you don't have a choice, Mr. Marschant. We're partners until I say different. Got it?"

Aiden eyed the stunning little redhead, wondering if she'd be just as much a spitfire writhing naked beneath him, her delicious body bucking as he plunged inside her.

Squelching that thought, he turned away, knowing he had to

get her away from him. Before he could accomplish that, she walked up and said, "If you're having trouble keeping up with this Ryben guy, maybe you need to change your tactics."

Suddenly the heat of her body hit him like a blowtorch, and he staggered back. Was it the bloodlust rearing its ugly head again? Swiping a hand over his mouth, he gripped the back of Marta's empty chair, then looked over at his vassals. They both watched him as if expecting him to burst into flames at any moment, or pounce on his unsuspecting prey.

He looked back at the thorn in his side, this woman he'd foolishly invited into his life to ruin everything he had worked years to build and maintain. His mind buzzed with so much burning anger and lust, he couldn't decide whether he wanted to kill her or kiss her. But he knew he had to do something fast to relieve the insanity that gripped him. "How," he rasped, "do you propose I change my tactics?"

She shrugged, seeming not to realize what her mere proximity was doing to his broken self-control. "Bait a trap for him."

He cocked his head, concentrating on making sense of her suggestion. "You mean ... dig a pit or set a net—"

"No. When you want to flush out a suspect, you set up a situation you know he can't refuse. You pick a location that will hide your team, your backup. Then you set your bait to attract him. And — wham!" She slapped her palms together with a loud smack, making him cringe with inner pain. "When he shows up to take the bait, you've got him. Okay?"

Still leaning on the chair for support, he nodded feverishly, unable to think straight. Finally he managed, "What kind of bait?"

"Me."

"What?" He shoved away from the chair and straightened, glaring at her through the reddish haze of his damnable bloodlust. "What are you talking about?"

"You said he looks for easy women." She shrugged. "All we have to do is spot him. I can play easy as well as the next girl."

"No! I won't have you go anywhere near him."

She got right up in his face. "Listen, Mr. Chivalry. It's not your call. I want this guy, and I'm prepared to do whatever it takes. Got it?"

He backed away from her, then saw Marta and Noel moving to his rescue.

"Let's discuss this another time," Marta ordered, trying to herd Shanna out of the kitchen. "It's late, and —"

Shanna shook her off and stood her ground. "If we wait for another time, more women will die." She turned on Aiden. "We have to settle this now and come up with a plan. Tomorrow night, we're going after Cameron Ryben. *Together.*"

Aiden shook his head in misery. He had no way of controlling the madness that overtook him whenever he got near this damnable female. How could he spend even one night with her and expect to concentrate on stopping Ryben? "No. I can't do what you're asking. It's … it's too —"

"Can't, or won't?"

He looked down to find the gutsy little deputy nearly toe to toe with him. Noel stepped over and grabbed her arm. "Lass, don't."

"Don't?" She shot Noel a quick glare and jerked free of his hand. "I thought you wanted us to get together. Isn't that what you've been winking and leering about all evening?"

Noel, properly chastised, ducked his head. "An idea mayhap I'd not thought through well enough, considerin' the present situation."

Scowling, she aimed her eyes back at Aiden. "I know you're attracted to me, and you think you can't control it. But trust me, it's not the end of the world. If you're like most guys, it'll fade just as soon as you see another pretty face."

She put a hand on his chest, and the contact burned like a brand. He groaned and moved back from her, but she took another step closer until she had him backed up against the island counter. "There's no need for embarrassment or awkwardness. We can actually make this work for us."

He raised one brow with a painful trace of concentration. "What?"

She smiled and whispered, "If this is the first time you've had trouble tracking one of these rogue characters, Cameron Ryben probably knows you're after him, and he's figured out a way to string you along, to taunt you. Don't let him get by with that crap anymore. Turn the tables on him and make his overconfidence be his undoing."

Aiden gazed at her through the shimmering haze of lust forcing his soul into meltdown. "How?"

"Give him a reason to think there's a way to get the best of you. Then make him go for it."

He squinted, not sure what she was suggesting.

"Give him the idea he's in a position to take something of yours, something dear to you. Make him think he's able to hurt you."

Slowly her meaning dawned on him. He exhaled heavily, feeling the pressure ease in his chest. "You mean, make myself appear vulnerable to him."

"Yes!" She grinned. "And right when he thinks he has you where he wants you, you'll have *him*. Trap set and sprung."

"But what would make me seem vulnerable to Cameron Ryben?"

"Me."

He shook his head. "No. I already said —"

"Yeah, yeah, I know. But look at the situation you're in. You admitted you can't outfox this guy. You always arrive too late to save his victims. And —"

"And the same thing could happen with you. I won't have it!"

"Just listen to me, will you, before you shoot my idea down?"

He huffed and gripped the counter behind him. "All right. I'll listen — on one condition."

"Which is?"

"You sit down at the table."

She looked over her shoulder at the table, then back at him. Frowning, she mumbled, "Sure. Okay." She turned and plopped down in the nearest chair, the one he'd hung onto for support earlier. He sighed with some relief.

"So," she hammered, "I was thinking, you let Ryben know you're *interested* in me..."

He gulped down his terror and eased out, "How?"

She shrugged with her hands up in the air. "I don't know. You're supposed to be the all-powerful vampire master. You tell me. Don't vampires mark their sex slaves somehow?"

He shook his head. She was treating this all as a joke, and that was a mistake. He looked at her half-serious, innocent expression and wanted to shake her, but the wondrous physical yearning and emotional pain gripping him left him only enough control to smile. "You're saying you want to be my sex slave?"

"No, that's not what I'm saying, and you know it. We're talking about a plan here, a ploy to trick that murdering bastard. Just listen, okay?" She shot up from the chair, obviously forgetting his request for her to keep her distance from him. "Do whatever woo-woo thing vampires do, and let everyone know you want me so they'll keep their hands off. Once Ryben thinks I'm yours, he'll come after me."

"*Woo-woo thing?*" He chuckled, feeling a little more at ease. "Deputy Preston, you've been watching far too many vampire movies."

"You mean you can't leave your mark on a person?" Sounding almost disappointed, she took a step toward him.

As his breathing smoothed and his senses sharpened, one thing became painfully clear to him. He *did* want her, whether or not she truly offered to be his sex slave. "You really want me to mark you, Shanna?" He smirked and moved away from the counter, closer to her. His body burned with a steady flame of background heat that didn't frighten him so much anymore. "What kind of mark would you like? A mental brand to make you pliant whenever I call? The scent of my body after we make love? Be forewarned that a properly mated Shanrak is bound to his significant other for life. Do you want the two of us bound together for the rest of our lives, Shanna?"

"No, that's not what I..." She gulped and stood very still as he stepped closer to her, as if she could sense the current of danger pulsing just beneath the surface of his calm exterior. "I-I mean ... that's not what I was suggesting." She let out a breathless chuckle, almost a sigh. "*Bound for life?* I thought vampires were supposed to be sexually promiscuous."

He smiled and felt the protrusion of his fangs peeking out. She blinked and staggered back against the table, mumbling, "Uh ... not all vampires are faithful, are they? Otherwise, there wouldn't be all that lore about—"

"You're right," he whispered, breathing down into her face. "Not all my kind mate for life. Some take many sexual partners and never bond fully with any of them. A few believe it is permissible to take human slaves for blood-drinking perversions, but the Enclave doesn't condone such activity."

She swallowed hard, and the sound drew his attention to the pulse beating in her neck. The feel of it pounded in his ears, and the warm, welcoming metallic scent of her blood drew him even closer.

"I thought," she squeaked, "that you could just ... bite me or something. Leave some fang marks for show. Isn't that what vampires usually do?"

"Bite you," he purred, his pulse quickening at the thought. The heat of her body so close made him feverish with lust. With lightning speed he grabbed her and shoved her backward over the table, scattering cups and silverware. She yelped in surprise and struggled to free herself, but with her ass pinned against the edge of the table and his hips wedged between her spread legs, she couldn't move. He gripped both her wrists with one hand and lunged over her. Grabbing her hair with his free hand, he pulled her head aside to expose her delicate, slender neck.

Both Noel and Marta rushed over and took hold of his arms, but they couldn't pull him off her. He ignored their protests as he moistened his lips and felt her trembling beneath him. She drove him mad with desire. "When I mark you," he growled, "you'll be *mine.*"

He barely heard Marta and Noel screaming at him as he touched his lips to Shanna's neck. The acrid smell of her fear drove him, and her soft skin made his mouth open involuntarily. He felt his fangs pressing against her racing pulse, then closed his mouth and sucked gently, drawing her skin against his tongue. He wanted to taste her blood in his mouth and down his throat, into the pit of his stomach roaring for satiation. He wanted to feast on her but knew it would be incomplete without their physical joining. Without him inside her, he would be left wanting.

Just short of breaking the surface of her skin and drawing blood, he pulled away. When he opened his eyes and looked down at her, at what he'd done, he felt sick — and pleased. Tears glistened in her eyes, and her chest heaved with terror as she shuddered beneath him. Finally he'd managed to make her take the situation seriously. "You want to lure Cam Ryben to you?" he snarled. "He can move just as fast as I did, and before you can blink your eyes, he'll have your throat ripped out." He let go of her hands with a toss and lurched back from her, breathing hard with pent-up lust and hunger.

As Marta rushed to pull Shanna from the table, Aiden stepped back. Marta glared over her shoulder at him, then escorted Shanna to the hallway.

"My God, man," Noel rasped, "I thought ye was gonna kill her!"

Aiden glanced at Noel, thinking for a second that he might be better off if he had.

* * * * *

Still shaking, Shanna stood in front of the hall bathroom mirror and craned her neck. The purplish bruise on her neck was a whopper. "He gave me a hickey!"

Marta scowled. "What did you expect? You asked him to mark you — an incredibly stupid thing to do."

"But a hickey! That's so ... sophomoric!" She wanted to be angry and indignant, but fear kept eating at her. She'd seen his fangs — big, white, wet, and sharp. They were real, and there was no telling herself anymore that she'd imagined them.

Slowly she faced Marta. "He really is a vampire, isn't he? And you and Noel along with him?"

Marta nodded.

"My God."

"Finally, you understand the danger, Deputy Preston. Now will you listen and abandon this foolhardy plan of yours? Aiden can't work with you. He can't afford to spend even a few minutes near you. You saw what happened when you put your foolish teasing ideas in his head, then got too close. We should all be thankful he didn't break skin. There's no telling how far things would have gone then." The woman shook her head. "Come now. You must leave."

Shanna glanced back in the mirror, trying to pull the neckline of her tee shirt up to cover her bruise, but it was too high up. Finally she swished her hair down to cover it. Turning, she exited the small, tastefully under-decorated bath. When she headed toward the kitchen, Marta caught her arm. "Don't go in there. Let him be."

Shanna lifted her hand to her neck, thinking maybe she ought to listen to the woman's advice. But she couldn't let things go unsettled, with that man — that *creature* — in the next room thinking he had scared her off with his boyish prank. She hadn't accomplished anything this evening, except to make herself look ineffective as a law officer, and she wasn't going to tuck her tail and run now. There was still the matter of the killer she needed to catch, and that unspoken *thing* looming between her and Aiden. Until they came to terms with it, neither of them would move forward. "I have to talk to him."

Marta threw up her hands, and Shanna darted into the kitchen, stopping short when she saw Aiden standing near the counter. The memory of him on top of her, sucking her neck, made her heat with embarrassment and fear. It was too much like sex to pass off as casual contact. She lowered her gaze, unable to meet his eyes. She didn't know what to say or do next. Talk about an awkward moment...

She looked up suddenly to find him standing before her. She gasped as he lifted his hand and brushed her hair from her neck. He raised his brows and smiled. "I've marked you, Deputy Preston. Satisfied?"

With a trembling hand she rubbed her neck and stared up at him. His smug look angered her. "You gave me a damned hickey!" she spat before she could stop herself. "I was expecting something more ... substantial."

He shrugged. "It's the best I could offer on short notice. I'll try to do better in our next foreplay session."

"There won't be a next session. I want my gun. Now."

"You're going to shoot me?"

"No. I'm leaving."

"So, I'll see you tomorrow at sunset?"

She shot a look at Marta standing nearby, then gave him a steaming glare. "You bet your sexy vampire ass you'll see me tomorrow night, Mr. Marschant."

* * * * *

At the sound of Shanna's tires squealing in the drive, Noel turned from the front window and grumbled, "I still say ye should've bedded her and got it over with, Aiden."

Marta slapped Noel hard on the arm. "Shut your mouth and leave well enough alone, you old fool! We're lucky nothing serious happened."

Aiden huffed and turned to the stairs. What could he say to either of them to justify his atrocious behavior this evening? He'd gone too far with Shanna, and now he would pay dearly for it. As he ascended the stairs, his body ached in protest, having been brought to the brink and then stopped short. He hurt all over and burned with need, but he would just have to get over it. Bedding Shanna Preston was not an option.

He arrived at his bedroom door, then turned instead to peek in at the baby who'd apparently slept through all his misery and misbehavior. She tossed fitfully. When he reached the crib, he placed a hand on her warm little body wrapped loosely in a soft blanket. She stilled under his touch, and he smiled.

Easing out of the room, he left the door ajar, then crossed the hall to his own room. After turning off the light and shedding his clothes, he got into bed, only to realize sleep would not come. With his hands clasped behind his head, he lay staring up at the dark shadows cast on the ceiling, wondering what in the hell he was going to do now. Shanna Preston had proved to be more than a match for him, and he had no idea how to handle her. He'd tried repelling her, but she was more tenacious than a junkyard dog.

With Cam Ryben still running loose on the rampage, and Shanna determined to lure him out in the open, Aiden knew they were all headed for one hell of a clash. Somehow, in the meantime, he had to figure out a way to keep his hands, and the rest of his body, off her. Heating at the mere thought, he knew he was royally screwed.

CHAPTER 6

When Shanna entered her apartment a little after ten, the first thing she noticed before turning on the overhead light was the red light blinking on her answering machine. She hadn't taken time to make any close friends since moving to Paducah six months ago, and her older sister only called at her convenience, which wasn't often. The message had to be work related. As soon as she pushed the playback button, she heard the droning voice of the evening dispatcher, Mary McDaniel.

Sheriff Grainger wanted someone to sub tomorrow for an officer at the county workhouse, who had to take his wife to the hospital. Grainger decided Shanna was the right woman for the job, so she'd be on litter-pickup supervisory detail with the officer's partner. And before she showed up at 8:00 a.m. at the workhouse, she was supposed to brief the sheriff on the FBI's progress in the murder investigation. What? Becker, the *real* liaison from the Sheriff's Department, was too damn busy to tell him what was going on with the task force? To see Sheriff Grainger and then get to the workhouse on time, she'd have to show up at the station right at the morning shift change. She groaned and erased the message, then called in to confirm.

Shrugging out of her shoulder holster as she marched into her bedroom, she flipped on the light and released the clip from her pistol and popped the round out of the chamber. Turning on her bedside lamp, she stowed the weapon in her nightstand drawer. She pulled off her tee shirt on the way to the shower and turned on the water to let it warm up as she finished peeling off the rest of her clothes. When she turned toward the mirror over the sink, her souvenir from Aiden Marschant glared back at her like an angry red rash. *Bastard!*

As she brushed her teeth and stepped into the shower, she kept going over the events of the day, trying to figure out when and how things had gone so wrong. Of course — it started the moment Aiden walked into her life. Everything she'd done since she'd first laid eyes on him had been a mistake of bad judgment. She should have pulled her gun in the restaurant and arrested him, cuffed him, and hauled him off to jail. Instead, she'd had an intimate chat with him over lunch. *Damn, she was an idiot!*

She squirted shampoo on her hair and scrubbed vigorously, trying to wash away the memory of her stupidity. She'd screwed up, not just once, but twice. No, more than twice. How many times? When she'd let him walk away in the restaurant. When she'd found his house and surprised him without backup. When she'd pulled her gun but somehow let him take it away from her. And to top it off, she'd sat down to dinner and listened to all the bizarre lies he and his house servants told her about the lot of them being vampires. But those weren't lies, were they? All three of them *were* vampires — at least they'd perfected their little routine to convince her they were. And she'd let Aiden *touch* her. Worst of all, she'd walked out, almost run, leaving Melody Hanks' baby with those nutty people. And on top of all that, she had vowed to go back tomorrow!

She growled and doused her face in the onslaught of the shower. What the hell was she supposed to do? Her duty as a law officer required her to report Aiden Marschant's known whereabouts in connection with the murder of Melody Hanks and the kidnapping of her child — regardless of his claim he'd had nothing to do with the murder and had taken the baby to protect her. Now he had Jewel Ann and refused to give her to her next of kin. By allowing it to continue, Shanna had become an accessory to the crime. Yet she couldn't make herself believe Aiden meant harm with his actions. Despite all the crazy things he and his helpers had told her, she felt in her gut she should trust him.

Was it because she wanted to trust him and wanted to believe him? She couldn't deny he enthralled her, and at the same time creeped her out. She didn't know how to connect with him on a professional level. He was weird, powerful, and attractive, yet vulnerable in a way she couldn't figure out.

She turned off the water and slashed back the shower curtain. Grabbing her towel from the rack, she fluffed her hair dry, patted herself down, and stepped out of the tub.

She was in too deep with that little vampire clan now not to go along with them in their scheme to hunt down Cameron Ryben, the man they claimed was responsible for the murders the FBI investigated. A horrid fear flashed through her mind — what if Aiden and his cronies had been stringing her along just to stall her and lull her into cooperating? What if, when she went back after work tomorrow, she found the house empty and them gone — along with the child?

Shaking her head, she grabbed up her discarded clothes from the floor and stuffed them in the hamper. She just couldn't believe they'd go to all the trouble of dining with her and explaining their odd situation to her, only to skip out and leave her behind. They could have done a lot more crude and horrible things to her if they'd wanted her out of the way. But they hadn't harmed her — except for that little hickey incident.

Flashing a look at the partially fogged mirror, she caught a glimpse of her temporary brand of ownership from Aiden. Had Aiden been showing his chauvinistic ass to dissuade her from working with him, or had he nearly lost his self-control as his housekeeper Marta suggested? She rubbed the bruise on her neck and frowned.

Stepping into her the bedroom, she grabbed a tee shirt and panties to sleep in, then flipped off the overhead light. With only her bedside lamp casting a soft glow, she sat on the edge of her bed and set the alarm to give herself plenty of time to get to the station tomorrow morning. Somehow she'd have to get a good night's sleep so she'd be in top form. She didn't know how she was going to do that with thoughts of that gloriously sexy and frightening man darting around in her head like rabid bats. Sighing, she turned off the bedside lamp and immersed herself in the cocoon of darkness.

* * * * *

"Whoa-ho, Preston! You must've had a real hot date last night, judging by that bruiser on your neck."

"Shut the hell up, Fenshaw." Shanna slammed her locker door then shoved past Jake, who had just come off duty. She knew this would happen. She'd arrived at the station before seven, but Grainger had kept her waiting around — like the fat bastard was *so* busy doing other things. Scarfing down donuts, probably. When he'd finally deigned to see her, she'd spent just enough time bringing him up to date on the FBI's investigation to emerge from his office at 7:45 a.m., right in the middle of the morning shift change. She had endured ribbing about her 'promotion' to FBI agent and then suffered the usual and expected comments about the hickey she couldn't hide with makeup or her uniform collar or her hair. It was just *there*, reminding her she was hungry for sex but didn't have any prospects for partners she could trust — least of all Aiden Marschant.

She headed for the main entrance and strode to her car. She had a full eight hours to spend with the work-release detail. A familiar oldies tune sneaked into her head, and she caught herself mentally paraphrasing the lyrics: 'A bunch of good ol' boys drinking whiskey and wine, picking up trash in lieu of jail time.' She laughed for a second, then cursed as she drove toward the workhouse. Nothing about her situation was the least bit funny.

* * * * *

Aiden awoke gradually in a haze from the all-night dream he couldn't escape. He felt as if he'd fallen into a shaft leading straight to hell, where he'd burned for Shanna continuously in nightmarish wakefulness. She was a beacon in the darkness of his agony, and he, the moth unable to resist her light.

Still dazed, he showered and dressed with careless disregard, letting his heavy, wet hair dry on its own. His body ached with a dull but persistent need that grew more intense whenever he came close to Shanna. He had to find her, to be near her, see her, smell her, touch her. He knew his heart would stop without her. He had to have her. All of her, all to himself.

Slinking downstairs, he found Marta at the breakfast table, feeding Jewel Ann. When the baby reached for him, he took her in his arms and sighed with relief. The baby helped quell his need. As long as he kept her near, the burning wasn't so bad. Funny how the baby's presence had opened him to the horror of bloodlust, yet her continued proximity seemed to curb it. Only when he thought of Shanna or was near her did the bloodlust overtake him.

How would he survive? He couldn't keep going like this. His obsession with Shanna drove him ever nearer madness. He had to find her and make it stop. Kissing the baby's soft powder-fragrant head, he handed her back to Marta and turned to leave.

"Where are you going, Aiden?"

He saw the fearful worry on Marta's strained narrow face and willed her to be calm, but her worry didn't falter. "I'm going for a drive ... to clear my thoughts."

"Is that wise?"

He shook his head. "Probably not, but it's something I have to do."

"Aiden..."

"It will be all right."

"Are you sure?"

He knew what she meant. He would find Shanna, and Marta feared for the girl's safety. "No harm will come to anyone."

"But what if you aren't able to control—"

"I won't hurt her. I promise."

Marta steadied Jewel Ann on the table as she rose to her feet. "Take Noel with you."

He shook his head again. "I must do this alone. I *can* do this alone."

Marta sighed and gave him a resigned look. "Call if..."

He touched her shoulder on his way past her. "I won't need any help. Everything will be fine. I just want to talk with her. That's all."

"Aiden—"

He ignored her protest and left the house.

* * * * *

At twenty minutes till twelve, Shanna sat in a dented, hundred-year-old white pickup truck bearing the county workhouse symbol on the doors. Okay, it wasn't a hundred years old, but it seemed like it. The cab had a vinyl bench seat, torn and worn vinyl floor mats, and no padding on the armrests or door panels, just faded black plastic over metal. The inside of the cab smelled like sweat and dirt and stale smoke — the typical halitosis of old vehicles.

74

Her stomach growled as Stan Bartow, her short, balding, shotgun-toting partner for the day, did a head-count of the workers piled in the back, then opened the creaky passenger door and hopped in the seat beside her. "All loaded up?" she mumbled with bland disinterest as she reached for the ignition key.

Stan, a perpetual grinner, nodded his head. "Ready to go back for chowtime."

Shanna started the truck. Looking in the cracked side mirror, she checked the road, then pulled away from the grassy shoulder to take them all back to their wonderful digs down from the jail. She glanced at Stan, still amazed he voiced no objection to her driving. Maybe he just wanted to see if she could handle a three-speed stick on the column. She could, and she had her father to thank for it.

Julie, her older sister by almost ten years, had always been closer to Mom. But Shanna was Daddy's girl — a tomboy surrogate for the son he never had. Her father, an investment counselor, had grown up a farm boy on a nice little forty-acre plot, the Preston family homestead about sixty miles south of Chicago. He taught her to drive his old Ford tractor and a beat-up Chevy pickup he'd inherited from his father. She'd hated to sell their house in the city after her father and mother were killed, but finances dictated it. She'd managed to hang onto the old farm and didn't want to think what kind of disarray it was now in, after more than a year of inattention. But she wasn't ready to give it up.

With a sigh she put away her memories as she pulled the truck into the workhouse parking lot. She hopped out of the truck and helped Stan escort the workers inside, most of them still wearing their neon-reflective pullover vests. As the last of them shuffled inside, she felt an uncontrollable urge to get away from everything for a while. With others to watch over the lunch proceedings, she made a quick excuse to Stan and hurried to her squad car. Just as she reached for her keys to unlock the door, she sensed a presence. Turning, she stared up at Aiden and gasped. "Don't sneak up on me!" He looked as stunning and sexy as he had last night, and she felt a swift tug in her chest, but didn't want to let him know how easily he stole her self-control. "What are you doing here?"

"Waiting for you."

When he smiled, she felt her knees go weak. Leaning against

the car for support, she ignored her reaction to him and announced, "I'm going to lunch."

She opened her car door, and he put a hand on hers. "May I accompany you?"

She withdrew her hand and looked around. "I don't think it's a good idea for you to show yourself around here."

"Because I'm a wanted man?"

She rolled her eyes at his statement of the obvious.

"I tied my hair back, and I'm not wearing my leather coat. I hardly think anyone will recognize me from the scant description in the FBI's APB, especially when I'm having lunch with a sheriff's deputy."

He grinned, flashing his pearly whites that lacked any residual sign of the overgrown canines she'd seen — felt — last night. His fangs looked like perfectly normal teeth for the moment, but she didn't trust him to keep them that way. "I ... uh ... I still don't think it's such a good idea for us to be seen together."

He gave her a pouting frown. "You're afraid of me." His eyes flashed at her neck, and his smile returned. "I see you're still wearing my mark."

She massaged her neck. "Yeah, like I could make it disappear."

He shrugged. "If we're going to spend time together tonight, we should become acclimated to each other."

She scowled at him. "Acclimated?"

"Yes. Chat, get to know each other, and become accustomed to each other's presence, to avoid any unexpected *unpleasantness* while we're working."

He raised his sharp black brows, and she almost regretted that his wonderfully thick, deep auburn hair was curtailed with a black leather tie, except that she was better able to admire the chiseled features of his exotically handsome face. As he grinned, his green eyes danced with something she preferred to think was just innocent mischief. "All right," she grumbled. "But I have to be back here in an hour. And no funny business."

He put up his hands. "You have my word."

She snorted. "Yeah, like that means anything, coming from a guy who claims to be a vampire."

He laid a hand on his chest. "Your cynicism wounds me. Shall I drive?"

She shrugged and locked her cruiser. "Fine. But I hope you're not a control freak who always has to be in charge."

He smiled oddly as he leaned close and whispered, "I'm perfectly willing to let you be the aggressor at least part of the time."

She glared at him, then accompanied him to his conservative sedan, noting the plate number and the little rental sticker on the trunk edge. As he unlocked the doors and held hers open for her, she gave him a warning look. "That 'aggressor' comment isn't supposed to be some sneaky sexual reference, is it?"

"Of course not." He shut the door for her, circled around to the driver's side, and got in. He started the car, then faced her, adding, "Unless you want it to be."

She sighed and sat back in the seat, wondering just what he was up to. Her better judgment warned her she could be making a monumental mistake agreeing to go off with him, but she didn't care. All she could think about was the sudden surge of curiosity and desire flooding her body, and the sexy man sitting close to her — close enough to touch.

* * * * *

What in the hell am I doing? Aiden looked over at Shanna sitting beside him in his car and felt a thunderous charge of lust overwhelm him to the point of nausea. He had no objective other than to get himself near her. He found it sinfully easy to locate her just by clearing his mind and focusing on her essence. Now that he'd caught up with her, he knew what he wanted to do with her, but that was absolutely out of the question. He couldn't let anything like that happen. He forced a smile. "Hungry?"

She glanced sidelong at him and gulped. "Not really."

"Neither am I," he lied. Oh, he was hungry all right, but not for food. He looked her over from head to toe and then made himself focus on backing up the car. As he faced traffic on the main road, he said, "Let's go for a short drive, shall we?"

"Where to?"

"Someplace secluded."

When she glared at him, he made himself laugh. "Just kidding." But he wasn't really. He wanted to take her where they could be alone together, where no one else would interfere. Not a good plan. "What do you suggest?"

"I don't care. Let's just get away from here. Turn right."

He did so, realizing that direction took them out of town, toward the less populated countryside. He felt tingling heat permeate his entire body.

A few miles down the road, he spotted what appeared to be a tree-cloistered turnoff into a hay field. Impulsively he slowed and pulled in.

Shanna glanced at him, her aqua eyes wide. "Why'd you stop?"

"I was tired of driving." He cut the ignition and turned to her. "We need to talk."

She looked around, then drew back and eyed him. "Maybe this isn't the best place to do that."

"I don't want any interruptions."

He heard her breath falter in her chest and sensed her fear and desire as her pulse pounded in his head like a tribal drumbeat. He wanted to touch her, but caught himself before he let his hands reach out to her. He licked his lips and felt the warning protrusion of his canines scraping his tongue. Why hadn't he listened to Marta? This was a terrible idea, allowing himself to be alone with Shanna Preston. He cleared his throat and murmured, "You have to give up this plan you've devised to catch Cameron Ryben. You have stay away from him — and me. I don't want you getting hurt, and I don't know how much longer I can control myself when I'm around you."

She sat very still, blinking her eyes a few times before she whispered, "Is it true you've ... never had sex?"

Her question caught him off guard. He felt himself heating from embarrassment rather than lust. He looked away and mumbled, "Yes, it's true."

He heard her breathing slow and deepen. He could almost feel her thoughts swarming around him, trying to touch that idea and make sense of it. Finally he faced her. "I assume you've had sexual experiences."

She blushed rosy pink, and the reaction made his chest warm.

He smiled, waiting for a confession. She shrugged and looked down at her hands clasped in her lap. "Yeah. But nothing spectacular."

"Would you *like* spectacular sex?" he prodded, immediately regretting the words as they slipped from his mouth.

She looked up at him with a start. "I thought you weren't willing to—"

He reached out and grabbed her by the back of the neck, leaning toward her as he pulled her closer. He pressed his mouth against hers, and the contact of her warm, soft, yielding lips on his ignited a roaring bonfire inside him. With gentle pressure, he enticed her mouth with his and snaked his tongue between her parted lips. When she touched the tip of her tongue to his, he groaned and forced himself to pull away with what shaky vestige of self-control he still had left. Breathing hard, he turned to his side window and raked the back of his hand across his mouth, trying to wipe away every trace of his dangerous indiscretion.

In a tremulous voice she whispered, "I know you want me, Aiden."

Refusing to face her, he managed a weak laugh that came out as a huff. "Obviously."

"Then why don't you just have me?"

He whirled around and glared at her. "I can't. I won't."

She unfastened her seatbelt, and the click drew his eyes to her lap — her crotch. When she moved toward him, he reared back against the door.

She eyed him with determination and something else he wasn't ready to acknowledge. "Listen to me. I haven't had sex in so long, I can't remember why I ever wanted it — well, that is until I met you." She smiled and touched her fingertips tentatively to his nearest forearm. "I admit I'm attracted to you. Maybe it's a bad idea, but I can't seem to stop it, and I'm tired of fighting it."

He drew his arm back, and she let out a ragged sigh. "I'm not saying we have to have a flaming affair. Just once is fine with me, if that's all you're up for."

"Shanna, don't..."

"Aiden, let's do this, so you can get over whatever it is between us that's keeping us from working together. I want Cameron Ryben's head on a stake, and I'll do whatever it takes to make that happen."

Was she offering him mercy sex, or suggesting this in the line of duty? Or did she really want him? He shook his head. It didn't matter, because it would never get that far between them. He wouldn't allow it. He sat forward and reached for the keys dangling in the ignition. "Buckle up. I'm taking you back."

"No." She reached out and pressed his seatbelt latch to release it. When he felt the seatbelt snake back across his chest and stomach, he turned and found her leaning close to him. "Kiss me again, Aiden. Please. And this time, don't hold back."

His heart fluttered in his chest like a frightened bird trying to beat its way out. Could he do what she asked? Should he? He shook his head, knowing he mustn't even consider the possibility. Engaging in sexual activity with this beautiful creature might endanger her life. "You don't know what you're saying."

"Yes, I do." She grabbed a fistful of his tee shirt and pulled him to her. "I want you to make love with me."

Make love? He felt the tug in his loins screaming for release as his mind fought for control. "I-I don't know how."

"You'll figure it out." She smiled and gripped his shoulders, bringing him toward her. "Start by kissing me like you did before."

Swirling in the unthinking fog of lust, he dived at her like a fox after a hen and welded his mouth to hers. The sweet taste of her lips left him wanting more as he drew back and sucked in a harsh breath. "I don't want to hurt you, Shanna."

"You won't." She ran a hand down his cheek, and he folded into her touch. "I trust you. Now trust yourself and make love to me."

He bit his lip, trying to stave off the vision of her naked body lunging under his. "I don't..."

She grabbed for the closure of his jeans, fumbling with the button. "Take off your pants."

He glared at her and pushed her hands away. "You don't want to do this. Not with *me*."

"Yes, I do," she insisted, undoing the top buttons of her tan uniform shirt. "We'd better hurry. I have to go back to work soon."

He sat dazed, watching her remove her shirt. Her perfect alabaster skin begged for his hands to slide all over. When she pulled down the straps of her bra, his gaze darted to her full breasts that bounced out unfettered. His mouth watered, and his loins writhed with need. A groan escaped him as she dropped her bra to the floorboard with her shirt.

After she removed her utility belt and sidearm, he leaned over and tentatively touched his fingertips to her naked breasts. The moment he made contact, he felt the flame rise within him. He smoothed his hands over her, squeezing her breasts as she slid her hands under his tee shirt. Before he could stop himself, he plastered his mouth over first her right nipple and then the left, sucking greedily.

She ripped his tee shirt over his head and then pulled him tight against her. Their nakedness blended like a roiling mist of lust swirling to make them one. He dove for her neck and nipped her, smelling the heat of her blood taunting him.

"We'd have more room in the back seat," she whispered.

As he held her in his arms, he felt the urge overcome him, and then heard her gasp. When he opened his eyes, he found himself leaning over her, with one knee on the back floorboard as she lay sprawled across the back seat.

"How did you...?"

Ignoring her shock at being transported with him to the back seat, he grabbed her trousers and parted the zipper, yanking them down over her hips along with her underwear. In a second he shimmied out of his jeans, kicking off his tennis shoes as he pulled off her black work oxfords. A moment later they were completely naked, their clothes strewn everywhere, tossed across the back of the seats and wadded up on the floorboard.

He eyed the prize he'd dared not want, and saw her looking up at him, willing him to come to her. He touched a hand to her flat, fluttering belly and felt her tense expectation. His gaze slid to the soft, reddish muff between her thighs. Could he do this? Could he pleasure them both without hurting her — without killing her? He sensed no urge within him to do her harm, but he knew how unpredictable the bloodlust could be, especially for someone like him, unaccustomed to its effects. Letting his doubts get the better of him, he tried to pull away, but she reached out and grabbed his arm. Sitting up, she coaxed, "Let me start."

* * * * *

Shanna couldn't get over what she was doing with this glorious man she barely knew. He was so beautiful, mysterious, and frightening. Somehow he'd managed to put them both in the back seat without any effort, but she couldn't think about that right now. Here they were, both naked, and she couldn't keep her eyes and hands off his wondrous body. She expected him to bear some kind of identifying marks like iconoclastic tattoos of his secret profession, but his muscular golden body loomed over her without a blemish of any kind.

Gawking, she wondered how he could be so gorgeous and well endowed, and still be a virgin. But he was just as shy and reticent as she expected someone with no sexual experience to be. She was sure this was not an act.

Her gaze darted to the prize straining between his legs, and she got more than the eyeful she'd bargained for. His long, thick cock appeared to be uncircumcised. With the terrific hard-on he sported, the foreskin all but disappeared. She'd never been much into cocksicles, but she knew she needed to pleasure him first before he'd take the initiative to consummate their relationship. And she did want him to consummate it — her. The tingling heat between her thighs left no doubt. But when she leaned forward to place her face closer to his magnificent appendage, he tried to push her away. Gently she moved his hands aside and murmured, "It'll be okay. Just relax."

When she wrapped her fingers around his shaft, he lurched. She held still until he rested his hands on her back, then she began massaging him with slow, careful strokes. Touching her wet tongue to the swollen head shining a lovely shade of purple, she tasted the sticky dew of his desire budding at the opening and slathered it all over the smooth, taut surface. He groaned and writhed under her touch, caressing her back and shoulders with grateful reverence, as if he'd never experienced anything so wonderful in his life. Realizing he truly hadn't, she dove down over the top of his cock with her mouth wide open to take in as much of him as she could. He cried out and thrust against the back of her throat, almost choking her.

When she pulled away to take a breath, he pushed her on her back. She shuddered at the dark, unholy look in his eyes. With his black pupils almost eclipsing the vivid green of his irises, he seemed like an animal about to devour her as he held her gaze and moved over her. When he parted her thighs and covered her body with the weight and heat of his, she moaned, entranced, wanting and needing him with her whole being, to the depth of her soul.

He pushed against her slick opening, and she thrust her hips upward to accommodate him. With her last bit of reason, she whispered, "You can't come inside me. I'm not on the pill." He didn't answer as he closed his mouth over hers. Sliding against her with slow, easy control, he nuzzled her neck, his hot breath brushing her damp skin. Her pulse jumped when he opened his mouth and clamped his fangs onto her throat. He didn't break the skin, but she feared he planned to. Pinned under him, she couldn't stop him from doing whatever he wanted. The thrill of her total helplessness drove her desire to the edge of madness.

* * * * *

Lost in the fever of lust, Aiden felt his hips moving of their own accord as his fangs found the hot pulsing prize at Shanna's neck — her jugular vein. His jaws ached, and his mouth watered to clamp down hard and draw blood, but he knew he wasn't ready yet. His penis, suddenly alive and working for the first time in his life, searched blindly for her opening. Covered in the juices of her desire, he slid closer and caught the inner folds of her vulva. With no self-control whatsoever, he plunged inside and groaned with her as her pain and pleasure and surprise mingled with his own.

The sensation of moving inside her deep, wet warmth drove him to distraction, and he pumped harder and faster until his mind went numb. He had no sense of time passing until the pressure surged deep within her, and she cried out in release, pleasure coursing through her body in waves that grabbed him hard, again and again. With his fangs aching to find anchor, he massaged her neck with his lips then bit through her skin. Hot blood gushed into his mouth, and he gulped it down his throat as his hips lurched and his loins exploded in awesome, electrifying relief that left him tingling and trembling. Slowing to a halt, he licked her neck and stopped the flow of blood with his saliva. Exhausted, he collapsed and buried his face in her silken hair, relieved that she still breathed beneath him.

* * * * *

Shanna felt weak but wondrously satiated. She let out a soft sigh, shifting under the weight of her lover. *Her lover.* She'd never thought of a man that way before. She'd had casual boyfriends and a bit of casual sex, but nothing like this. This was different. This was — she grinned, recalling their earlier conversation — *spectacular.*

She turned her head to eye the man who'd managed to elevate himself to the esteemed position of Her Lover. He breathed evenly but seemed unusually still. Had he fallen asleep? Gently she touched his shoulder. "Aiden, are you all right?"

He pressed an arm against the seat and lifted himself up. The dreamy soft look on his glorious face told her right away he was just fine. Except — was that blood on his lips? "Aiden, what happened? You're bleeding." When she reached up to touch his mouth, he lunged off her. She sat up and felt his seed evacuating from inside her. *Oh, God!* "Quick! Get some napkins or something."

In a flash he wedged himself between the front seats. She heard him pop open the glove compartment. A moment later he returned with a package of moist wipes she assumed he'd put in the car for Jewel Ann. Pulling two out, he handed her the package, then turned away. She stuffed several wipes between her thighs and watched him clean his mouth with a quick swipe, then tidy his groin area. While he had his back to her, she opened the car door and tossed out the evidence of their lovemaking. When she slammed the door shut, he looked over at her. She pulled on her panties and trousers with haste. *Stupid, stupid, stupid!* "I have to get back to work," she croaked, trying not to lose her composure. *Why did I let this happen?*

As he grabbed his jeans and shoes, she opened the door again and climbed out. Scurrying to the front passenger door, she got back inside the car and wrestled with her bra as she pondered the consequences of what they'd done. She hadn't planned on this happening and hadn't come prepared. Inexperienced and obviously trying to avoid their sexual interlude, Aiden had failed to exercise self-control or provide the necessary protection. As quickly as things happened, she'd been unable to stop the inevitable mistake.

She took several deep breaths, trying to calm her rising hysteria. Once she had her shirt buttoned and tucked in, she fastened her utility belt and looked over to find Aiden dressed and positioned in the driver's seat. He seemed hesitant to look her in the eyes, and she guessed he was ashamed of what he'd done, regretting, even fearing his slip-up. And well he should, after she'd warned him she wasn't on the pill. A sudden rush of tears flooded her eyes, and she covered her face with her hands.

She jerked when she felt his hand on her hair, stroking her. "I'm so sorry, Shanna."

She swiped at her eyes and nose and jerked at her shirt collar. "It's my fault, not yours. I shouldn't have pushed you."

With his hand still resting at the back of her head, he pulled her close and touched his feverish forehead to hers. "My biology differs from yours enough that I'm reasonably sure nothing will result from just one time." He kissed the top of her head, adding, "But as incredibly satisfying as it was, we can never do this again."

She shot him a look, then pulled away. Trying to swallow down her fear and shame, she eyed her lap and mumbled, "Um, yeah, right. You'd better take me back to work before I'm late."

CHAPTER 7

Shanna repeatedly stole glances at Aiden as he pulled his car out of the field and drove her back to work. He didn't speak and never once met her eyes. His stoic profile revealed nothing. How could he be so calm? She frowned and looked away. Perhaps now that he'd sampled what he'd been lusting after, the thrill was gone. When he parked beside her cruiser in front of the workhouse, she glanced at him again. He still didn't look at her.

When she reached for the door handle, he said, "What time do you finish your work shift?"

She found him contemplating her with a chilling gaze. "Why?"

"Do you still wish to assist me in tracking Cameron Ryben?"

Did she? Suddenly her quest to capture the murderer didn't seem quite as important as before. She had other things on her mind now. She shrugged. "Yeah, sure."

"I'll pick you up at your residence after you get off work. Tell me when and where."

Eyeing him, she tried to figure out his angle with this new cold, cooperative attitude. Why had he changed his mind about letting her get involved in his hunt for Ryben? Unable to come up with a satisfactory explanation, she sighed and gave him her address and directions to her apartment. "I get off work at four. It'll take me a little while to get home and shower. Five o'clock should give me enough time."

He nodded once.

Frowning, she surveyed him. "Are you okay?" Other than appearing slightly flushed, he seemed determined to maintain a placid demeanor. She suspected he tried a bit too hard to be cool and collected, and she feared something was wrong.

"I'm perfectly fine," he said without batting an eye.

"Maybe we should talk about what we—"

"I'll see you at five this afternoon, Shanna."

Assuming she'd been dismissed because he didn't want to discuss the ramifications of what they'd done, she got out of the car, shut the door, and stepped away. He backed up the car and drove off. She couldn't shake the feeling she'd been used and dumped, and doubted he'd show up at her place as promised. The hollowness growing in her chest threatened to engulf her. "Bastard," she grumbled under her breath.

As she walked toward the tiny front office of the workhouse, Stan Bartow, her temporary partner, swung the door open and held it for her. "Didn't think you were gonna come back, Preston, after you left in such a hurry with your boyfriend." He winked.

Shanna blinked at him, startled that he'd been watching her, and thankful he hadn't recognized Aiden Marschant as the man wanted by the FBI for questioning. She was tempted to correct his error in categorizing Aiden as her boyfriend, until she realized that's exactly what he'd become. He might not hold the title very long, but that's what he was, for now.

She walked away from Stan, trying hard to ignore the smirk of the county officer sitting behind the beat-up counter with a backdrop of cheap paneling. "Come on," she called over her shoulder to Stan. "I bet our crew can't wait to resume picking up trash along the highway. I know I'm chomping at the bit."

"Hey, hold on a minute, Preston," Stan said, walking up beside her. She turned, surprised when he leaned close to peer at her neck. "Is that blood on your collar?" She touched her fingertips tentatively to her neck, then scowled when she felt sticky residue.

"I know you didn't nick yourself shaving." He straightened and winked again. "By the look of that hickey on the other side, I'd say your nooner got a little out of hand."

She darted into the bathroom and slammed door. Fumbling around for the light switch, she turned on the stark overhead light and rushed to the tarnished mirror over the grungy standalone sink. She craned her neck and pulled her hair back to see the clotted blood that had oozed from deep, full-mouth teeth marks. "Son of a bitch! He *bit* me!"

"You okay in there, Preston?"

"Yeah, yeah, just peachy," she snarled, grabbing some paper towels from the dispenser mounted on the wall. Wetting them, she dabbed at the quickly bruising area, noting the indentation where Aiden's teeth had pressed down hard on her flesh, just short of tearing her skin. When she cleared the blood away, she saw the four neat round puncture wounds from fangs—both upper and lower. "Son of a bitch!"

She jumped at the sound of Stan tapping on the door. "Hey, you need some help?"

Swallowing hard, she dared another glance at the fang marks. They looked deep. She probably needed to disinfect them and bandage them. Maybe she needed stitches. "Can you ... um ... find me a first-aid kit?"

"Yeah, sure. Hold on a minute."

As she heard Stan ask the other officer for the first-aid kit, her stomach rolled, and her knees started to fold. Grabbing the sink, she waited for the wave of nausea to pass. Through the fog filling her head, she barely noticed the door swing open.

"Jesus, Preston! You better sit down before you fall and knock yourself out." Stan slammed down the toilet seat lid and took her by the arm to help her find a safe perch. Once she was settled on the toilet, her head stopped spinning. She took a deep, tremulous breath, then managed to look up at Stan holding a slightly rusted blue metal first-aid case in his hand. "You want me to call a doctor or something?" he offered.

She grimaced and looked down at the dirt-encrusted beige linoleum floor. She'd skipped breakfast to get to the station early enough to talk with Grainger this morning, then skipped lunch too — to do the wild thing with Aiden. No wonder she was woozy. "No, I just ... maybe I need to eat something. Could you get me a package of cheese crackers and a soda out of the vending machines?"

When she started to dig some change out of her pocket, he said, "No problem. I got it. You just sit there and take it easy." He moved to the door, then turned back. "Maybe you ought to report off sick and go home. You aren't pregnant, are you? When my wife—"

"No!" she roared, instantly regretting it. Her head reeled and pounded as if it were about to explode. Carefully she swallowed down the nausea rising in her stomach and rubbed her temples with her fingertips, admitting, "Maybe I *should* go home. I'm not feeling so hot all of a sudden."

* * * * *

Aiden slogged up the curving stone walk to the front entrance of the half-million-dollar executive home he'd leased short-term. The red aura tinting his vision gave the tan brickwork a bloody tinge. His stomach rolled and growled with an acidic burn mimicking hunger and nausea combined. He knew what he was hungry for, and why, but he'd sworn never again to taste that forbidden fruit. He'd just have to ride this out and hope for the best. Still, an unsettling feeling nagged him. Across the miles he sensed Shanna's growing unease. Despite her valiant determination to cope, he knew she was in trouble, and it was his fault. He had to do something, but wasn't sure what. He was in over his head and needed help.

He reached for the brass handle on the front door, and the door swung open as if by magic. The hint of magic disappeared, replaced by Marta's long, glowering visage. "Where have you been?" She grabbed him by the arm and jerked him through the doorway, making him stumble across the threshold.

Aiden straightened, trying to repair his damaged composure by smoothing his palms over the front of his black tee shirt. The moment he did so, he recalled hastily tucking the hem into his jeans while dressing in the car, after his torrid encounter with Shanna. He glared at Marta and let out a harsh sigh.

She sniffed the air near him. "Is that *blood* I smell on your breath?" She reared back. "By all we hold sacred, Aiden, tell me! What have you done?" She glanced over her shoulder when Noel came hurrying into the foyer to investigate the commotion.

Aiden tried to ascend the stairs, but Marta's grip on his arm tightened like a vise as she repeated louder, "What have you done, Aiden?"

"Let him be, woman!" Noel ordered, hobbling over to pull her off Aiden. "Ain't it plain that he done what was needed?"

"What of the girl?" Marta demanded.

Aiden's stomach clenched at the thought of Shanna. He wanted to see her, hold her, taste her, love her again. He wanted to make her *his*. Caught in the haze of his feverish musings, he turned toward Marta, barely able to make out the worry lining her face. "She's not been harmed."

"But ye bedded her, didn't ye?" Noel prodded. "Just to take the edge off the bloodlust."

Aiden moved his head with effort to face the old man frowning up at him. He saw no benefit in lying as he admitted, "Yes."

Noel put a gnarled hand on Aiden's shoulder and gave him a hearty pat. "'Twas the best thing. Ye fought it valiant, but a time comes in every man's life when he must face the demons of his lust. Ye've battled yers far too long, Aiden."

Marta slapped Noel's shoulder and pushed him away. "Stop blathering, you old coot." She jerked on Aiden's arm, forcing him to look at her. "You lost self-control and partook of her blood. For her sake I hope you had the good sense to use discretion and keep your seed from spilling into her. Tell me you used protection!"

Aiden's composure crumbled. He grabbed the stair newel and held his stomach. "I need to lie down."

Marta tightened her grip on his arm, digging her fingers into his tense muscles. "Not until you tell me exactly what you did to that poor girl."

He shook his head as tears filled his eyes — tears of fear and regret. "I wasn't prepared. I didn't intend for anything to happen."

"Of course you intended for something to happen," she said in calm rebuke. "You sought her out and put her in a situation that would allow you to do exactly what your body demanded."

He groaned and leaned against the banister. "I've shirked my duty and put her in danger. What can I do?"

"You have some hard decisions to make, Aiden. Go upstairs and lie down. You must think about what you have done, and make amends as best you can. We must warn the girl of what might happen, and explain what she may expect. She must be told the truth." Marta let go of him. "I'll be up in a minute with a tonic to help ease your distress. Then we'll discuss how to best handle the girl and this hellish situation you've created."

She shook her head and walked away, growling at Noel on her way out, "And you, egging him on to relieve himself in the bloodlust, as if it were a mere youthful indiscretion. He may have ruined his future as a Protector — and he could have killed. Do you not have a bit of sense, you horny old goat?"

Noel hung his head. "I was just thinkin' of his best interest."

She spun around and glared at him. "Spare us all and refrain from thinking from now on!"

* * * * *

Lying on the bed on his side with his back to the door, Aiden heard Marta's footsteps on the stairs. He'd managed to regain a small semblance of his composure, but still couldn't believe how quickly he'd fallen apart when confronted with the terrible thing he'd done to Shanna. He assumed it was the bloodlust weakening his resolve and getting hold of his emotions. He'd have to maintain a stronger front and not allow his fear and debility to get the better of him again. Such behavior was inappropriate for a Protector. Of course, he might not be a Protector for long.

He refused to move when he heard Marta push the door open. The soft scuff of a side chair being pulled across the carpet to his bedside alerted him that she sat nearby. "Have you calmed yourself sufficiently to talk now?" she asked. "Sit up and drink the tonic I prepared."

He lay still for a second, not wanting to confront Marta. Finally he turned and pushed himself up, swinging his legs over the side of the bed to face her. He dreaded this conversation, knowing what must be said, but he couldn't avoid it. He met her steely gaze as she handed him the steaming cup.

Bringing the yellowish tea-like liquid close to his mouth, he sniffed. It smelled of roots and grass, and something acridly pungent he couldn't identify. Marta prided herself on being well schooled in the traditions of their people, and this was a longstanding remedy to ease the symptoms of bloodlust. He didn't know how effective it was, having never suffered bloodlust until now, but he wouldn't shun any reasonable aid offered. He took a sip and winced as the hot liquid seared his mouth and throat.

"That's it. Drink up. In a little while you'll want to take a cool shower to wash away your body's toxins, once you begin perspiring. It should start working soon. Swallow it all quickly so you can get the full effect."

He assumed by 'toxins,' she meant the raging hormones flooding his bloodstream. He took another gulp. Strangely it didn't burn as bad. To get past the horrid taste, he guzzled the remainder, then handed the empty cup to her.

Cradling the cup in her palms, she rested her hands on her closed knees and leaned forward. "We've much to do, Aiden. Now tell me exactly what happened between you and Shanna Preston, and don't be shy. There's no time for bashfulness at this point."

He lunged off the bed and paced away from Marta. "I don't know how it happened. Everything just ... progressed so quickly, I didn't realize what I was doing until ... until it was over. And then, of course, it was too late." He turned to her and grimaced.

"Did you force yourself on her?"

"No!"

"Then how did things get out of control?"

He looked aside, trying to recall what had taken place between him and Shanna. He couldn't deny he'd wanted something to happen, even before he left the house this morning. And he didn't doubt for a moment Marta knew that. He'd been under the influence of the bloodlust almost from the instant he met Shanna, and only now admitted it to himself. When Shanna offered herself to him, he couldn't resist.

He sighed miserably and wandered back to the bed, plopping down on the nearest corner. "How could I have let this happen? I never imagined I would give up all my years of training and discipline so easily. And why now? It makes no sense."

Marta got up from her chair and came over to sit beside him on the edge of the bed. She placed a hand on his knee. "Something about Shanna drew you, Aiden. It is the chemistry of emotion, of our bodies, and who can explain how that works? Sometimes we fall in love when we have no intention of doing so. Many would look at Noel and me and wonder how we ever became matched. We are so dissimilar and seemingly ill-suited, and he is a stubborn and ornery old goat no woman in her right mind would want. Yet we are still true to each other to this day. That's just how it happens, Aiden, even considering how odd it is you would be attracted to a human female after rejecting so many of your own line over the years. You could fight this thing between you and Shanna with all your might and will, but if it is truly what you want, you will find a way, despite your higher reason and sense of duty, to let it come about. And that is just what you have done."

She patted his knee in an uncharacteristic attempt to comfort him. "You have given many years of faithful service to the Enclave Protectorate, Aiden. Perhaps your body is telling you it's time to retire."

He glanced sidelong at her. "Protectors are not allowed to retire until they can no longer do their job."

"Which may be the fate that has befallen you since your bout with bloodlust. We must inform the Enclave straight away, so that another Protector can be sent to deal with Cameron Ryben in your stead."

Aiden shook his head and stared at his hands clasped between his knees. "The Enclave will have my head on a stake for disregarding my vow of celibacy."

"Maybe. Maybe not. That remains to be seen. Certainly they are sticklers for their traditions and rules, but the demands they make on Protectors have long been debated. It would be a shame indeed if they chose to ignore your previously spotless record of service. Of course, all this is moot until you appear before them to state your case. In the meantime, we cannot afford to guess how they will rule. Our immediate problem is to fetch Shanna and keep watch on her here at the house until we know for sure whether she will succumb to the effects of your attempt to mate with her."

Attempt? He'd already mated with her successfully, and his bloodlust instinct drove him to finish it — to make it permanent. Another intimate encounter with Shanna, perhaps two, with a real blood exchange between them, and she would be his forever. His mind, body, and soul would be linked with hers in a bond so strong, only death would sever it. If old lore could be believed, even death might not break it.

"Do you know where to find her?" Marta asked.

Aiden nodded.

"Then take Noel with you, to ensure nothing else untoward happens between you and her, until we can be sure of her condition. I know it will be difficult for you to abide her in the house without touching her again, but that you must do. Another incident would only make things worse for the both of you. If she shows no symptoms of turning, we will release her. But if she does, you must be prepared to do whatever is necessary."

He glared at her.

"You know what I'm talking about. Don't pretend otherwise. If she cannot survive the change, she will go mad and must be put down, just as if she were a Shanrak rogue. Because, truly, she will be every bit as bad, hungering for the flesh and blood of others like an insatiable animal."

Aiden scowled and looked away. Turning humans to Shanrak, even if they remained at the lowest blood-power level like Noel and Marta, had been taboo for ages. If Shanna survived the change successfully, she would no longer be just human. She would be something else — something the Enclave strictly forbade. Yet, from time to time, it happened, usually when a rogue in the throes of bloodlust failed to kill a victim. But without the proper follow-up for that victim, what resulted was often just as bad as a rogue — a creature that could not be allowed to continue living. Aiden felt his self-control falter when he thought of Shanna descending into gnashing madness because of his carelessness. He couldn't let that happen.

"If that fate bypasses Shanna," Marta continued in a calm voice, "and she does go through the change successfully, you must be prepared to finish the mating in a way that will not bind you permanently to her. It simply would not be appropriate for you to tie yourself to such an inferior creature for life. If you are forced to leave the Protectorate, there are still many of your own bloodline suitable and eager to become your life mate."

Aiden wouldn't consider discarding Shanna in favor of some one else. No other interested him like Shanna. "If need be, I will complete the mating bond to ensure Shanna will have the best chance of coming through the change without bad results."

Marta scowled at him. "Just remember, Aiden. Even if you complete the mating bond, she will always be dependent on you, never to have the strength of will or pureness of blood to become a creature whole, in and of herself. Do you truly want a once-human weakling tugging at your shirttails the rest of your days? You could grow to resent her, even hate her. It has been known to happen."

He shook his head. He could never hate Shanna. He loved her. He hungered for her. Even now, in the throes of his need for her, he could barely think of anything else.

Marta got up from her perch next to him and walked to the door. "Take Noel with you, Aiden. Find Shanna and bring her back here. You mustn't have unprotected intercourse with her again or drink her blood — or allow her to ingest yours. Doing so will not bode well for either of you. Once she's in our care, we'll deal with things as they come."

Aiden got up from the bed, feeling weak in the knees and sweaty all over. He needed to shower. He glanced at the clock at his bedside, noting it was almost two-thirty. Being with Shanna again occupied his thoughts as he watched Marta exit his room. No matter what his caretaker said, he had his own agenda for handling the situation with Shanna. He'd done what he'd done, and now he alone was responsible for her. If that meant for the rest of her life, so be it.

CHAPTER 8

After gobbling some cheese crackers and washing them down with a soda, Shanna convinced herself she felt well enough to finish her work shift. Bandaging her neck to hide the evidence of Aiden's bite, she helped Stan get the workers to their assigned area, albeit an hour later than scheduled. When three-thirty rolled around, she was more than ready for them to pack it up and return to the workhouse. Prudently, Stan offered to drive the truck while she rode shotgun.

"You gonna be okay driving home, Preston?" Stan asked.

Shanna nodded. "Yeah, I think so. Sorry about earlier."

"No problem. Just get yourself checked out."

She managed a quick smile as she unlocked her patrol car. "I'm fine. Really." But she was lying. As soon as she got in the driver's seat and Stan went to his vehicle, she buried her clammy forehead in her palms. Her head had started pounding an hour ago, getting steadily worse. Now nausea had set in again. She assumed this was the worst case of flu she'd ever had, but a nagging worry in the back of her mind told her it might be something else. She couldn't dismiss the fear that she'd caught something horrible from Aiden.

She shook her head and fastened her seatbelt, then started the car. What kind of virus would work that fast? She knew her paranoia ran wild. She just suffered from a stomach bug, and it was a coincidence that it hit her right after she'd spent intimate time with Aiden. But as she drove home, she changed her mind when her stomach tried to eat her alive. By the time she reached her apartment door, it was almost four-thirty, and she felt on the verge of collapse.

Knowing Aiden had promised to arrive at five, she fumbled for her door key, feeling woozier by the second. She hoped showering before he got there would help her feel better. But as soon as she opened the door and stepped inside her living room, she sensed something amiss — somebody was in her apartment! Tensing, she pulled her gun and froze, glancing around for evidence of the intruder.

A second later, Aiden appeared in the doorway leading from her bedroom. As soon as she set eyes on his tall, muscular form, her fear turned to need. God, he was sexy. She wanted him beyond reason. The very thought of touching him made her tremble uncontrollably, and her need was so intense, she came close to nausea. She couldn't understand her overboard reaction. Swallowing carefully, she lowered her gun to her side. "What are you doing here? I told you five o'clock. And how'd you get in?"

He shrugged and crossed his arms in front of his chest as he leaned against the doorframe. "You invited me to come, which gave me the necessary permission to enter your dwelling."

"Is that lame vampire joke supposed to be funny?" She tried to laugh, but it came out as a weak huff. "What comes next — the Svengali hypnotizing stare to put me under your spell?"

He raised his brows. "Excuse me?"

She looked into his emerald green eyes, suddenly wanting to be put under his spell — and under his yummy body. She held his gaze, willing him toward her, but he stayed near the doorway.

Realizing how ridiculous she was acting, she snorted and moved toward her bedroom, but stopped a foot short when he failed to step aside to let her pass. Her body heated in his proximity, and she had to make herself stand her ground as she glared up at him. "I need to go to my room."

He moved out of her way and followed her inside. Her room had warmed to a brassy gold as afternoon daylight approached evening. She pulled off her gun and radio and dropped them on her nightstand. When she turned to confront Aiden standing behind her, she noticed the old man, Noel, lurking in the shadowy corner by her overstuffed flowered chair. Recalling how eager he'd been for Aiden and her to get together, she frowned. "What's *he* doing here? Not chaperoning, I hope."

Aiden's lips twisted in a smile. "He is, in a manner of speaking."

She looked from Aiden to his aide, then turned toward her bathroom. "I need to shower."

Aiden followed her, slipping inside before she could slam the bathroom door and shut him out. "We need to talk."

"Fine. Give me some privacy and let me shower, then I'll be all ears."

"We need to talk *now*."

The door creaked open, and Noel ducked his head full of shocking white hair into the small room. "It is unwise for the two of ye to remain alone together in this confined space."

An inhuman rage lurched in Shanna's chest. "What the hell is it to you, old man?" she roared. Blinking, she staggered back a step, shocked by her uncharacteristic aggressiveness.

Noel looked to Aiden, then shot her an apologetic grimace. "Marta bade me keep an eye on the two of ye, to make sure nothin' else untoward transpired between ye."

Shanna glared at Aiden. "You *told* them?"

He lifted his palms. "I had little choice. There are important issues we must discuss."

She gave him an impatient huff, then reached up and ripped off the gauze pad she'd taped to her neck. She caught Aiden's pained look as she tossed it in the trash, but it didn't matter how pained he acted. She was the one with the bruises and bite marks on her neck.

"So, talk," she snapped, unbuttoning her shirt. "I can listen while I get cleaned up." She glanced at Noel with his head still poking into the bathroom. "And you — is it necessary you watch?"

Noel gave a little indignant cough, then mumbled, "I'll be right on the other side of the door, in case ye need anythin'."

Shanna watched the door until it clicked shut. Quickly she peeled off her shirt and dropped it to the floor. Flicking a hot gaze at Aiden, she caught his eyes zeroing in on her cleavage. She heated, feeling oddly charged at the thought of him watching her undress. Her head started to swirl, and her stomach gnawed a reminder that she hadn't overcome her nausea. Pausing in her partial state of undress, she breathed carefully, trying to maintain control.

"You're not feeling well," Aiden said, approaching her.

She stepped back from him. "Your toady's right. I don't think it's a good idea for you to be in here."

"I need to tell you something."

She put a hand over her breasts still covered by her bra. *Uh-oh. Here it comes.* "You better not say you have some kind of terrible, contagious disease."

"Not exactly." He grimaced.

"Oh, my God!" She turned away, flinching when his hands lit on her shoulders. She shuddered under his touch, wanting desperately for him to release her and step back. But the burning deep within her flared like a flash fire, and she knew she wanted him closer — a lot closer. Gulping down her maddening confusion, she let out a few quick breaths and whispered, "I really need to get cleaned up. Please, give me some space."

He let go of her and stepped back. Trembling, she reached behind the shower curtain and turned on the water to let it warm up. Without facing him, she mumbled, "I could use some privacy right now, Aiden."

"I'm sorry. What I have to tell you can't wait."

She gasped for breath, trying to calm herself, but it was no use. She whirled on him. "Then talk!" When she reached around and undid her bra, pulling it off, his eyes darkened at the sight of her naked breasts. She let him take in the view, then kicked off her shoes and pulled off her socks. Undoing her trousers, she skimmed them down along with her panties and stepped out of them. When she straightened, she found his gaze traveling the length of her naked form, but the roar of her lust masked whatever embarrassment she might have suffered.

Sealing her lips with determination, she turned and raked back the shower curtain. She reached to test the water temperature and stepped into the tub. Jerking the shower curtain shut, she surrendered her flushed face to the onslaught of water. With her eyes closed and Aiden so close, she felt the rush of desire leap inside her with a vengeance. As warm water cascaded over her, she put a hand over her mouth and held her stomach to keep from vomiting. She knew something was wrong — terribly wrong — and she suspected Aiden could tell her exactly what it was. He wanted to tell her, but she didn't want to hear it.

She lurched and turned as the back end of the shower curtain slid open. With water shedding down her back, she paled when she saw Aiden, completely naked, step into the tub with her. He closed the curtain, faced her without smiling, and surveyed her from head to toe. Slowly he raised his gaze back to her face. "First," he said in a low tone barely audible over the spray of the shower, "I want to apologize."

Her heart thudded in her chest. Despite the warm water cascading down her back, her body felt cold and lonely, devoid of his touch. She wanted him near her, plastered against her, with not a breath of air to separate them. She stifled the urge to leap on him and wrap her arms around him. Standing her ground, she stared up into his luminous green eyes while the heat of the shower and her lust enveloped her.

Involuntarily her gaze dropped to his protruding shaft. Despite his professed need to talk, she saw a more pressing need. Dragging her stare back to his face, she waited. He swallowed hard and clenched his fists. She knew he was near losing control. "Wh-What did you want to tell me?" she croaked.

He opened his mouth, but no words came forth. His face looked pained as he stared at her. She knew he wanted to touch her, to hold her. But she also knew it was a bad idea. He had something very important to confess to her — so important that he hesitated to blurt it out. It had to be something regarding their intimacy.

In a flash he moved so close that her nose almost touched his chest. She eyed his smooth golden skin and sucked in a breath heavy with humidity and the scent of his lust. She could smell his skin, smell his hair, smell his *need*. How, when had she gained that ability? Drawing another breath, she took all of him in and let him fill her senses. He had become her drug of choice, and she wanted to OD on him. Without thinking, she slid her arms around his waist and pulled him close. He wrapped his arms around her. The shower sprayed them both, but nothing could wash away the desire swirling between them.

"Make love to me again. Please." She hugged him tight and buried her face in his chest. The feel of his body pressing against her turned her nausea to something sweeter and more intense that moved lower inside her and spread like a warm elixir through her veins.

He held her close, stroking her wet hair under the spraying water. "I must explain the situation, Shanna. When I do, you might not want to remain so close to me."

She hugged him harder. "I don't want to hear it. I just want to be with you."

"And I with you. But you must listen. Please."

She nodded her head, unable to form words.

His chest heaved with a deep sigh. He reached down behind her and turned off the water. As the showerhead gurgled, dribbling out the last of the water down her back, he took her by the shoulders and searched her face. When she planted her palms against his chest, he closed his eyes briefly, then opened them and looked down at her. His expression seemed even more glum than before.

"What's wrong?"

He grimaced and tightened his grip on her shoulders. "I may have ... done something terrible."

She frowned, trying to imagine what he was getting at. "Did you hurt someone?"

He swallowed hard. "Perhaps."

"Who?"

"You."

She blinked her eyes, surprised, then let out a breathless chuckle. "If you're talking about earlier today in your car —"

"That's exactly what I'm talking about."

A twinge of dread tweaked her chest. "I thought you said nothing would happen because of your —"

"I was wrong. I think something *has* happened."

"T-To me?"

He dropped his hands from her shoulders and took a step back. "Yes."

As her dread graduated to fear, her breathing came fast and shallow, and her knees turn to jelly. When she started to sink down, Aiden slid his arms around her waist and pulled her up against him. Vaguely she realized she was near shock. She wasn't ready to be a parent. Was he? Dazed, she looked up into his eyes and found them full of passion — and regret. "I-I don't think..." She gulped and tried again. "I can't handle being pregnant right now."

His eyes widened, and she felt her knees regain their former strength. She stood on her own and backed away from him. "Isn't that what you meant?"

Slowly he shook his head. Renewed fear chilled her to the pit of her stomach. It was worse? "What then?"

"I'm sorry." He shot her an aggrieved look, then stepped

forward and gripped her shoulders again. "I'm so very sorry, Shanna. I didn't realize what I was doing until it was too late."

"What are you talking about?" Apprehension blossomed like cotton balls in her throat, threatening to choke her.

"When we made love ... I..." He shook his head and glanced down, then eyed her and started again. "I partook of your blood *and* released my seed into you. That begins the mating ritual. Now..."

"Now *what*?" She tried to calm her panting, but her chest felt so tight she had trouble breathing. "What, Aiden? What?"

"It's possible you will undergo the change. You already show the preliminary signs."

"Change?" she echoed, trying not to shriek. "What the hell are you talking about?"

He hardened his mouth and turned away. She grabbed his nearest arm and pulled him around to face her. "What's going to happen to me, Aiden? Tell me!"

He tried to caress her face, but she knocked his hand away. "Tell me right now, damn it!"

"Your body is changing, and so is mine. Our mating has initiated a bond between us. It would be strengthened, made permanent, if we were to complete the mating ritual. If we do not complete the ritual, it is possible we could both suffer irreparable damage."

Shanna swallowed several times to moisten her cottony throat. She ran a hand over her wet matted hair. Turning away, she tried to stave off sudden tears, but they cascaded uncontrolled down her cheeks. She swiped at them and faced Aiden. "What kind of damage?"

He let out a harsh sigh. "Madness. A killing madness, with insatiable lust for blood and flesh and sexual domination that will not stop, ever — until death."

Suddenly she wanted to laugh, but she was sure he was not joking, and this was not a laughing matter. He was serious — *dead* serious. She waited a moment to regain control of the tittering fit about to explode from within her. When she felt the butterfly tickles in her stomach subside, she took a couple of deep breaths and calmed herself. "Are you sure?" Her voice sounded shaky and unfamiliar, as if she were listening to someone else talk in another room.

"Yes. I'm sorry. I didn't mean for any of this to —"

She put up a hand to silence him. Useless excuses after the fact wouldn't fix anything. "Is there something we can do?"

She saw his chest heave repeatedly with excitement. His cock pointed up at her like an accusing appendage waiting for her apology of flesh and blood and love. She blinked at it, then looked back to his face. "Do we have any options at all?"

He shuddered and clenched his fists repeatedly, obviously having trouble calming himself. "Marta wants you to come to the house and remain under close observation. She thinks there's a chance you'll come through this relatively unscathed."

Shanna blinked her eyes, trying not to think of herself as a rampaging killer on the loose, looking for hapless victims to prey upon. She gulped hard. "What do *you* think?"

Aiden's eyes darkened as he looked down at her. "I think," he rasped, "that we shouldn't wait. We should complete the mating ritual before it's too late, to ensure neither of us suffers needlessly or goes beyond the point of no return."

The idea of joining again with this man erased whatever fear had gripped her moments ago. She looked up at him with longing and acceptance, then moved forward and wrapped her arms around his naked waist. Pressing herself against him, she felt his hardness dig into her belly. One thought overtook her — she wanted him inside her, and nothing else mattered.

As if he could read her mind and body, he grabbed her ass and lifted her up to meet his cock. She locked her arms around his neck and wrapped her legs around his waist as he eased her over his swollen head, onto his thick, rock-hard shaft. Slick with anticipation, she slid down on him and groaned with relief as he stretched her and filled her to the limit. Her entire body shuddered with lust. She wanted him inside her, all of him, until she couldn't tell where she ended and he began. In that one moment she knew she'd waited all her life for this man.

With his powerful arms holding her in place, he effortlessly rocked her against him and hunched under her as she held tight and rode him. Their moans and groans echoed in the confined space of the curtained tub, and the heat of their exertion permeated the musky sex-scented air like a jungle rainforest.

She squirmed against him, and he stopped, letting go of her long enough to drop her to her feet and spin her around. She braced herself against the slippery, tiled tub wall as he hunched over her backside and shoved himself inside her again. He ground into her, then pumped hard and fast. The repeated slapping sound played like tribal music in her ears. Her body burned all over, and the feel of him sliding in and out drove her to mindless madness. She arched her rear high in the air and braced herself with her arms to keep him from ramming her head against the wall as he slammed harder and harder. With each impact, her heart came nearer to exploding until finally the release washed over her, then socked her in the loins. She bucked and cried out, rocking and writhing as the spasms gripped her entire body.

Still pumping from behind, Aiden shoved his wrist up to her mouth and growled, "Drink of me."

She saw blood dripping from the jagged tear he'd made by biting open his own skin. Moaning in the throes of orgasm, she could barely stand up and couldn't respond. He jerked her hair, pulling her head aside to expose her neck. As he opened his mouth wide and clamped down on her jugular, he shoved his dripping wrist against her lips. Pulling his mouth back, he demanded, "Drink!"

Unable to resist his commanding voice, she opened her mouth and touched her tongue to the warm, wet flesh he offered. Instantly the musky scent of his sex and the metallic sweet smell of his blood drove her orgasmic madness to a new level of ecstasy. She swallowed small dribbles of his blood, and it burned her throat all the way down to her stomach. She felt the pressure of his fangs puncturing her neck, but rode it in pleasure rather than pain. Her eyes dimmed, and she lost herself in the moment.

Holding her tight by the waist, he lurched and groaned and slowed to a stop. Weak and shaky, she let him pull her up and ease her back against him as he leaned on the tub wall. His rock-solidness steadied her, and she felt his heart hammering as his chest rose and fell with hard, fast breaths. He stroked her sweaty, trembling body, running his hands all over her stomach and breasts until she relaxed and regained control of her legs.

Still in the circle of his arms, she turned around to face him, offering her mouth to his. The sight of her own blood covering his lips didn't faze her. She wanted to taste him, to taste the two of them mingled inseparably together. It occurred to her how odd and repulsive this would have seemed just hours ago, before they'd first made love. But now everything was different, surreal. She wasn't sure why she was so accepting.

He bowed his head and kissed her softly. The tangy taste of her own blood and his permeated her mouth with a tingling sensation. She rolled her saturated tongue over his. Lower, between them, his spent member rejuvenated to another full-blown erection. She wriggled against him until he pulled away and whispered, "Let's shower, my love. We could use a few moments to recuperate."

She turned from him and giggled like a silly schoolgirl, realizing she was acting intoxicated. She *felt* inebriated — drunk with love. Turning on the water, she drowned her face under the soft blast, then whirled around and swiped water from her eyes and mouth. "Am I really your love, or is that just what you think you should say after you've been in my panties?"

Chuckling, he wrapped her in his arms and spun her around so he could steal the water. "I saw no panties involved, my love."

She snuggled against his drenched chest, inhaling the lingering earthy scent of their lovemaking. Vaguely it occurred to her she was acting irrational and out of character with this near stranger who'd taken her twice in one day. A stranger who professed to being a vampire — and had proved it.

She glanced down at his wrist he'd torn open and offered up to her. The water had washed away every trace of the blood she'd sipped, and all that remained was a jagged red line indicating his flesh had closed up on its own. How could that be? She looked up at him, but a quick kiss from his mesmerizing soft lips made her forget her question. Her eyes slid shut as she leaned against him and let him support her. For now, being in his arms was enough. She never wanted to be anywhere but with him.

CHAPTER 9

"What in blazes do ye think ye're doin', Aiden?" Noel rasped when Aiden emerged, fully dressed, from the bathroom.

Aiden smoothed a hand over his damp hair. "Don't concern yourself, old man."

"Don't concern meself?" His buggy eyes ran the gamut of Aiden's height, from his head down to his feet, and back again to his face. "Old man I am, I don't deny it, but not so addled with age I can't figure out what's happened. Ye think I'm deaf as a post and didn't hear ye both beyond that door, and blind to what I see now? Ye've torn open yer wrist, man, and I know very well what ye've done! What I'm askin' is, have ye gone completely daft?"

Aiden shot a look over his shoulder, then scowled at Noel. He moved away from the bathroom door. "I know what I'm doing."

"Oh, do ye, now? And what of the consequences? Did ye even consider them before goin' right ahead and doin' exactly what Marta told ye not to do — takin' the lass again and givin' up yer own blood to her?"

Noel shook his head and gave Aiden a glare of wide-eyed amazement. "Now ye've bound her to ye, and her sorry soul will be yers to tend for the rest of yer miserable days! And what'll ye do with her when ye find one of yer own bloodline to take as yer *true* mate? Have a bloody threesome?"

"Shanna *is* my true mate! There will be no other." He held up his hand. "No more of this. I don't want your idle speculation worrying her. She'll have enough to deal with."

Noel furrowed his bushy brows. "Aye, that she will."

A moment later, Shanna emerged from the bathroom, wearing nothing but a fluffy white cotton robe. When she spied Noel, she lowered her gaze, most assuredly suspecting the old man had heard everything she and Aiden had done in the shower.

Aiden's heart melted at the sight of his new love. Gods, she was beautiful, wet hair and all. He couldn't get enough and instantly felt himself harden at the thought of touching her again. He shot her a swift smile, then turned back to Noel. "Help me gather some things so we can take her to the house."

Noel let out a disagreeable snort and stomped off to the opposite corner of the room, plopping down in the flowered chair. "I doubt ye'd care to have me fondlin' her dainties."

Aiden frowned. "I'll handle her *dainties*. All you have to do is help carry her bags once they're packed."

He looked over and caught Shanna examining her neck wounds in her dresser mirror. She hadn't said a word since coming out of the bathroom, and he worried about her state of mind. She seemed preoccupied with the wounds, but he was certain they wouldn't remain a problem long. He'd bitten both sides of her neck in the two times they'd made love. He assumed once the mating ritual was complete and the two of them were fully bonded, she would possess some of his attributes and heal more quickly. But he didn't know how many times it would take before she exhibited overt abilities from the change. When he walked over to her, she eased away from him, letting her hair drop to cover her neck.

"How do you feel?" he whispered.

"Great. Wonderful." She managed a smile.

"No more nausea?"

She shook her head, lowering her gaze demurely. Her shyness after what they'd shared surprised him. He reached out and brushed her hair from her neck. The bruising from the first time had almost disappeared, and the fang marks he'd left had closed up to tiny puffs of white skin. Soon they would completely disappear. He moved her hair back and exposed the other side of her neck. Those puncture wounds were almost healed as well.

Before he could lower his hand, she reached up and pressed his palm against her warm neck. The gesture made his loins lurch, and instantly he found himself moving in to kiss her. As their lips touched, Noel cleared his throat, then warned, "We should go. The sun's gettin' lower in the sky, and soon it'll be dusk."

Aiden nodded and stepped back from Shanna. Noel was right. There was more to worry about than his new mate. He had a killer to catch, and Cameron Ryben would definitely be on the prowl tonight. Aiden hadn't cleared his emotions for the past day and a half to pick up on Ryben's mood, but in his gut he sensed something foul and knew it was Ryben's killing urge coming out to play.

His heart filled with warmth as he linked gazes with Shanna. Patting her on the ass, he said, "Gather up what you'll need for at least a week, and don't spare extra time. We need to move quickly."

"Aiden, I have to go to work tomorrow." A frown creased her brow, as if she wasn't sure how he'd react.

The fact that she worried about his feelings made him all the more protective. He grimaced. "You'll have to call and report off-duty. You're not going to be in any shape to work for the next couple of days, maybe longer."

"But I feel fine now."

"That's only temporary." He shot Noel a look over his shoulder, then managed a smile for her and whispered, "You're going to want me in a bad way again very soon. And it will be intense, I promise."

She stared at him open-mouthed. He laughed and ducked down to kiss her. "You didn't think it was going to be easy to become my life mate, did you?" He felt the need for her rising in him again and hoped he could stave it off until after he dealt with Ryben. He couldn't let his own lust mingle with Ryben's unholy urges and interfere with his duty.

Still gaping at him, Shanna stood motionless. He smacked her gently on the hip. "Come on. Once darkness falls, I have work to do."

"So, we're still going after Ryben tonight." She pulled her robe tight over her chest. Her tone sounded as if she'd regained a bit of the professional eagerness partly responsible for the situation they were in now.

"Yes. *I'm* going after Ryben. *Alone.* You're going to the house and stay put. There's no way I'll let you near that animal."

"You're not going after him without me," Shanna challenged.

Aiden eyed her face taut with anger and smiled. Her tenacity made him want her all the more — and want to protect her. "I need to make sure you're safe."

"Aiden, you promised—"

"I promise to take care of you, my love." He caressed her

cheek, adding in a low whisper, "My life depends on it. Do you not understand that? If something were to happen to you..."

She screwed up her face and turned away from him. In the mirror he could see the hurt and worry dominating her emotions. But he didn't have to see her reflection to know how she felt. Her feelings permeated his heart like a song matching the melody of his. They were a duet, and soon would be inseparably joined in the music of love and life.

She raised her eyes to the mirror and met his reflection. "What if ... what if something happens to *you*?"

He spun her around to face him and held her shoulders tight. "Nothing will happen to me. That is my promise to you. But I have a job to do, and I must do it. Alone."

She dropped her gaze and frowned. He felt her resistance, but somehow he would have to convince her to obey his wishes. He couldn't have it any other way. She was too precious to him to risk foolishly.

He turned to Noel, who grumbled, "Are ye finally ready then?"

Aiden nodded. "Just a few minutes to let Shanna dress and pack, and we'll be off."

"It's bloody damned well time. Not that I'm eager to get back to the house and face Marta when she learns I let the two of ye do just what she told me ye wasn't supposed to."

"Let me handle Marta," Aiden said with newfound authority. Shanna was his love, his mate, the one woman in the world he never dreamed he'd have. The one person he couldn't afford to lose. He managed a smile to soothe her worried look. "Make haste, my love. We must hurry and get you safely home."

* * * * *

The moment Aiden ushered Shanna through the front doorway of the house, he felt Marta's anger like a dark cloud hanging in the air. Untrue to Noel's earlier misgivings, Marta said barely a word as she held the baby in her arms and ordered Noel to carry Shanna's bags upstairs. In her cold silence, she shot Aiden a disapproving scowl, leaving no doubt that she knew exactly what he and Shanna had done.

As Aiden faced Marta, Jewel Ann reached out to him and whined, eagerness shining in her bright blue eyes. Taking the baby from Marta, he smiled and hugged her close. Glancing over, he caught Marta glaring at him. She quickly turned to Shanna and urged, "Go on upstairs and get yourself settled in. Last door on the right."

Aiden raised his brows. Apparently Marta had prepared the bedroom next to Jewel Ann's for Shanna. It was just a door down from his, across the hall. So much for keeping her segregated from him. But there was little point in that now, as he was sure Marta was well aware.

"Once I see to Shanna," Marta snarled, passing by him on her way upstairs, "I'll have a word with you privately."

Aiden watched Marta ascend the stairs, then shook his head. More likely she'd share several words with him. *Fool* and *idiot* would be at the top of her list.

* * * * *

As soon as Shanna reached the top landing and was out of sight of Aiden, terror gripped her. She rushed back toward the stairs to find him, but Marta blocked her path. "You must learn to control the urge," the older woman coached. "The sooner, the better — for both of you."

Shanna gulped. Her mouth had gone dry, and her stomach lurched, threatening to spill its meager contents. "H-How long does this last?"

Marta touched her shoulders and prodded her toward the end of the hall. "It is part of your life now. It will never truly stop."

Shanna halted in her tracks and glared at Marta. "What?" She couldn't believe she'd feel this fluttering illness every time she was separated from Aiden, even for a moment. "How—"

Pushing her gently toward the last door, Marta grumbled, "This is all new and unfamiliar to you. You need time to come to terms with it. Unfortunately Aiden hasn't allowed you the luxury of time. Now that this situation is upon you, you must accept it and learn to deal with it quickly."

"But—"

"Fretting will do you no good. Try to be patient until I can spare a few moments to explain."

Marta opened the bedroom door, and Shanna eyed the modest room drenched in the warm golden glow of sunset spilling through the one large window. Sparsely furnished, it offered only a Hollywood double bed with a blond Shaker nightstand. A white wooden candlestick bedside lamp with a beige shade cast a dull circle of light on the equally bland beige bedspread. Definitely rental furnishings. Of course Aiden couldn't be expected to drag a houseful of custom furniture with him every time he had to relocate while tracking his latest prey.

Shanna glanced away from the Spartan accommodations and found Marta eyeing her with distaste written all over her long, stern face. "I ... I'm sorry," Shanna mumbled. "I know you told me not to let anything happen—"

"Yes, that I did. But you chose to ignore my advice."

Shanna turned toward the window showcasing the reddening sun dipping behind the horizon of trees and three-story houses in the meandering subdivision. "I just didn't realize—"

"How could you possibly know?"

Shanna looked over her shoulder at the woman who seemed to want to blame her for something she didn't even understand. "I should have listened to you. I'm sorry."

Marta screwed up her face, then smoothed out her distress with a harsh sigh. Clasping her hands in front of her, she shrugged simply. "What's done cannot be undone. Now we must deal with it as best we can."

"What about Aiden? Will he ... will he be all right?"

Marta shook her head slowly and turned to the door. "Only time will tell. He'll never be the same, I can assure you of that." Before shutting the door behind her, she ducked her head back into the room and warned, "Stay here until I come for you. Please, if you can do nothing else I ask, observe that one simple request."

Shanna grimaced, then nodded. The door closed silently, shutting her off from Marta's palpable disapproval. Only a hint lingered, and it alone was enough to make Shanna feel like a total heel. What had she done to Aiden's life by forcing herself in and becoming part of it? And would she remain a part of it, or would powers beyond their influence interfere? She had no idea what to expect, and not knowing made her jittery with worry that all but drowned her lurking hunger for Aiden.

* * * * *

When Marta breezed into the kitchen like a frigid north wind, Aiden had just finished feeding Jewel Ann pureed peaches. Marta snagged Noel's attention with a stern glance. Right away Noel darted over to relieve Aiden of the baby.

Aiden rose from the table and faced Marta, knowing she intended to have it out with him. As Noel left the room, cooing to the baby with uncharacteristic softness, Aiden smiled. Despite the old man's vehement objections, he'd obviously developed quite a fondness for Jewel Ann, like everyone else had.

"The Enclave has grown impatient." Marta folded her arms across her chest.

Aiden blinked and stepped back. He expected to be lambasted for his behavior, not face reprisal from the Enclave this soon. "I'm handling the situa—"

Marta put up a hand to silence him. "You've done enough harm to yourself and others. You're out of control, Aiden, and you know it. I shudder to think what else you'd do if you continued *handling* things much longer. The Enclave has informed me they're sending another Protector tonight to take down Ryben."

Aiden sank down in the nearest chair. His work was his life — at least it had been until Shanna came into the picture. But Marta's blunt announcement cut him to the bone. Staring at the tile floor, he mumbled, "What did the Elders say?"

"They acknowledged you've experienced unusual difficulty hunting Ryben. They suspect you can't finish the job."

He whipped his head up and stared into Marta's steely eyes. "Did you tell them about Shanna and Jewel Ann?"

"No, but the Elders aren't fools. They have access to news broadcasts, and I'm sure they've speculated what happened to the baby reported missing from the murder scene."

Marta's face softened a bit as she took a seat opposite him. "Aiden, sooner or later you're going to have to face them. But for now, you need to concentrate all your effort on weathering the bloodlust and bringing Shanna through the change." She stiffened her back and glanced away momentarily, then eyed him again. "While I don't approve of your choice, I respect your right to choose. I just wish you'd given Shanna a choice in the matter. She still has no idea what's to come, and I don't feel it's my place to tell her. That's your responsibility."

He nodded and stood. "You're right. I can't leave her hanging like this. I'll take care of it now."

Marta moved away from the table, mumbling as she headed for the stove, "And I'll see to dinner." She shot out a last caveat over her shoulder. "Try to control yourself, Aiden. Remember, Shanna's still human at this point."

He nodded again, then headed for the stairs, wondering how long his new mate would remain human, and what exactly she would become when she could no longer maintain her humanity.

* * * * *

When he reached the top of the stairs, Shanna bounded toward him with a wild, terror-stricken look. "I was afraid you'd leave me here alone," she said breathlessly as she leapt up and wrapped her arms around his neck. "Don't leave me, Aiden."

"I won't, my love." Gently he peeled her off him and slid an arm around her shoulders. Guiding her toward his room, he whispered, "For the next few days, we'll be inseparable — I'll leave only long enough to hunt when Ryben emerges from hiding. And when I dispense with him, I'll return to your side so fast, you'll barely notice I was absent." He stopped her at his door and faced her. "But I need you to promise me. No matter what happens, no matter what I tell you, you will do everything as I ask. Promise me, Shanna."

She nodded her head eagerly, bouncing her hair around her face. He touched a hand to her chin and lifted her face to meet her eyes. He sensed something amiss with her, but couldn't pinpoint the cause. She seemed insecure suddenly, and he didn't know why. Was it simply worry, or was she losing herself already to the madness of the change?

He managed a smile as he pushed his door open and escorted

her inside. It didn't matter. He would do everything in his power to ensure she came through it unscathed. She was his to take care of, from now on, forever. It was his duty, his privilege, his pleasure. "Make love with me," he urged, closing the door behind them. At the mention of it, his body sprang to sexual alertness.

Shanna glanced over her shoulder at his king-size bed dressed in plush, chocolaty satin. "What? No car seat or shower curtain? Can this be right?"

He laughed, hugging her to him. At least she still retained her sharp humor. She wasn't losing her mind, only a bit of her self-confidence as she left her old existence behind. "Yes, finally we have a proper bed to muss."

She lunged at him with her teeth bared and grabbed him by the back of the neck to pull him down to her. Nipping him on the neck hard enough to cause pain, she whispered, "Take me now. I want you inside me."

His loins burned with need for her. He scooped her up in his arms and marched to the bed. Tossing her unceremoniously into the middle of the bedspread, he straddled her and ran his hands up her sides, squeezing hard as he reached her breasts. She wrapped her arms around him and pulled him closer, making him lose his balance. Collapsing on her, he pushed the breath from her. Quickly propping himself up on an elbow, he recalled Marta's warning to be gentle. "I'm sorry. I need to be more careful—"

With speed and strength that surprised him, Shanna lunged up and pushed him over on his back. "You don't need to be careful on my account. I can handle whatever you can dish out." She laughed in a low teasing tone, planting herself atop him and riding his crotch. Even through their jeans he could feel her heat calling to his hardness.

"Whatever I can dish out?" he taunted, flipping her down on her back. She wrestled with him, trying to get the upper hand again, but he held her wrists flat against the bed and pinned her legs with his shins. He looked down at her breathing hard and glaring up at him. He felt the expectation and the desire rising in her like a scream about to rip out of her chest. He knew she needed to be appeased quickly. There was no time for gentleness.

In a fumbling frenzy they undressed each other. When he shoved himself inside her, her slick warmth enveloped him like a cocoon, welcoming him as if she'd been waiting for him forever. He pumped hard and fast, pushing groans from her with each thrust. She clawed his shoulders and wrapped her legs around his back, drawing him deeper. Red madness overwhelmed him, and his body bucked with animalistic instinct, sliding into her harder and faster until she cried out and lurched under him.

His mouth filled with saliva, and he found himself sucking at her neck as if it were something he'd always done without a second thought. Her blood rushed into his throat with the delicious sweet metallic heaviness he savored. His orgasm came in a flash of heat and light and intense tingling all over. He drank her blood in hard, greedy gulps, pumping the last of himself into her. He slowed to a stop, wallowing in his glorious release until he realized she lay limp beneath him.

Flooding with terror, he pulled away from her and touched her chest. She still breathed, but her breaths seemed weak and shallow. Had he drunk too much of her? Had he brought her to the brink of death?

He shook her shoulder. "Shanna, love ... are you all right? Talk to me, please!"

Tears of relief filled his eyes as her eyelids flutter open. Slowly she moved her head and gazed at him. Her mouth twitched, then spread in a smile. "Wow," she croaked. "I ... must have ... fainted."

He grabbed her up in his arms and squeezed her tightly to him. "Gods, I thought—" He caught himself before he blurted out his ultimate fear. "I'm sorry. I went too far too soon. I should have known better, but I..."

She dangled a hand then managed to move it up to stroke his arm. "I'm okay, Aiden."

He kissed her hard on the mouth, thrusting his bloody tongue inside. When he pulled away, he left her gasping. A breathless chuckle fell from her lips, and she whispered, "Can we do it again?"

He started to laugh, then stopped. A visitor had just arrived. Someone he once knew—

"Aiden?" Shanna called out.

He looked back and saw that he'd vacated the bed and stood near the door. He glanced down at himself, completely naked. "Quick." He rushed back to the bed to help Shanna up. "We need to shower and dress."

"Why?"

"We've got company."

"Company?" Shanna stumbled to her feet, then pulled her hands from his. She glared at him. "You know her."

He eyed Shanna, startled that she had picked up on the fact that their new houseguest was female. Was she sensing others on her own, or sensing old memories — feelings — from him? "Knew," he clarified.

"She's your old girlfriend?"

Aiden shook his head as he bustled Shanna toward the master bath. "She wanted to be, but I had already committed myself to the Protectorate. When I rejected her, she moved to another clan. It was a long time ago. I haven't seen her since."

He turned on the water in the tiled shower and looked back to find Shanna considering him with doubt and mistrust. He took her by the shoulders, pulling her close. "There's never been anyone in my life but you. And there never will be." He pushed her back to look into her eyes. "You can feel it in me and know it's true."

She swallowed hard and nodded. Her eyes softened with love, and he felt the specter of jealousy slip away just as quickly as it had appeared.

"So, what's she doing here now?" Shanna challenged.

Aiden kissed her and led her into the huge tiled surround with twin showerheads. As the soothing warm water cascaded over his face and chest, he turned and eyed his new life mate, his other half drenching herself under her own waterfall. "I assume she's here to replace me and bring down Cameron Ryben, where I've failed."

Shanna swiped water from her face and blinked at him. "She's a Protector, like you?"

"Apparently so."

CHAPTER 10

"Talya Yvanna Zhakovika," Aiden announced as he stepped off the bottom stair landing and circled around a few pieces of black leather luggage. Shanna followed him from the stairs to the great room, hurrying by his side so she could see for herself the woman from his past who'd vied for his affection and lost.

"Aiden," a deep, feminine voice responded. Shanna blinked, startled to see a tall, muscular woman garbed from neck to toe in black leather, rising from the couch. She looked like a professional wrestler and stood facing Aiden as if she were braced for battle. Her hair, a mountain of shiny black ringlets, surrounded her pale angular face and cascaded down her back. Her sleeveless black leather vest showcased small odd markings on both her bare shoulders — tattoos of a sword piercing an anatomically rendered heart. The artistic detail was impeccable. When Shanna glanced back at the woman's face, she found herself ensnared by luminous black eyes. She gulped and stepped closer to Aiden, instinctively touching his arm. She didn't like the dangerous vibes emanating from their visitor.

"It's been a long time," Aiden said, moving closer to this ghost from his past who'd come to haunt their present.

"Yes, a very long time," Talya Zhakovika agreed in a cold tone. Shanna tried to detect a hint of an accent, Russian she presumed by the sound of her name. But with her antiseptically bland newscaster dialect, the statuesque Amazon revealed nothing of her origins. Shanna guessed the Protectorate taught their assassins how to sublimate all traces of individuality so they'd blend better with whatever human population they might infiltrate on their rogue hunts. However, as she looked from Talya to Aiden and back to Talya, she realized neither of them was close to mundane in appearance. How they blended escaped her for the moment.

Knowing Talya was sizing her up, Shanna tensed and pushed

forward. "Hi. I'm Shanna Preston." She held out her hand in greeting. Talya made no move to complete the customary gesture. Instead, she continued to glare at Shanna for another second, then turned her attention back to Aiden.

"You're looking well," Aiden said, as if he hadn't noticed the slight.

"As are you." Talya cocked her head of shimmering black curls, then narrowed her equally black eyes. "But I sense something different about you." She shot a pointed glance at Shanna, then looked back to Aiden. "What's happened?"

Aiden circled an arm around Shanna's shoulders and drew her close. Holding her tight, he announced, "We've mated."

Shanna looked up at Aiden, then glanced at Talya just in time to see a flash of anger whisk across her face. In the blink of an eye it disappeared, leaving her features hardened with resolve and perhaps regret. "Yes, I sensed it was so, but could not believe it. I would congratulate you, but that hardly seems appropriate, considering you are in the midst of bloodlust, in clear violation of your status as a Protector."

Shanna tried to empathize with this woman's feelings, but couldn't deal with the stone-cold treatment. Without acknowledging Shanna, Talya eyed Aiden and demanded, "Has your Clan Enclave been apprised of this disastrous development?"

Aiden withdrew his arm from Shanna and took another step toward Talya. Before he could say anything, Marta breezed into the room, smiling like a viper about to strike. "Aiden, you've already welcomed our guest. Good. I'll have Noel transfer Shanna's bags to your room, then carry Mistress Talya's luggage up to the guest bedroom."

Marta turned to Talya. "As to your inquiry regarding our Enclave's knowledge of Aiden's situation ... no, the details have not yet been revealed to the Elders. I reported to them only that Aiden seemed unable to fulfill his Protector duties with regard to Cameron Ryben. That was two days ago, right after he brought the baby here."

"*Baby?*" Talya growled. "*What* baby?"

"Found at the scene of a murder. You didn't hear about it?"

Aiden cut between the two woman and towered over Marta. "So, you contacted the Enclave behind my back? I thought it was the

Elders who contacted you!"

Marta looked up at him, not fazed a bit as she said, "Of course I contacted them."

"Why? How could you?"

"Aiden, be sensible. Noel and I have been with you so long, you tend to forget we were assigned to you by the Elders. We are loyal to you, but we serve the Enclave also."

"You cannot have two masters! Either you are with *me*, or —"

"With you? Of course we're with you. We've been with you every painful step of the way on this assignment. You've followed Ryben's trail for weeks but haven't been able to find him. The Enclave contacted me privately last week, asking for a report on your progress. The closest you came to catching Ryben was the night you found the baby. But there was another murder after that, and will be again tonight if he's not caught. The Enclave is nervous, and we can't afford more slip-ups. If that rogue isn't stopped soon, we're all at risk. You know that."

Aiden whirled away, stopping short when he almost ran into Shanna. He looked as if he'd forgotten she was there, and she didn't like seeing that impersonal disregard in his eyes.

"I was summoned by my own Enclave," Talya clarified, "and instructed to provide assistance with the rogue Ryben."

Aiden turned to face her. "Assistance? I thought you came to replace me."

A flicker of a smile skittered across her lips, then disappeared. "Your Enclave sent word to neighboring Enclaves, requesting an outside Protector to aid in Ryben's capture. I was available and came as soon as I could."

Shanna wondered how fiercely Talya Zhakovika had fought to win this assignment. Obviously she wanted to see Aiden again. Shanna's suspicion was confirmed when the woman added, "Apparently I came a few days too late to prevent your fall from duty." Shanna tensed when the woman shot her another piercing glare.

Aiden shook his head and turned back to Marta. "*You're* responsible for this. I trusted you, depended on you. And this is how you demonstrate your loyalty? By betraying me and whispering behind my back that I am no longer fit to perform my duties?"

"Aiden!" Marta barked. "I merely suggested the Enclave bring in another Protector from outside our clan to help you."

"Knowing of my past, did you ask specifically for *her*?" he roared, pointing at Talya. "When did you learn she had become a Protector, and why did you not inform me of it? Did you think bringing her here and surprising me would sway me from Shanna?"

"*Can* you be swayed?" Talya asked, taking a step toward him.

Aiden shot a look at Shanna, as if he just realized what he'd said. Her heart clenched in her chest. She caught her breath, waiting for his answer. Finally he lowered his eyes and turned back to Talya. "Forgive me. I have not been myself of late. I appreciate whatever assistance you can offer in bringing down Cameron Ryben. He has been a thorn in my side for too long."

"Yes," she agreed. "Far too long."

Shanna glared at Talya Zhakovika, not liking what she sensed from the interloper. Not only would there be a battle to stop Cameron Ryben, apparently Shanna had a serious rival for Aiden's affection.

* * * * *

A quick switch of bags put Shanna in Aiden's room with him, so that his old flame Talya could occupy the room across the hall. Standing in his bedroom, Aiden shook his head. Marta had engineered a cruel and unusual punishment for him, taunting him with a woman who clearly still harbored feelings for him. Did Marta think Talya would be enough to draw him away from Shanna? And what did she think that would accomplish, except to lure Talya to disobey her Protector duties, and leave Shanna in the lurch? But, no. Marta would not have suggested Shanna move into his room if that were her plan. He raced his fingers through his tangled hair, wondering if it was the bloodlust teasing him with these insane thoughts, or if it was his own guilt for failing his duties as a Protector.

He looked at Shanna staring out the window at the darkening sky. He sensed something had faltered between them since Talya's arrival. He knew Shanna approached the worst of the change, and his only option was to bring her through it and finish it. Once he did that, she would become a new kind of creature and his life mate forever. But she kept her distance, refusing to cleave to him for lifeblood and love, despite the need he sensed in her. She seemed to have suddenly developed more self-control than he imagined her capable of, quickly overcoming her recent clingy behavior. Certainly she demonstrated more willpower than he'd shown lately.

He sucked in a quick breath. Was she having second thoughts about their commitment to each other and their new life together? Was *he* having second thoughts too, now that he'd seen Talya again?

He shook his head and turned away to smolder in the darkness creeping into the bedroom. Talya was still a beauty, looking every bit as striking and powerful as he remembered. And it was no secret she still had feelings for him. He sensed her anger and disappointment the moment she realized he had taken Shanna as his mate. But diving deep into his own feelings, he found no hint of wanting Talya. She did not stir his need like Shanna. He felt no different about Talya than he had when he'd told her he'd chosen the Protectorate over her. He hadn't wanted her then, and he didn't want her now. He wanted only Shanna.

He turned to tell Shanna the truth in his heart, but when he set eyes on her, he sensed doubt emanating from her. Perhaps she didn't want him as much as he wanted — needed — her. Perhaps the bloodlust affected only him. Perhaps Talya's arrival had somehow halted Shanna's change.

He walked up behind his mate, his love, but she didn't stir from her stance before the window. When he placed his hands on her shoulders, she flinched but refused to face him. Slowly he spun her around and saw tears glistening in her eyes. He'd somehow hurt her, slighted her. Or maybe it was just the awkwardness of the situation. He drew her into his arms and held her close, caressing her back as he pressed his lips to her hair still smelling flower-fragrant from their recent shower. "I love you," he whispered, "no matter what happens or what anyone says. And Talya Zhakovika being here changes nothing."

Shanna shuddered and wrapped her arms around him. "But I thought ... the way you looked at her, what you said to Marta—"

"I know, but it's not as you fear. Nothing could sway me from you. Talya begged me once to love her as I do you, but I couldn't. It wasn't simply my honor in agreeing to become a Protector that held me back from caring for her. She is as strong and beautiful as she was then, but I just didn't have those feelings for her — and still don't."

"But did you ever..." Shanna blinked her eyes and looked up, searching his face for a hint of holding back.

He smiled. "You're the one who introduced me to love and stole my heart. There's no room for another in my life."

Sighing, she rested her head on his chest. "I'm sorry, Aiden. I'm trying not to be jealous, but I think Talya still has feelings for you."

"You're probably right, but don't worry about it. I'm committed to you, and only you. The problem is, Cameron Ryben is still on the loose, and Talya and I must work together to catch him."

Shanna lifted her glistening gaze to him once more. "What do you think she can do differently, that you haven't been able to accomplish yourself?"

He shrugged. "I don't know. But I fear there's nothing I can do. My attraction to you may be a symptom of my ongoing failure to bring him down."

She pushed herself away from him. "You make me sound like some kind of disease you caught when your resistance was low."

He reached out and smoothed a hand over her hair. "I'm sorry, but that might be exactly the case."

"And I was just some wandering virus at the right place at the right time? A happenstance who infected you with something you've now decided is love?" She scowled at him as new tears brimmed in her eyes.

He shook his head. "No. I'm not explaining it well because I don't fully understand it. But somehow, while I was tracking Cameron Ryben, I lost my focus. And the moment I set eyes on you..." He sighed and smiled, moving close so he could take her in his arms again. "The moment I set eyes on you, I knew my life was changed forever. It just took me a while to realize and accept it as truth."

He stroked her back. "I don't want to question or analyze it anymore. I just want us to be together. Always." He felt her relax in his embrace as they stood together with the last rays of light fading into dusk.

While they held each other, the sun disappeared completely, allowing darkness to carry a chill into the room. But just as the coolness settled in around them, a sudden fire of emotion exploded between them. Everything turned red before Aiden's eyes, and he gasped. A hunger not his own enveloped him, burning him as it demanded satisfaction. He staggered away from Shanna and heard her moan. Looking over at her stumbling toward a nearby chair, he realized she felt the same thing that had overcome him. Ryben, drenched in need and madness, was on the prowl again and had taken both of them along for his death hunt.

Aiden gripped his stomach and lurched toward the bedroom door. "Stay here, Shanna. I have to find Talya and—"

Before he could finish his sentence, the door swung open, revealing Talya wearing twin sabers sheathed in scabbards hanging from leather straps crossing her chest. "Our prey is calling, Aiden. We must hurry."

He straightened, trying to appear in control, even though he knew it was obvious he was not. He looked back at Shanna, draped on the chair against the far wall, and warned, "Promise me you won't leave this room. I'll be back as soon as I can."

Shanna let out a soft moan and nodded.

"I'll send Marta up to tend to you." He gave her one last look, then turned and headed for the door.

Once Talya closed the door behind them, she whispered, "She can sense him too?"

"Unfortunately."

"Because of your bond with her?"

"Apparently."

"I feel Ryben's hunger in the air, so I know he must be close. But by your reaction, I'm guessing I don't feel it with near the intensity the two of you do."

Aiden stopped at the head of the stairs and turned back to frown at his new hunting partner. "It is quite intense. Worse than anything I've ever felt from a rogue."

Talya blinked. "With a hunger this strong, how could you not have already caught him, Aiden?"

"It was never this strong before."

"You mean, before you mated."

Aiden eyed Talya, then turned away. By pointing out the obvious, she'd reminded him that both he and Shanna could be at risk. Because he'd established a link with Ryben to track him, he was tied to him mentally. With the onset of bloodlust, that link had grown and become so strong that it might be hard to sever. And when Ryben died, as he surely must when Aiden and Talya carried out their duty as Protectors, Aiden and Shanna both might suffer the pain and agony of his dying — perhaps so much that one or both of them might die along with him.

CHAPTER 11

"He's very close, Aiden," Marta warned, grabbing Aiden's arm as he headed toward the basement. "So close, Noel and I can sense him. Even the baby's fretting."

Aiden swiped a hand over his face. "I'm doing the best I can, Marta. Please, go upstairs and see to Shanna. She's been ill ever since Ryben revealed himself. And take the baby with you. I want all of you — Noel as well — to stay in my room until Talya and I return. It is imperative all of you remain there until I say otherwise."

Marta nodded and stepped back to let him by so he could retrieve his weapons. Like Talya, when he hunted, he wore a long coat to conceal his sword of choice, an engraved *katana* presented as a gift by his mentor, Fadim Kalmud, upon his completion of Protector training. He wanted to ask Talya how she'd acquired her very fine weapons, but that small talk would have to wait. Right now they had a killer to stop, and no time to spare. Ryben could strike at any moment — perhaps in this very neighborhood. It pained Aiden to think he'd drawn that animal here.

Once suitably armed and garbed, Aiden met Talya in the foyer. He considered taking his car to scout the area for Ryben, when Talya objected, "Too cumbersome. Ryben is on the move, probably transporting himself from spot to spot, to prevent us from pinpointing his exact location."

Aiden nodded, refusing to be annoyed by the fact that Talya had invaded his thoughts without his permission, and he hadn't even been aware she'd done it. He'd been so unfocused, so rattled by Ryben's proximity, he hadn't bothered to shield his mind from wayward probing. And that was a serious mistake. Once in his mind, Ryben could do serious damage. Had he slipped that badly?

Talya placed a large, slender hand on his shoulder. "You'll be fine, Aiden. You just need to concentrate on what you're doing. You can't let yourself be distracted with fears about those you're trying to protect. You've instructed them to remain in the room where your presence has been strongest. Your lingering power will shield them from intruders. Not even Ryben would dare cross that threshold. Now you must trust them to do as they're told. Continuing to worry about them will accomplish nothing but make you hesitant or unable to perform your duty — the whole reason the Protectorate forbids its members to take mates in the first place."

"I *know* that!" he snapped, jerking the front door open. "I've been a Protector much longer than you have."

"Not that much longer," she corrected, following him outside. "I entered Protectorate training almost immediately after I changed clans. I figured if it was good enough for you..." She closed the door behind them.

He grimaced. "Talya, I'm sorry. I never meant to hurt you. You would have been a mate any man could love and honor. It's just that I ... we were so young then, and I had other priorities."

She sucked in a deep breath and scanned the well-lit neighborhood with her head held high. "No apology is necessary, Aiden. You did nothing wrong. You made it clear to me that the Protectorate was your choice. I hurt myself with expectations you were unwilling — unable — to fulfill."

He looked away, not sure he could trust the sincerity of her words. He knew he'd deprived her of the chance for love by not giving in to her when she'd wanted it. He suspected she'd gone years trying to convince herself that she was not unworthy of love, just simply didn't need it. Perhaps her refusal to lay blame was more for her own benefit, to show that she'd outgrown her desire for him, rather than to ease his guilt.

"Come," she said, walking away from the house. "We have a murderer to find. Now where do you suppose that slippery rogue is hiding?"

Aiden searched the darkness and beyond, waiting for Ryben's killing urge to engulf him. But nothing happened. The night stayed clear and warm, with a slight hint of summer in the soft breeze. "I don't sense him now."

"Neither do I." Talya's eyes all but glowed in the dark as she looked at him. "This one's very clever. It's almost as if he's stringing us along. With the Protector training he's had, I can see why you've had difficulty stopping him."

Aiden sighed. That was little consolation now, after he'd been reported to his Enclave as ineffective. "I'm sorry. I don't have any suggestions. If I knew how to lock in on him, I'd already have neutralized him."

"But you do get a clear sense of him right before he kills."

"Yes — not that it does me much good. By the time I reach the victim, he's already disappeared."

"Perhaps, together, we can find a way to make him *not* disappear."

Aiden scowled. He wasn't used to working with a partner. Protectors were trained to be self-sufficient and function alone in the field. "What do you have in mind?"

"If we both focus on his location, we should be able to find him, then combine our energies to hold him where he is and keep him from dematerializing and transporting elsewhere. At the very least, we should be able to follow him wherever he tries to go. If he's constantly on the move, and we're right behind him, he'll have trouble stopping long enough to kill and satiate himself. Eventually he'll tire of the frustration and the drain on his reserves, and he'll face us off."

"But we can't even find him!"

"Don't worry. We will, once we get another whiff of him. He'll reveal himself — he can't help it."

Aiden didn't want to wait for Ryben to reveal himself. He'd had been very close by, which meant he knew right where Aiden was. And so far, waiting for Ryben to make the first move had resulted only in death. He feared he and Talya wouldn't be quick enough to stop Ryben from killing once again.

* * * * *

Shanna lay on the bed in the dark, trying to keep still so her head wouldn't pound and her stomach wouldn't lurch up through her throat. The sound of Jewel Ann whining in Marta's arms didn't help. And Noel's constant pacing and muttering about the killer on the loose nearby only made things worse. Slowly Shanna sat up and turned on the bedside lamp. "I feel like hell. Why ... why am I so disoriented?"

Marta got up from her chair across the room and handed the baby to Noel, who then stopped muttering. "I'm not sure," she said. "Usually the nausea and headaches pass after the second mating. But with a human, the process can be unpredictable. Perhaps your change is progressing to a new level. I'll go to the kitchen and prepare you a tonic to help ease your distress."

"No. I'll be all right. You need to stay here with the rest of us. You said Aiden wanted us all to remain together in his room."

Marta sighed. "You need relief. I'll just be downstairs, and it won't take a moment."

Shanna scowled and looked around. Something didn't feel right. She looked back at Marta. "I don't think we should leave. You said Aiden was adamant about us staying in his room."

"Masters always assume they know best, but age and experience count as well — and I have more of both where Aiden's concerned. His training notwithstanding, he's still suffering bloodlust and can't help being overly protective. How can he think straight with you in his blood and weighing on his mind, while he wonders and worries about that rogue roaming around town? A Shanrak Master's realm of power is strongest where he resides, encompassing all who remain inside under his cloak of protection. We'll be fine here in the house. No one can enter who is not a friend or has not been invited by a member of the household."

Invited? Shanna pressed her hands to her aching temples in muddled confusion, trying not to picture some old vampire movie rerun she'd seen on late-night TV. She couldn't handle outrageous mythical lore right now. She needed guidance. She needed reassurance. *She needed Aiden.* "If Aiden specifically said we were supposed to stay right here in this room, then we shouldn't go anywhere else."

Marta waved a hand and marched to the bedroom door. "You need the tonic to help alleviate your symptoms. Surely Aiden wouldn't object if he were here to have a say in the matter. I'll make quick work of it, and he'll never know I left."

Shanna squeezed her burning eyes shut and grimaced. "Are you sure your concoction will work?"

"I know from the tales of others who practice our herbal arts, this tonic definitely can help."

Shanna eased a hand over her queasy stomach. "All right. But I'm going with you." When she grabbed her Glock from Aiden's nightstand drawer, Marta drew up with a start.

Noel stopped jostling the baby and looked at the gun in dread. "Lass, that cannon's not gonna do ye a bit of good against the likes of Cameron Ryben."

Shanna rammed the loaded clip into the butt of her pistol. "And why not?"

"Ryben's a Shanrak Master — or close enough to it to masquerade as one, when he's not pretendin' to be somethin' else. Masters have abilities that would amaze ye. They're difficult to harm and near impossible to kill. In minutes a Master can heal himself of minor wounds, and in mere hours be rid of serious injuries that would kill most others. The only way to make sure a Master stays good and dead is to take his head clean off." Noel raked a crooked finger across the front of his shriveled neck to emphasize the statement.

Shanna scowled, finally understanding why Aiden and Talya armed themselves only with swords. She stuffed the gun in her waistband anyway. "If it won't kill him, maybe it'll slow him down."

"Or bloody well piss him off."

"Come on," Shanna urged, approaching Marta near the door. "If we're going to do this, let's get it over with. The faster the better."

"I'm not stayin' here alone, with that beastie about!"

Shanna glared over her shoulder at Noel clutching Jewel Ann. "We'll only be a few minutes, Noel. Aiden said to stay here. Keep the baby with you."

"Aye, and he said for *all of us* the same, to stay within this room. If any one of us is to leave the confines, we should stick together, don't ye think? Together we should be safer."

Shanna scowled. The old man's suggestion made sense, she supposed. Safety in numbers. But according to Marta, Aiden had been adamant about them all staying in the bedroom. And he specifically made her promise not to leave. She sighed. "Maybe we should just forget it and stay put." As soon as she said it, her stomach turned in on itself. She doubled over, grabbing her gut.

"You definitely need the tonic," Marta announced. "We'll do as Noel suggested and all stay together. Come now," she said, taking hold of Shanna's arm.

Shanna straightened slowly and took several careful breaths to ease the tightness in her abdomen. When she felt like walking again, she nodded in silent agreement. She didn't want to go through hours of this misery if Marta could whip up something to alleviate it in whole or in part.

Grimacing, she drew her gun and led Marta and Noel with the baby from Aiden's room. But as soon as she stepped into the hallway, she feared she'd made a grave error. The sense of security and strength she felt whenever she was with Aiden seemed to fade the further she moved from his room. She didn't understand how or why that was so, but the feeling of wrongness increased even more as she set foot on the top stair. And the pounding in her head grew worse.

Clutching her gun, she looked over her shoulder at Marta with Noel bringing up the rear. Jewel Ann whined and wriggled in the old man's arms, obviously also feeling it was wrong to leave.

Shanna caught Marta's glance, and the older woman shooed her forward. "Go on. Let's get to the kitchen, make up the tonic, and get back up here as fast as we can. The longer you dawdle, the longer it will take us."

"I ... maybe we should go back to Aiden's room. I don't think—"

"You'll feel much better after drinking the tonic."

"But—"

"Trust me. Your symptoms have been mild so far. I thought you'd be one of the lucky ones and skip most of the ill effects. But if you're having this much trouble now, chances are your situation will get worse before it improves. You don't want to weather the height of the change without whatever aid you can find."

Shanna stopped on the third step down and turned to look back at Marta two steps above her. "Are you saying this ... whatever it is that's happening to me ... gets worse?"

"I've not personally witnessed a human in the throes of the change, but there are stories a plenty gathered and passed about through the years. If you thought things were bad so far, you haven't felt anything yet."

Shanna's foot slipped, and she stumbled down the next step, then turned to catch herself. Maintaining a firm grip on her gun, she hurried down the last of the steps with Marta and Noel right on her heels. To hell with home-brewed Shanrak tonics — she needed a gin and tonic.

* * * * *

"What of your vassals?" Aiden asked as he stood near Talya under the oak trees at the perimeter of the subdivision. They had tracked Ryben to this area, where his trace had then disappeared. "Why did they not accompany you? A Protector always brings his assigned backup along during a hunt, for footwork support or other background aid. You've severely limited yourself by coming here alone and leaving your servants behind."

In the darkness, Talya shifted her weight, causing her coat to rustle. Aiden eyed her, able to see her with the cool gray clarity of his night-vision. She wore a distressed look, and he felt a wave of pain and sadness ripple from her. In that moment he knew. "How, when did it happen?"

She sighed and stared at the grass as she leaned against the tree behind her. "Over a year ago I was assigned to take down a rogue pair that had joined forces to hunt together. As I closed in, they launched a strategic attack from two flanks. One lured me away while the other lay in wait. My vassals got caught in the middle. I failed to protect them."

"You mean you couldn't protect them."

"I *failed*," she repeated, glaring at him. She turned away with a huff and crossed her arms over her chest. "I should have anticipated—"

"How could you, with two rogues teaming against you, working to deliberately mislead you? Unfortunate situations do occur in our line of work. That is to be expected. Even the best trained cannot foretell all danger, especially when it involves particularly crafty rogues. Surely your Enclave Elders didn't lay blame on you."

"No, their final judgment matched your gentle assessment, but the result is still the same no matter what excuse is used to explain my failure. Those who served me died because I—"

"Because you could not be in two places at once."

Talya shrugged.

"And you didn't request replacement vassals?"

"The Elders suggested a new couple, but I declined."

"Afraid the same thing would happen to them?"

She shrugged again.

"Talya, you can't do this completely alone. You must have others you can trust and depend on to be there when you need support or just simple conversation. You know what will eventually happen to your sociability if—"

"Everyone is better off staying away from me."

Aiden sighed. He couldn't win this argument and convince Talya of her faulty logic if she was determined to isolate herself. He knew her reasoning was flawed with fear, but he was in no position to give her advice. Look what he'd done to his own life in the last few days.

He gazed at the houses rising up like chiseled outcroppings in the night landscape of the subdivision. Lights dotted the sprawling structures, betraying the people inside, busy going about their lives, unaware danger lurked in their midst and waited for an unsuspecting victim to wander into range.

He scanned again for some sense of Cameron Ryben, expecting it to rise in the air like the stench of death. Instead, fear gripped him — *Shanna's* fear.

His chest seized. He'd left his own household unguarded to prowl around in the wilds, hunting for prey that had circled around behind him to turn on him and become the hunter. "We have to go back to the house. *Now!*" He took off running and willed himself to Shanna.

* * * * *

As soon as Shanna and her small parade reached the kitchen, a yellow tabby tomcat appeared out of nowhere, suddenly standing in the middle of the kitchen floor, staring up at them. Shanna stalled in confusion, and Marta gasped. The cat shimmered like a mirage, then billowed upward, transforming magically before Shanna's eyes into a six-foot man with shoulder-length blond hair...

Cameron Ryben!

"Hello, beautiful," he purred, surveying her with his mesmerizing brown eyes. "I've been dying to meet you."

She raised her gun, but with a flick of his wrist he caused it to fly out of her hands as if knocked away by an unseen assailant. The gun spun across the floor, and his low chuckle floated through the kitchen like soft romantic strumming on an acoustic guitar. Shanna shuddered as the sound surrounded and caressed her, reminding her of the casually probing hands of a sick molester. She'd never had such a horrible experience, but suddenly she knew exactly what it was like, as if she were suffering the memories of someone else — one of Cam Ryben's past victims?

She blinked and staggered back, bumping into Marta and Noel. The baby wailed and sobbed as if frightened out of her wits, and Shanna was tempted to join in the caterwauling. When her mind screamed for Aiden, Ryben grinned. "Yes, that's it. Call to him. Bring him to you — to *me*."

His voice possessed a soft hypnotic quality, nothing like what she'd expected. She gulped, trying to make her mind work, but all she could think about was how stupid she'd been to disregard Aiden's instructions. Now she'd exposed all of them to danger. But how could she have known? Aiden hadn't explained to her what he'd done to keep Ryben from entering his bedroom. Why couldn't he shield the rest of the house? Perhaps his realm of power resided strongest where he spent most of his time—

"The Protector's private area, no, I can't go there. But anywhere else, yes. You see, I was invited into his house after all." His burning gaze darted momentarily to Marta, then back to Shanna. "The mental link he and I have shared for the past several weeks is a bond stronger than he suspected, not unlike friendship, which I'll always treasure." Ryben's chuckle sent a shiver down Shanna's spine.

"Don't worry. He'll be here any second now," he said, taking a step closer. "I can feel it. And soon all our differences will be settled."

Getting a hold on her raving thoughts, Shanna dared a glance at Marta. Before she could tell her and Noel to run for their lives, Ryben cooed, "Everyone stay right here. You won't want to miss the—"

Shanna looked back as his face went slack, then suddenly

warmed with a smile. "The Protector comes at last — oh, and he brings a friend. An old friend from his past." His eyes lit up as he surveyed Shanna. "My, my. A love triangle? How deliciously quaint. Even better, considering what I have planned for us. The more the merrier — isn't that what you humans say?"

Before Shanna could think of objecting to that suggestive comment, Aiden and Talya materialized in the kitchen, their feet hitting the floor as if they'd just leapt in from another room. As soon as Aiden turned on him, Ryben moved in a flash. Shanna gasped as he grabbed her and pulled her to him. Holding her tightly from behind, he positioned his mouth near her face while his arm pressed intimately under her breasts.

Aiden stared at them, frozen in terror, but Talya flung back her coattails and drew both swords with simultaneous zings, lifting them midway in front of her. "Don't!" Aiden barked, stopping Talya in her tracks. She lowered her swords slightly.

"That's right, Protector. I'll tear out your lovely mate's throat before you can touch me. Let me leave here with her, and I promise to be gentle as I take her to my bed at my leisure. Or I can kill her now. Your choice, Protector."

When Ryben ran a finger suggestively over her neck, Shanna flinched and tried to break his hold. He tightened his grip around her chest, lifting her feet off the floor as he dragged her further into the kitchen, away from everyone. "Don't make this more difficult on yourself," he growled in her ear. "You can't escape me — unless you die trying."

Knowing she couldn't fight him off or get away from him, she concentrated on calming her wild breathing. Rather than the mindless killer she'd imagined, he seemed rational in a perverse way, bent on using her to taunt Aiden. If she could keep her wits about her, she might be able to reason with the maniac, or at least talk him down until she could find some way out of this—

Talya rushed forward in a shimmer, but Aiden grabbed her, pulling her back. "Don't! He means it."

Talya shot Aiden a quick glare, then focused on Ryben. "He'll kill her anyway, Aiden. We—"

"No!" Aiden swallowed hard, his gaze beseeching as he looked from Shanna to her captor. "Let her go, Ryben. Take me instead."

Talya whipped her head aside. "Aiden—"

"A lovely gesture, Protector, but I'll have you both soon enough." Ryben laughed, and the sound cascaded through the house in concert with Jewel Ann's shrieking. "We're all connected, Protector. You, me, and your lovely human mate — who won't be quite human much longer, thanks to your disregard of your training. How fortunate I arrived just in time to insinuate myself into your private little love link. After I share my blood and semen with her a time or two, she'll be tied to me as strongly as she is to you. And once I'm done with her, the three of us will become an eternally mated triangle. All of us bonded forever, lusting for each other, tasting each other, loving each other, killing together..."

"No!" Aiden yelled. "You bastard, let her go!"

Ryben's demonically seductive laugh echoed in the air as the kitchen — and Aiden along with everyone else — wavered out of Shanna's sight.

CHAPTER 12

Aiden started to follow Ryben, but Talya grabbed his arm hard and held him back. "You know where he's taken her, but you also know he must have set a trap. He's had time to plan."

Aiden jerked his arm from Talya's grasp. He knew she was right, but he didn't want to face the obvious. "I have to protect her!"

"How will you protect her, Aiden? He has her. One stray blink of your eyes, and he could kill her right in front of you. Do you want to go there merely to watch him torture her while he does as he wishes—"

"I have to go *now!* Can't you understand? She's trying to be brave, but I can hear her fear screaming in my head. I can feel her pleading for me to save her."

"Aiden—"

Noel and Marta rushed over. "Aiden," Marta interrupted, taking the squalling baby from Noel's arms. "Talya's right. You cannot go. Shanna's gone, already past saving. You—"

Before anyone could say more, Aiden swept himself away from the grim truth, speeding like a bullet across the plane of matter-energy. Shanna's life force and her overwhelming fear drew him like a rope through churning waves, pulling him to her. He didn't know what waited for him on the other side, but he had to get to that other side, to Shanna.

* * * * *

Shanna yelped when her feet hit a solid surface. Immediately Cameron Ryben let go of her. She staggered forward on a warped plank floor. Regaining her balance, she spun around in time to see her captor stalk away as if ill-tempered and disturbed. His tan trench coat hit him mid-calf and flared behind him like a cape.

She sucked in a shaky breath, inhaling the musty air in the poorly lit, unheated building. Rubbing her arms, she congratulated herself on still being alive and unharmed, but she had no idea how long she'd remain that way. She scanned her surroundings quickly, trying to get her bearings and look for an escape route — not that she had any real hope of escaping this maniacal killer. She didn't want to think about the foulness Ryben had planned. As soon as her mind conjured frightening possibilities, she shut them down. She'd drive herself nuts if she started worrying about uncertainties. She could deal with danger only when it presented itself. So far, Ryben hadn't hurt her, but the night was still young, and he seemed determined to cause Aiden as much agony as possible.

In the eerie bright light coming from the far wall, she focused on Ryben standing about twenty feet away, with his back to her. Maybe he was meditating — or jacking off. She couldn't tell exactly what he was doing. Convinced he wasn't going to attack at that particular moment, she eased out the breath she'd been holding and dared to cast another more careful look around.

She guessed the building was an abandoned warehouse that had been used as some kind of factory. The floor was littered with piles of refuse. Near the far wall a battery-operated lantern cast cold, bright light onto an old wooden wheeled desk chair. On the floor beyond lay a lumpy stained mattress with a ratty pink blanket tossed haphazardly across it. Apparently this was Ryben's home away from home.

She checked on Ryben again. He still had his back to her and hadn't moved from his spot. What was he up to?

Dragging her gaze from him, she surveyed the open space, searching for any details that might help her out of this nightmare. Strategically placed metal poles covered in flaking turquoise paint supported rusty metal roof trusses high overhead. Uniform rows of casement windows lined the bare brick walls. The glass panes had been covered with an uneven film of turquoise paint. Some of the panes were broken or missing. She focused on a set of double metal doors, also covered in turquoise paint, centered in the end wall. Near the doors, a turquoise metal handrail surrounded a hole in the floor that she assumed led to stairs. The idea of escape sneaked into her head again, this time with a real punch. Maybe, if she was very quiet...

She eyed Ryben again. He still stood the same distance from her, but had turned around and now stared her down with his arms folded across his chest. "Don't even think about it," he growled.

She realized he knew exactly what she was thinking. "I have to try," she countered, knowing it was a foolish thing to say. Why taunt him and remind him of her predicament? Still the resistance pushed out of her chest and up her throat, forming the challenging words.

He shrugged. "Be my guest. See how far you get before I tear your head off like a bottle cap and drink your blood from the stump of your neck."

She cringed and fought the disgusting, gory image he described. Instinctively she raised a hand to her forehead, making sure her head was still where it should be. That's when she realized her headache and nausea had dissipated. She didn't understand why, but she was thankful for the relief.

"You can thank *me*," Ryben said.

She stared at him. "Thank you?"

"For sparing you the misery of the change, at least for a while. Aiden's been a very bad boy, taking a mate. But bringing a human over ... that's *so verboten*. The Elders will roast him on an open pit." One corner of Ryben's luscious mouth lifted in an evil smirk.

Shanna scowled. She already knew Aiden was going to be in big trouble when the Elders found out about her. But how could Ryben have any effect on her inner well-being? Aiden's proximity certainly influenced her — but Ryben?

"It's not that difficult to understand," Ryben said in a tone laced with boredom. "Aiden and I have been mentally linked for weeks, ever since he opened himself to my emotions so he could track me. I knew the exact moment he became attracted to you, and I've been waiting for just the right time to move in."

She hugged her shoulders, feeling a sudden chill through her short-sleeve tee shirt.

Ryben uncrossed his arms and smiled. "I'm also linked to *you*, Shanna, just as Aiden is. I feel your emotions and know your thoughts. Aiden invited me to your private little party without even realizing it, and I've been there with you like a voyeur every time the two of you mated." Tilting his head, he added in a sultry tone, "Although I've not yet had the pleasure of fucking you personally, I'm anticipating it with keen delight."

She staggered back a step from the heat blasting from Ryben. She knew he wanted to touch her, to feel her, to force her, and the thought of it made her shudder. But beneath his unholy desire, she sensed steel-hard control. He was holding back ... waiting.

He took a step toward her. "I am not as detestable as you imagine. I can be a very accommodating sex partner."

"Until you rip out your victim's throat." She stepped backward to maintain distance between them, not that she believed it made any difference. She'd seen him move faster than she could think, and knew he could pounce on her anytime he pleased. She didn't know what he was waiting for.

His lush lips twitched with the hint of a wry smile as he strolled closer to her, like a panther relentlessly moving in on its prey. "If I were the crazed animal I'm purported to be, my dear Shanna, you'd already be dead." His brown eyes twinkled when he added, "What puzzles me is that you know my reputation, yet you aren't begging me to spare your life."

She studied him across the short distance separating them. When he stopped and put his hands behind his back, she instinctively surveyed his lithe body casually garbed in faded jeans and a sage green chambray shirt under the long tan overcoat. He was a handsome, intelligent man who oozed sex appeal, and she couldn't understand why he'd resort to murder — over forty times! Was he so sick, he derived some kind of orgasmic pleasure from it?

"So," she ventured, her voice cracking. She cleared her throat. "What's the game plan here? Am I *supposed* to beg for my life? Is that what you made all your other victims do?"

He laughed with ease, tossing his head back. She saw his glistening fangs and gulped. When the fangs came out, somebody was going to bleed. She didn't want it to be her.

He leveled his gaze on her. "My other victims didn't have time to beg. They were too busy fucking me, and were too unaware of their impending fate to even consider pleading for mercy. Their dying came quickly, easily, joyfully."

Shanna bit her lip and backed away from him, shuffling

through a pile of wadded up newspaper and rags. She couldn't see how bleeding to death and choking on one's own blood after having one's throat ripped open was a particularly quick and easy — or joyful — way to die. So many sad and hopeless women needlessly lost their lives. Tears stung her eyes, and she blinked rapidly to clear them away. Sucking in a shaky breath, she stopped her retreat and whispered, "Why did you murder all those women?"

"I didn't murder anyone, Shanna." His tone was tender, beseeching, as if he were calming a distraught child.

She scowled. "I think your victims would have a different opinion, if they were still alive to voice it."

His mouth twitched with another smile, and he parted his lips to show off his enlarged canines. "I simply loved them ... to death."

Shanna shook her head vehemently. "What you did to those women wasn't love."

"They believed it was," he said in a deceptively soft tone, moving forward again. "Because they wanted it to be."

She retreated further, sensing their friendly conversation was about to escalate to something hazardous to her health. She stumbled and looked down just in time to keep from falling over a splintered two-by-four lying behind her. In that split second when she looked up again, she found Cameron Ryben's hypnotizing brown eyes only inches from her face. "They wanted love," he purred, "and I gave them lust instead. But it didn't make any difference. I fucked them all equally well, and they enjoyed it."

"Until the end, when you sucked them dry of blood." Shanna felt her insides quaking, but she couldn't back down, couldn't let herself fall apart.

"You'll enjoy it too, Shanna — more than any of them ever could, more than you can possibly imagine right now. Trust me, you'll like it so much, you'll beg for it again and again."

She scowled, wondering how dying at his hands would become such a delicious experience that she would beg for it again — not that she would have the opportunity if he bled her to death.

When he moved his hand, she glanced down to see him rubbing his groin area swollen beneath his jeans. He grabbed the denim outline of his cock, big and hard under his grip. She froze in her tracks and stared back at his eyes, bottomless pools of deep brown. How much time did she have before he pounced for the kill? Why hadn't he killed her already? Was he toying with her, testing her? He'd said something about forcing himself into a threesome with her and Aiden. Was he joking? What did he hope to accomplish with that ploy, if not merely to increase Aiden's suffering? She could almost see the wheels turning in his head. He was plotting something, but what? And how could she possibly get away from him before he carried out his scheme?

With quick shallow breaths, she dared another swift glance around, but still saw no easy escape. She knew she'd never outrun him. He'd transported her through thin air like Aiden had. How could she outmaneuver a power like that? She blinked, trying to think, but her mind simply wouldn't work. She caught him smiling at her and sizing her up as he stroked himself. He eyed her like a cat about to swallow a canary, reveling in the imminent kill. Yet he didn't advance on her. He waited for something ... someone ... *Aiden.*

"Don't," she croaked. "Don't hurt him. Please."

"*Now* you beg? For *him*?" He whirled away and plopped down in the wooden swivel desk chair nearby. It creaked under his weight as he lounged back and propped his arms on the wraparound back. The lantern shined up on his shimmering blond hair, making it look like spun gold cascading around his shoulders. The lantern also highlighted the contour of his raging hard-on, but Shanna looked away when her neck and cheeks heated.

"Most people live in self-imposed ignorance, Shanna. They take advantage of very little life has to offer. If they only knew the excitement and pleasure that awaited them, they'd chuck their silly rules and do what comes naturally."

She raised her brows. "Killing indiscriminately, without remorse? That's not natural behavior."

He waved an elegant hand in the air. "For the cowardly, bloodlust amounts to nothing more than a pitiful orgasmic phase lasting only a few weeks. Once that thrill is gone, what else is there?" He smiled at her, his eyes glittering with inner excitement. "If cultivated properly, bloodlust can be made to last much longer than most lovers have the stomach for. It can become a continuous orgasm, a permanent high that overtakes you with an intensity you can't imagine until you've experienced it. But to maintain that level of excitement, you have to keep stoking the fire and feeding more wood to the flame."

"A new victim every other night?"

"Yes — unless a partner comes along who's strong enough to join in and elevate the high and keep it going." He ran a palm over his crotch, and his eyes flickered as he stared at her.

"A partner," she said, furrowing her brows, "presumably strong enough to survive the experience without dying from it."

He lunged smoothly from the chair and strolled toward her, closing the space between them until he stood just inches from her. "Precisely."

Like a deflating balloon, she let go of the breath she'd been holding. Apparently Ryben thought he'd found that partner in the form of her — and Aiden.

He elevated his chin and assessed her. "Despite the fact that you are — were — human, Shanna, you're very strong-willed. Aiden chose well. Or perhaps you chose each other." With a dreamy smile, he cooed, "Together the three of us will reach heights of ecstasy beyond your wildest dreams."

"And the killing will continue."

"Yes, but there are so many willing victims waiting out there for us, it will be child's play to hunt and take them. You'll see."

She shook her head slowly. When he took a step closer, she shuffled backward, stumbling over more debris behind her feet. "You can't just go around killing people!"

"Why not?" He shrugged, then gave his distended crotch another slow rub as he closed the space between them. "There are so many worthless, stupid humans, the world is overrun with them. They ruin the earth, waste its resources, and destroy everything, while breeding like a rampant infestation of roaches. Yet the Enclaves — the elite who are supposed to lead us — do nothing. Our quaking Elders turn away and shield their eyes and whisper to our people, 'Lie low, stay quiet, follow our longstanding rules, and we will yet survive.'"

His eyes darkened to nearly black, the kind of black that sucked in all light and reflected nothing back. The eyes of a shark, an unstoppable killing machine. "I'm tired of lying low and simply surviving. I'm tired of all the restricting rules that make us act like vermin hiding in the shadows. I'm tired of trying to blend among humans. Shanrak are better than your inferior race that's overtaken our lands and our lives. I want to live as I am, to rule the earth as the superior being I know I am!"

When he spread his lips wide to bare his glistening fangs, she knew she was in trouble. All along she'd assumed he could be reasoned with. But now she realized that wasn't so. There was nothing sane or reasonable about him. She continued backing away from him as he advanced relentlessly.

"Once we separate the wheat from the chaff, we will use up and discard the refuse. Those we deem worthy to live, we will turn, so they might join us in our war to rise up and rule."

She tripped over something big and sturdy behind her and almost fell on her ass. He laughed. "Just a little while longer, my sweet Shanna, and you'll know exactly what I'm talking about. He's here, very close by. Soon we'll all join together to become the greatest hunting, fucking, blood-sucking team the world has ever seen."

* * * * *

Aiden shimmered to solid form outside the dilapidated three-story brick warehouse surrounded by weeds sprouting through the cracked concrete pavement. It was easy to follow the breadcrumb trail of Shanna's fear and find where Ryben had taken her. If only he'd been able to track Ryben that easily, he could have avoided this hellish scenario. But Ryben was too clever to be tracked so simply.

Aiden looked up. Behind the turquoise institutional casement windows, he saw the faint glow of light on the third floor and knew Ryben had Shanna cornered — trapped like a helpless animal fearing imminent death.

Sensing Shanna was unharmed despite her revulsion and stress, Aiden had stopped short of his destination. Ryben was on the verge of indulging his impulses, but he held back, waiting for Aiden to show up. Aiden hoped by staying away he'd keep Ryben from hurting Shanna. He knew the bastard wouldn't waste the opportunity to make him suffer by forcing him to watch his beloved endure his perverse sexual gratification. But he wasn't sure how much longer Ryben would — or could — control himself.

Taking a deep breath, Aiden smelled decaying garbage overpowering the brackish scent of asphalt and concrete and the bitter stench of weeds. He glanced aimlessly around the area, trying to come up with a plan. Sporadically stationed streetlights cast a pinkish-yellow glow in the cool foggy night air. Building after building stood unoccupied and unattended. Warehouses and light industrial buildings, vacant and unused, spelled economic death for this part of Paducah that had apparently once thrived. He didn't know what happened to kill its prosperity and didn't care. His focus narrowed on the building in front of him, its third floor, and the occupants inside.

Clenching the hilt of his sword, he prepared to mount his rescue attempt. Just as he stepped forward to propel himself up inside the third floor, Talya appeared nearby. "We'll go together," she said, her swords drawn. "Two of us may provide enough distraction to keep him from harming her."

Aiden nodded and faced the building. With Talya at his side, he shimmered and lunged toward whatever trap lay waiting.

* * * * *

Anxiously watching for Aiden to appear, Shanna stood with her back to Ryben, afraid to breathe as his hard-on pressed against her through his jeans like a loaded pistol in his pocket. Ryben had his arm wrapped tight around her middle, and a sword clenched in his other hand. She knew he'd have no trouble wielding the weapon while maintaining his hold on her. If Aiden tried to rescue her, Ryben would do his best to kill him. If she resisted Ryben's promised assault, he'd hurt her, possibly kill her. But then if he killed her, who would he use as a hostage to keep Aiden off him? If Aiden arrived to find her already dead from Ryben's capriciousness, would he be motivated that much more to bring the rogue down with vengeance? If she were going to die at Ryben's hands eventually anyway—

"Prodding me to kill you so you can sacrifice yourself for Aiden's benefit will accomplish nothing," Ryben whispered in her ear. "If you're a good girl and do as I tell you, no one will die, and everything will turn out just fine."

"Fine for you, maybe."

"No time to argue now..."

Aiden and Talya appeared in the middle of the large room like glittering dust swirling and solidifying into human form right before Shanna's eyes. She couldn't get over the surreal effect. She was surrounded by superheroes and felt woefully inadequate.

"Patience, my chrysalis," her captor soothed. "Soon you will change into a wondrous butterfly with many of the powers we possess, although not to the same extent. Still, I sense you will become one to reckon with."

"Cameron Ryben," Aiden challenged, pointing his sword, "stop hiding behind Shanna and face me as an equal."

Ryben chuckled in a low sultry tone, and the sound traveled down Shanna's spine, making her tremble like a tuning fork. "I'm not interested in fighting you, Protector. I merely wish to show you how to properly excite and satisfy our soon-to-be shared mate. Already she's bonding with me. Can you feel it? My touch makes her tremble with anticipation, and under my expert sexual tutelage, she'll be linked as strongly to me as she is to you." As he stroked her hair with his free hand, Shanna realized he must have sheathed his sword under his coat.

When Talya lunged forward, brandishing her swords, Ryben pulled Shanna tighter to him and placed his hand at the side of her head. "One step closer, and I'll snap her neck like a twig."

Talya stopped mid-stride and backed up a step, lowering her swords. "Kill her and you'll have no buffer to protect yourself from us."

"Funny how Shanna was thinking the same thing when you two arrived. She even contemplated sacrificing herself to hand me over to you. What a loyal little soldier she is. She'd have made a terrific Protector, don't you think?"

Aiden walked toward them with a slow, sure gait. "Ryben, I'm telling you for the last time, release her."

"Or what? Just what do you plan to do, oh mighty Protector? Rush me and hope you can get to me before I kill your lovely little cock-squeeze? Come on, Aiden. You know that approach won't accomplish anything but her death."

Aiden halted and held his sword at his side. "If you planned to kill her, you would have done it by now."

"That's not to say I still can't." Ryben stroked Shanna's hair again, making her shiver with revulsion. He pulled her tighter against him, blocking off her air. Shanna struggled to loosen his grip, but the harder she pushed on his arm, the harder he squeezed. "Look, Aiden, how she yearns for my touch. In another second I'm going drop her pants and mine, shove my dick into her, and release my cum inside her while you stand there and watch. And you won't do a thing to stop me. You'd rather let me fuck her than see me kill her. And you'd still have her, tainted by my touch, but not dead." He chuckled evilly.

"Ryben! Damn it!" Aiden raised his sword and lunged forward.

"Ah-ah-ah! Stop right there if you want Shanna to live to enjoy her next breath." Shanna threw her head back, struggling to suck air into her collapsing lungs. With her head tilted back and her vision hazing over, she saw Ryben in the corner of her eye, glancing down at her with open lust. "Oh, look," he taunted. "She's turning a lovely shade of blue."

"Stop it! You're killing her!"

Just as Shanna felt her head floating near unconsciousness, Ryben eased his hold on her. She gasped in huge breaths, her lungs burning with rage to get oxygen.

The blurred vision of Talya materialized beside her. She felt herself being pulled aside as Ryben moved to deflect the attack. Shanna saw a flash of metal, heard a soft hiss and a groan, then felt the dull thud of a body dropping to the floor at her feet, accompanied by the clatter of falling swords.

"Talya! No!" Aiden yelled.

Before Shanna quite realized what was happening, Ryben dipped her down like a dance partner and reached out, whipping one of Talya's swords up in his free hand. Shanna glimpsed Talya lying on her back with her bloody chest skewered to the floor with Ryben's sword. Her eyes stared up at nothing, and her breathing ceased. "You killed her!" Shanna shrieked, wriggling wildly and elbow-jabbing Ryben to free herself.

Ryben swung the edge of Talya's sword blade against her throat and snarled, "Keep it up, and I'll do the same to you."

In that instant Aiden shimmered toward Shanna and lunged forward, aiming his sword for Ryben's head. Shanna yelped, fearing

Aiden would get himself killed like Talya. "Back off, Protector, or I'll slice her open."

Aiden let out a harsh sigh and stepped back without a word.

"That's it, Protector. I know you'd rather see your lovely mate take me inside her and accept me as her lover than see her blood paint the floor. Behave yourself and you'll both live to love and fight another day. A better choice than letting her die to save your male pride, don't you agree?"

Ryben switched the sword hilt to his hand braced firmly against Shanna's chest. With his arm encasing her shoulder, he shoved his free hand behind her. She felt him maneuvering, then heard his zipper open. Her chest seized when she realized he really intended to carry through with his threat to rape her in front of Aiden.

"Unfasten your jeans," he purred in her ear, "and pull them down to your knees."

"Fuck you!" she yelled, trying to elbow and shin-kick him.

He squeezed her tight with another death grip and shut off her air again. "That's exactly what I intend to do. Now obey me, or I'll wait until you pass out, then take you while you're unconscious. It won't be as much fun, but it'll still accomplish what I want."

The heat of anger and the teary rage of frustration rose up in her as she looked into Aiden's pleading green eyes. She knew he didn't want to watch her die like Talya, but neither did he want to see her being heartily fucked by his nemesis. She didn't know what he expected her to do. She couldn't imagine this scenario playing out the way Ryben planned, yet Talya lay dead right beside her, with Ryben's sword plunged with such force into her chest that her body was pinned to the floor. How could Aiden bear to stand there, helpless to save Talya, and helpless to do anything but watch while Ryben bent her over bare-assed and rammed his dick into her with joyous abandon? Ryben couldn't have all the aces. He couldn't be allowed to win. Someone had to act, to stop this insanity. But she couldn't visualize how. Maybe once she had Ryben distracted with sex, Aiden could—

"Undo your jeans!" Ryben yelled in her ear.

She cringed and pushed against his arm, but he held her like a vise while gripping the sword. She couldn't budge him, and she knew it wouldn't be her that stopped this insanity. It had to be Aiden. But she'd resist as long as possible to give him an edge. "Let go of me, or my pants stay on."

Her hips jerked to one side, and she heard the loud rip as Ryben literally tore her jeans from her. Yanking at the remains of her pants, he forced them down to her knees and pushed her forward. She screamed a blood-curdling protest that sent a tremor of rage thundering through her body.

In surreal slow motion she saw Aiden move in. Ryben let go of her as he raised Talya's sword still clutched in his hand. Shanna screamed again, but heard no sound as she spun aside, out of Ryben's grasp. Just as Ryben plunged his sword into Aiden's abdomen, Shanna's hands landed on the hilt of Ryben's abandoned sword still pinning Talya's body to the floor. With a force of will that came from a depth she didn't know she possessed, Shanna pulled the bloody sword from Talya's body and lifted it up as she swung around. Aiden fell backward from the thrust of Ryben's sword, and Shanna's swing just barely missed him as the blade in her hands swooshed around to make swift, unerring contact with Ryben's unprotected throat. Blood sprayed out in an arc as Ryben's head tilted and flew backward off his body.

By the time Shanna's swing came full around to stop, she'd staggered aside and doubled over to rest on the sword hilt for support. Aiden lay writhing on the floor on his back, struggling to pull Ryben's blade from his gut. Talya lurched with a gasp and opened her eyes as she awakened from her untimely death. Only Cameron Ryben seemed unable to recover. His body lay sprawled chest down, with the last of his blood pouring out around him. His head lay some distance away, a mass of bloody blond hair tangled around it like a cat's abandoned ball of yarn.

Shanna tried to go to Aiden, but her shredded jeans hobbled her at the knees. She fell to the floor, slamming her knees down hard. She groaned, wanting to cry out and make sure he was all right, but she could barely draw a breath and certainly couldn't form words.

Free of the sword, Aiden threw it aside with a clatter and held a hand to his bleeding stomach. "I'm all right, Shanna," he rasped. "Are you okay?" He managed to roll over and rise to his knees.

She let out a trembling moan, not sure whether she'd vomit

from shock or burst into tears of relief. When neither happened, she felt the tickle of manic laughter start in her stomach and bubble up to her chest.

"Talya," Aiden called out.

"Alive..." Talya whispered, still lying on her back.

Shanna looked over at Aiden and then back at Talya, reassured that they would eventually heal and be all right. When she looked down at herself, violently denuded from waist to knees, she freed the urge she'd held back and chuckled. Her chuckle turned to giggles, then to an outright belly laugh.

It was over, finally over. Even after nearly dying, somehow they'd all come through it unscathed. All of them but Ryben. She glanced over at his headless body drenched in blood, and her manic laughter stopped. He'd never rise up to kill again.

Tears slid down her cheeks as she looked up at Aiden shuffling over to her. He pulled her to her feet and held her close, hugging her tight like he never intended to let her out of his grasp. She placed a hand over his bloody hand holding his stomach. The bleeding had already stopped.

Noel had told her Shanrak Masters could heal themselves of terrible wounds. As she glanced over her shoulder at Talya slowly getting to her feet, she believed it. Talya had been dead. She had stopped breathing. She'd lain on the floor with a sword shoved through her chest, and minutes after Shanna had removed it, she was up walking around.

"You did it, my love," Aiden whispered. He kissed the top of her head. "Your aim was true, and you brought down that bastard rogue when no one else could. You have the skill of a true Protector, and that's not something that can simply be learned. It must already have been a part of you."

He lifted her chin with his fingers and looked into her eyes. "You've become Shanrak, Shanna. You've completed the change in a way better than I ever dared hope." He kissed her softly on the lips. She knew the gesture said more than 'I love you.' In his mind and heart she had become his equal, his partner, his one true mate.

She swiped at her nose and rubbed the tears running freely down her face. With a heavy sigh she rested her head against his chest and whispered, "I'm tired, Aiden. Please, take me home."

CHAPTER 13

Aiden whisked Shanna straight to his room, leaving Talya to relay the situation to Marta and Noel so they could make necessary arrangements. It would not do to let human authorities get possession of Ryben's body, or any biological evidence beyond what they already had. If they came upon the raw scene at the warehouse, they'd ask the inevitable questions regarding Ryben's death and look for someone to blame. The Enclave always had crews strategically located and ready for such emergencies, and everything would be cleaned up in no time. No one would ever find out Shanna had been involved, much less that she was the one ultimately responsible for bringing Ryben down. She'd done the Shanrak a great service, but human law enforcement would not see it that way. It was best not to let them see it at all.

After helping Shanna out of her ruined clothes, Aiden held her naked in his arms, vowing never to let her out of his sight. He'd come so close to losing her—

"Aiden," she said, touching a hand to his shirt crusted and damp with his own blood, "we need to check to make sure you're all right."

"I'm fine. I want to hold you and never let you go." He squeezed his arms tighter around her.

"Let's get you out of those clothes so I can make sure for myself that you're fine," she insisted. "Then we can shower and get some rest."

He eased his hold on her and looked down at her, realizing they would not make love tonight. After what they'd been through, neither of them was in the mood. He hoped that wouldn't last long.

She looked up at him and smiled, her aqua eyes glassy with leftover tears. "I love you. I'm so glad—"

He put his fingertips to her lips. He knew what she was going to say, and nothing more needed to be said. They were both lucky to be alive, in each other's arms, with no real harm done.

"Come," he said, taking her by the hand. "Lets shower and get you into bed. We'll enjoy peace tonight, and face the inevitable problems tomorrow."

* * * * *

Squeaky clean from showering, Shanna lay in Aiden's arms in the darkness, wondering why she was wide awake. She'd felt so exhausted earlier, near mental and physical shutdown, and now her mind tormented her by working overtime like a hamster scrambling in a squeaky wheel.

With a huff she readjusted her position. Aiden rose up on an elbow and looked down at her. Somehow the darkness didn't seem so dark anymore. She could clearly make out the features of his face and naked torso. Before she could ponder that odd development, he whispered, "Neither of us can rest with so many loose details to take care of. Why don't we go downstairs and see what Marta and Noel and Talya have arranged?"

Shanna touched a hand to his shoulder when he started to turn and leave the bed. "Aiden, how are we going to handle this? You'll have to report to the Enclave, and I've got my job. I can't just blow it off and not show up."

He leaned over and kissed her on the forehead, then rolled out of bed. Turning on the bedside lamp, he pulled on fresh underwear and a silken robe. Tying the sash, he said, "Those are some of the details we'll have to work out."

She grimaced, then crawled out of bed. She hadn't had time to think about anything, now that her life had taken this strange and unexpected turn. She had her apartment, her furniture, clothes, and a few personal effects — and, yes, her not so wonderful job with the McCracken County Sheriff Department. With Aiden in her life, expecting her to drop everything and go off with him, she found herself in the difficult position of seeming to have no choice in the matter. But she knew she did have a choice. She could simply say no to him and stay behind to pick up where she left off before he breezed in and screwed everything up.

But was everything really screwed up, or was it just different? Definitely different from what she'd imagined her life to be. What the hell had she expected? Her life as it was hadn't been going anywhere. She'd just been marking time. But now ... now she had a whole new set of problems to face, one of the most important being the new powers Aiden promised would continue to surface as she adapted to the changes her body would experience.

She glanced up and found him staring at her across the bed. His face looked serene, but she guessed he knew everything that was going through her mind. After all, Marta did say most Shanrak Masters possessed telepathic abilities — as Cameron Ryben had aptly demonstrated. When Ryben first dragged her off, she hadn't had the presence of mind to analyze the details of her situation. But now that she thought back on it, Ryben seemed to answer aloud her every thought without her voicing it. If Ryben could do that, she had no doubt Aiden could too.

Aiden frowned as he slid his hands into the roomy pockets of his navy silk robe. The subtle woven stripes shined discreetly under the soft light of the bedside lamp. He looked so sexy and powerful, so damned delicious. She imagined them in bed, her on top, riding his big, beautiful cock like a jockey on the winning racehorse. When she looked up in embarrassment, she found him grinning at her. And she knew — he could read every naughty little thought in her head. "That's not fair!" she objected, circling around the bed to stand in front of him. "You have all the power, all the advantage—"

He gripped her shoulders, stroking her arms to calm her. "I'll teach you."

"But I—"

"If you want to keep your thoughts to yourself around the Shanrak, you have to learn to exercise control. Shanrak children are schooled in such arts at an early age, but this is all new to you, and you need to be taught how to manage it. I'm quite sure you've already developed a knack for reading others' emotions through body language and perhaps a bit of latent empathy. But soon you may start overhearing stray thoughts, and if you don't develop the skill to handle it, you could have serious problems."

She sighed as he drew her into his arms. She didn't want to have these kinds of problems. They weren't natural. They weren't human—

She pulled away from him as soon as that awful realization popped into her head. She looked up to see if the thought had hurt him. She didn't want him to feel bad because they were so different. But then, perhaps he didn't feel bad for himself. Maybe it was her he looked at in lesser light. No. No matter what he might think of humans in general, she knew he didn't look down on her as inferior. Did he?

With a sad frown, he stroked her shoulders. "You have much to reconcile. Much newness to adjust to."

"Aiden, I didn't mean—"

"I know, love. The truth is, you and I *are* different. There's no getting around that. But the longer we're together, the more alike we'll become. I can't guarantee you'll develop full Shanrak abilities and qualities, but I sense your latent potential. Cultivated properly, that potential can be made to blossom to the fullest."

She shook her head and turned away from him. "I ... this is all too much too soon. I don't even know if I want to..."

She turned back to him, but instead of meeting his steady gaze she could only give him a sidelong glance. "I don't know if I really want to do this."

With a half laugh he gripped her shoulders and spun her full to face him. "Shanna, you don't have a choice. You have to embrace the change, or..."

She looked up at him and narrowed her eyes, trying to catch a hint of what he'd been about to blurt out. "Or I'll be in limbo the rest of my life?"

"Yes. Exactly. You're never going to be quite human again. And if you don't embrace the change, you'll never be quite anything else. You'll have yearnings you won't be able to satisfy, and you'll become distraught, frustrated. Or worse."

That sounded like her life before Aiden had come along. She let out a little laugh. "Nearly everybody feels that way ... disconnected, unfulfilled, always thinking there should be more to life, but they can't seem to find it. They turn to drugs, religion, family, work, hobbies, sex, whatever. And it's almost always less than what they hoped it would be."

Aiden sighed. "We all have to find our own answers, and

sometimes the questions change when we least expect it. I convinced myself being a Protector, devoting my life to that calling, would be all I'd ever want. But I know now I was wrong. I was just as disillusioned and burnt out as you described, and didn't realize it until I found you."

He gripped her hard and pulled her closer, staring down into her eyes with such intensity, she wanted to turn away. But she couldn't. It was like gazing into the sun, so bright, so awesome, she had to look no matter how painful and damaging it might be.

"Shanna, together we are better than each of us could ever be alone. You know that, don't you? You feel it. I know you do. There is no alternative. We *have* to be together."

She cringed, realizing she'd wounded him with her indecision. "Aiden, I'm not trying to be difficult, and the last thing I want to do is hurt you. I do love you. You know that. All I'm saying is, I need time to ... to get used to the idea. Two days ago, I didn't even know you existed! Now you're telling me I have to give up everything I know to become something I never asked to be."

He grimaced and loosened his grasp on her. "I'm sorry. To the depth of my soul, I'm sorry I put you in this position. It was wrong, I know. But it's done now, and I can't undo it. I don't want to undo it."

"Aiden—"

"I don't want to go on living without you, Shanna. You've opened a new awareness, a sense of wholeness and satisfaction in me I never knew could exist. Before, I'd been trying to achieve that through discipline and self-denial. But now you've presented possibilities so much more fulfilling, so much better. I know what it means to love, and that is such a wondrous gift. You gave that to me, Shanna. Don't take it away. Please."

"Aiden..." Her eyes filled with tears, and she snaked her arms behind his back as he circled her with his. "Just give me a little time. Please. That's all I'm asking. I have to wrap up my life. I can't just leave everything dangling and walk away."

He kissed the top of her head. "I know. You're right. You deserve that consideration, and I'll give you all the time I can. But you have to understand that some things are already out of my control. I must face the Enclave and answer for what I've done. And you'll be counted as one of the major wrongs I've committed. Both of us will have to deal with that — on the Enclave's timetable, not ours."

She pulled back to look up into those brilliant green eyes softened by love. "What will they do to you?"

He shrugged. "I will be reprimanded, of course. Most assuredly banned from the Protectorate. Maybe banished from the Clan." His exquisite mouth warmed with a little smile when he added, "I'll be lucky if I'm not executed."

Shanna gasped. "They wouldn't—"

"It's hard to tell what the Enclave Elders will do. They take preservation of the Protectorate very seriously, and I've betrayed their trust in me as a member of that elite force."

"Aiden, I'm sorry. It's as much my fault as it was yours." She bit her lower lip and gently extricated herself from his arms. "Here I've been whining about how my life's screwed up, and look at yours. What will you do if you're forced to leave the Protectorate?"

"You mean, assuming I'm allowed to live?"

"Aiden—"

He chuckled and headed for the bedroom door. "I haven't really thought about it. Come, put on your pajamas and go downstairs with me. It's best we discuss our possible options now rather than later."

She scurried over to the dresser where Aiden had cleared out a few drawers for her. Pulling out a set of soft, lightweight, pastel blue pajamas, she turned. "What about Jewel Ann?"

Aiden stopped near the door and faced her. "You know I want to keep her and raise her as our own."

"But, Aiden, I don't think we can finagle that." She stepped into her pajama pants and pulled the shirt over her head. "There are too many obstacles—her grandmother for one. Once we turn Jewel Ann over to the proper authorities—"

"Who said anything about surrendering her?"

Shanna straightened the hem of her pajama shirt and stood with her bare feet planted in the carpet as she scowled at Aiden. "You've been plotting this since you first brought her home, haven't you?"

He shrugged. "Maybe not right at first, but ... yes, soon after, I started thinking how I might manage it."

"Aiden..." Shanna shook her head and walked over to him.

155

"You can't just abduct her and keep her."

"Why not? She'll have a much better life with us as her parents than she would with her drug-peddling grandmother."

"But that's not our decision to make."

"I don't want to see that sweet, innocent child come to any harm. I want to protect her."

"Aiden—"

"Shanna, I've devoted my entire life to protecting others. I don't know how to do anything else. And Jewel Ann needs to be kept from the environment her grandmother's wallowing in. I simply won't allow her to be subjected to that."

His eyes lit up, and he grabbed Shanna's arms. "We could change her name to Julianna Marschant. Jewel Ann ... Julianna. They're similar but different. And she's young enough that she won't remember her name was changed."

"But we'd have to get her a fake birth certificate, a new Social Security number, and—"

"Easy enough. I have several alternate personal identification documents. I know where to get whatever we'll need."

Shanna glared at him in amazement. He really and truly wanted this child. "Assuming you can pull it off, will the Enclave let you keep and raise a human child you stole?"

"Removed from harm."

She rolled her eyes at his semantic splitting of hairs. "Whatever."

He gave her a wry smile as he let go of her arms. "If they'll let me keep you, why would they object to letting me keep Jewel Ann?"

Shanna shook her head and stared at the floor. "She's a sweet child, but why are you so eager to keep her, besides the fact that you've grown attached to her?" She met his gaze and found reticence lurking there. "What are you not telling me?"

He reached out and stroked her hair. "I love you, Shanna, and I feel privileged to be your mate. But..." He glanced away.

"But what?"

With a deep sigh he faced her. "You must know there is one drawback to our mating. Because we are different biologically and may never become totally compatible genetically, it's possible we'll never be able to have children of our own."

Shanna felt a wave of shock wash over her. She'd been angry and afraid about the possibility of getting pregnant when Aiden had first made love with her and they'd failed to use precautions. But now that she'd been informed he might never be able to get her pregnant, her take on it changed. She hadn't seriously considered children, because she wasn't married and wasn't that close to running out of time to reproduce. She guessed everybody thought they'd have all the time in the world to decide to have children when the circumstances were right. But now those circumstances might never be right for her and Aiden. She stared off at nothing as tears blurred her vision.

"I'm sorry, my love. Truly I am." He caressed her hair gently. "But we have healers who may be able to provide help. It's not hopeless. It's just that ... Jewel Ann was there and needed protection, and then you came along, and..." He sighed again and fell silent.

She sniffed and swiped a finger under her nose, then blinked away her tears with a smile. "You're right. It's too early to mourn about what-ifs when we don't even know which what-ifs we're facing. Let's take care of our immediate problems, then worry about the future later."

He bowed his head and placed a soft kiss on her lips. "I love you. And I promise, whatever happens, I'll be with you. Always."

She ran a hand over his silk-covered arm and felt the ripple of muscle beneath. "I love you too." She laid her head on his shoulder for a brief moment of comforting closeness, then followed him out the door.

* * * * *

"The cleaners are on their way to the warehouse," Talya informed them.

Seated at the dining table, Aiden nodded, wondering how close the team had been to respond so quickly. He knew the Enclaves kept sweeper teams close by whenever Protectors hunted, but he hadn't really thought about it until now. The crew must have been holed up in some hotel, waiting for the call.

He glanced at Shanna sitting beside him, then let his gaze jump to Marta and Noel, who'd been at the table much longer, conferring with Talya. The baby had been put to bed some time ago.

"It will probably take them several hours to finish," Talya elaborated. "We left quite a mess for them. They'll call when they're done."

Aiden nodded again in approval. But he knew Talya would have much more to say, to which he certainly would not be inclined to nod his approval. He twisted his mouth at the thought and lifted the cup of decaf tea Marta had made for him. The soft, aromatic steam rose up to greet his nose. He sipped the comforting warmth, then set the cup down with care. Finally deciding to take the bull by the horns and ask the difficult questions before they were asked of him, he pierced Talya with a direct stare. "What about the Enclave? What have the Elders said of me?"

Talya shifted her black eyes from him and sat sideways in her chair, propping an elbow on the tabletop. "Of course they're pleased that Ryben was brought down, but they do have concerns." She turned her head to eye Aiden, and he nodded in acquiescence. He knew what else had to be said, even though she didn't seem eager to voice it.

As Talya continued to sit in silence, Aiden gave her a quick once-over. She'd cleaned up and changed clothes, shedding her leather overcoat while in the house. With the back pierced through by Ryben's sword, her coat would have to be repaired or replaced. He eyed her muscular arm, noting the tattoo of their trade on her shoulder — the same sword-through-the-heart image he'd refused to wear as a brand on his own shoulders.

At the time he finished Protectorate training and was to be marked for life as one of that elite force, he declined the brand. His excuse was that he felt it was more important to sublimate all overt signs of his profession, to remain anonymous among the human masses he would have to infiltrate while performing his services for the Enclave. But now he realized it was simply resistance on his part in an attempt to maintain his individuality. Had he always resisted giving in fully to the calling that had ruled his life? Was that why he'd so easily failed himself and the Protectorate by taking Shanna as his mate when the opportunity presented itself?

He glanced at Shanna sitting in the chair next to him. When she smiled up at him, he smiled back, wondering if he'd subconsciously left himself a backdoor escape route ... a slender, secret hope that one day he could be something other than a Protector. Someone more, with a real life and aspirations for a future, not damned to walk forever alone. Now that hope seemed close to becoming reality. He just didn't know *what* he would become if he would no longer be a Protector.

The Protectorate had always funded his wants and needs without limit, without question. They provided everything he'd ever required — until now. Having no thought for personal resources, Aiden had saved back nothing for his own comfort and support. Without the Enclave's limitless financial backing, he would have to find a job. But what business sector within the Clan would accept him? He had no skills other than those developed to track and kill the undesirable of his kind. As a former Protector, the stigma of failure would follow him everywhere among his people. And he couldn't fathom working with humans. They would not appreciate his unique talents, assuming he would be at liberty to divulge them.

And what of being a father and husband? Those roles in life had always been off-limits to him, and he never considered them as possibilities. Could he fulfill them adequately, superbly, or end up woefully inadequate? Would those roles fulfill *him*? He glanced aside at the fringed oval oriental rug accenting the hardwood floor beneath his feet. How could he possibly know until he tried? And if he tried and found his life lacking, what would he do then?

He sighed and looked toward the windows. He had no options. The Protectorate would never accept him back into their fold after he'd betrayed their code. Perhaps he'd never truly belonged in the first place.

"They gave you one week," Talya announced finally.

Aiden looked at her as she swung around in her chair to face him across the table. "They decided that would be sufficient time for you and Noel and Marta to clear up loose ends here ... cancel the lease on this house, return the furniture, and pack up your personal effects."

Aiden nodded, surprised by the generous offer. One week to get his life in order, before they decreed his sentence. "Did they set a time for the hearing?"

Talya shook her head, and her glistening black ringlets shifted under the chandelier. "Not yet." She cast a sidelong glance at Marta and Noel sitting quietly to her right, then leaned forward with earnestness in her black eyes. "I'm sorry, Aiden. Of course I'll appear to speak on your behalf, but you know—"

He put up a hand. "I appreciate your support, Talya. Not that it will do much good."

She whirled aside again and slapped a palm against the tabletop, making Aiden's teacup clatter in its saucer. "It's not right. You've given them ten years of your life for Protectorate training, then over forty years of exemplary service after that. And now, all they care to do is—"

"Forty years?" Shanna squawked. "And ten years before that?"

Aiden turned to her, surprised at her outburst. As Talya turned to look at her, so did Noel and Marta.

Glaring up at him, Shanna whispered, "Just how old were you, Aiden, when you started your Protector training?"

He stared softly at her, letting his hands slide to his lap where he folded them in repose. There was no use lying to her. She would have to know eventually. "Seventeen."

She blinked at him, doing the math in her head. When she came up with the result, she glared at him in horror mixed with awe. "You're ... sixty-seven years old?"

"Sixty-eight."

She coughed and turned aside, trying to laugh as if it were a joke, but failing miserably. After a second she whirled back around and pointed at Talya. "Her too?"

Aiden glanced at Talya, then forced a smile as he looked down on his shocked mate. "Actually, she's a year younger."

Shanna blinked her eyes and leaned forward to look at Noel and Marta sitting opposite her. "And them?"

Aiden turned his head to appraise his vassals. Calmly he said, "Noel is over two hundred years old. And Marta is close to one-seventy. They mated later in life. Each of them outlived a previous mate who died prematurely."

"What's ... what's an *expected* lifespan for a typical Shanrak?"

Aiden surveyed each of the others sitting around the table. None of them held his gaze, and he knew he was on his own this time. He turned to Shanna and said, "It's difficult to estimate. Some of our people have been known to live only a little over two hundred years, while others are reported to live to six-hundred-fifty, sometimes longer. Those living past seven hundred are rare."

"Rare!" Shanna burst out laughing, then stopped abruptly. Swallowing several times, she whispered, "Are you counting in dog years or human years?"

His lips quickened with a wry smile. "To simplify things, we measure time by the generally accepted human method."

Shanna sat there for a moment in silence, staring at the tabletop, then shoved her chair back and catapulted to her feet. Whirling around, she headed for the kitchen.

Aiden started to rise and follow her, but Noel put a hand out and murmured, "Give the lass a few moments alone to mull things over on her own."

Aiden sighed and settled back into his chair. Not only did he have a potentially devastating confrontation with the Enclave to face, he could look forward to many more issues with his new mate, who had no idea what he'd gotten her into. He only hoped she had the strength to bluster through it and come out the other side, still wanting to be with him.

* * * * *

"Seven hundred years," Shanna grumbled as she paced barefoot on the tiled floor, blindly following the perimeter blocked off by the kitchen cabinets and appliances. "Ten times longer than a typical human. *Ten times!*"

She halted and crossed her arms over her chest. Aiden had been a virgin until he was sixty-eight years old. That was past the time some human men stopped being able to have sex. And Aiden had the staying power of a horny teenager. How would she ever keep up with—

"As part of your change from human to Shanrak," Aiden whispered behind her, "you'll undoubtedly gain an extension to your lifespan."

She whirled to face him, stunned and angry that he'd sneaked up on her, and infuriated that he'd kept this information from her. But why would he want to tell her he would outlive her to mate with

161

another, long after she'd turned to dust?

"I can't predict how many years you'll have," he said gently. "I can't predict how long I'll live. No one knows that." He walked up to her and rested his hands on her shoulders. Tentatively he smiled. "But I promise you this—we'll enjoy whatever time we have together to the fullest. It may not last long after my hearing with the Enclave, but it will be fabulous until then."

She raked at the tears suddenly pouring from her eyes. She didn't want to be angry and didn't want to feel cheated, but she did. She feared if the Enclave had its way, Aiden would be taken from her before she ever had a chance to enjoy the fulfillment he promised. They simply couldn't live a lifetime in a week. And that's about all he had, if the Enclave decided to hand out the ultimate punishment or declare that the two of them could not remain mates. The tears continued to flow as she wailed, "What are we going to do, Aiden?"

He pulled her into his arms and kissed the top of her head. "It will do us no good to rush and worry and live in angst. We'll prepare for the worst tomorrow, then set our decisions aside until the time comes to face fate. In the meantime we'll make love and live as if we have all the time in the world."

He rubbed his palms over her back, warming away the chill of fear that had settled between her shoulder blades. "Come back upstairs with me, love, and we'll start living right now."

CHAPTER 14

Shanna lay next to Aiden, amazed at the gentleness with which he'd undressed her and carried her to his bed. Every other time they'd made love, they'd joined in a heated, hurried frenzy of passion akin to animal lust. Now that Aiden feared he had only a week left to enjoy her company, he seemed intent on taking his time with her and leisurely tasting her with roving kisses all over her legs and stomach. Finally he settled between her legs to taste her there.

As he flicked the tip of his tongue over her tingling nub, she lurched with tickling surprise. He massaged her thighs, then moved in again, taking her clit gently between his lips and rolling his tongue over it. Snaking his tongue lower, he dipped it into her slit. She moaned, enthralled by the slippery sensation of him sliding in and out. Probing her with his fingers, he stroked her inner lips until they were hot and wet from delicious need.

"I want you inside me." She clawed her fingers across his shoulders. He craned his neck back and looked up at her, his face partially curtained by his hair. Smiling, he dipped back down and sucked hard on her, drawing an intense cry of shock and pleasure from her. Impatient, she reached out and grabbed at him, trying to coax him up to plunge into her. "Please, Aiden. Now."

Finally he moved forward like a panther creeping across its prey and settled his hips between her thighs. When he pushed inside her, she groaned with relief and thrust up to meet him, slamming her pelvis against his. With his hands planted on either side of her, he pushed slow and deep, forcing another groan from her. Bending down, he welded his mouth to hers, and she smelled the musky scent of her own desire. He undulated with fast, easy strokes and worked his mouth across her lips and her jaw and finally her neck ... kissing, licking, nipping. She felt his fangs graze her skin and knew he was close to the height of passion. Turning her head, she closed her eyes and felt his teeth sink in with welcome pressure as his hips worked their magic, moving like a well-oiled machine to bring her to the brink of ecstasy.

She rolled in a heated daze under the pressure of his thrusts as he drank from her. Sinking down to a netherworld of semi-consciousness, she literally fell into orgasmic bliss, moaning a song of satisfaction in dreamlike satiation.

Gradually she became aware of the heaviness of Aiden's body resting atop her. His hot breath caressed her wet exposed neck with the regularity of near sleep, and she drifted off.

* * * * *

Shanna blinked her eyes as a cloudy dawn peeked through the parted drapes, promising gloom for the day. She looked over at Aiden stretched out beside her, seeming dead to the world as he breathed in deep sleep. Glancing at the alarm clock beside his bed, she rubbed her bleary eyes until the numbers came into focus. Five forty-seven. If she got up now and got ready, she'd make it to the task force office in plenty of time to fetch donuts for everyone.

She rose from the bed, suddenly tense and alert, her heart pumping hard and fast as if her body had geared her up for a coming confrontation. But her mind felt like mush. She couldn't seem to put two coherent thoughts together. Shuffling toward the bathroom, groggy and a bit unsteady on her feet, she knew she hadn't rested sufficiently, but still needed to go to work.

Showering quickly so she'd have time to go back to her apartment and change into a fresh uniform, she let her mind toy with the worries that still plagued her. But she came up with no answers. If she and Aiden tried to run, she was sure the Enclave would send a Protector to hunt them, just as if they were rogues to be brought down. Whatever decisions would be made about her life and Aiden's would have to wait until the powers that be convened to hand down their decree. In the meantime, she had to go through the motions of appearing normal. She sure as hell couldn't let anyone know what had happened to her in the last couple days. She ran her fingertips over her neck, amazed that the marks from Aiden's frequent biting had left no permanent evidence.

* * * * *

Aiden lay in the bed, oddly relaxed as he listened to the water in the bathroom running. He could almost feel the warm shower cascading over Shanna's wet breasts — breasts he'd suckled with abandon while she writhed beneath him. He felt himself get hard at the thought and willed it away. She was going to work today, and he would not try to dissuade her. He knew she needed to keep up appearances to deflect suspicion — not that any of her colleagues would suspect her of colluding with the enemy to thwart their hunt for the unidentified serial killer, Cameron Ryben.

He sat up, propped his pillows against the headboard, and leaned back. Without inquiring, he knew Talya had not yet received the call confirming the cleaning crew had finished with the warehouse. He seemed especially keen to every stray thought in the house, and wondered if the other occupants knew his and Shanna's thoughts as well. He hadn't bothered closing his mind after Ryben's death, and he sensed Talya had suffered the joy of his ecstasy while making love with Shanna.

With a sigh of apology, he bowed his head and closed his eyes, waiting for Shanna to emerge from the bathroom. It was too late to change what had already happened, and no amount of regret or pardon would fix any of it. He just had to deal with the fallout the best way he could. But whatever happened, he would not let his love for Shanna be diminished, even if the two of them were damned to remain apart. Somehow he would find a way to be with her, no matter what the Enclave decreed.

* * * * *

When she emerged from the bathroom, naked and clean, Shanna found Aiden sitting up in bed, leaning against the headboard as he admired the view she presented. He didn't ask where she was going — obviously he knew. He watched her hastily dress in silence. Sitting down on the chair across the room, she put on her tennis shoes, then stood up and faced him. "I need to go. I have to check in with the task force."

He nodded once with a somber look in his green cat eyes.

She felt a strong twinge of guilt at leaving him. "I want to see where they stand with the investigation," she elaborated, feeling as if she still hadn't adequately justified herself. "I'll be back after work this afternoon."

"What will you tell them?"

She stared at Aiden, sitting like a king with the silken comforter concealing his nakedness from the waist down. He was so regal, so beautiful, she suffered a sudden urge to cry just looking at him. She wanted to stay in bed, wrapped in his arms all day, but she knew she had to take care of the regular duties in her life the best she could.

What would she say to Special Agents Reissenor and Norris? What could she say? Was there any way she could suggest to them their search for the elusive predator they'd been tracking was over? She shook her head slowly. "I don't think I'd better say anything. I just want to monitor whatever progress they think they've made."

"Yes," Aiden said softly. "It's probably best you don't volunteer any information. When they finally figure out the killings have stopped, perhaps they'll assume their target has moved on, or is simply taking a break from his arduous schedule of mayhem."

Shanna frowned. That didn't fit the profile the FBI was working with. Without knowing his name, without knowing anything about him except his body size and coloring, and the fact he had a serious hemoglobin deficiency, they'd pegged the Bloodsucker — Cameron Ryben — as a relentless killer who thought himself above the laws of man. A man who would not stop killing because he liked to kill, he needed to kill. And they were absolutely right about him, except for one glaring detail. Ryben *had* stopped killing — because he was dead.

Shanna shuddered inwardly when she remembered the sight of his headless body pouring out blood onto the old wood plank floor of the warehouse — blood she had spilled without remorse in one swift, smooth act. As she thought about it now, she still didn't feel sorrow for what she had done. Was something wrong with her? Had she lost her humanity in the change to Shanrak? No. She simply felt relief that a vicious animal had been stopped and would kill no more.

But how could the cleaning crew sent by the Enclave eradicate all traces of that much blood? Aiden said they had special techniques that would render the site totally void of clues. How could he be so sure? With the technology available to law enforcement today, clues that would never have surfaced before might suddenly become available. Still, would it matter? The FBI had no reason to search that particular warehouse.

She sighed, then managed a smile as she walked over to Aiden. Bending down, she kissed him tenderly on the lips. "I'll call you if something develops."

He returned her smile. She walked away, feeling his eyes on her as she approached the door. Turning back to look at him one last time, she murmured, "You'll be here when I get back, won't you?"

He nodded again, still maintaining his smile. She held his gaze for another instant, then opened the door and walked out, closing it softly behind her.

The moment she left Aiden's sight, she suffered an overwhelming urge to run back to his arms. But she knew she had things to take care of, things that might help Aiden when it came time to face the Enclave Elders for the misdeeds he'd committed. She sucked in a shaky breath and forced herself to walk down the hallway one agonizing step after another.

The tug to run back to Aiden turned into roaring need. She ignored the blood-rush pounding in her ears and carefully took the first step at the top of the stairs, then another step. But her drive to see Aiden did not diminish. By the time she reached the bottom of the stairs, she was sweating and on the verge of tears. Still she forced herself toward the door, to wait outside for the cab she'd called. As it pulled up, she shuddered, willing one foot in front of the other until she stood at the curb. Reaching for the back door of the cab, she opened it and climbed inside, promising herself she'd return to Aiden soon. That was the only way she could talk herself into leaving him and going to work.

* * * * *

At 7:49 a.m., Shanna arrived at the task force headquarters, surprised to see the flurry of activity and excitement. Everyone acted as if there'd been some startling new development in the case. There had been, thanks to her, but she knew they couldn't be aware of it.

She watched tall, slender Agent Victoria Reissenor, busy relaying information in clipped sentences via her cell phone. "A call from a couple driving by." She paused, then said, "The investigating patrolman was first on the scene." She shook her head. "Unknown. The vehicle license was bogus, either fake or reported incorrectly." She paced a short distance, then turned abruptly. "Not necessary, sir. Norris and I took the sample and had it typed at the local hospital." She sighed. "Don't know yet. Still waiting." She looked toward the ceiling then down at the floor. "Yes, sir. Of course. Every possible courtesy. Yes, sir."

Shanna ducked over to bulldog-faced Agent Roger Norris standing in front of the fax machine, chewing on a toothpick as he waited for the fax to finish spitting out a multi-page transmission.

"So," she whispered as she glanced at two new plain-clothes detectives she hadn't seen before, moving in a hurry to leave the office. "What's going on?"

Agent Norris pulled the mangled toothpick from his mouth and glared at her. "You didn't hear?"

She frowned, trying to look put out. "How could I hear? I got reassigned to litter-pickup detail yesterday. Guess nobody missed me, huh?" Not that she was considered an essential member of the task force. She doubted Norris had bothered to learn her name yet. The last time she'd been in here the day before yesterday, he'd pointed at her with a "Hey, you,"' or "Yo, deputy," to get her attention.

Snorting, he grabbed his fax pages and plopped down in a nearby chair at an unoccupied desk. As he picked up the phone receiver and punched in a long-distance number, Shanna glanced at the top fax page lying on the desk. The info header sported the FBI's logo with the address of what she assumed was a Virginia field office below it. Sprawled under that in big bold letters was the word 'confidential.' Below that she skimmed a list of names with 'M.D.' and similar impressive medical titles strung behind each. Last she read a flight registry number followed by 'ETA' and a time, plus some other coded nonsense. She guessed it was notification that a forensic pathology team was flying from Virginia to Paducah via government jet or helicopter. Obviously some heavy stuff was going down.

Before she could ply Norris for answers, he started talking into the phone. "Norris here. Yeah, got it. We'll have a van waiting at the airport within the hour. No, the warehouse is secure. Yeah, the locals are guarding all the entrances, with explicit instructions to stay out. Nobody's been in there since Reissenor and I took the sample to have it tested."

Shanna stepped away from Agent Norris, feeling an imaginary hand grip her throat. Was he talking about the warehouse where she'd killed Cameron Ryben a few short hours ago? She swallowed hard and glanced at Agent Reissenor still on her cell phone, speaking in hushed tones. This was too much furor to be a fluke. Somehow the task force had gotten wind of the site of Cameron Ryben's demise. But what had happened to the Enclave's cleaning crew? When she remembered Agent Reissenor mentioning a fake license number, she knew. The cleaning crew must have been spotted and interrupted before they could finish scouring the warehouse to render it free of clue residue.

Taking a quick look around to make sure no one noticed her, Shanna slipped out of the office and marched purposefully down the corridor to the outside entrance of the building complex, trying to look like she was on official business. As soon as she stepped away from the main entrance and stood among the mostly vacant parking spaces, she grabbed her cell phone and speed-dialed the number to Aiden's house she'd programmed in. She had to let him know what had happened. By now he probably already knew more than she did, but still, she had to talk with him to find out just how bad things were.

When Marta answered, Shanna asked to speak with Aiden but was told he and Talya had gone out on important business. "It's about the warehouse, isn't it?" Shanna prodded.

Marta went silent for a second, then said, "What does the task force know?"

"I'm not sure. I just got here and discovered they had the warehouse cordoned off. They're bringing in some forensic medical team from Virginia — Quantico, maybe." She grimaced and asked, "How bad is it?"

"The crew barely had time to remove the major ... objects. Most of the ... residue ... was left behind, unattended."

Despite Marta's euphemisms, Shanna immediately guessed

the blood was the residue left behind — including some of Aiden's and Talya's. "Shit." Shanna glared at the asphalt at her feet, then looked up just in time to see Agent Norris standing at the building entrance, motioning to her. "Uh ... I gotta go. I'll call again later."

Marta started to say something else, but Shanna hit the end button and hid her phone in her palm at her side as Agent Norris called out, "Hey, Deputy ... Cupcake ... whatever the hell your name is. Talk lovey-dovey with your boyfriend later. I need you to go to police headquarters downtown and pick up a van. I've got nine people arriving at the airport with a load of equipment and luggage, and you're the only chauffeur available."

Shanna cursed under her breath and put her phone back on her utility belt. The last thing she needed was to be stuck on gopher detail when all this heavy crap was going down. She wanted to find out exactly what was happening, so she could keep Aiden informed.

Marching toward Agent Norris with a grim look, she took little satisfaction in realizing she was right — he hadn't paid enough attention to her feeble presence on the task force to bother learning her name. "Yeah, okay, *Chuck*," she snarled. "I'm on it."

He held the door, giving her a what-the-hell glare as she brushed past him. She shot him a mean grin over her shoulder. "If you can call me *Cupcake*, I get to call you *Chuck* ... as in Chuck Norris."

He laughed out loud, surprising her with his hearty guffaw. She stopped and turned, amazed the gruff bulldog was capable of smiling, much less laughing.

"Move it, Cupcake," he said, trying to stifle his lingering snicker. "We don't have all day."

"Wow," she sniped, turning back around to head for the task force office. "You're a real chauvinistic charmer, aren't you, Chucky-Boy?"

He laughed again, this time with a low and throaty chuckle. Without glancing back to see, she knew instinctively that he was admiring her ass. She didn't care. He could look all he wanted, as long as he didn't try to touch. "Enjoying the view?" she taunted as she walked ahead of him down the corridor.

"Sure thing, Cupcake," he answered without missing a beat. "You're not gonna tell your big, bad boyfriend, are you?"

She peered over her shoulder at him as she swung open the

office door. "Why? Are you scared?"

He grinned, his creased face assuming the look of a squashed beach ball as he grabbed the door and held it for her. "Me, Chuck Norris, scared? Hell, no. I'm a big-time, movie-magic, kick-ass karate expert with my own lifelike action figure."

"Uh, yeah, right. That was years ago. You're way past your prime now, and so is your *action figure*."

The door ease shut behind him as he followed her into the office. "*Old* doesn't keep me from looking, Cupcake."

Shanna laughed and sang, "Whatever," over her shoulder.

* * * * *

Shanna left her patrol car downtown, in the back lot behind police headquarters. Maneuvering the long white unmarked van through late morning traffic, she headed down Route 60 toward Barkley Regional Airport, with little time to spare before the expected flight arrived. After Agent Norris called ahead to clear her way, she showed her badge a couple of times and experienced little fuss getting permission to drive straight to the tarmac to pick up her passengers and their gear.

As the seven medical experts — five men and two women — disembarked from the small, business-class government jet, Shanna swung open the back cargo doors of the van and walked over to see how much stuff needed to be packed inside. A couple of suits with sunglasses and ear-bud communicators had stacked the various small crates and cases in a neat pile, and stood at ease near the plane's fold-out steps.

Shanna gave the scientists a quick once-over, noting that all of them had packed light with one suitcase and one small carry-on per person, almost as if they'd coordinated their travel preparations. They were all under fifty, she guessed. The two women were slender and fit, and both wore similar nondescript dark skirts and jackets. Neither was particularly pretty or ugly. They just looked normal, like people you'd pass on the street and never give a second glance. One was slightly taller than the other, had straight, dark hair, blunt-cut at the shoulders. The other wore wire-rim glasses, had wavy dishwater blonde hair, also shoulder-length but pulled back at the neck. Both were taller than Shanna. The men seemed similarly well groomed and fit, as if they were true-blue government slaves, conditioned to obey orders. They all looked like they'd spent most of their time encased in a hermetically sealed lab, staring at microscopic specimens, the only live contact they had with the world.

Only one of the men seemed to stand out from the rest. He was nice-looking with dark hair and dark eyes, but there was something about him that seemed out of kilter. Although he appeared clean-shaven, he had a slight beard shadow, even this early in the day. But it was his eyes that made Shanna give him a more thorough once-over. They were tinged with red, making him appear not to have slept well in weeks, perhaps months. He possessed a haunted, tortured air, and she couldn't help imagine that something terrible had happened to him to make him look that unsettled.

She forced a smile and stepped forward. "Welcome to Paducah. I'm Deputy Shanna Preston with the McCracken County Sheriff's Department. Please take a seat in the van. Your luggage and other gear will be packed in the back. I'll drive you to the hotel where you'll be staying. You'll have half an hour to freshen up, then meet me at the van so I can take you to task-force headquarters, where you'll be briefed on the situation." She hoped she'd get to listen in on that briefing, because she wanted to know what the hell was going on.

As the two suits hauled the crates and cases and luggage to the back of the van, the scientists filed toward the passenger area and opened the doors. Shanna watched the suffering one, wondering why in the hell he had been allowed to accompany the group. Obviously he wasn't feeling well. Clutching a slim black briefcase to his chest, he shot her a quick look over his shoulder, then turned and climbed into the last row of seats.

Walking over to make sure everything was loaded and the doors were secure, Shanna stopped in surprise as the two suits got into the van, one in front and one in the rear. She glanced back when she heard the steps of the jet being folded up. As she strolled around to the driver's side of the van, she figured these scientists were important enough to warrant at least two government bodyguards. What was up with that?

* * * * *

Shanna stood in the lobby of the Drury Inn with its dark patterned carpet, real potted palms, and one-hundred-thirty-dollar-a-night rooms. Definitely a cut above regular government standards. She checked her watch yet again, figuring good ol' Agent Chuck would chew her ass if she delayed much longer to give the weird, sickly guy time to show up. Everybody else in the Virginia science team had been standing around ready to go for the last ten minutes, but nobody complained or looked the least bit put out at having to wait on their tardy colleague.

Shanna glanced at the elevator once more, then eyed the two suits, having no idea what their names were. They glared through their sunglasses at her like she was a bug. Unfazed, she strolled over with a smile and murmured, "Looks like somebody's got a punctuality problem. I'm supposed to already be on the road with your folks, and I'm going to catch hell if I wait any longer."

The two bodyguards, both tall and muscular with shorn heads and identical charcoal gray suits, looked at each other, then stared down at her. Neither one of them bothered to speak.

She huffed with exasperation. "So, one of you clowns want to go upstairs and check on him, to see what's taking him so long? Maybe he's sick or something. He didn't look too good on the way over here." She recalled catching a glimpse of him in the van's rearview mirror. He was holding his stomach like he was about to toss his cookies, and she was pretty sure it wasn't from her driving.

The tree trunk on her left looked over at the other science team members, then turned back and grumbled, "Give Dr. Burkhart another two minutes."

She glared up at them for a second, then huffed again. "Fine. I'll go see what's keeping him."

She started toward the elevator, then swerved and went to the front desk. "Dr. Burkhart's room number?" she demanded of the thirty-something woman wearing an emerald green vest and a hotel staff tag that said Gloria.

Gloria started to open her mouth, but Shanna already knew what she was going to say. She put up a hand and growled, "Don't give me any guff about privacy policies, Gloria. I just drove Dr.

Burkhart here forty-five minutes ago. I'm a law-enforcement officer, and this could be an emergency. Now tell me what room he's in, and give me a key while you're at it."

Without further hesitation, Gloria tapped on the computer keyboard below the counter. She turned around and reached into a drawer at the workstation. Turning back around, she whipped a keycard at Shanna. "Room 219."

"Thank you." Shanna yanked the card from her hand, then marched to the elevator.

* * * * *

Shanna tapped louder on the door and called out, "Dr. Burkhart, I know you're in there. I have a keycard to your room. If you don't answer, I'm coming in."

She waited another few seconds, then cursed under her breath and slipped the card into the lock mechanism. The green light flashed. She turned the handle and pushed on the door. It opened a crack, then stopped with a clunk as the inside security chain held. "Damn it," she grumbled. "Come on, Dr. Burkhart. Don't make me kick the door in and bust the chain. I'm just here to make sure you're okay. Say something, will you?"

She stood there, holding the door open against the chain as she listened for some sign of movement. Finally she heard the slight creak of a mattress and the soft shuffle of unshod footsteps coming toward her. A second later she heard a deep, gruff male voice rasp, "I'll be down as soon as I can." The cloying stench of hard liquor filtered out past the door opening. "Just … give me a minute."

"Sure, take all the time you need," Shanna retorted in a singsong tone. "We got all day. No need to worry I'll get my chops busted for bringing you all in two hours late."

She caught a flash of one red-rimmed brown eye as he glared through the door opening at her. He ducked back quickly. She heard him sigh long and hard, and smelled the whiskey scent again. "That's some cologne, doc. Eau de Bourbon?"

He huffed again, hard. "If you don't mind, deputy—"

"Look, it's none of my business what you—"

"You're right. It isn't any of your business," he growled, still hiding behind the door. His voice seemed stronger. So did his breath.

She frowned. "The thing is, I don't really give a damn about your drinking problem. But I do give a damn about my job. And right now, my job is to see that you get your fanny downstairs with everyone else, so I can drive you to the task force office. I'm not leaving you alone until you either unchain this door and let me in, or you come out here and go downstairs with me to the van. Your choice. I can stand out here and blather away until I get tired of it and kick the damn door in and drag you out by your collar, or—"

"Okay!" he snapped. "Let me close the door to unhook the chain."

She stepped back. "Great."

The door slammed shut. She heard the chain rattle, then a second later the door swung open to reveal six-foot-one Dr. Burkhart standing in front of her, sans tie and jacket, with the sleeves of his rumpled white shirt rolled halfway up his corded forearms, and the hems of his sleek-fitting brown trousers skimming his sock feet.

"Sorry," she said, pushing past the door before he changed his mind and closed it in her face. "Did I wake you from a nap?"

"No such luck." He shot her a tortured glance with those big sexy brown eyes of his that looked squinty and tired from lack of sleep. Turning his back on her, he ran a hand through his thick black hair cut in a casual business style, and let out a ragged sigh.

Standing in the opening leading to his sleeping area, she frowned and watched him head for his jacket draped across the chair tucked under the desk against the wall. Quickly she skimmed the room's details — fabric recliner, king-size bed, real cherry headboard, nice ornately framed painting of a flowery garden above. Big fifth of bourbon, three quarters empty, on the nearest nightstand.

As he rolled his sleeves down, she focused on him. The guy was definitely good looking. Nice body. But he had a serious problem, and she didn't think it was just a hankering for booze. Something truly painful bothered him. She couldn't avoid feeling sorry for him. "Drinking never helps anything," she said softly. "Just disguises it."

Finished buttoning his cuffs, he rolled his broad shoulders to settle into his shirt. "Numbs it," he clarified, pushing his tie knot tight to his throat. He slipped his jacket on, then eyed her. "I'm ready to go now. Satisfied, deputy?"

"Whatever your problem is, Dr. Burkhart, you can get help."

He forced a mean laugh. "Trust me. There's no help available for my problem."

She let out an exasperated sigh. "Well then, maybe you should sit this one out. Get some rest. You don't seem to be at the top of your game right now."

He strolled purposefully toward her and stopped just inches from her, invading her personal space with the sour-sweet stench of his liquor-laden breath. "You don't know anything about me, about my situation. How can you stand there and make snap judgments about me and presume to give me personal advice?"

"Humanitarian concern," she grumbled, glaring up at him towering over her. She refused to back down and give him the mistaken idea he could intimidate her. "One person caring about the welfare of another. That's all it is, Dr. Burkhart. Want to discuss what's bothering you?"

His eyes, already red and scratchy-looking, glistened with sudden tears. He whirled away. "It was my fault. *My fault!* If I hadn't stayed involved with the damned research, Anna wouldn't have been there with me, and —"

He covered his face with his hands. "I can't stand to even think about what she..." Shaking his head, he lowered his hands and looked toward the window darkened by the closed drapes. He sucked in a hard breath and mumbled, "This is the first time I'll have access to enough of the biological sample I need. What if I can't figure it out? I'm afraid to even try. But I can't afford to stop working on it. Not now..."

Shanna scowled in confusion. "Exactly what are you working on, Dr. Burkhart?"

With his back to her, he sucked in another ragged breath, then let it out slowly. "A cure."

She took a tentative step closer to him. "Are you ill?"

He shook his head again, refusing to face her as he choked out, "My wife."

"What's ... what's wrong with your wife, Dr. Burkhart?" Shanna felt a sinking sense of dread in her chest.

Dr. Burkhart turned slowly to face her. Clenching his fists, he fought valiantly to maintain emotional control as he whispered, "That murdering animal attacked my sweet Anna a month ago and nearly killed her. Now she's ... infected with something, some kind of virus that's driven her completely mad."

Shanna staggered back. "Oh, my God..."

CHAPTER 15

Shanna didn't ask any more questions, and Dr. Burkhart didn't offer any more information. They rode down the elevator together in prickling silence. He rubbed his eyes with his thumb and forefinger, obviously trying to erase his tortured thoughts, while she wondered what in the hell the poor man had been going through since his wife had become ... whatever she was now.

His wife had been raped and nearly killed by Cameron Ryben. But how — why? Surely she hadn't been Ryben's usual flavor of choice, some hapless barfly looking for a good time. Obviously Anna Burkhart had been loved and cherished by her husband who, for whatever reason, blamed himself for the gruesome fate that had befallen her.

Shanna couldn't let herself believe Mrs. Burkhart's apparently foul transformation was the same that both Aiden and Marta had warned could happen to her too if she didn't come through the change well. Had Cam Ryben's attack turned Mrs. Burkhart into a ravenous rogue-type creature lusting after blood and sex like a mindless animal? Shanna grimaced, wondering if it might still happen to her. She had no way of knowing for sure that it wouldn't, despite Aiden's assurances that their being properly mated would prevent it.

On the flip side of awful was terrible — Aiden and Talya had both been stabbed by Ryben at the warehouse, and the cleanup crew sent by the Enclave had not had time to eradicate all the evidence. Not only would Dr. Burkhart's team have access to copious amounts of Ryben's blood, they'd have Aiden's and Talya's too. What the hell kind of research had Burkhart been working on that caused him to cross paths with Cameron Ryben?

Shanna's stomach growled in distress as the elevator door slid open with a ding, startling her from her troubled thoughts. She shot a glance at Dr. Burkhart, who'd chewed some breath mints on the way down and had buttoned his jacket so he almost looked and smelled like a regular guy, not some emotionally haunted and boozed-up wraith. He waited for her to step out, then followed her to the rest of the team. No one met his eyes. No one met Shanna's.

"I'll go get the van," she blurted. Pulling the keys from her pants pocket, she jingled them nervously as she charged for the lobby doors.

Once outside, away from the hotel entrance, she grabbed her cell phone and speed-dialed Aiden's home number. It rang and rang. Finally Marta answered. "I need to talk to Aiden," Shanna demanded as she marched toward the van in the parking lot behind the three-story building.

"He and Talya are still out working. I'll tell him to call you when he returns."

"Yeah, okay. No, wait. I might be with some other people and won't be able to tell him what I need to. Just ... I'll call when I can. When do you expect him back?"

"Any time now."

"Fine. I'll call later. Um ... what's he doing, anyway?" Shanna suffered a twinge of jealousy in her gut. Aiden had been gone with Talya for over an hour, maybe longer.

"Trying to repair the damage."

"Damage?"

"The *situation*."

She felt her face blanch as she stopped at the van driver's door. "Did they go where I think they went?"

"It's best not to discuss particulars over the phone, don't you agree?"

"Okay." Shanna wrinkled her nose. Who did Marta think would eavesdrop on their conversation? Was she being overly cautious, or paranoid — or just damned uncooperative? Was she trying to cover up for Aiden? Shanna shook those suspicions from her head. "Tell him I called, will you? And I'll call back again when I can."

"Certainly."

Marta's super-calm tone irritated her. She knew she shouldn't blame the woman for being a rock in times of stress, but it made her pissy all the same. "Damn it, why doesn't he have a cell phone?"

"Can you imagine the inconvenience of it ringing while he's *working*?"

With the key inserted in the door lock, Shanna froze. Yeah, right in the middle of chopping some rogue's head off, Aiden gets a call he just can't afford to miss. And while he's fumbling around with his phone... She sighed and forced the image from her mind. Aiden wouldn't be so careless. Anyway, she just couldn't picture him as a cell-phone kind of guy, a player with the headset and the whole bit, making deals and putting callers on hold so he could answer other calls. That just wasn't Aiden. He was so much more sophisticated than that.

"Incidentally," Marta added, "he wouldn't need a cell phone if you were fully Shanrak, Shanna."

Shanna started to curse then hit the end button. She realized then she would never live down that stigma. Jamming the phone onto her utility belt, she unlocked the van.

* * * * *

When Shanna escorted Dr. Burkhart and his team to the task force office, she immediately realized the FBI was no longer in charge of things, as she'd first assumed. The taller woman from the Virginia team, with the straight dark hair, conferred briefly with Agent Reissenor, who deferred to her in every way — verbally as well as with subtle body language. And Victoria Reissenor did not strike Shanna as a woman who readily deferred to anyone unless she had to.

All the while Tall Scientist Chick conversed with Agent Reissenor, the rest of the team swarmed around the office, checking things out like bloodhounds sniffing a new area. They casually glanced at papers, opened file drawers, and perused the map on the wall with red pushpins indicating the locations of all the Bloodsucker's kills — except one.

Shanna didn't recall seeing Anna Burkhart's name on the victim list she'd reviewed the other day. But then again, she didn't claim to have a photographic memory. She shot Dr. Burkhart a quick look. He still stood off by himself, staring toward the windows, apparently not focusing on anything at all. Poor guy was probably zoned out in his own little world of agony and denial, which was fine with her for the moment. At least he wouldn't catch her checking the file containing the victim list to make sure his wife's name wasn't on it.

On her way to the file cabinets, she spied the fax papers her good buddy Chuck had left on the desk he no longer occupied. On top still sat the list of names of the folks coming from Virginia, who were now here. Her eyes zeroed in on Dr. Burkhart's name. Dr. Peter Maxwell Burkhart. Did he go by Peter, or Pete, or Max? She glanced over at him once more. He still stood like an autistic child trapped in his private inner hell of regret and self-recrimination.

The rest of the Virginia team acted like she was invisible as they went about the casual business of assessing minute details of the office while their hawk-eyed lady leader continued laying out the game plan to Agent Reissenor. Good Buddy Chuck Norris seemed happy to stay out of their way as he watched them with his beady teddy-bear eyes. At least he didn't call her *Cupcake* in front of everyone and draw undue attention to her as she nonchalantly strolled over to the file cabinets.

Quickly finding the file containing the master list of the Bloodsucker's victims, Shanna confirmed her suspicion that Mrs. Burkhart's name wasn't on it. Mrs. Burkhart hadn't become a murder statistic in this investigation — she was merely a rape victim. *Merely.* Shanna grimaced at the term, thinking it was so unfitting. Having spent just a short time with Cameron Ryben herself, Shanna guessed Mrs. Burkhart had suffered much more than rape. She'd most likely been terrorized mentally and physically, not to mention getting her throat ripped open. But why had Ryben attacked her? How had she come into his realm of mayhem in the first place? Dr. Burkhart had blamed himself because of his mysterious research. Shanna still didn't have the whole story on the Burkharts, and she needed to know more.

As she looked to Agent Reissenor, wondering if she'd be a good source of information, Tall Woman Team Leader started making noises about wanting to go to the warehouse. Shanna shuddered inwardly with dread, wondering how she could possibly keep these people from getting their hands on the biological evidence that had been left behind. Once they had it, there was no telling what repercussions would filter down to Aiden and Talya, and the rest of their people. But in the same moment she recalled Dr. Burkhart's dilemma. She looked over at him standing motionless by the window, entranced by his tortured thoughts. He desperately wanted to find a way to get his wife back, and all his hopes were pinned on the same damning biological evidence Aiden and Talya wanted destroyed.

Shanna made her way over to Agent Reissenor, who seemed to be packing up for the ride to the warehouse. Somehow Shanna had to convince Reissenor to let her go along.

"You still have the keys to the van, Deputy Preston?" Agent Reissenor prodded.

Shanna stopped in her tracks. "Uh, yeah." She fished them out of her pocket and held them out in the palm of her hand.

Reissenor shook her head without disturbing a single blonde hair pulled back and held in place with the slim barrette at her nape. "You can drive. *Chuck* and I will take the rental car."

Shanna managed a smirk in response to Reissenor's acknowledgement of her besting her chauvinistic partner. Shanna glanced over and found Chuck wearing a good-natured glower, seeming to enjoy the notoriety of their private joke.

* * * * *

Shanna sweated the drive over, her fear and dread growing more intense the closer they got to the warehouse. She'd never seen the outside of the building, and it looked like any typical abandoned brick factory, except for the yellow police tape everywhere, and the squad cars parked all around. As of yet, she'd suffered no horrendous flashbacks from last night's mayhem. But she knew enough about trauma victims to realize she might experience some unpleasant episodes when she revisited the scene of the crime. After all, she'd beheaded a man who'd tried to rape her. If that wasn't traumatic, she didn't know what was.

Her good buddy Chuck had been kind enough to spill a quick summary of the details before she left the office to drive the science team to the warehouse. Apparently the task force had been given strict instructions that the crime scene was not to be disturbed by anyone after the initial report made by the city patrolman on duty last night.

An elderly couple on their way home had called in about a suspicious vehicle at the premises, and gave a license number. By the time an officer reached the warehouse, the unmarked white van — probably a van very similar to the one Shanna drove today — was gone. Shanna guessed that as soon as the Enclave cleanup crew's posted lookout spotted the couple's car stopped in the road near the van, the crew panicked and left — with just enough time to remove Ryben's body and the swords before the cruiser with blue lights flashing pulled up to the building.

The license number turned out to be bogus, chalked up to the poor eyesight of the elderly at night. But the light on the third floor of the building with no active electric service piqued the patrolman's curiosity. By the time backup arrived, the investigating police officer had taken it upon himself to wander upstairs. As soon as the patrolman saw the horrendous pool of blood still lit by the battery-operated lantern, he knew he'd stumbled onto something big, and reported it to the task force.

Soon after, Agents Reissenor and Norris took a small blood sample from the largest puddle and had it tested, confirming the blood was a probable match for the Bloodsucker. Immediately word came down from higher up to leave the scene undisturbed. Now Shanna would find out firsthand just how bad things were, assuming the mystery team of scientists decided she was worthy to pass the do-not-cross tape.

She parked the van on the cracked concrete near the building's main entrance and stood by as the team of seven scientists and their two muscular football-fullback escorts vacated the van and removed several cases of equipment. She saw some city and county vehicles parked nearby and realized somebody must have put out the word to the rest of the task force team that the big event was going down now.

She waited for a signal that she was welcome to come along. When everyone ignored her, she scurried up beside Agents Reissenor and Norris. They didn't object as she crossed the tape with them and approached the metal stairs where a crew of technicians garbed in white paper suits, caps, booties, and Latex gloves were busy dusting for fingerprints and taking pictures. Apparently the Virginia team had decided to go all-out on this crime scene, from bottom to top.

A uniform from the city police department handed her a sealed cellophane packet containing a lab-wear kit. Shanna followed the agents' cue and ripped open her packet, unfolding the one-piece paper suit. When she stepped into it and pulled it on over her shoulders, it hung on her like a molted snake skin three sizes too large. By the time she put on the paper shower cap and the rest of the ensemble, she felt as if she were a dough-factory worker. As she glanced around, she realized everyone else looked equally ridiculous, like actors in a low-budget sci-fi flick.

"You know the routine," the tall woman from the scientist team announced, fanning her deadpan gaze toward Shanna, Agents Reissenor and Norris, and the other various and sundry members of the task force that had showed up. "Touch nothing, disturb nothing. You, as members of the local investigative team, are being allowed at this crime scene merely as a professional courtesy. You may make whatever recordings, photographs, or other notations you wish, but we reserve the right to review everything before it's distributed or filed. We will confiscate anything we feel would jeopardize our efforts. Understood?"

Shanna didn't understand exactly what their efforts entailed, but she nodded like everyone else standing in the dark and drafty first floor of the warehouse. At the rear of the procession, she filed past the busy technicians. They seemed so engrossed in their collection of possible evidence, they failed to look up, and barely moved out of the way.

Reaching the second floor, Dr. Tour Guide made a curt announcement Shanna missed by the time she stepped onto the plank floor. Apparently everyone was supposed to stay put until Tour Guide and her team made the first round alone. The group of scientists returned quickly, seeming dissatisfied by the lack of interesting evidence mixed among the piles of trash and liquor bottles strewn about.

The task force members stepped back to allow the science team to lead the way back to the stairs. They all proceeded up to the third floor. By the time Shanna reached the landing, some kind of ruckus was already in progress. Dr. Burkhart apparently had lost his shaky control and was screaming at the rest of his team members — something about *betraying* him and *undercutting* his objective to save his wife. Shanna managed to squeeze around the rest of the stunned task force members to see just what Dr. Burkhart was so upset about. She glanced over where he and the others stood, and saw the blood was gone. All of it. In its place was a huge bleached-out area where some of the floorboards appeared to have been partially eroded by a caustic substance.

So, that's what Aiden and Talya had been doing this morning ... surreptitiously destroying the evidence while police stationed below guarded the crime scene, unaware it was being desecrated just three stories up. Shanna guessed now why Aiden and Talya had been the ones to do this dirty work. They were Shanrak Masters and could enter and leave the premises by dematerializing at will — most probably something the Enclave cleanup folks were not capable of doing themselves.

"Calm down, Peter," the female scientist in charge ordered. "You have to know we aren't responsible for this. We're as shocked as you are by this development."

The two bodyguards held Dr. Burkhart by his arms. He flailed to the side, seeming on the verge of complete collapse as his handsome face crumbled in rage and distress. "How can I ever help Anna now?" he wailed, covering his face with his gloved hands as he broke down and sobbed openly.

Shanna felt her eyes burn with tears and started to wipe them away until she realized her hands were still covered with Latex gloves. She blinked furiously and swiped her sleeve across her face.

"Hey, don't sweat it, Cupcake," Agent Norris whispered, leaning sideways toward her. He'd removed his silly cap and gloves. "Those spooks will take care of their own."

"Spooks?" Shanna echoed, wide-eyed. "You mean CIA?"

"NSA, Black Ops, who knows? All they told me was this investigation was classified, and not to ask questions. Looks like somebody beat them to it, and cleaned everything up. Or maybe they had their own people do it, to keep us out of the loop. And this little show is just to convince us it's all legit."

Shanna frowned as the two bodyguards escorted Dr. Burkhart toward the stairs. His cap had fallen off, and he'd removed his gloves. He'd stopped crying, seeming to have descended into a blue funk so deep, Shanna feared he might never recover. No matter what Agent

Norris said, she could tell Peter Burkhart was not putting on an act. He was a broken man, and it was partly her fault. As the bodyguards approached with him, she stepped forward impulsively. "Do you want me to take him back to the hotel?"

The two suited goons looked at each other, then glanced over their shoulders to their leader. She nodded and turned back to her tight little band of coconspirators, as if Dr. Burkhart were a mere afterthought.

"Help me get him into the van," Shanna ordered. "I think I can manage him by myself from there."

The two suites looked indecisive for a moment, then proceeded toward the stairs as if they intended to follow her instructions. She raised her eyebrows at how easy that was.

* * * * *

Having shed her lab wear, Shanna looked over at Peter Burkhart strapped in the seat beside her, leaning against the door glass with his eyes shut. The two goons had peeled off his paper suit and booties, leaving him in his street clothes. She knew he wasn't sleeping, just so emotionally drained that his mind had shut down on him. He seemed to have lost all hope, and that frightened her. A man without hope was a man who didn't want to live.

She tried to think of something encouraging or comforting to say, but what could possibly make this man feel better? Her own mate had destroyed Dr. Burkhart's last hope of recovering his wife from a fate worse than death. Just how much of a hope had it been to begin with? She wanted to know more about his mysterious research, but she knew he was in no condition right now to answer any questions.

She straightened and started the van as the two suits stood between her and the building, watching her. They gave her the creeps, like they were a couple of guard dogs just waiting for her to make one wrong move so they could leap on her and tear her to pieces. She decided that was stupid and paranoid thinking, but as she glanced at them again, she felt maybe she wasn't too far off the mark. They were spies, weren't they? Spooks, as Agent Norris had pointed out. Trained to kill on orders. They'd kill her in a heartbeat if they even suspected she'd had anything to do with the destruction of evidence in the warehouse.

She wanted to try giving Aiden another call. He ought to be home by now, and she needed to talk to him, bad. But right now was not a good time. Not with those two men watching her. They'd probably think she was reporting to someone, and suspect her of collusion, which she was certainly guilty of.

With a quick glance at Peter Burkhart, she pulled the van out of the parking lot and headed back to the hotel. She'd just have to wait until later to call Aiden and pick up her car at the police station. She hoped the other science team members could bum rides with the task force people at the warehouse. Right now her main concern was to get Peter Burkhart stabilized and off suicide watch.

* * * * *

"Watch your step ... there you go," Shanna encouraged as she coaxed Peter Burkhart from the van to the ground. "Oops, oops," she said, catching him as he started to crumble to the ground. He caught himself finally and leaned against the side of the van with a heavy sigh. She closed the van door, then circled an arm around his waist. "Ready? We'll get you to bed so you can rest. You look exhausted."

The closer they got to the back entrance of the hotel, the stronger Peter seemed to become. When Shanna stopped to dig his room card out of her breast pocket, he mumbled, "You can let go. I'm fine. Thank you for your help, deputy. I can make it from here."

She frowned at him, then shook her head. "I wouldn't be doing my job if I didn't make sure you made it to your room, safe and sound."

He grimaced and shot her a wounded look. "I'm sorry to be such a pain. Normally, I'm not ... like this."

She shrugged. "Hey, everybody has a bad day now and then. You going to open the door, or shall I?" She flipped her keycard out of her pocket and waved it with a grin.

She caught just a hint of something that looked almost like a smile flicker across his mouth before he turned to the door and mumbled, "I'll get it." He pulled his wallet from his jacket and extracted his keycard, slid it into the lock, then pulled the door back for her.

She walked inside the back entryway with stairs leading upward, and a hall leading to the front lobby and the elevator. As the door closed behind him, she turned and said, "Walk or ride?"

He gave her a big sigh and actually looked her in the eyes as he said, "Ride. I'm not up to climbing more stairs right now."

They got into the elevator, rode in silence, got out, then walked down the long hall to his room. He turned to her and managed a perfunctory smile — the second one she'd seen in less than five minutes. Maybe he was feeling better.

"Thanks," he said softly, glancing at her, then looking down at the carpeted floor. "I really do appreciate your help."

When she touched his arm lightly, he looked at her, then at her hand resting on his arm. She realized that was probably the only friendly physical contact he'd had since his wife ... since she'd changed. Feeling suddenly odd about touching him, she withdrew her hand and covered the awkwardness with a bright smile. "Why don't you change into something more comfortable, and I'll take you to get a bite to eat?"

His wide, expressive mouth stretched into a wry smirk — as close to a genuine smile as she'd seen on him yet. "Really, deputy..."

"Preston." She tapped her breast pocket with her last name sewed on the top edge. "Shanna Preston. Call me Shanna."

When his face clouded, she realized her name sounded close to his wife's name. Just hearing it probably made him think of her. "Or," she amended quickly, "you could just call me 'Cupcake,' like Agent Norris has been."

He tried to laugh at her obvious attempt at levity, but the sound that came from his throat was closer to a broken sob.

She grabbed his hand and drew it up, squeezing hard. "Everything's going to be okay, Dr. Burkhart."

He lowered his head and shook it slowly. "No, it's not. My Anna ... she's ... you don't know ... you can't imagine..." He pulled his hand from hers and swiped his palm over his face.

"Yes, I can. I can imagine what you're going through, and I can sympathize. I may not be able to do much right now to help you, but I'm going to do what I can to make you stop torturing yourself." Shanna slipped her keycard into the door lock and pushed the door open. "Come on. You need to freshen up and relax. You've had a very crappy morning."

As he walked inside, he let out a huff that could have been a laugh. "And the afternoon's not shaping up to be much better."

"That's where you're wrong, doc," Shanna countered as she let the door slam shut behind her. "Got any jeans in that suitcase of yours?"

He turned and shot her a quizzical look.

"First thing is to get you out of that suit."

"Really, deputy, you don't need to stick around and play nursemaid. I promise, I'll be all right on my —"

"Off with the tie, doc," she whispered, feeling oddly intimate reaching out to unclasp his tie clip. It was a delicate thing with a tiny gold chain and a line of glittering diamond chips across the front. She studied it with absent admiration.

"Anna gave me that for our third anniversary."

She looked up at him, amazed that he hadn't fallen to pieces saying that. His voice didn't even crack when he spoke his wife's name. Maybe he just needed someone to listen, so he could talk about her.

"How long have you been married?"

He looked down and finally managed another smile. "Almost five years." As he reached up and loosened his tie, he said, "I don't see you wearing a wedding ring, deputy."

She smirked then glanced at his tie tack resting in her palm. "I'm working on it." As she started to hand the tie tack back to him, it flipped over in her hand. She noticed something peculiar stuck on the backside and held it up for closer inspection. She wasn't a surveillance expert, but she could swear the tiny appendage on the back was not part of the tie tack.

"What's so interest —"

She put a finger to her lips to silence him and spun the tie tack around, holding out for him to see her discovery. He got a peculiar, sick look on his face and flicked her a horrified glance.

She rotated her hand in front of her with a rolling motion to indicate he should play along. "I'm going to use your ... um ... facilities, and give you a little privacy while you change clothes, doc."

"Okay..." he said hesitantly, standing there waiting for some further signal from her.

She started toward his suitcase, then caught a glance at her black sports watch. Turning, she pecked the crystal of her watch with her finger. He shrugged with a puzzled look. She rolled her eyes then started to undo the clasp. He nodded with understanding and undid his watch. She grabbed it from him and set it on the dresser near his suitcase, along with his tie clasp.

Looking him over, she tried to decide what else might be bugged. Immediately her eyes zeroed in on his gold wedding band. She pointed to her naked ring finger on her left hand, and he shook his head, understanding exactly what she wanted him to do. Obviously he had no intention of ditching his wedding ring. She sighed and motioned for him to take it off. Finally he did. She looked it over carefully, noticing the tiny engraving on the inside. 'Always—Anna.' She swallowed down a sudden burn of impending tears, then slowly handed it back to him. He put it back on his finger and watched her intently for more prompts.

She mimicked unbuttoning her shirt. He did the same, only for real, parting his shirt to reveal a broad, solid chest under a low-neck A-line tee shirt, barely exposing the sparse vee of black hair above his breastbone. He pulled the shirt off and handed it to her. She had a hard time not openly staring at his bod. He evidently worked out. Feeling around on the shirt collar and down the placket, she decided there was nothing suspicious hidden inside and tossed the garment on the bed.

Looking down at her feet, she put a heel in front of the toe of her other shoe. He nodded and slipped out of his business oxfords, expensive oxblood leather, almost new. She tossed them over by the bed, knowing some kind of tracing device could have been hidden inside the heels. Not that she had a plan that would require ditching a tail. She just didn't want them to be spied upon, eavesdropped on. Because what she had to tell Dr. Burkhart might put him in danger if what she suspected was true.

At that point she darted over to his open suitcase and pulled out a light blue chambray shirt and a pair of jeans, plus a pair of scruffy running shoes. She inspected them all for evidence of tampering, but could find nothing suspicious. She handed them to him, then pulled at her trouser legs to let him know what to take off next.

Arching his black brows, he gave her a wry smile and pointed his index finger down, twirling it in a pirouette to indicate she should turn around. She grinned and turned her back to him, realizing she wanted to take a peek, which she easily did in the mirror. About the time he revealed the nice healthy package cuddled by his tidy-white briefs, he looked up and caught her staring in the mirror. He paused for a second like a deer caught in headlights, then smiled broadly and peeled off his trousers, obviously unfazed by her voyeurism. As he stepped into his jeans, she looked away, wondering what the hell had gotten into her.

When she was fairly sure he was decently covered, she turned back around, catching a glimpse of her naughty grin in the mirror. Suddenly the idea that the mirror might have a camera behind it made her lurch with fear. She moved to the side and tried to spy at it from an angle, to see if there was any hint of a light or lens reflection. She saw nothing.

Tucking his shirt into his jeans, Peter came over to see what had her tensed up. She shrugged, then smiled and stepped back to take a good survey. He really was a looker, and those dark eyes and hint of a beard shadow gave him a bad-boy edge. Anna Burkhart had been one lucky woman — until Cameron Ryben entered the picture.

"Come on, doc," she said, heading for the door. "Let's get some lunch."

CHAPTER 16

Shanna traded in the van for her patrol car at the city police department, then took Peter to lunch at a hamburger joint filled with noontime diners amid the din of beeping French fry alarms and counter help calling out receipt numbers. She figured spooks would have a hard time blending in and listening in with all this noise and confusion, since the majority of folks frequenting the place were overweight, middle-to-lower-income worker-bees who made fast food their lunchtime routine. Then there were the grandparents taking the finicky grandson out for lunch, and the stressed-out mom with three wild kids too busy playing in the rumpus area outside to eat their cheap, high-fat burgers and salty fries. Not to mention the five teenage boys scrounging for sustenance while pissing away their summer vacation from school. And a group of four Hispanic construction workers in dusty work jeans. Yep, spooks would have one hell of a time blending in with this diverse crowd. Of all the patrons, she and Peter probably stuck out the most – her in her deputy uniform, and him with his sexy model looks and tortured bedroom eyes.

Sighing, she sipped her diet soda and sat back in the tiny booth they occupied, to study the man sitting across from her. "So, doc, what are you doing hanging around with a bunch of spooks?"

In the middle of taking a sip of his soda, he almost choked. "Spooks?"

"Agent Norris said your team was involved in some kind of classified operation. What's going on? How'd you get mixed up with them? You don't seem to fit in."

Peter lowered his gaze and stilled in his seat. She'd hit the quick with that last round of questions.

"I'm not at liberty to say," he mumbled, still not looking up at her.

"Bullshit," she whispered, leaning forward. "You've already told me too much about what happened to your wife. And with your little outburst at the warehouse, plus the discovery of that micro-electronic modification to your tic tack, I think you know you're on the outside looking in." She waited for her declaration to sink in, assuming he already suspected it was true. "Obviously your colleagues feel they can't trust you anymore."

His eyes flicked up at her, and his face darkened. "I'm sick of constantly being watched, monitored like I'm some kind of liability."

"Are you a liability?"

He looked down again and crumpled his empty sandwich wrapper in his fist. "I didn't know in the beginning what they were trying to do when they recruited Anna and me. If I had..." His brown eyes hardened with anger and pain.

"What *are* they trying to do?"

When he glanced away, she feared she'd lost her grip on the slender thread connecting them. Turning back to face her, he smiled briefly. "I'm sorry, deputy. This is information you don't want to know. Trust me."

"Why don't you let me be the judge of that? What's this about you and your wife getting recruited? For what? By whom?"

He sighed and sat back hard against his seat. He studied her for a long time, probably trying to calculate his odds of surviving the night if his colleagues learned he'd trusted her and spilled his story. But she knew he wanted to tell someone. She could feel his need like a palpable entity looming between them.

Looking down, he fiddled with his crumpled sandwich wrapper and mumbled, "Anna and I both worked at a company outside Richmond, called GenCon. We were brought into their genetics research division at about the same time. After we'd worked together for about two years, we decided to get married." He glanced up briefly and added, "It was a beautiful private ceremony with just our immediate families. Anna..." His eyes started watering, and he grabbed for his soda. Taking a sip, he calmed himself with a couple of deep, slow breaths then whispered, "She was the best part of my life."

Shanna grimaced. He'd said '*was* the best part,' as if his hope of redeeming that life, that love he'd cherished so much, had died. She wished somehow he could eventually turn that *was* back to *is*.

Sighing, she forged ahead. "What exactly is this GenCon place?"

"A private facility, a dedicated research corporation. Our division performed genetic testing and research. GenCon also contracted certified DNA testing for various organizations — law enforcement, and so forth — to help fund research. Our work required a lot of sophisticated cellular and molecular imaging equipment, and that doesn't come cheap. We had the best of everything that was available, and we were being paid very, very well."

He huffed. "When I think back on how naïve I was, believing it was a legitimate, self-sufficient private company..." He shook his head. "Anna suspected long before I did that some secretive branch of the government was using the company as a front for covert, unapproved research. Turned out she was right. If I'd listened to her and agreed to quit when she wanted to..." He shook his head again.

Shanna sat back to digest this revelation. Peter didn't say anything for a long while, just stared down at the table. "So..." she prodded finally, "what happened?"

He sighed and studied the ceiling for a moment, as if he were waiting for some inspiration from above. Looking down at the table once again, he made a pile of confetti by tearing tiny pieces of paper from his sandwich wrapper. "Shortly after we started at GenCon, we were given a blood sample to examine and put through a battery of standardized tests. We weren't sure of the sample source, whether it was human or ... something else. We inquired but were told not to ask questions, just use extreme caution handling the sample."

"What was unique about the blood sample that made you question where it came from?"

He looked at her and stopped shredding his wrapper. "The hemoglobin molecular structure had been altered significantly. At first we thought it was the result of sophisticated gene splicing, but the closer we studied the genetic structure of the cells, the more we realized this was something we'd never seen before in a lab, or in nature."

"But it appeared to be of human origin?" Shanna prodded, fearing she knew exactly what the source of that sample had been.

Peter shrugged. "At first glance, yes, it could have passed as human blood. But it wasn't. Not really."

"Because of the strange hemoglobin?"

"And other significant differences. The cells contained an extra chromosome strand not found in typical human blood. At first we mistook it for a viral DNA strand."

"Some kind of infection?" Shanna concluded, trying to follow his explanation. She'd never been an avid student of genetics and feared he'd start talking over her head.

He nodded. "To test the hypothesis, we introduced the foreign DNA strand into one cell of a normal human blood sample. In no time the foreign DNA replicated its coding and attached itself to RNA, to spread to other cells. Once the coding was given to neighboring cells, the DNA strand replicated itself inside the nucleus of each infected cell, attaching itself to the existing DNA in a geometrically increasing cascade effect."

He sucked on his soft drink straw and met her eyes with renewed energy, as if talking about his research fanned a dormant ember in his nearly deadened core. Surrounded by those thick, black, pretty-boy lashes, his deep brown eyes suddenly looked livelier, more alluring. She lowered her gaze and cleared her throat, but he seemed not to notice her interest.

"Because the DNA replication process mimicked the action of a viral infection," he continued, "we had a hard time deciding whether we were dealing with just a DNA strand or a true virus. But we knew whatever we decided, this thing we had in our lab could turn out to be deadly."

Shanna flashed him a look and blinked, trying to swallow down her astonishment. "Deadly? How?"

"In modifying normal human genes to carry its own signature DNA structure, the chromosome strand also changed the function of the cell to conform to its DNA coding. That's exactly what happens when a virus spreads through the body, replicating itself until the entire host is overrun and destroyed because it can no longer function without its original DNA intact."

"Sounds like some kind of ... cancer."

He shrugged and took another sip of his drink. "The end result might appear similar, but in many types of cancer, the affected cells simply reproduce out of control, creating tissue that has no viable function in the body except to replicate the same out-of-control cell reproduction again and again in other parts of the body. But this DNA strand appeared to have a specific agenda ... find new cells and replace their DNA with its own until it was in total genetic control of the host organism."

Shanna raised her brows, startled by the revelation, but also wondered how this could possibly be of interest to the government. Unless... "Did the altered blood cease to function properly?"

Peter shrugged then rested his elbows on the table, propping his chin on his clasped hands. "We had no way of knowing for sure, since we were dealing with a small sample. Without knowing the symptoms of the source individual, we could only conjecture about the functional quality of the mutated blood."

"So, you concluded this was a fluke, a genetic disease?"

"Until we were given more samples to test. Each of those samples bore a different genetic signature."

"What do you mean?"

"Each individual has a unique DNA stamp — specific characteristics present that identify that person as different from every other person. Short, tall, blue eyes, brown eyes. That sort of thing. Anna and I verified the later blood samples came from individuals different from that first sample."

Shanna frowned, wondering how many people that secret government agency had captured or deliberately infected for the tests Peter Burkhart and his wife were conducting. "What were you testing for?"

"Cell lifespan after alteration, plus a battery of chemical and irradiation tests to determine survival rates of the cells in a given sample. Some of the samples were more stable than others and withstood extreme testing amazingly well."

"Better than human blood?" Shanna asked, trying to keep her voice from betraying that she knew more than he thought.

"Yes. Significantly better."

"How long did you and your wife continue the tests?"

"From the beginning? Six years ... two years before we were married, and four years after."

"What did you deduce from all that testing?"

Peter gave her a darting look, then sat back with his lips pressed together.

Realizing she'd reached an area of discussion he felt uncomfortable revealing, she diverted the conversation. "So ... what happened then?"

He eyed her again and sighed. "Anna and I were asked to transfer to another facility, to continue our work. It was a secret underground lab we knew was run by the government. After we agreed — as if we really had a choice at that point — we realized our work was just a small part of a bigger research program."

Shanna nodded, figuring she knew exactly what kind of program it was. Either the government was trying to create their own Shanrak rogues by altering — infecting — humans, or they were trying to isolate the life-extending benefits of being Shanrak by extracting some key element in the blood. The question was, where were they getting their infected blood samples?

"Your wife ... how did she manage to be attacked by..." Shanna winced and let Cameron Ryben's name wither on her tongue. Peter knew him only as the Bloodsucker, and there was no reason now to attach a personal name to the nemesis in his life's nightmare.

Peter opened his hands and covered his face, almost as if he were just resting his eyes for a bit. Dragging his hands away, he leaned back against the booth seat. "Two months ago, when the ... killings began, Anna and I were mobilized and set up with a temporary lab in every city the killer hit, so we could perform immediate tests on each of the ... victims. A month ago Anna and I were working in the makeshift lab in the basement of a hospital in Wisconsin."

He glanced around as if trying to stay grounded in his current reality of a daytime hamburger joint. With a heavy sigh he flicked Shanna a quick glance and whispered, "I had planned to work through the night and finish some tests for results they wanted in the morning. Anna was exhausted and decided to go to the hotel early to rest. She was..." He gulped and exhaled harshly. "Two months pregnant with what would have been our first child."

Shanna straightened in her seat, shuddering inwardly as the chill of shock washed over her.

"Not far from the hospital," he continued in a ragged tone, "the rental car she was driving broke down, and she called me on my cell to come and get her. But by the time I got there..." He shrugged, putting his palms in the air in a gesture of helplessness as his eyes clouded with tears.

Shanna reached over and touched his shoulder. "Let's go. It's awfully noisy in here."

He nodded and rubbed his eyes with his fingertips, as if to remove some grit. Getting up, Shanna grabbed their trash and tossed it in the nearest receptacle. He followed her outside to her car.

* * * * *

Aiden paced in the great room, not bothering to gauge Talya's black eyes as they followed his every move. She sat on the couch expectantly, waiting for him to blow up and go after Shanna, but she was too reserved to taunt him by saying so aloud.

Did she gain some perverse satisfaction, watching him wallow in jealousy because he was too proud to bluster in and take his woman back with a commanding hand? He turned on Talya lounging on the couch as if she were a large lap cat — no, lioness.

She looked up at him openly, and he knew in his heart she took no pleasure in his misery, which was not nearly so private as he would like. Having spent many hours in her proximity, he had inadvertently opened a link with her, and their thoughts now flowed freely between them. He had not bothered to close himself off, thinking nothing of it at the time. But now he chastised himself, wondering how the newfound mental intimacy he shared with Talya was any different from the link Shanna had unwittingly formed with the man she irreverently called 'doc' aloud, but thought of as 'Peter' privately.

He glared at the phone. It did not ring as he commanded with his strongest wish of desperation. While he could not sense Shanna's every thought at this distance yet, he knew he would be able to eventually, once she gained more Shanrak abilities. For now, all he could sense were her overt feelings and a few key thoughts. And he had sensed several in the last hour. He could not see exactly what she'd been doing alone with Peter Burkhart, and that tortured him most evilly.

"She will call," Talya reassured, getting up from the couch with a heavy sigh. "She called several times while we were away this morning, and she will call again when she feels it's appropriate to do so."

"But it's been hours since her last call. Surely she knows by now we have returned."

"Don't vex yourself, Aiden. I have felt her love for you, and yours for her. You have performed the proper mating ritual with her, and she is bound to you, even though you shared your blood with her only once. You have no reason to worry she would be easily swayed by casual concern, even affection, for another."

He turned away, wishing he had thought to shut Talya out of his mind long before he'd been startled by Shanna's coy excitement at secretly watching Peter Burkhart undress. What had made her do such a thing? Even now, he felt her warring with her attraction to this man.

He whirled around and headed for the door. "I have to go to her." As he touched the doorknob, the phone rang. He knew it was Shanna calling. He could feel it. He rushed to the phone and snatched up the receiver before it could ring a second time. "My love," he said, breathless, "I've been waiting anxiously for you to call. Is everything all right?"

"I have something important to tell you, Aiden. You need to come to my apartment right away."

He closed his eyes and sighed with relief. "I'll be there in a moment." Feeling Talya's smirk at his back, he turned and glared at her, then hung up the phone.

"You see," Talya said. "Everything is just fine."

He gave her an impatient toss of his head. "Come with me. I fear I'll need a referee once I face this Peter Burkhart."

Talya chuckled wickedly, making him want to throttle her. Before he could finish the thought, she shimmered out of sight. A second later, he followed.

* * * * *

Shanna sat on her couch and watched Peter pace nervously in her small living room. "Will you please calm down? Everything will be fine."

He shook his head. "I shouldn't have left the hotel with you.

They'll suspect I've told you things, and you'll be dragged into this mess too." He stopped and turned to her, his dark eyes echoing pain and remorse. "I'm sorry, Shanna. I put your life in danger. But I needed to talk to someone, and you seemed so—"

Shanna shot off the couch when she saw the shimmer near her bedroom doorway.

"Oh, my Lord," Peter said. "Wh-what...?"

"Peter," Shanna said, going to Aiden's side as he materialized before her. She took his arm in hers and felt an immediate sense of calm and relief as she turned back to face Peter. "This is my ... *partner*, Aiden." She patted Aiden's arm softly and smiled up at him, then leaned forward and added, "And that is his ... um ... business associate, Talya. They've come to help you."

Peter gulped and staggered backward. "What ... what *are* you people?" He glared at Shanna, looking at her in a new and horrified way.

She shuffled forward, taking care not to startle him. "It's okay, Peter. Really. They're here to help. Please, don't be frightened."

"Are you..." He let his eyes dance from Aiden to Talya, then back to Shanna as he whispered, "Are you one of *them*?"

Aiden laughed. "One of *us*? Just what do you think we are, Dr. Burkhart?" He moved in on Peter with the muscular grace of a panther. Shanna caught herself admiring her mate with definite lustful intent until he flicked her a knowing glance over his shoulder. She'd forgotten he could read her like a book, could sense what she felt. She blushed when she recalled her indiscretion earlier, watching poor Peter undress like he was nothing more than a convenient piece of beefcake dangling in front of her, a wanton alley cat. Had Aiden sensed *that*?

Aiden shot her another look over his shoulder. His face heated with subtle anger until he smiled. She bit her lip. He knew, but he forgave her. Why was he being so generous?

Because you are my love, he answered. She blinked and stared at him in awe, realizing he'd never opened his mouth to speak.

Aiden turned to Peter, barely extending a hand. Peter staggered back against the front door, drawing her attention from Aiden. Peter's knees gave out, and his eyes slid shut as he sank to the floor in a crumpled heap.

"Peter!" she yelled, rushing past Aiden to get to him. She knelt down and rested Peter's head in her lap as he slouched over to one side. She touched a hand to his stubble-roughened cheek, trying to figure out what was wrong with him.

Aiden knelt down beside her and looked her in the eyes. "He's all right, Shanna. I put him under a calming sleep to sooth his nerves. He's a very distraught man. And he seems quite afraid of Talya and me. Why would he fear us?"

Shanna grimaced, then looked down at poor Peter and stroked his thick dark hair. "Oh, Aiden, you have no idea what he's been through."

"Let me put him on the couch where he'll rest more easily." As if he were lifting a small child, Aiden picked up Peter's limp form in his arms and carried him to the couch. Once he positioned him comfortably, he turned to face her. "So, what is this important thing you have to tell me, Shanna?"

* * * * *

Aiden scowled after hearing the rambling discourse Shanna had spewed out for him and Talya to consider. It appeared, despite the Enclave Protectorate's best efforts, a powerful and highly placed human government sector — a rogue authority — possessed intimate knowledge of the Shanrak, and probably planned to use that knowledge for nefarious purposes. One look from Talya confirmed that she agreed with his dire assessment.

He turned to eye the sleeping form of Peter Burkhart, the troubled man he'd suspected was a rival for Shanna's affection. But after hearing Shanna's heartfelt plea to help Peter, Aiden admitted he was wrong.

Shanna may have inadvertently formed a bond with Peter Burkhart out of sympathy and compassion, but Aiden knew her love and loyalty lay firmly with him, her mate. Peter Burkhart still loved his wife so much that he convinced himself he could use the magic of his medical arts to bring her back from the tormenting animal transformation she'd suffered at the hands of Cameron Ryben. Unfortunately, he too was wrong.

Aiden watched Shanna watching him with nervous

expectation. Smiling gently, he took her aside and ran his hands down her arms with comforting caresses. "Shanna, my love. I need you to understand something."

"What, Aiden?" Shanna glanced at Peter Burkhart on her couch, then looked back at him.

He sighed. "After our recent mating, you are still emotionally vulnerable. Your body is going through many changes you are not even aware of, which will impart many new abilities, some of which I'm sure will cause difficulties for you. Until you stabilize and learn to control those abilities, it is very important for you to exercise extra care in your dealings with others." He squeezed her shoulders intimately. "Do you understand what I mean?"

She scowled at him. "No."

He sighed again. "I discussed this with you before, but did not see the need to go into detail. Now it is painfully obvious I should have taken more care in explaining."

Twisting his mouth, he tried to think how best to put it so he would not sound as if he were chastising her for something she simply didn't understand she was doing. "The bond we've formed between us through mating is very strong, but still tenuous. Cameron Ryben hoped to use that tenuousness to create a permanent triangle link between him, you, and me."

She blinked her eyes, still not getting what he was saying.

"Until we share blood again, perhaps several times, our bond with each other will remain somewhat vulnerable to outside influence." He stroked her arms again. "Do you understand now?"

Biting her lower lip, she looked deep into his eyes, then glanced back over her shoulder at Peter Burkhart. When she looked Aiden in the eyes again, her face held a dawning tinge of hurt embarrassment. "Aiden, I didn't mean to—"

"I know you didn't. I mention this only to make you aware of the possibility. It would be very easy to draw someone else into our bond unintentionally, and very difficult to extricate ourselves from that third link once it is established."

Her eyes glassed over, and she blinked, looking away. "What ... what am I supposed to do?"

He wrapped her in his arms and drew her close. "Nothing. Don't worry about it. Just remain aware of it. Once we have the opportunity to complete our mating ritual and strengthen our bond permanently, there will be no chance for another to intrude, either by accident or by design."

She nodded and gulped back her tears. He released her, and she stepped away, unable to look him in the eyes. He feared for a moment the tentative bond she'd formed with Peter Burkhart was stronger than he'd first suspected, but when she finally looked up and smiled, whispering, "I'm sorry," he felt secure in his position as her one true mate.

"Don't apologize. It was my fault for not explaining the risks related to our incomplete mating. I simply didn't think it would become an issue again, after Ryben was eliminated. Now I see the danger can come from anywhere." He glanced over at Peter Burkhart on the couch and frowned. "I am eager to seal our mating bond permanently."

She stepped forward and wrapped her arms around him. "Yes, we'll have to do that soon. But right now, we need to figure out a way to help Peter and his wife."

"There is no way to help his wife," Talya announced coldly from the bedroom doorway.

Aiden looked up, suddenly reminded the Protector was still in the room. When Shanna pulled away from him and turned to confront Talya, he knew there'd be trouble. "Shanna," he said, grabbing her by the arm, "Talya and I have dealt with this sort of thing for over forty years. We know what we're talking about."

She shook her head, biting back the tears that threatened to flood her eyes. "But he loves his wife so much. And he wants her back. There has to be a way—"

"There is no way to bring her back after she's gone through the change and turned rogue," Talya reconfirmed, stepping further into the living room. "The man is deluding himself if he thinks he can conjure some potion to cure her as if she suffers from a simple disease. There is no cure, no vaccine. Period. Sometimes those we least expect to suffer the change turn rogue. No matter how much we hate losing a friend or relative, there's no turning them back. Peter Burkhart's wife must be put down."

"No!" Shanna yelled, pulling out of Aiden's grasp.

He rushed up behind her and gripped her shoulders as she

charged at Talya. "Shanna, there's no use arguing. It has to be done."

She whipped around and glared at him. "You're just afraid maybe Peter *can* find a cure. Then all you Protectors would be out of a job!"

He grimaced and shot a glance at Talya, whose hardened face betrayed nothing. He sensed her steadfastness and looked back at Shanna. "If there were some possibility for a rogue cure, don't you think we'd be the first to celebrate it — and the end of the Protectorate? Do you think we live to kill? We don't, Shanna. Seeing those suffer from turning rogue is a horrible sight, and we know from experience putting them down is doing them a great favor. No one should have to suffer that way, including Peter Burkhart's wife. She is no longer the woman she once was. She has gone mad with agony. She deserves relief and final peace from that hellish torture."

"Well, good luck on finding her," Shanna spat, crossing her arms as she turned away from him. "Peter doesn't know where the hell they're keeping her. He says they moved her since the last time he saw her, and they won't allow him to see her anymore. They've probably got her locked up somewhere in the same place they've got the others."

Aiden eyed Talya. She scowled and strolled over to take a closer look at their problem slumbering on the couch. "There have been infrequent Shanrak disappearances in the recent past," Talya admitted. "But with no reported rogue activity, the Protectorate traditionally wrote them off as voluntary exiles."

Shanna exhaled roughly and turned to look at the man she had hoped to help regain his wife. Aiden felt a wave of remorse as she wiped her eyes and tilted her head in Burkhart's direction. "Well, what are we going to do? Once the people he works for realize he's told me about everything, they're going to come after me to shut me up. Permanently. And they're going to reassess his usefulness to them, maybe deciding they can't afford him as a liability any longer."

Talya leaned over Peter Burkhart and perused his sleeping face. "You," she said to Shanna without turning from Peter, "will have to keep close to home. Him, we'll have to keep an eye on from a distance. We may not be in position to protect him, but perhaps he'll lead us to his wife's location. The Enclave Council will have to be informed of this new information straight away, so that a plan of action can be developed."

Aiden sighed, realizing this situation had just added more fuel to the bonfire the Enclave Council was building to roast him alive next week.

CHAPTER 17

Shanna didn't like Aiden's suggestion that Talya take Peter back to his hotel room the quick way. She knew Aiden wanted her alone so he could further seal their mating bond immediately. With Talya gone to the hotel to keep watch on the man Aiden obviously feared had jeopardized their closeness, they could join in bliss without fear of interruption. But Shanna didn't trust Talya, even though she'd promised to protect Peter faithfully as he slept, and stop anyone who might try to harm him. With Talya's unrelenting belief that Peter's wife must die, Shanna couldn't expect Talya to keep Peter safe when she might just as easily decide he was expendable too.

Wanting to iron things out and be sure of the expected outcome if she released custody of this man she'd taken into her care, Shanna blurted the first objection that came to mind. "How do we know what Peter will do when he wakes up? He might go straight to his superiors and tell them all about us."

Aiden frowned thoughtfully. "I doubt it. Why would he trust that information to the very people who've hidden his wife from him, presumably to study her as the change takes its toll? Revealing more about the affliction she suffers would give them more power, and certainly wouldn't further his objective to help her." Arching a brow, he glanced at Peter lying on the couch and added, "I assume he is smart enough to realize that."

Aiden sounded as if he thought everything was settled, but Shanna couldn't let go yet. It seemed wrong to send Peter away and unilaterally decide his wife must die without even trying to find an alternative. He'd be right back where he'd started — lost, with no hope or will to live. "If Talya whisks him off to his hotel room, how are we supposed to explain his magical reappearance? The bodyguards saw me leave the warehouse with him. They'll expect me to drive him back to the hotel."

"Did you notice anyone following you? Perhaps they're unaware you brought him here to your apartment." Talya narrowed her coal-black eyes in obvious disapproval.

"No, I didn't notice anyone following us, and maybe they don't know where he is right now. But they'll assume he's *somewhere* — most likely with me. They bugged at least one article of clothing they figured he'd wear every day while he was here on assignment. And the security cameras at the hotel entrances would show us coming and going. If they wanted to, they could track our every move, probably without our realizing it."

"How many of them did you see, Shanna?" Aiden asked.

She shrugged and glanced at the window with its closed blinds, allowing pale gold afternoon light to filter through. Soon it would be dark. She was surprised no one had showed up to kick her door down and take Peter into custody. She looked back at Aiden. "I picked up nine of them at the airport, including Peter and the two bodyguards. But the big shots in charge back at the secret clubhouse may have sent more agents earlier, to scout out the situation right after the first murder here in Paducah."

Aiden shot Talya a warning look. "They'll be watching. Exercise care when you deliver Dr. Burkhart to his room. We can't have anyone see you materialize with him."

Talya nodded in acknowledgement.

"But how are we going to ... I mean, how am I supposed to explain..." She huffed. "I tried to make sure his clothes weren't bugged. They're going wonder what we were up to while they couldn't monitor him."

"A dilemma you should have considered before you freed him from his keepers," Talya admonished in a superior tone.

Shanna started to retort, then caught Aiden's reprimanding frown. She let her scalding comment drift away with a sigh of exasperation.

"Now that you've taken him in, so to speak," Aiden said, "the damage is done. All you can hope to do is divert suspicion by giving those watching him something else to believe."

Shanna frowned. "Like what?"

"If they think he's gone off with you to tell you all the classified information he knows about their covert research, you're both in trouble — we all are. But if you can convince them you were merely comforting him in his time of distress and personal need, they would probably accept it with a wink and a nod. People will always be eager to believe sexual dalliance first, over any other suspected violation."

"What?" Shanna felt her face heating. "Are you saying I should pretend that he and I..."

"Slept together? Precisely."

"Aiden!" She snorted then shook her head. "I can't do that!"

"Of course you can."

"But you and I—"

"We can assume no one knows you and I are together, except for that deputy at the workhouse who saw us leave for lunch. I doubt he has any connection with the people Dr. Burkhart is involved with, so we have no reason to suspect they would find out about us. Your only task is to convince them you and Dr. Burkhart have been intimate."

She glared when he smiled with catlike ease. He made it all seem so simple, yet the idea forced her to a new level of discomfort. He obviously enjoyed putting her in this delicate and awkward position. Just because she'd seen Peter Burkhart in a state of partial undress didn't mean she'd seriously toyed with the idea of having sex with him. In fact, the idea never crossed her mind. But for a fleeting moment Aiden must have believed she'd considered it. Knowing it wasn't true, he still wanted to rub her nose in it. Did this qualify as a lover's quarrel?

"I can't do what you're suggesting," she objected. "And I doubt Peter could either. He loves his wife too much. His superiors wouldn't believe our pretense for a moment."

Aiden shrugged as if it made no difference. "People can do strange things in times of extreme stress or emotional upset, with no reasonable explanation. If Dr. Burkhart is distraught over his wife and hasn't slept well in weeks, he might be close enough to the edge to behave irrationally. In a moment of weakness and despair, he might submit to his intolerable need to connect with another caring person and find comfort in the arms of a beautiful young woman like you. He would surely regret the betrayal of his wife's memory the morning after, possibly for the rest of his life. But I wager the fear of regret would not stop him from enjoying that one small oasis of relief in the desert of turmoil he's been suffering night and day for the past month."

Shanna stood there, staring at Aiden with her mouth agape. Was that how their relationship had started? With Aiden's betrayal, not of a wife, but of his oath as a Protector? Did he still feel regret?

I regret nothing, my love, he whispered in her mind. She stepped back, jolted by the intrusion of his words when his mouth hadn't moved.

Smiling, he turned to Talya. "It's settled, then. You will take Dr. Burkhart to his hotel room now, and stay on guard with him to ensure he remains safely asleep. At dawn you will bring him back here to Shanna's apartment so that we can wake him and explain our plan. Then Shanna will drive him back to his hotel room to carry on the charade of their tryst. In this way, we will avert the possibility of Shanna being targeted for silencing, and Dr. Burkhart will maintain his status with those who employ him. I assume we will want to keep him in place. He may be of further service as the Enclave investigates the human government's research perversions Shanna has brought to our attention."

With a private smile he walked over and took hold of Shanna's shoulders. "And you, my cherished mate, will ensure this charade with Peter Burkhart remains a pretense only. Your physical and emotional love belongs to me alone." He bowed his neck and placed a lingering kiss on her slightly parted lips.

Glancing over his shoulder, Aiden nodded to Talya. She strolled to the couch and lifted Peter's limp body in her arms, seemingly with as much ease as Aiden had earlier. "I'll return with him at dawn," she said, and disappeared.

Aiden wrapped an arm around Shanna's shoulders and guided her toward her bedroom. "Now that we are alone at last, we can continue our mating ritual."

Frowning, Shanna pulled away and looked up at him. "I want you to promise me nothing will happen to Peter's wife."

Aiden shook his head. "You know I can't make a promise like that and expect to keep it. Even if I agreed with you that she should be spared to wait on Dr. Burkhart's research, I have no sway with the Enclave at this point. I cannot control what happens when it is not my situation to control, Shanna."

She sighed miserably and stared distracted at the floor. "It's not fair. It sucks, Aiden. He loves her so much, and—"

"I know, but there is absolutely nothing you can do about it at this moment."

She sighed again, swiping at her eyes as they threatened to tear up from her frustration.

He took hold of her shoulders and pulled her to him. "Let me think on the situation. Meanwhile, you can do something about *this*." Grasping her hand in his, he pressed her palm against his bulging crotch. "I'm already hard for you. Let's not waste this opportunity to seal our mating bond in seclusion."

Chuckling, she forced her worries away. Aiden was right. For now, she could do absolutely nothing to help Peter. But as determined as she was not to give up on his situation, she realized she shouldn't use sex with Aiden as bargaining leverage to make him see things her way. She laughed low in her throat as she gripped his tremendous hard-on through his jeans. Rubbing him slow and hard, she brought a growl from deep within his chest. "You seem to be in an awfully big hurry to make me yours."

He turned her forward and prodded her into the bedroom. When they reached the foot of the bed, he spun her around to face him and kissed the top of her head. "I've held my need for you in check far too long and fear I'll ravish you. But it's a chance I'm willing to take. Remove your clothes and let me feast my eyes before we enjoy the feast of each other's bodies."

She laughed softly, feeling the heat of his nearness permeate her loins. She didn't want to give in to him so easily. He'd made her squirm earlier, in regard to her involvement with Peter, and she suffered the perverse desire to punish him — in a loving, drawn out manner. "So, you're jealous of Peter, aren't you, Aiden?" she teased.

"Me? Jealous, over you?" He growled again. "Apparently so — as much as you are about me spending time with Talya." His green eyes glittered with mischief as he bowed his neck and captured her mouth with his.

She surrendered to his embrace. So much for holding out...

* * * * *

Aiden looked into Shanna's glazed eyes after they'd shared a deep kiss with full tongue exchange. She pulled back with a slow sigh and focused on him. With a coy smile she murmured, "Would you ever seriously entertain a threesome?"

Aiden's anger flared, heating his possessive desire for her. "I would gladly kill any who dared intrude." He leaned down and nipped her neck hard, almost breaking the skin. She yelped and pulled away from him. His gaze danced over her face full of alarm. Her expression indicated she realized she'd truly riled him.

He sucked in a swift breath, then forced a smile as he eased the air out of his chest still tight with desire and jealousy. He rested his hands on her shoulders. "Do you, or have you ever desired a threesome, Shanna?"

"Not with Cameron Ryben," she answered quickly, frowning.

"But with Peter Burkhart?" Aiden tensed, waiting for her response.

"What about you — with Talya Zhakovika?" she countered, surprising him with the suggestion.

He dropped his hands from her shoulders and glanced aside. Obviously she'd picked up on his weak link with Talya, formed only by his recent close association with her. It was a harmless thing he could fix instantly by shutting himself off from Talya's thoughts. Yet he hesitated doing it. He didn't mind sharing his thoughts with Talya while they worked closely together. It made communication so much more quick and efficient, with no room for error. But now, what excuse did he have for continuing to allow Talya free access to his mind and feelings — and him to hers?

He huffed and looked down at Shanna. He had no real excuse, but still he didn't want to end the casual association. Did that mean he was being unfaithful in some small way to Shanna by desiring the mental closeness of another woman in addition to his mate?

He tried to be honest in his assessment of his motivation. He felt no desire for Talya. Even as close as they'd been in the last two days, he never yearned for her touch, or desired the heat of her body against him. He felt no excitement when she was near, only a sense of comfort and familiarity. Camaraderie. Talya was a partner, a coworker, not a lover or potential secondary mate.

He shook his head and gripped Shanna's arms gently. "Talya is a friend. I apologize if that makes you uncomfortable, but I humbly and sincerely ask for your understanding and acceptance, that you not require me to choose between you and her. There is no choice to be made. My allegiance, desire, and love belong to you alone. But by asking me to make a choice, you elevate Talya to a level of importance in our lives she truly does not occupy. And forcing me to denounce the casual friendship and working relationship I have with her would deny me an innocent pleasure of companionship I do enjoy and wouldn't want to give up."

Shanna looked up into his eyes for a long time, thinking about what he'd said. He could feel her confusion and gradual command of that confusion as she made sense of her thoughts and said, "Everything you say about your relationship with Talya is also true of my association with Peter Burkhart, Aiden. I love *you*." She skewered his chest with her index finger to emphasize the point. "And, most probably, I'll never see that poor man again, once he goes back to whatever underground laboratory he's damned to slave away in. I only want to help him find a way to redeem his wife and bring her back to her former self. I only want to see him happy again. It goes no further than that. So, please, can we both swear a truce? I promise I'll try to be tolerant of Talya for as long as she has to be around, even if sometimes she deliberately tries to be a pain in the ass."

Aiden smirked. "And I agree to try to show the same courtesy in regard to Peter Burkhart, even though his mere proximity to you has been a royal pain in the ass for me, as you so eloquently phrased it. Let's not speak of it further. I have a more urgent issue to address."

He kissed her quickly, then unbuttoned her uniform shirt, parting it to see the inviting bulge of her breasts. She reached down and unfastened her utility belt, letting it slide to the floor with a soft thud. He pulled her shirt hem from her trousers, exposing the last of the bottom buttons, which he quickly released. He snaked a hand across her flat stomach as she unbuckled her belt and undid her trousers, sliding the zipper down. When he reached for the waistband of her trousers, she caught his hands in hers and winked. "That's far enough. Now it's your turn."

He smiled as she slid her fingertips under the hem of his olive green tee shirt, raking her nails softly across his skin while pushing his shirt upward. When she reached his uplifted arms, she gripped the bunched shirt and pulled it off over his head. Leaning forward, he drew his shirt off his arms and dropped it on the floor.

He straightened, naked from the waist up, and shook out his ruffled hair. He caught Shanna's eyes gleaming as she watched him and knew the simple act excited her. He shook his hair again and widened his smile, feeling his fangs lengthen as his body heated in anticipation of their joining.

She grabbed for his jeans and unfastened them with quick roughness, parting them to expose the lowest part of his abdomen. She ran her fingers across the vee of dark hair leading downward to his bulging prize. He ran his hands under her loosened shirt and raked it back off her shoulders. She shrugged out of it, exposing her lacy black bra. Reaching around her, he pushed the hooks apart and pulled the sexy harness forward off her arms, releasing her lovely breasts into his eager hands.

Squeezing and rubbing, he dipped down to flick his tongue over one nipple, then the other. She purred like a cat in his arms as he pulled her to him, pressing herself against him, her erect nipples pricking his hot naked skin. He grabbed her butt cheeks with both hands and drew her to him, pressing his denim-covered erection against her exposed belly. She ran her hands over his arms and licked his burning skin, cooling it as her tongue flicked away to find another place to tease. Pursing her lips, she drew the taut flesh of his left nipple into her mouth, sending hot pulses down his belly straight to his cock, making it lurch with eagerness.

He tantalized her mouth with his as he Shoved his fingers into her trousers, beneath her panties, and rubbed the fluff of hair just above the curve of her mound. With teasing caresses, he thrust his fingertips lower and lower until he reached the slick moisture gathering to ease his entry. Slipping two fingers across her slippery clit, he massaged in and out, darting deeper with each downward thrust of his hand. She moaned, shoving her hips forward to give him better access.

Licking and nipping her chin and jaw, he made his way toward her neck, while below he spread her inner lips, slipping three fingers inside her. She groaned and sighed, grappling with his jeans to push them down out of the way to free his cock. Finding it with her hands, she gripped the shaft and stroked it with squeezing pressure, pulling her thumb and forefinger up the neck and just over the rim of the head. He pumped steadily into her grip as he drove his fingers deeper inside her channel.

Unable to do more without greater wardrobe freedom, he released her long enough to toe off his shoes and shove his jeans off over his feet. He kicked his pants aside as she shed her trousers in a similar rush. Lunging at her, he pushed her back on her bed, spreading her legs to rub the length of his shaft along her wet slit. She writhed under him, undulating her hips as she alternately nipped and kissed his arms and chest, and ran her hands over his back and ass, squeezing his cheeks hard.

Wrapping her legs around him, she grabbed his arms, supported his weight, and leveraged him off balance. He fell on his side, letting her push him on his back. Straddling him, she grabbed his pulsing dick and positioned the taut head inside her hot, wet opening, mounting him like a stallion as she eased down into the saddle, engulfing the entire length of him with her welcoming tight tunnel. He growled with joy and grabbed her ass as she braced her hands on his chest and rocked her hips, riding him hard and fast. With a soft litany of moans, she closed her eyes and threw her head back in lustful abandon. The last blaze of sunset shone through the open drapes of her bedroom window, setting her red hair aglow with a fiery halo.

His eyes narrowed to slits, and his nostrils flared as he smelled the earthy scent of their mingling sex. His mouth watered and ached to clamp onto her neck. He needed to drink her while he made love to her. Lurching up, he flipped her on her back and pushed a groan from her as he plunged back inside her. Thrusting hard and fast, he claimed her mouth with his. She twisted her lips hard against his and twirled her tongue inside, raking it across his fangs as her fingers clawed down his chest.

Slowing for a moment, he bent down and twisted his head to reach his left arm. He bit through the inner soft skin just above his wrist and, with his other hand, pushed her head close, forcing her mouth to close around the wound blossoming bright red. She drank, sucking his lifeblood down her throat, making him shudder with joy. He lunged for her exposed neck as she pulled her mouth from him and panted frantically on the edge of orgasmic bliss. He planted his wide-open jaws on her thundering pulse and sank his teeth in deep. The hot rush of liquid filled his mouth, and he swallowed it down with exquisitely sweet satisfaction as his entire body shuddered and tingled with the prickling warning of his coming explosion.

She bucked and cried out beneath him, her waves of pleasure engulfing him, pulling him down into her undertow of satiation. He groaned as his release burst out of him. The heady elixir of pleasure flooded his entire body, making him dizzy with passion. He pulled his mouth away from her and breathed in great gasps of air as he collapsed alongside her, rolling onto his back.

Once he was able to turn his head and open his eyes, he looked at her lying on her back, her chest rising and falling with deep, heavy breathing as her heart pumped visibly beneath her breasts. She licked her lips, smeared with his blood, and opened her turquoise eyes to mere slits to gaze at him. He leaned over and kissed her, tasting his warm tangy blood on her, then collapsed on his back again.

She gave a long sigh. "I don't know if we can survive much more of this."

He managed to lift a hand and stroke his fingers across her cheek. His body felt happy and whole, telling him at least for now he was satisfied. "The need to share blood will fade soon. I feel our bond is nearly sealed."

Frowning slowly, she seemed to have trouble formulating what she wanted to say. Finally she mumbled, "Will we stop enjoying sex then?"

He smiled, licking his lips as he felt his fangs receding. "The bloodlust only lasts until the mating bond is complete."

"And then ... you won't desire me as much anymore?"

With some effort, he turned on his side to face her. Running a hand over her warm, moist belly, he said, "Our desire for each other will not diminish, but will be strengthened by the sealing of our bond. The bloodlust is the catalyst that brings about the change we both must experience to become attuned to one another. Our need to satisfy each other will remain strong and constant."

She frowned, obviously not understanding what he was trying to tell her. He sighed, stroking her soft, sex-scented skin until he felt himself growing hard again. He checked his desire, realizing he'd exhausted her with this joining. She wouldn't be ready again for at least an hour, perhaps longer. "Don't be concerned that we'll drift apart, that our love and desire for each other will fade. In time, perhaps, as we grow older and our bodies lose some youthful vitality, our lust will also diminish. But that is not an immediate concern for either of us. For now, just trust me when I say we will not need the bloodlust to remain happy with each other, or to pleasure each other fully. It is but a temporary first stage. What develops from it is what lasts."

She managed a smile, and he feasted his eyes upon her for a long span of wondrous silence, until the room darkened and her eyelids grew heavy. He touched her shoulder, and her eyes fluttered open. "We should clean up. I want to give you your first quick lesson in avoiding mind-probing."

She lifted her head to look at him. "What?"

"It's time you learned how to defend yourself from casual mental eavesdropping." He propped himself up with one elbow and looked down at her. "It is well past the time I shut Talya off from reading my thoughts and feelings. It is a two-way connection we share, but as long as I keep my door closed, the connection will be stopped. We will remain friends, of course, but the sharing of mind-blended intimacy I want to reserve for you and me. You need to make a similar effort to keep yourself closed off. Otherwise, Talya will still be able to get to me through you, if you don't shut her out."

Shanna sat up, propping herself on an elbow to face him. "You mean like Cameron Ryben did?"

He nodded.

"But I know nothing about—"

"You'll pick it up easily. Your progress in the change has been surprising so far. You exhibit no outer distress as you did following our first intimacy." He leaned forward and gave her a peck on the mouth. "Don't worry. You'll do fine. But we must be quick. Dawn will come much sooner than you think." He patted her ass and urged her up.

CHAPTER 18

Shanna opened her eyes to the darkness, wondering for a second where she was until she heard the comforting sound of Aiden's quiet breathing and felt his warmth beside her. Carefully she pulled back the covers and rose from bed, padding barefoot and naked toward the bathroom. As she pushed the door open, she glanced back at Aiden still sleeping, then caught a glimpse of her alarm clock. She figured she had a little over an hour and a half before dawn, before Talya returned with Peter Burkhart.

Having slept fitfully, Shanna recalled fading in and out of dim nightmarish scenes where she seemed to be in constant peril. The last one she remembered most vividly featured her slogging through a river thick as molasses, breathlessly trying to escape the gnashing fangs of a female creature flying through the air with her clawed hands outstretched, and her dark long hair streaming out behind her. When Shanna hadn't dreamed about outrunning monsters, she'd dozed in a semiconscious state as her mind desperately scrambled to come up with some way to help Peter Burkhart save his wife.

Hoping to dismiss those thoughts for a few moments of relief, she refreshed herself with a quick shower and brushed her teeth. Exiting the bathroom, she stood motionless until she heard the reassuring sound of Aiden snoring softly, still asleep. She crossed the darkened bedroom to her closet to get a clean uniform, glad she'd taken the time after her training session with Aiden last night to tidy up and return all her things to their proper place. With her shoes in hand, she pulled open her dresser drawers to fetch underwear and socks.

Sitting on the chair in the corner of the room, she looked up when Aiden stirred and turned on his side, pulling the covers as he rolled over. She stilled, hoping not to wake him. When he settled back to sleep, she finished dressing and grabbed the utility belt she'd left near the nightstand on her side of the bed. Slipping out of the bedroom, she buckled the utility belt and headed into the kitchen. She turned on the overhead light, then checked her firearm and extra ammo clips. Satisfied everything was as it should be, she grabbed the coffee package from the refrigerator and filled the percolator with water.

As the scent of fresh brew filled the room, she caught sight of the time glowing on her microwave. Dawn would arrive in about forty-five minutes, then Talya would return with Peter in tow. She sighed deeply, trying to calm her unsettledness, but she couldn't shake the feeling that she'd failed the man. She'd hoped by bringing Aiden into the situation, she'd find additional avenues of help for Peter, but she'd only managed to make things worse. Now, instead of being able to give him some hope that his wife could be rescued, she'd damned the woman to certain death. If the Enclave ever found out where Mrs. Burkhart was being kept, they'd do their best to see that she was executed rogue-style by a Protector.

Shanna grabbed a cup from the cabinet and filled it with coffee. What else could she have done? If she hadn't told Aiden right away that one of Cam Ryben's victims had survived, he would have found out eventually, by the sheer fact that he could read her pitiful little mind. Even if he'd showed her earlier the mind tricks he'd taught her last night, she doubted she could have kept him from knowing her thoughts.

Leaning against the counter in her small eat-in kitchen, she practiced visualizing a door to her mind slamming shut, and could almost hear the thud of it. But just because she could think up an imaginary door, that didn't guarantee she could keep someone like Talya from scanning her thoughts. Aiden seemed to think she had a good grasp of the exercise he'd showed her last night, but she wasn't so sure.

She shook her head and sighed miserably as she set her cup aside on the counter and crossed her arms. There had to be some way to help Peter, but how? He'd seemed encouraged by the blood found in the warehouse, tentatively identified as belonging to the same individual who'd attacked his wife. But when he realized it had been completely destroyed, preventing him from retrieving a sample large enough to work with, he'd become distraught. Obviously he believed finding the source of the infection ravaging his wife's body was the key to her cure. He had seemed sure that, with a blood sample from his wife's attacker, he could somehow devise a serum to change her back from the barely human creature that she'd become in just one month after the attack. Could he have been right? There was no way to ever know that now.

Shanna grabbed her coffee and took a deep gulp, then settled back, thinking about her relationship with Aiden, and what he'd told her last night about their mating. Up front he'd warned her if she wasn't properly mated, she could turn into the same kind of crazed animal Anna Burkhart had become. After the first time she and Aiden had made love, she felt on the verge of madness with her uncontrollable nausea and weakness. But after their second interlude, those symptoms seemed to fluctuate, growing stronger in cycles as if to push her to mate with him again and again. Now she felt a deep sense of need for him, but it wasn't a gnawing, maddening drive. And through the entire transformation, she still maintained control of her faculties, without descending into raving madness like Anna Burkhart. She could look back now and view her association with Aiden as a choice rather than an affliction — certainly not something that required a cure.

After their lovemaking last night, Aiden seemed sure they were close to moving past the need to share blood. She assumed the exchange of body fluids between them through raw, unprotected sex, in addition to outright blood-drinking, had caused the change in both of them. What was different about their mating that kept them from turning rogue like Cameron Ryben and Anna Burkhart?

She rubbed her forehead wearily, trying to sort things out. Ryben had raped Mrs. Burkhart and drunk her blood, just short of killing her. He'd most probably left his seminal residue in her, as he had done to all his other victims who hadn't survived. But the one thing he hadn't done that Shanna and Aiden had was share his own blood with any of his victims.

She looked up and stared off at nothing. Was that the difference? If he had shared his blood with his first sex partner and let her live, would he have kept himself from going rogue, going mad? She shook her head. After meeting Ryben and almost falling prey to him, she suspected he'd already been quite mad before he'd gone rogue.

She shoved away from the counter, refilled her cup, then took a deep draft. Perhaps Peter needed to see a blood sample from someone who'd been altered successfully by mating with a Shanrak, not ruined by unwanted, incomplete interaction with a rogue. Maybe the difference would give him the proper research direction and show him what his wife lacked to return to normal, assuming a reversal of her change was even possible. Shanna knew she had the necessary ingredients in her own blood to show him the way.

Glancing at the kitchen doorway in sudden guilt, she realized Aiden would never approve. The idea of volunteering a sample of her blood for use by a human researcher trying to investigate the intricacies of Shanrak biology went against everything Aiden had trained for and worked for over forty years to accomplish. It would reveal the secret of Shanrak existence, negating his Protector oath to preserve that secret. But hadn't the secret already suffered serious exposure if the US government was conducting experiments to replicate Shanrak genetics? What difference would it make if she gave Peter a sample of her blood to help him discover a way to aid his wife?

She shook her head and paced across the small kitchen. She couldn't betray Aiden that way. But she couldn't leave Peter and his wife to the wolves either. She stopped in her tracks and looked back at the doorway, expecting Aiden to pick up on her treasonous thoughts and barge in to confront and berate her. But he didn't.

She went back to the counter and leaned against it, sipping her coffee again. If she were to do such a thing, how would she slip a sample to Peter without anyone else finding out? More importantly, should she even consider it? She had no idea what potential liabilities she'd create for herself, Aiden, and all his people, if she betrayed them this way. Yet she couldn't let go of the idea. It was the one way she might help Peter, and she felt sure he would do his very best to keep her contribution confidential.

Setting aside her cup still a quarter full, she darted over to a drawer and pulled it open to reveal a rudimentary collection of storage items, aluminum foil, and plastic wrap. Her eyes focused on the two boxes of different sized resealable plastic bags. The pint-size bags ought to do, if she double-bagged the —

No, she couldn't really do this. Aiden would...

What *would* he say if she suggested this crazy idea? He'd betray his Protector position if he knowingly allowed her to give Peter a sample of her changed blood. But Aiden had already betrayed his position as a Protector by changing her. How could he make any objection now, since he was unofficially relieved of his duties and being called back for review and possible severe punishment?

She shook her head and backed up a step, straightening as she stared with longing and distress at the baggie container in the open drawer. If she didn't do this, she'd regret it the rest of her life. She had to try to help Peter.

Impulsively she grabbed the box of baggies, then slid the drawer shut. Turning to eye the kitchen doorway, she tapped the box against her open palm, wondering how she could manage to get away with this, without letting Aiden find out and jeopardize him with complicity. Maybe she could somehow refocus and shield her thoughts of this act long enough to let Peter slip away with the evidence before Aiden caught on.

God knew she didn't want to hurt the man she loved, but it just wasn't right to let someone else's loved one die if there was even a slim hope of reprieve. The Enclave was wrong to damn Mrs. Burkhart to death without giving Peter a chance to save her. It wasn't her fault she'd fallen victim to Cameron Ryben. Shanna couldn't stand by and do nothing. The Enclave would just have to deal with that.

With the decision made, Shanna cast a last wary glance at the kitchen doorway, praying Aiden would stay asleep a little longer. Turning, she pulled open her silverware drawer and drew out a sharp steak knife. Pushing the drawer shut with her stomach, she huddled over the counter and pulled two baggies from the box. Eyeing the pointed tip of the steak knife, she gave herself one more chance to rethink this, but quickly dismissed her nagging worries. She had to help Peter help his wife. She couldn't let them go on suffering. If something like that happened to her, she'd want whatever help was available.

Determined to go through with it, she gripped the knife handle, then paused, wondering just how she was supposed to let blood without maiming herself. Aiden had torn open his own wrist with his teeth to bleed for her, but he had healing abilities far swifter than hers. She touched her fingertips to her neck, feeling for the evidence of his latest vampiric assault. The puncture wounds from his bite last night seemed to have totally disappeared. Maybe—

"Need some help, love?"

Shanna spun around, dropping the knife on the floor as she gaped up at Aiden towering over her, barefoot and wearing just his jeans. His auburn tresses flowed softly about his broad naked shoulders, as if an unseen gentle breeze tickled the air around him. He zeroed his glittering green eyes on her without smiling.

She gulped and stumbled back against the counter. "I was just ... I—"

He put up a hand to silence her. Of course, he knew exactly what she was up to. He could read her like an open book, and that imaginary closed door in her head meant nothing to him. He'd taught her the trick and surely saved a secret backdoor access for himself, to come and go freely in her mind as he pleased.

He crossed his arms over his naked chest. She eyed his muscular arms in distraction as he said, "You know this goes against everything I stand for. I've dedicated my life to preserving the secrets of my people. And with this act, you could expose us all."

She glanced at the floor, feeling the heat of embarrassment and fear mushroom outward through her pores. "I ... I don't want to put anyone in danger, Aiden. Most of all you."

"But still you're doing it. For *him*."

She glared up at him. "Not just for Peter. For his wife too, and all the Shanrak who might turn rogue."

He shook his head. "If a cure were possible, don't you think my people would have developed it long ago?"

She studied him, saw the pain in his eyes, and knew he felt betrayed. But she hadn't betrayed him in favor of another man, or for any reason that opposed their union. She wanted — needed — to try another way to redeem a broken man's wife from the hell to which she'd been damned. If there was even the slightest hope her ploy would succeed, she had to try.

She stiffened and glared up at her love, her mate, the man she feared right now might want to kill her for her treasonous behavior. "No, Aiden, I don't think your people have ever considered trying to

222

develop a cure. From what I gather, those crusty old Elders that run the show where you come from are too steeped in their own traditions to consider alternatives. And they sure don't want anyone challenging their authority. They have a longstanding system in place to deal with the rogue problem. I'm sure in their minds they don't see any valid reason to chuck that system to try something different. They've built an industry to deal with it, of which you're a part. Think of all the people — trainers and assassins — who'd suddenly be out of a job if Peter Burkhart, or anybody else, managed to figure out a way to keep people from turning rogue, or to cure them when they did. Think what that would mean to your society, how it would change things, how it would diminish the power of life and death the Elders hold over everyone now. You think they're going to give that up?"

He looked down, frowning in thoughtful silence. Finally he uncrossed his arms and dipped down to retrieve the knife she'd dropped on the floor. Straightening, he held it out to her. "I suggest you make a shallow vertical slice across the underside of your index fingertip." His gaze skated over her face as he added, "Would you like me to do it for you?"

She blinked at him in confusion, surprise. "You're really going to let me do this?"

He nodded once.

"Why?"

"Because I know you believe in your heart this is the right thing to do. Because it is not about you and me. You're simply trying to help others in need. Because it could change the safety and future of my people, your people, for the better. And because I love you."

"Aiden..." She felt tears of gratitude flood her eyes.

He pulled her forward and kissed her on the forehead. "We must hurry. We haven't much time before Talya returns with Peter."

She grabbed the baggies and stuffed one inside the other. Holding her finger over the nested openings, she tensed as Aiden ran the knife tip slowly across her fingertip. She winced as it stung, wondering why the much more violent wounds he'd inflicted on her neck hadn't seemed to hurt at all.

"My saliva contains a natural pain blocker," he explained. It took her a second to realize she hadn't asked the question aloud.

She glanced up at his face intent on his task as he squeezed her finger to hasten the bloodletting. With surreal detachment she watched her blood drip and dribble down into the bag, oozing along the sides to collect in a dark red pool in the bottom.

After a few moments he said, "That should be enough for what he'll need." He pulled her hand from the baggies and leaned down, wrapping his lips around her fingertip still blossoming red. He sucked greedily on it for a moment, and she felt his hot mouth and tongue close in with erotic intensity. When he finally pulled his mouth away, the tip of one of his fangs scuffed her fingernail. She twisted her hand, still gripped in his, and saw the bleeding had slowed. With a flick of his tongue, he lapped up the last of the blood to reveal a thin red line that seemed to have already started closing up. Examining her fingertip, he announced, "You shouldn't need a bandage."

She pulled her hand away from him and looked up to see him holding up her bag of blood, studying it with keen interest, as if he planned to dump it or drink it. Finally he lowered it and pushed the air out to seal first the inner bag, then the outer bag.

Setting the blood gently on the counter, he frowned and sighed hard. After a moment, he pulled two more baggies from the box, then picked up the knife. Looking at his own fingers, he murmured, "If we are to truly help Peter and his wife, he will need more than just your blood alone to find the secret he seeks."

Shanna scowled in shock. "Aiden, I don't want you to—"

He shook his head. "It is beyond my worry now. I have committed so many other wrongs against the Enclave this past week, this infraction will make little difference. And Peter will need this if he hopes to cure his wife."

Before she could object or question him further, he stuffed the baggies one inside the other and handed them to her. Holding his finger over the opening, he made a quick slice down his fingertip as he'd done to her, then set the knife aside. His blood flowed freely, and he held his hand over the bag until they'd collected about the same amount as before. Withdrawing his hand, he held his dripping finger to her. She hesitated, then slipped her mouth over it and sucked the warm metallic liquid until she felt it magically stop. When Aiden withdrew his finger, she saw the wound he'd made had closed to a thin pink line. She glanced up at him in awe as he sealed the bags and set his blood sample next to hers.

When he reached for the box of baggies again and withdrew two more, she frowned. "What are you doing?"

"He'll need one more sample."

"Of blood?"

Aiden shook his head then eyed her with a slow smile. "You were correct in your earlier musings about the bloodlust and the mating ritual."

"You were listening in on my thoughts the whole time I assumed you were sleeping?"

He shrugged with a smirk and nested the two baggies in preparation for collecting another sample. "Shanrak seminal fluid contains an important ingredient necessary to make the mating change successful. I am not an expert on medical arts, but I do know that much. Without a sample of my semen to go along with our blood samples, Peter's research will go much slower, perhaps nowhere."

Shanna laughed with breathless embarrassment. "But—"

"He's a scientist. I'm sure he's handled human biological samples of all types. Certainly this will not offend him so much as it will aid him in his quest to cure his wife."

Blushing, Shanna hedged, "What about a similar sample from me?"

Aiden handed the doubled baggies to her. "It will be more difficult to collect a sample of your vaginal fluid at the moment of orgasm. And I doubt it will further his research very much, since you were not Shanrak in the beginning and would not have had the necessary ingredients to aid in the mating ritual. Your changed blood should be enough to show him what a human mated to a Shanrak should become."

She watched in amazement as he undid his jeans and pushed them down just past his hips to reveal his already whopping hard-on. He wrapped a hand around his cock, then smiled down on her. "This would become a much faster, sweeter experience if you would lend assistance, my love."

She gawked at him and laughed softly, then stepped aside to drag a chair over from the nearby dinette table. He leaned his bare ass against the edge of the counter and waited as she sat down on the chair to face him. He stroked his shaft a couple of times, pointing the distended purple head at her as she licked her lips. Leaning into position, she slid her mouth over the crown of his cock, and he arched his hips forward, easing himself further into her orifice. She sucked him hard as she pulled back, making him groan in delicious agony.

Wrapping one hand around his shaft, she cupped his balls with the other and gently massaged the hot, heavy spheres as she slid her mouth back and forth over his cock with delicious ease. He moaned again and pumped his hips slowly, bracing his hands on her head to steady and control her ministrations.

She looked up to see him entranced in bliss as he held her head with his hands, pushing himself deeper into her mouth, then pulling back to push in again even further. She felt the head of his cock hitting the back of her throat and tried to swallow as her mouth gushed with saliva. He let out a growling, "Oh..." as she pulled back on him, swallowing and slurping her tongue on the head of his cock to keep from drooling.

He gave her a second, then pulled her toward him again. She grabbed him hard and slid her mouth down full on him, sending his hips into overdrive. She let him hold her head in place so he could fuck her mouth faster and faster until her lips tingled, almost going numb from the repeated rubbing. She felt her panties getting moist with anticipation and wished he were pumping her pussy instead of her mouth.

He tightened his buttocks and pulled back with a moan, grabbing the baggies from her just in time to shove them over the head of his penis. Milking his shaft hard with his hand, he thrust his hips and sent the first spurt of thick white come into the bag. Another shot followed, and another, until his hips slowed and stopped. Crouched over, breathing hard, his muscles taut with the sheen of sweat, he finally withdrew the baggies and straightened. With his cock hanging wet and semi-hard, he caressed it softly and leaned back, breathing out a long sigh of satisfaction.

Shanna sat on the chair, looking up at him as she swiped her hands over her mouth. She still tingled with lust and wished Aiden had fucked her instead of those damned baggies. She let the fleeting thought of finishing herself off drift away as she got up from the chair and grinned. "You really enjoyed that, didn't you?"

He looked down at her with hooded eyes and smiled.

Straightening, he sealed the baggies then set the sample aside with the rest. Pulling up his jeans, he buttoned them and said, "A wasted mating opportunity. I would much rather have expelled my seed inside you as we enjoyed making love together. As it is, I'm spent, and you're still wet from the excitement."

She blushed at his accurate description.

"I hope this new friend of yours appreciates the sacrifice we've made. And I hope he's worth the possible consequences."

Sighing, she looked down at the floor. "I hope so too." Then she glanced at the baggies, wondering what they should do next. "How am I going to get these to him without anyone finding out?"

Aiden looked at the baggies, then stroked his stomach, as if he were still reliving the ecstasy he'd enjoyed while supplying that last sample. "We need to keep it cool for transport. Wet some cloths with cold water and double them up between and around the individual packs. Do you have some kind of insulated container?"

"Yes, somewhere I've got a wide-mouth soup carrier."

"That should preserve it for a little while. If he's going to be delayed returning more than a day, he'll want to put these on ice."

She returned the chair to its place at the table, then dug through the cabinets. Finally she pulled out a short wide insulated container with a removable screw-top lid. Grabbing several dishrags out of the linen drawer, she wet them and wrapped them between and around the samples as Aiden suggested. Fetching a larger zipping bag, she carefully rolled the entire sample packet and slipped it into the larger baggy. Stuffing it into the soup container, she screwed on the lid. She thought for a moment, then bent down and fetched a small soft-sided insulated carrying pouch from the cabinet. Putting the soup carrier inside, she zipped it up and dangled it by the hand strap like a little purse. "There. As far as anybody knows, this is lunch."

Aiden wrinkled his nose. "I'll take the red. You can have the white."

She laughed and started to give a retort about wine choices, but he stiffened and stepped away from the counter. "It's almost dawn. Talya will be here any moment with Peter. You remember what I taught you last night? It's very important we don't give away any hint of what we've done. Talya would be obligated to inform the

Enclave of our betrayal, regardless of whether she agrees with our motive."

"Aiden, I don't know if I can—"

"Yes, you *can* do this, Shanna," he said, leaning down to give her a quick kiss. "Your mind is strong enough, and you know how to shut out the thoughts of others, because I've taught you."

"But this morning, you knew—"

"I am your mate," he countered with a grin. "I'm much more difficult to shut out." He urged her forward into the living room. "She's coming. Just remember, you're doing this for Peter. If you let Talya get wind of what's in that lunch carrier, all our efforts are for nothing. You and I will be in big trouble, and Peter will go back empty-handed with no way to help his wife."

She grimaced. "Oh, great. No pressure there."

He wrapped an arm around her shoulders and squeezed gently. "Stay near me, and I'll help you remain mentally strong. And try not to provoke Talya."

CHAPTER 19

Talya glimmered into solidity, wearing her leather coat and boots and sleek-fitting pants. With her mountainous shock of glistening black curls, she looked like an urban Amazon huntress carrying her dead prey. Shanna frowned, thinking Peter did look rather lifeless as Talya strode over to the couch and unceremoniously dumped him, not bothering to put him in a comfortable position. When Shanna saw his head was cocked forward against the arm of the couch, she started to pull away from Aiden to rearrange him, but Aiden tightened his arm around her shoulders. She stayed put and glanced at her coffee table, staring adrift as she tried to focus on nothing but the closed door to her mind, the way Aiden had taught her last night.

"Any problems, Talya?" Aiden asked casually.

"None. He was a very good little boy and slept like the dead. Didn't make one move or sound all night. I was bored senseless."

Shanna looked up, wondering why Talya didn't watch TV or something, then remembered the tie tack with the listening device attached. If she or Peter had made any noise, whoever might have been monitoring the tie-tack transmission would have guessed there was someone in Peter's room and gone in to investigate.

"You swept the room for additional surveillance devices?" Aiden prodded, still holding tight to Shanna's shoulders so she wouldn't step away from him.

Talya narrowed her eyes and looked at them carefully for a second, then nodded. "Apparently his superiors didn't consider him a great enough risk to plant devices in his room before he arrived to occupy it."

"Apparently," Aiden said in a tone of agreement.

Talya cocked her head and took a step closer. "Something's ... different." She narrowed her eyes again, then glared at Aiden. "Why have you blocked me?"

Aiden sighed, still not removing his arm from Shanna's shoulders. "It was time. Shanna and I are mates, and there are some things we don't wish to share with others." Shanna glanced up to catch him grinning.

Talya snorted. "I take no more pleasure in being made aware of your private activities than those of the rogues I hunt. You should have done me the favor earlier." She turned away with obvious disgust.

Finally Aiden withdrew his arm from Shanna's shoulders. She met his eyes, and he gave her a cautionary look. Motioning subtly with his hand, he urged her to follow and stay close to him as he walked toward Talya standing near the couch, staring down on Peter. "You will wake him now?" Talya asked, eyeing Aiden.

Aiden nodded and knelt down beside the couch. Touching a hand to Peter's forehead, he smoothed away stray locks of his hair. With a slight tilt of his head, he looked at Peter with detached but gentle consideration, like an angel watching a sleeping child.

As Peter moaned and licked his lips, Aiden stood up and stepped back. Peter's brows knitted, then his eyes flashed open. He looked around, startled, then pushed himself up. Immediately he sat down again and leaned forward, groaning as he cradled his head in his hands.

"The discomfort will soon pass," Aiden said, stepping forward to stand over him.

Peter craned his neck as he squinted up at Aiden's face. "Wh- What did you do to me?"

"Merely induced a deep sleep, to keep you on ice, so to speak, and to give your body and mind time to rest and recuperate."

"Who the hell are you people? *What* are you?"

"You will learn that as we explain what you must do for us."

Blinking, Peter frowned and glanced away. Before he had time to contemplate his situation, Talya put her hands on her hips and stepped forward, towering over him. "Now it is time for you to listen and cooperate with us, Dr. Burkhart."

He leaned back to look up at her. "Cooperate? What are you talking about?"

"I said listen first, then cooperate."

He raised his dark brows and waited in silence.

"Your wife's condition, as well as your ongoing research, present a serious problem for us."

"*Us* being...?"

Talya shot Aiden a glare, obviously having no patience to explain things. Aiden stepped forward and took over. "Who we are is not really important for you to know right now, Dr. Burkhart. *What* we are — I think you already know."

Peter's eyes widened. He scooted sideways on the couch, away from Aiden. Managing to get to his feet, he backed toward the door. "You're like that creature that hurt my Anna!"

Aiden shook his head, making his hair shimmer like silken animal fur. "The creature that hurt your wife was an anomaly of our kind. I was sent to hunt him down and exterminate him. That task is now completed."

"So ... you're the one who destroyed the evidence in the warehouse?"

Aiden nodded.

"Why? Why would you—"

"Because it was also my task to keep the secret of our kind from humans. But it appears now that secret has already been discovered."

Peter swiped a hand over his face, then blew out a harsh breath. "My research..."

"Yes, your research."

Shaking his head, Peter glared at the hardwood floor. "I didn't know! All I had were samples. I never saw anyone with the ... symptoms ... until Anna..." He shook his head again and slumped against the door, covering his face with his hands.

Aiden moved in and placed a hand on his shoulder. "That doesn't matter. What is important is finding out exactly what information has been gathered, who has it, and what they plan to do with it."

Dropping his hand to his sides, Peter scowled at Aiden. "I don't think you're going to like what I have to tell you."

Aiden patted his shoulder then stepped back. "I know, Dr. Burkhart. But I still need to hear it."

"Whom do you work for?" Talya interrupted, charging

forward like a tag-team wrestler.

"I don't know exactly," Peter said, stepping away from her as she herded him back to the couch.

"Unacceptable!" she yelled, moving in on him. "You go to work every day. You know the location. You see other people there. You know what kind of work you are doing. Tell us!"

With the sheer presence of her body, she forced him to plop down on the couch and crane his neck to look up at her. Shanna wanted to kick her ass for deliberately intimidating him, but as soon as that thought leapt into her head, Aiden turned on her with a glare. She concentrated on the imaginary door in her mind. *Closed.* It was closed tight and locked securely.

"I-I work in an underground lab facility outside D.C., on the Virginia side. I have no idea how big the place is, because it's underground. The building aboveground is a front, complete with a corporate logo with the company name Biotech Industries."

"And...?" Talya prodded, leaning over him, making him rear back.

"The main lobby leads to offices assigned to company executives. They're with the *Company*, all right, but not BioTech Industries. That's not even a real corporation from what I can tell. It's just a front."

"More!"

Shuddering visibly, Peter tried to scoot away from her. She stepped over to keep him pinned in her sights. "Talk!"

He sighed and raked a hand through his thick dark hair. "Everybody has a security clearance, just like in the government. I have one to do my research, but I don't have access to certain files or certain areas of the facility. I suspect there are other, more intensive, experiments going on in other sections of the facility."

"Yes, that's what I want to know. Give me the location of this building."

Peter blinked, then blurted out the building's physical address. "I think my wife is being kept in one of the restricted areas. They moved her after ... after she started getting worse."

"I'm sure." Talya whirled away, giving Aiden a harsh look.

He stepped forward and tried to smile as he looked down at Peter. "Dr. Burkhart, your wife is very ill."

232

Peter looked aside. "You don't think I know that?"

"In her condition, she may not survive much longer, confined."

He flashed his dark eyes full of pain and lunged up from the couch. "She has to survive! I'm going to cure her! She's pregnant with our first child, and I want her — and the baby — back with me! The way she was ... before..." Tears flooded his eyes, and he put his hands over his face, sinking back down on the couch.

"Gods!" Aiden exclaimed, turning to glare at Shanna in shock. "She's pregnant?"

"I-I forgot to tell you." She looked down at Peter hunched over, with his face still buried in his hands as he sobbed silently.

"How far along?"

Shanna shrugged. "Two ... three months."

"And that little detail slipped your mind?" Talya snarled.

"What difference does it make?" Shanna felt herself trembling with apprehension as she looked at Aiden.

He shook his head and whirled away, then turned back to her and growled, "Take Dr. Burkhart to your car and wait there with him." He eyed Talya. "You'll scan her vehicle for foreign devices — and plant none of your own."

Talya nodded.

He turned back to Shanna. "You'll have to explain the plan to Dr. Burkhart in the car. I'll meet you at the hotel room. Once you're there, remember your little playacting, and make it good for the listening device on his tie tack. This will be your only chance to convince his superiors that you and he had a good time last night. Both your lives may depend on your performance. Just don't make it *too* convincing."

Shanna blanched as she stared at Aiden. He turned away from her and shook his head again. She walked up behind him and whispered, "What about Peter's baby?"

"This changes everything," Talya said. "The Enclave might have condoned killing Mrs. Burkhart, but they won't destroy an unborn innocent, even if it's steeped in rogue blood. They'll want to know first if it's Shanrak or human before they decide to terminate it."

"What are you talking about?" Peter roared, shooting up from the couch. He glared from Talya to Aiden with reddened eyes. "Nobody's killing my wife or my child!"

Aiden marched swiftly to him and jerked him by the arm, dragging him aside. "Whatever cure you might come up with to help your wife could kill your baby. In the womb, the child will be affected by the blood exchange with its mother. Since she has been changed, so might the child. I cannot guarantee that an attempt to reverse your wife's rogue symptoms won't abort the child. If you wait until the child's born..." He shook his head and turned away from Peter.

"What do you mean? What am I supposed to do?"

Shanna looked at Aiden lost in his own thoughts, then walked over to Peter and took him by the arm. "Let me take you back to your hotel room. I need to talk to you on the way."

* * * * *

As soon as Peter closed the passenger door, Shanna glanced through the windshield at Aiden and Talya standing in front of her apartment, arguing quietly. The post-dawn light peeked over the tree line behind her, warming the top edge of the apartment building and moving further down the face of the building in swift progression. She turned to Peter as he demanded, "What is going on?"

"We don't have much time. Fasten your seatbelt. We need to go."

"But they were talking about killing my wife!"

She glared at him. "Right now, your wife's already dead to you, Peter. If you don't shut up and listen to me, she's not going to have a ghost's chance in hell of being resurrected."

He pressed his lips together and put on his seatbelt. She started her patrol car and backed out of the parking space in front of her unit. Directing the car onto the main street, she glanced at him and sighed. "I'm sorry. This has all gotten out of hand, and it's my fault. I should have known Aiden and Talya would have some weird take on the situation regarding your wife. The important thing is," she said, patting the lunch carrier sitting next to her in the seat, "you do have a fighting chance to develop a cure for her."

Peter looked down at the lunch carrier. "What's in that?"

"Some ... homemade soup. But I guarantee you're not going to want to taste it."

He scowled at her and looked straight ahead. "I don't have any earthly idea what you're talking about."

"Aiden and I are ... mates."

He shrugged. "I figured that, once I saw you two together."

"He's sort of like the man who attacked your wife. Only not exactly. The man who hurt your wife was ... he did something that caused a horrific change in him, making him want to kill."

Peter looked at her wide-eyed. "And Aiden is like that?"

"No. Aiden and I have mated." She huffed, realizing she wasn't explaining it well, and couldn't really concentrate on doing a better job since her main concern at the moment was to drive her car. "Because Aiden and I have mated, we've been changed, like Cameron Ryben, only in a different, better way."

"Who's Cameron Ryben?"

She pulled up at a red light and glanced over at him. "The Bloodsucker. The man who attacked your wife and killed over forty other women."

Peter gulped, grinding his throat as he swallowed. "And now he's dead?"

"Yes."

"So, I don't have a snowball's chance in hell of ever developing a cure for Anna." He grimaced and touched his fingers to his eyes.

"Now you have a better chance, because of this." She touched the lunch carrier.

He glared at her in confusion. "I don't understand."

"You need blood samples to study the DNA mutations, to try to reverse them."

"Yes."

"There are some samples inside this insulated carrier."

"I thought you said it was homemade soup."

She glanced at him, then eyed the road again. "Made right in my own kitchen, just before you arrived."

He scowled, not getting her private joke. She huffed, realizing they were almost to the hotel. "These samples are different from any you've seen previously. They contain DNA mutations from a successful mating, which should be much different from the mutations in your wife's blood. If you can't reverse the mutations that have taken over her body, maybe you can alter them to something different, something not quite as bad, so that maybe she won't suffer so terribly. At the very least she might regain her sanity."

In her side vision Shanna saw him staring at her, assessing her. Finally he said, "It's your blood, isn't it?"

"And Aiden's. Plus..." She wrinkled her nose and felt her cheeks get warm. "Something else. Something that may help you better see how the mutation process works overall." She gave him a quick glance and added, "It's not about just the blood, Peter."

He arched a brows, then sat back in the seat to look ahead as she drove. After a moment, he murmured, "Why are you doing this? I don't think your mate really wanted to help me. And I'm sure his friend Talya didn't. Does she even know what you two are doing?"

"Well..." Shanna hedged, hesitant to tell him the rest of the plan as she pulled the car into the back parking lot of the hotel. "For now, we're keeping this a secret from Talya. And don't hold it against Aiden if he acted cold toward you. He's just a little jealous." She put the car in park and turned off the ignition, turning to Peter just in time to see him glaring at her in surprise. "I know. It's stupid. But he's a man. What can you expect?" When Peter smirked, she added, "I don't mean all men are—"

"It's okay. I know what you meant." He grinned, glancing aside as he mumbled, "So what gave him the idea you and I..." He looked back at her, still smiling. "He wasn't hiding under the bed, was he, when you watched me take off my pants yesterday?"

She blushed and cleared her throat, not wanting to hash over her indiscretion, or get into the whole Shanrak telepathy issue. It would just freak him out more. "The thing is, Aiden's decided that you and I need to pretend that something *is* going on between us. At least enough to convince your superiors that's the only reason you left with me and stayed gone all night."

He raised his brows again, giving her a swift once-over, as if he were considering the pros and cons of having a fling with her.

"We won't be getting naked, or anything like that," she clarified, squirming slightly in her seat. "We just need to talk the talk and walk the walk as long as we're being watched, or someone's listening in."

He nodded slowly, refusing to take his eyes off her. She huffed and flipped open her seatbelt. "It's just a way to keep down suspicion, so your superiors don't think you're a danger to their project."

"So," he prodded in a teasing tone as he released his seatbelt, "just how in love are we?"

She gave him a deadpan stare. "Assuming you'll be going home soon, possibly today, I'd say we're just a one-night stand."

"But at least I'll get a goodbye kiss out of it, right?" He flicked her a hot glance with his soft dark eyes, then turned and opened his door.

She reached over and grabbed his arm, making him turn to face her. "This is serious, Peter. I'm betting the people you work for play for keeps."

He pivoted toward her and touched a hand to her face. "You're right. They do. But so do I."

When he turned and left the car, the tingling sensation of his touch still lingered on her cheek. She lifted her fingertips gingerly to the spot as his last declaration rang in her mind. What did he mean by that? Surely it wasn't directed in any way toward her...

Grabbing her lunch carrier, she exited the car and locked it, then quickened her gait to catch up to him halfway to the hotel back entrance. She held out the insulated carrier and said, "Don't forget the lunch I packed you."

He stopped and turned to eye the carrier in her hand. "They won't let me set foot in the lab without inspecting that thoroughly, and they don't allow anything foreign into the research area. As soon as they see what's inside, they'll want to know where it came from. And they'll have ways to make me talk, I assure you."

She frowned and lowered the carrier to her side. "Then how can you use it?"

"Let me worry about that. Just give me the package before I leave. I should be okay with it on the trip home. As far as getting it into the lab, if I have to, I'll smuggle the samples inside my pants. The guards don't usually pat me down, and if they do start the practice, they'd better not plan on patting me there, unless they're prepared to do a lot more follow-up." He winked.

She laughed in spite of their situation. Good ol' Dr. Burkhart apparently had a wicked naughty streak.

237

* * * * *

They rode up the elevator to the second floor in silence. As the door opened, Shanna turned to him. "Are you up for this?"

He smirked. "Yeah, I think so."

She almost let her gaze drop to his crotch to see just how up he was, but she caught herself and walked out of the elevator. She had no business checking him out, even if they were supposed to play footsies to impress his watchers.

He opened the door to his room and let her step in first. She glanced around to make sure they were alone — not that it would make a bit of difference, with the little tie tack sitting nearby to pick up any noise they might make.

About two seconds after Peter shut the door, the room phone by his bed rang. He gave her a look, then strolled over and answered it. He listened for a moment, then responded, "Yes, I'll be ready."

He hung up the phone and eyed her. "The team's leaving this morning. One of our security people will be coming around to pick us up in the van in about thirty minutes. We'll stop by the task force office to wrap things up, then head to the airport from there."

Shanna felt her heart lurch. She didn't want him to go. She enjoyed his company, and she wanted him to have a measure of relief just a little longer. She feared as soon as he returned home, his worries would overwhelm him. Stirring in an empty house, knowing his wife would not rejoin him for a long time, if ever, might break the tentative resolve he'd built. But as she looked into his soft, dark eyes, she saw a flicker of determination. Maybe he would be all right. He had to be.

"I'm sorry we didn't get to spend more time together," he said as he headed for his suitcase. "I need to take a quick shower and change into something more appropriate." He gave her a wink and a wicked grin over his shoulder as he added softly, "Would you care to join me?"

Startled by the brazen invitation, she blinked and laughed breathlessly. Surely he wasn't really serious. He was just doing this to make their pretense believable for the benefit of the tie-tack eavesdroppers. "I think I'd better get to the task force office. They'll

238

be screaming for donuts and coffee."

He chuckled. "Your loss."

Smiling, she walked up to him and handed over the insulated carrier. He stuffed it gently in his carryon. She touched his arm. "You'll be all right?"

He nodded then impulsively ducked down and kissed her lightly on the lips. "Thanks, Shanna. For everything."

Feeling her cheeks heat, she lowered her gaze and nodded. "I better go so you can get ready. I'll see you later."

She turned and left his room, realizing it was a good thing he was leaving today. She didn't need any more complications in her life. It was messed up enough the way it was, with Aiden nursing his jealousy and anticipating charges from the Enclave Council. She sighed and strolled to the elevator, hoping things would eventually work out — for her and Aiden, and for Peter and his wife.

CHAPTER 20

Shanna slid more files into a box on the desk. She'd packed two others in the last half hour, after Tall Woman Team Leader marched in and disbanded the task force, dismissing everybody except FBI Agents Reissenor and Norris. Shanna stayed behind only because Agent Norris spoke up and said they could use her help. It was a good thing Chuck liked her, otherwise she'd have been booted out without so much as a thank-you. She wanted to stick around as long as possible to make sure Peter would be all right.

She surreptitiously watched Skinny-Ass Stepford Scientist march over to the desk where Agent Norris sat with his arms crossed and his butt perched on the edge. "You were instructed to help pack the files, Agent Norris," she said.

By this time Shanna knew Deadeye FBI-Ass-Kicking Boss Lady's real name was Roberta Kramer, with a string of fancy letters behind it, including Ph.D. and the like. But Shanna still enjoyed secretly assigning the woman an ever-changing array of goofy-sounding titles like Irate Pencil-Pushing Doctor Bitch. It made her seem less scary somehow.

Not moving from his perch, Norris glared up at her with his mean little teddy-bear button eyes. "I think I've already helped you spooks enough by collecting all this crap together in one nice, convenient place, so you can waltz in and steal it out from under us."

"Norris!" Agent Reissenor called from across the room, scowling at him as she stopped in the middle of shoving some files into a box. She swiped the back of her hand across her forehead, where her normally pristine blonde hair now strung down in stray wisps. "The AD said we were supposed to cooperate fully. Grab a box and start packing like everyone else."

"Sure thing. Right after I go get a pedicure." He lunged up from the desk and swung his arms out in a wide back-and-forth motion, looking like he was trying to accidentally on purpose smack Surprised Scientist Spook Supervisor in the gut. She backed away and glared at him as he strolled to the door. He stopped and turned, eyeing Shanna. "Come on, Cupcake. You could use a pedicure too."

Shanna gazed around the office and found only Agent Reissenor and Evil-Eyed Laboratory Rat Killer Kramer looking at her. Everybody else from the science team continued to pack as if nothing fazed them. Involuntarily her eyes darted to Peter across the room, who, like everyone else, had been busy stuffing boxes as soon as Dr. Kramer announced the science team was taking all documentation. Not copying it — *taking* it. That's what had Norris pissed off. They had no damned right to take crime documentation he'd helped collect and construct, and he had no reservations whatsoever when he told them so.

Peter shot Shanna a furtive smile. She smiled back at him, then laid her stack of files down beside the partially packed box. "I think I will check out that pedicure, Chuck. Is there a two-for-one special?"

"Going on right now. Big sale. The more the merrier." He gave her a thumbs-up and held the door for her.

Once they stepped into the main corridor lined with windows facing the parking lot outside, Norris growled, "This whole shitty deal really burns my ass. When I called the AD, he just said let them do whatever they want." Shanna had to trot to keep up as he marched toward the outer exit. His short, piston-like legs could cover a lot of ground surprisingly fast. "They're our goddamned files," he groused, "and those spooks are just walking off with them!"

"Well, what were you going to do, except haul all that paperwork back with you and stow it away in some basement storage room to wait for shredding and incineration?"

He stopped to hold the outer glass door open for her, and she stepped outside. "The FBI doesn't destroy case files, Cupcake," he announced, following her and letting the door close on its own behind him. "We keep them for decades. Eventually it'll all get saved electronically, and the papers will be dumped, but destroying evidence of what was done — that's strictly a spook routine."

Standing on the sidewalk under the building overhang, he continued grousing. "And I'm still pissed as hell. Those assholes come breezing in here and take over, then up and disband the task force and tell everybody to go home, like everything's over with, game canceled. How the hell do they know it's over with? That bloodsucking monster could still be out there, planning his next kill!"

Shanna shrugged. "Now that they've got what they came for, everything *is* over with, isn't it?" She eyed him, careful not to say too much and give away what she really knew. "And all that blood..."

"Yeah," Norris said with a huff. "It was his blood, all right. At least that's what our preliminary test showed. They took the only sample we had." He pulled a pack of cigarettes from his inner jacket pocket.

"When did you start up smoking again? I thought you said you quit."

"For the fourth time this year." He flicked a cheap turquoise plastic lighter and sucked on the cancer stick till the end glowed orange. Blowing out a plume of smoke, he said, "So, Cupcake, did you and Pretty-Boy have a good time last night?"

Shanna shot him a surprised glare.

"Oh, come on," he said, laughing as he held his cigarette down at his side. "I'm not the only one who thinks there's something going on with you two. Burkhart's a cutie-pie with tons of emotional baggage and a manly 'just shaved but still got a five o'clock shadow' look. Women eat that shit up. Hell, I'm not a woman, and *I'm* in love with the guy."

Shanna snorted and giggled. "You go both ways, Chuck?"

"Nah. Just making conversation." He grinned and took another puff on his cigarette as he looked her over. "You're an absolute doll, Cupcake. Somehow I knew you and Burkhart would get together for a little belly-bumping."

She scowled at his unglamorous euphemism and crossed her arms with a huff. "He's married. And we didn't *bump bellies*."

"Okay, doggie-style. Whatever."

She took a step back as she uncrossed her arms and gawked at him.

"Don't give me that innocent look, Cupcake. From what I hear, his wife's in a loony bin, and she ain't coming out anytime soon. And then there's your mythical big, bad boyfriend I have yet to see, who's supposed to come and kick my ass for admiring yours. But I'm starting to think he's just a figment of my guilty imagination, especially after Burkhart's tits-of-steel boss grumbled something about you and him gone missing yesterday afternoon and not showing up till early this morn—"

"I just took him out for a frigging hamburger!"

Norris took another draw on his cigarette, letting smoke stream out his nostrils as he said, "Uh-huh. Sure, Cupcake. Just how big was that hamburger? And how many hours does it take to eat a hamburger in your time zone? Me thinks the lady doth protest too much. And judging by the bright pink color of your cheeks, I'd say you and him had a *real* good time eating hamburgers last night."

Shanna rolled her eyes and looked away. Norris had it right except for one tiny detail — she'd spent last night with Aiden, not Peter.

"Since Burkhart's leaving today with the rest of the spook squad," Norris said, "does that mean I have a shot now?"

She looked at him and laughed out loud.

"Ouch, Cupcake!" He put a hand to his chest. "You could've let me down easier than that."

She laughed again and shook her head, then turned toward the building door. "What a charmer you are, Chuck. So classy and smooth. Really smooth."

"Hey, so I'm a little out of practice. What do you expect from a washed-up, has-been, karate action hero? You can't blame a guy for trying."

* * * * *

Shanna stood outside the building with Agents Reissenor and Norris, watching the Virginia team — and Peter — load up the last of the file boxes.

The whole time she'd been busy doing the spooks' dirty work of stealing files, she'd tried to catch Peter's attention and lead him outside so they could say goodbye properly. But with Whip-Cracking Kramer on the job, they had no time to exchange more than an occasional furtive glance.

Now, as she watched him preparing to actually leave, she knew this was her only chance to tell him goodbye one last time, but she didn't know how to approach the team without drawing attention to herself and Peter. Then she reminded herself, maybe that's just what she needed to do. Norris already believed they'd spent the night together, so why shouldn't she confirm his hypothesis and give the rest of the science team something to be jealous about?

She walked over to Peter just as he was about to get in the van with everyone else. He saw her and stepped away from the door. Walking over to meet her, he took her hands in his and squeezed them gently as he smiled. "Too bad we didn't get to—"

She widened her eyes in warning and lunged up to plant a swift kiss on his mouth to keep him from blurting some inadvertent clue that would destroy their illusion of intimacy. He blinked his eyes in surprise that turned to something she suspected was longing. She disengaged her hands from his and touched her palm to his chest, over his eavesdropping tie tack. "Good luck, Peter. I hope something works out for you and your wife very soon."

He nodded and swallowed hard, obviously reminding himself he had another life full of unpleasant responsibility, the worst of which was his self-imposed burden of healing his wife and unborn child. "Maybe ... maybe someday you can meet her. And the baby."

She managed a weak smile, trying to hold back sudden tears. "I'd like that."

She backed away from him, knowing it was useless to exchange phone numbers or mailing addresses. The way things were going for both of them, it was iffy whether they'd be in the same place a year from now. "See you," she said, waving and quickly turning to walk away. She reached the building and turned around just in time to see him wave as he climbed into the van. The door shut, and a minute later the van drove away, taking Peter away with it. She watched until it rounded the corner out of sight. Then she went back inside the building, leaving Reissenor and Norris staring after her.

Rushing into the ransacked task force office, she looked around in dismay at all the file drawers and desk drawers hanging open, empty boxes scattered about the walls and floor, and the blank bulletin board covering the back wall. The science team had confiscated everything but furniture and electronic communications equipment supplied by the city. They even took the map and every single pushpin. But worst of all, they took Peter. She slumped down on the edge of a desk. Would he be all right? She'd probably never know.

The door to the office opened, and Agents Reissenor and Norris walked in. "We're heading out now," Victoria said, trying to smooth her slightly frazzled hair back into place. "We've got a plane to catch."

"And reports to do, dumb-ass bosses to shoot, yada-yada-yada," Norris chimed in.

Shanna stood up slowly from the desk and managed a smile for them. "I guess you want me to check in with the city and take care of the keys and all the rest of the left-behind stuff."

"Like I said, Cupcake, you're a doll." Norris came over and put an arm around her shoulders, giving her a big teddy-bear hug. "And I'll check up on Pretty-Boy for you. Give you a little status report."

He let go of her, but not before she planted a quick kiss on his creviced cheek. "Wow," he said, stepping back in feigned surprise. "If only I wasn't leaving..."

She chuckled and pushed him away. "Get out of here, you crusty old karate has-been."

She went to Agent Reissenor and shook her hand. "I enjoyed working with you." Reissenor grinned then looked over at her partner. "I think Chuck had more fun than either of us."

"Oh, now, I wouldn't say that," he said, winking at Shanna as he walked past her. "Come on, Vic. Let's ditch this town. We got other criminals to catch, other police departments to lord it over."

They both turned and waved as they walked out the door. Shanna collapsed back against the edge of the desk with a deflated sigh, looking around the abandoned office. She was the last one to leave the party, and she was stuck cleaning up the mess.

* * * * *

While she finished tying up the details of decommissioning the task force office, Shanna managed to call Aiden on her cell phone. After a lengthy and somewhat heated conversation, she agreed to his demand to go ask for time off work.

At three-fifteen she walked out of the city office building, having dropped off the office keys everyone on the task force had left behind. She wondered why Aiden was so adamant about her going with him to Connecticut, to his Enclave. Supposedly they'd called a multi-Enclave Council meeting specifically to deal with his case. Was he afraid that, while he was gone, something would happen to her? Or did he simply want her moral support when he faced the wrath of the Council? He never would say specifically what his reasons were, but she couldn't blame him for wanting her to go along. She wanted to go along. It was just that she had her job to think about.

She didn't have vacation coming yet, so she'd have to ask for administrative time off. She doubted Grainger would give it to her, if he knew she wanted it badly enough. Aiden had told her to go in and say the Bloodsucker case had shaken her, and she needed personal time to adjust. She didn't want to do that and admit she was too emotionally weak to handle the rigors of her job. That was a death sentence to her career as a policewoman. But Aiden couldn't really see clear to understand that. He just wanted her to come up with some way to be relieved of duty so she could go with him. What he didn't consider was that this crappy, low-paying job of hers might be the only income they'd have, if they were allowed to stay together after the Council's ruling. He'd be dependent on her, and she'd have to make sure she had a job waiting when she came back with ... or without him.

She sighed miserably as she drove to the Sheriff's Department office the next street over. She'd called ahead to make sure Grainger was there. She was surprised he wasn't out on a personal day, shooting fish in a barrel or whatever good-ol'-boy bullshit he did to entertain himself. She curtailed that thought, remembering that she was going in to ask him for a favor. It wouldn't do to march in with her usual 'yeah, you're my boss but you're an asshole' attitude.

When she parked her car in the underground garage and went up to Grainger's office, it was a little after three-thirty, close to his quitting time. The young, perky little officer acting as his assistant looked up and smiled faintly, saying, "He'll be with you in a moment, deputy. Have a seat."

He kept her waiting fifteen minutes. She didn't know whether the uniformed brunette at the desk was a ding-a-ling and just forgot to buzz him, or whether he was deliberately piddling around with junk on his desk just to waste her time. He sure wasn't making any important phone calls. Finally Shanna cleared her throat. "He knows I'm here, doesn't he?"

The young brunette batted her pretty brown eyes and looked through the glass plate windows of his office enclosure. The blinds were open. "Um, yes, I'm sure he does."

Shanna glanced over her shoulder again for the hundredth time and caught him looking straight at her. He started to look away, but she shot to her feet. After a second, he got up and motioned her in. With a huff she grabbed the doorknob and jerked his door open. Closing it behind her, she stood at ease with her hands behind her back. He reseated himself and looked down at his desktop again. She leaned aside slightly to glance around a line of code books decorating the edge of his desk and saw a damned plastic miniature golf course sitting in front of him. He was in the middle of making a put with a toothpick-sized golf club.

She rolled her eyes, then cleared her throat. He missed the put. Looking up in disgust, he opened a side drawer and shoved the toy inside, slamming the drawer shut. He clasped his fat hands together on his now empty desktop and smiled. His puffy eyes turned to piggish slits as his great jowls lifted in the act of pretended friendliness. "So, what can I do for you, Deputy Preston?"

"The task force has been disbanded, sir."

"Yes, Becker told me this morning. Damned shame. They never did figure out who destroyed the evidence in the warehouse, did they?"

"No."

"But they're pretty sure the Bloodsucker's dead."

She cleared her throat again. *She* was sure. "Yes, sir. Even without a body, they're fairly certain it's safe to assume he died."

"So ... I guess you're ready to return to the regular duty roster."

"Well, sir, that's what I came to talk to you about. The thing is..."

Gazing at her body in an openly lustful manner, when he realized she'd stopped talking, he looked up at her face and smiled. "What is it, Preston? Spit it out."

She wanted to spit, all right — in his fat, ugly face. But maybe she'd get fired. And if she filed a sexual harassment claim, she'd probably get fired for that too — but officially, for other reasons, of course. She frowned and sucked up a breath to start again. "The thing is, sir, I'd ... I need to take some time off. I know I'm not eligible to take leave yet, but—"

"How much time do you want?" he asked, leaning back and rubbing his big belly.

She glanced at his hands stroking the mountain of flesh under his tan shirt the size of a circus tent. She didn't know they made shirts that big. The movement of his hands caught her attention ... stroking, stroking, gradually moving lower. She flashed her eyes back to his face. "Two weeks. Maybe three."

"You want to tell me what the problem is, Preston?" He leaned forward, and his chair creaked under his weight as he settled his arms back on his desktop.

"Uh ... family situation, sir."

"Hmm." He picked up a glass paperweight with a silhouette of a golfer inside. He mentioned once his wife had given it to him.

His wife. She'd never seen the woman, and couldn't imagine anyone being married to the lascivious creep sitting before her. She wondered how many women under his supervision he'd propositioned — successfully, assuming they wanted to keep their jobs. But why would they want to keep their jobs after being touched by him? She'd heard the rumors, but so far she'd escaped with just his lecherous staring and leering grins. She didn't want to have to be in a position to bargain with him.

"You want leave without pay then?" he said, finally looking up from the paperweight engraved with some bullshit saying. Maybe it was a religious saying. She didn't know, and didn't care. But she'd bet it was religious. Grainger's wife had to be a sexual teetotaler to live with the likes of him.

"Preston?"

She blinked, realizing she'd zoned out, going long on her evil suppositions about her lecherous boss. "Uh, yeah. That's fine, sir. If that's what I have to do. I just need the time off."

"And when do you want it?"

She blinked again as she looked at his leering grin full of short, dull teeth. She wondered if he was thinking of something else besides a leave of absence when he said that. "As soon as possible."

He leaned back again and rubbed his giant stomach that strained the buttons of his shirt. "Fine, whatever you need, Preston. See Mandy at the desk. She'll take care of the paperwork for you."

Shanna swallowed hard. "Thank you, sir."

"My pleasure, Preston." He looked her up and down with his puffy hooded eyes as he rubbed his belly lower and lower.

She turned and swung the door open before he could say or do anything else to make her want to rush home and take a shower. No, two showers. One to wash away the grime of being in his presence, and another to wash away the memory of being in his presence.

* * * * *

When Aiden heard the car pull up in the drive, he rose from the couch and handed Jewel Ann to Marta. He didn't recognize the sound of the engine but knew it was Shanna driving. She'd just turned in her patrol car and had a coworker drive her back home, after securing Sheriff Grainger's permission for time off.

Aiden opened the front door and watched her circle around her small gold Honda. Her hair glowed like fire in the late afternoon light. He walked out and met her at the point where the sidewalk joined the edge of the concrete drive.

She gave him a wan smile. He circled an arm around her shoulders and escorted her to the house. "Are you all right?" he murmured, knowing she was not. She seemed depressed, as if she'd just lost her best friend. He knew it was a combination of temporarily leaving her job and worrying about what the immediate future held. But he also wondered how much of her stress was due to Peter Burkhart walking out of her life forever. She had grown quite fond of him very quickly, and that set his nerves on edge.

He hugged her gently for reassurance, determined not to let his continual surges of jealousy ruin whatever time they had left to spend together. "Marta has dinner ready. We've been waiting on you."

"I'm sorry," she said with a heavy sigh. "Everything took longer than I thought it would."

"That's to be expected," he said, hugging her again as they

reached the front door. "Everything always seems to take longer than it should. Anyway, it's not that late, and I wanted to wait until you got here to have dinner."

She nodded her head without looking up. He let go of her so she could step through the doorway ahead of him. In the foyer, he shut the door and turned to her. She glanced at everyone sitting in the great room, then flicked him quick smile. "I need to change."

"Of course. Would you like me to accompany you?"

She shook her head. "That's okay. I'll just be a minute."

He smiled and gave her a soft kiss on the lips. "As you wish. Come down when you're ready, and we'll dine."

She nodded wearily and trudged up the steps, not giving him a second look. He frowned as he watched her go. Had all this become too much for her to handle?

"Give her time to adjust," Marta said, walking up behind him as he stood puzzled in the foyer. "She'll come to terms with everything soon enough. She just needs to get her bearings. There have been many changes in her life in the last several days."

"And more to come," Aiden added with dark foreboding. He turned from Marta and walked down the hall straight to the kitchen, passing Talya and Noel who held the baby, bouncing and cooing at her to keep her entertained.

Stepping out on the patio, Aiden shunned the warm light, heading for a shaded corner protected by the side of the house. He sat down in a wrought-iron lawn chair and leaned back, clasping his hands over his stomach. What was he to do with Shanna? Could Marta be right, that she just needed some time to herself to come to terms with all the changes in her life? Or was it something else? *Someone* else? He burned to scour her mind and find out, but he'd promised himself he wouldn't intrude on her privacy more than their bond dictated, until she was ready and willing to share fully with him. Sighing, he closed his eyes and tried to ease his mind of those plaguing worries.

CHAPTER 21

With the driver's seat pushed as far back as it would go, Aiden leaned forward and squinted through the smeary windshield. "We should stop and replace these wipers before we get on the interstate. These are only making things worse, and I don't want to drive at night without being able to see where I'm going."

Shanna looked at him and then frowned back at Jewel Ann, whining fitfully in her car seat. Clearly the baby wanted someone to hold her, but that wasn't safe or legal while they rode in the car. "Fine," Shanna snapped. "Whatever you think is best."

Aiden raised his brows as she turned around in the passenger seat and crossed her arms, staring straight ahead. She knew there was no reason to object to his suggestion — after all, it was a valid safety issue. But she felt an unreasoning urge to grouse, simply because she'd been forced in the last week to do everything his way. Her whole life had changed because of him. The more she thought about it, the more she resented it, even though some of the changes had given her existence new depth and meaning. She knew she shouldn't be angry, but she couldn't help it.

"We have plenty of time to make it to my home in Hartford," he said, "and get settled in before the Council meets. There's no need to worry."

She waved a hand in the air, feeling a sudden urge to burst into tears. "I'm sorry," she said. "I don't know what's wrong with me!"

He placed a warm palm on her denim-covered thigh and sighed. Pulling her car into an auto-parts store, he shut off the engine and leaned to watch in the side mirror as Noel and Marta came lumbering up in the small moving truck. Shanna turned around to see Noel pulling over to one side in an attempt to give himself maneuvering room to get out of the parking lot.

Undoing her seatbelt, Shanna grabbed her wallet and reached for the door latch. "I'll go in and get the wipers. Maybe I can find someone to put them on for me."

Aiden gave her a bland smile. She shut the door and cowered under the pelting raindrops as she rushed into the parts store. As she glanced around at the maze of aisles, looking for the wiper section, she wondered what the hell was wrong with her. Why couldn't she just get her act together and behave? She was worse than Jewel Ann, whining about nothing and being a pain.

At least she could be thankful for one small favor. She wouldn't have to put up with Talya's dirty looks. The Protector had gone on ahead, leaving the day before in the rental she'd driven down here.

It was a shame they had too much stuff, too many people, and couldn't just zip wherever they needed to go, as Aiden and Talya did when they were working. But Talya with her luggage, Aiden with his mysterious paraphernalia in the basement, and Marta with her shelves of herbs and weeds for those foul-tasting tonics she brewed all required vehicles. Why none of them could fly on a plane, Shanna understood perfectly. Airport security cameras would take their pictures and put them on the government's suspicion radar. That couldn't be good in any scenario. But still, she wished they would get this damned trip over with.

She located the store's windshield wiper booklet and looked up her car model to find the right replacement wipers. Glancing around, she saw a young, acne-ridden guy wearing a red polo shirt with a nametag sporting the store's logo, pinned to his breast pocket. She smiled fetchingly at him, and he immediately came over to help her. At least this one little detail she'd be able to pass off for someone else to take care of.

* * * * *

The trip turned out to be every bit the nightmare Shanna figured it would be. They drove through the night and into the next morning while it rained nonstop the whole way. They took short breaks to feed and tend to Jewel Ann, and once tried to nap at a rest stop, but no one could sleep with the interstate noise and the diesel racket of refrigeration trucks constantly running while parked, combined with Jewel Ann's intermittent squalling. The only time the baby stayed quiet and fell asleep was when the car was moving. So, someone had to stay awake and drive. Shanna traded off with Aiden a couple of times, and each of them tried to nap in the passenger seat while the other drove, but that didn't provide the deep sleep Shanna craved. She suspected Marta and Noel had no better luck, despite not having the baby with them.

And now Shanna was still awake at noon, after having virtually no sleep, shuffling around in a huge, unfamiliar house that felt like nobody had lived in it for a long time. In the buzz of sleep deprivation, she wondered what in the hell she was doing here. It was as if someone had kidnapped her and set her down in another life she neither recognized nor wanted as her own.

"This is the formal living room," Aiden announced, leading her from the huge foyer facing a waterfall of a staircase, into a large arched doorway on the right. She gazed in deadened awe at the room resplendent with antique furniture, heavy painted moldings, high arched windows, and a two-story ceiling sectioned off with molding, each panel featuring murals of birds flying around cherubs perched in clouds. The room looked like the salon of a chateau she'd expect to find in Europe. It was too overdone for her taste, and she couldn't imagine Aiden preferring it. Of course, maybe he didn't really like it. Maybe it was just something he'd been stuck with, because it was available when he'd needed a home base.

Earlier, when he'd mentioned *his* home, Shanna didn't realize he meant it was just his temporary residence when he wasn't away on assignment. He really didn't have a home, she learned after he explained how the Protectorate handled things. It was sadly similar to the rules of the Roman Catholic Church. All property belonging to an individual entering into the service of the church had to be donated to the church, so the cumulative wealth could be maintained and distributed as needed. Of course the Protectorate, run by the Enclave Elders, decided exclusively what was needed. Therefore Aiden owned nothing, but had free use of whatever might be put at his disposal in the form of income or tangible assets.

That meant all these expensive antiques sitting around looking pretty had come from who knows where, to decorate this house he occupied intermittently like a hotel. He couldn't sell or give away anything, because none of it was his. Essentially, he was screwed if the Enclave kicked him out on his ass.

She guessed that policy prevented a lot of Protectors from defecting. No wonder Cameron Ryben didn't want any part of the deal when he'd been asked to make the commitment. No sex, no wealth, only constant training to kill those who went too far. Did the Protectorate also target those who tried to leave the Enclave's influence, or that were political adversaries? She looked at Aiden, wondering. She couldn't imagine he'd kill someone who didn't need to die to protect the safety of others. Of course, if the Enclave perceived someone as a liability out to expose the Shanrak people, they might decide that person, although not a killer, would present just as much danger as a rogue.

She sighed and gave the formal living room a parting glance. "Could we maybe save the tour for later? I'm exhausted."

"Of course," Aiden said, stroking her cheek with his free hand as he held Jewel Ann in his other arm. He kissed Shanna softly and led her upstairs, leaving Marta and Noel below to tend to everything else.

* * * * *

As Aiden settled Jewel Ann in the crib Noel had hastily reconstructed, he tickled her chin softly and smiled to reassure her. Placing a light blanket over her, he whispered, "Sweet dreams, my princess. I'll see you soon." She waved her arms erratically at him, but he patted her belly rather than picking her up again as he knew she wanted. "Sleep, my child." In response to the special tone of gentle command coloring his words, Jewel Ann stilled, and her eyes grew heavy. He watched her float gently to sleep and left the room.

Returning to his own room, now occupied by Shanna, he stepped inside and closed the door. She lay fast asleep in the ornate, king-size bed with an overhead canopy supporting fringed drapery that could be pulled around to completely enclose the bed in privacy. None of that made any difference to Shanna as she lay on her side, breathing heavily in slumber.

He smiled, undressed quickly, and joined her in the bed. He

wasn't nearly as tired as she obviously was, being used to keeping odd hours and going for days without sleep. He didn't have the same biological rhythms as humans, but still his body reminded him of those rhythms, and he did need rest occasionally. And this would be as good an opportunity as any, since he knew he would not be making love with Shanna for several hours.

He frowned as he settled into the plush bedding, wondering when he and Shanna would join again. He missed the bliss of their bodies fused in passion. The very thought of it made him harden, and he sighed with regret. When she was ready, he would approach her. He hoped that happened before the Council meeting tomorrow night. He wanted to join with her again and strengthen their bond before they faced the wrath of the Council Elders. He couldn't have her shaken by them and possibly betray thoughts of what they'd both done to help Peter Burkhart's research. If the Elders discovered that breach of trust, they'd surely have him executed for treason against his own people.

That thought gave him pause, and he stared at Shanna's tee-shirt-clad back for a long time before finally drifting off to sleep.

* * * * *

When Shanna awoke, she faced unfamiliar surroundings. This wasn't her apartment. She sat up with a start and looked around at the semi-dark room and its ornate furnishings. Slowly she remembered this was the place Aiden called home. This was his bedroom — elaborate, overwhelming. She immediately wanted to redecorate. Glancing at the empty bed, she wondered where he was.

She looked out the window, not sure whether it was dawn or dusk until she noticed the reddened sky seeming to grow lighter right before her eyes. Dawn, she realized, recalling she'd tumbled into bed around noon. Had she slept through the afternoon, and on through the entire night? She glanced around and then rose from the empty bed, disgusted at sleeping so long. But she'd obviously needed the rest. The last several days had been filled with harrowing experiences and revelations that ensured her life would never be as it had been one short week before.

Shuffling around, she saw her packed bags stacked neatly

against the far wall, near a carved dresser of dark veneers and gilt edging. The oval mirror startled her with her reflection — disheveled hair, light-blue A-line tee shirt, and bikini panties. She looked like one of those drugged out skinny broads modeling underwear on those stupid TV commercials that men drooled over. Running her hands through her stringy hair, she decided to shower.

The sculpted marble sink bowl and gilded fixtures accentuated the French palatial feel of the rest of the house, but did nothing for Shanna's decorating sensibility. She turned and rummaged in her bags for her toothbrush and other toiletries. Once she got over the ornate overboard décor, she rushed her shower and hurried to dress. Anxious to find Aiden, she skipped down the wide curving stairway and reached the marble foyer resplendent with arching palms on either side of the double front doors. Weak light shone through the beveled leaded glass doors. She stopped and listened for some clue as to Aiden's location.

Voices drifted faintly from the rear of the house. She hurried into the huge French country kitchen. Gleaming modern appliances sat proudly amid rich carved wood cabinets and granite countertops complementing the rough slate floor. Copper cookware dangled from a wrought-iron ceiling rack centered over the island cooking area. She saw movement in the sunroom enclosure off the end of the kitchen. Beautified with tropical plants placed strategically around the glass walls, the sunroom sported a large glass-top dining set with bamboo and wicker upholstered chairs. Marta and Noel sat at the table, watching Aiden feed Jewel Ann. The sweet domestic scene seemed totally incongruous with their situation.

Soon Aiden would face the Enclave Council and be formally charged with his transgressions against the Protectorate and the Shanrak people. Yet he sat in the dim overcast light of the sunroom, playing with a baby that wasn't his, as if everything had already been settled in his favor. How could he be so calm when he should be planning his escape? Running might be the only way he'd stay alive.

Shuddering inwardly, Shanna blinked as Aiden, Marta, and Noel all looked over at her simultaneously. She flicked Aiden a desperate glance, and Marta immediately shoved away from the table. "I'll make breakfast, now that you're up." Noel came out of his chair and took Jewel Ann from Aiden. Once they left Shanna alone with Aiden, she sat down next to him at the table.

"I trust you slept well," Aiden said, turning to face her.

She nodded her head slowly, trying to figure out what she should say or do. She felt so disconnected and confused, she couldn't seem to think straight. She reached out to him, then let her hand drop to the tabletop.

He placed his large, warm hand over hers, and instantly the comfort and solace she didn't even know she sought eased from him to her, settling her jittery feeling. She sighed with relief.

He smiled. "As soon as we have breakfast, we'll go upstairs where we will remain undisturbed so we can go over the things we must do this evening at the Council meeting."

She wanted to open her mouth and express her anxiety, but she knew that would solve nothing. He already knew she was worried, as obviously he was too. He patted her hand. "Everything will work out as it should, and we must prepare ourselves for whatever decisions are made, as they will be final. The Council makes no second guesses about its own rulings, so it would be futile for us to object or argue our case, once a decision is made."

She let out another sigh and nodded, sliding her hand away from his to put it close to her other in her lap.

"But there are some things we can — must — do to ensure the consequences of their decisions will have the smallest negative impact possible."

She cocked her brows, waiting for him to explain, but he only smiled and said, "After breakfast."

* * * * *

As soon as Aiden entered the bedroom behind Shanna, he felt his cock thicken with desire, but didn't feel his fangs lengthen. Realizing the bloodlust had already wound down, he felt a twinge of the worry Shanna had expressed days ago about their need for each other dwindling with it. He shook that thought from his head. He had no real mating experience except this upon which to base his assumptions, other than what he'd been told. The one thread of all the common knowledge and advice he'd heard regarding mating was that if the mating were true, the lust for physical bliss would remain long after the desire to share blood departed.

He led Shanna to the bed and then turned her to face him. "We should mate again to further seal our bond before we attend the Council meeting this evening."

She nodded, her eyes betraying her fear of what would result from that meeting. He stroked her face and kissed her softly for reassurance. "We must remain strong together. Mentally, emotionally, on all fronts. The Council members are all Master Shanrak and will expect to pierce our innermost thoughts and feelings to see that we speak true when it is our time to come forward in our own defense."

"But if they read our thoughts—"

"Exactly. They will discover what we have done for Peter Burkhart, and that revelation will seal our doom. We therefore cannot let any of the Council members enter our minds."

"But..." She shook her head and staggered back. "Aiden, there's no way I can withstand the probing of those people, if they're as powerful as you say."

"They are indeed very powerful, and our love bond will be put to a dire test tonight."

She shook her head again. "I won't be able to—"

"Talya could not break through our shield. We already know that." He sighed and stepped closer to take her in his arms. "You'll just have to trust me. This is our only chance."

"Maybe we'd be better off running."

"No, my love. Without resources, without help, how long do you think we could evade a team of Protectors sent to neutralize us?"

Shanna sighed miserably. "But—"

"Our love is strong. I have faith."

"But, Aiden," she said, looking up at him as she tightened her arms around him, "if we block them from probing our minds, they'll know we're trying to hide something."

"That they will, but if we stand firm, they'll have no inkling what it is." He let go of her and took her by the hands to lead her closer to the bed. "Making love will strengthen our bond."

She grimaced. "And drinking each other's blood?"

He knew exchanging blood was her least favorite aspect of their lovemaking, even though she couldn't deny it drove her orgasmic experience to a feverish pitch. She participated only because he made her do it. If left on her own, she would not initiate it. And he understood why. She had not been raised Shanrak, so it was not something she was led to believe was safe or sanitary or acceptable. But she would have to worry no more. His fangs stayed as normal teeth. He no longer desired the taste of her blood, even as his pulse quickened at the thought of taking her to him.

Pushing her tee shirt down over her shoulders, he nipped her left, then her right shoulder, then kissed each place tenderly to soothe the teasing pain. "No more blood drinking," he said softly.

She blinked in surprise, then slowly smiled. "But you still want to—"

"Oh, yes," he growled in reassurance, as he grabbed the hem of her shirt and pulled it over her head. He did the same to his, tossing it on the floor next to hers.

She giggled and pushed him, making him fall on his back on the bed. Straddling him, she kissed his face and neck and chest as he fumbled behind her, unclasping her bra. He pulled it forward on her arms, releasing her breasts as he strained to meet them with his mouth. Sucking hard on one nipple and then the other, he drew her far into his mouth until he could fit no more inside. She undulated on him, then tossed her bra from her wrists, and reached for his jeans. He whirled her over and pulled his pants down, kicking them off behind him. Working her jeans and panties down over her hips, he slid them down her legs and tugged them off, letting them drop to the floor.

He crawled between her spread thighs and lowered his throbbing cock to her slit, wet and ready to receive him. Sliding in just far enough to push the head past her lips, he pulled back as she yipped with pleasure. He pushed in again, a little further, and she thrust up to meet him. He pulled back. "Not yet, my sweet. You'll have all of me inside you in good time. Let me tease you for just a little while."

He bent down and buried his mouth on hers, working her lips softly as he darted his tongue inside, mimicking his cock stroking inside her just far enough to make her want more. With her arms wrapped around him, she pulled him down on her, flattening her breasts against his chest. "Make love to me, Aiden," she growled, pushing her hips up to meet his. "Harder, please." As his cock slid deep into her warmth, he groaned in pleasure and rotated his hips, grinding himself hard inside her. She wrapped her legs behind his back, offering her tight channel freely. He pumped faster, shoving himself in deeper each time, making her groan with each thrust.

She bit him on the arm, and he dove for her throat, nipping and sucking the soft flesh with the remembrance of his fangs digging deep to find purchase. As if by his will alone, his fangs pushed out, making his gums ache with pleasure as he sank the points into her neck. Her blood rushed into his throat, warm and thick, and he swallowed greedily. *Come for me, Shanna. Come all over me*, he ordered, invading her mind and willing her to yield her passion. He felt her fall into that momentary abyss of almost — and she lurched hard, bucking under him as he slammed into her and pressed his mouth against her neck, sucking down the quenching drug of her lifeblood. She was his, his, his alone. All his. In a blinding instant he stiffened, and then broke in shattering bliss as his body let go and shuddered to a halt.

He pulled his drenched mouth from Shanna's neck and felt her weak pulse at the tip of his tongue. Tears filled his eyes as he realized he'd pushed beyond the bloodlust and forced his body to drink of her when there was no longer a true need. Had he allowed himself too much leeway in the throes of passion? Would he turn the corner to rogue? He shook his head slowly as he lifted himself off Shanna, only gradually realizing she barely breathed.

Panic shot through him. He'd drunk too much of her to the point of satiation, and now she lay on the brink of death. Lifting his wrist to his mouth, he bit his own flesh and felt his blood spurt over his lips. Pulling Shanna's limp form up to cradle her at his chest, he forced his bleeding wrist over her mouth. *Drink, love. Swallow!*

She didn't respond until his blood dribbled out the side of her mouth. Then slowly her throat moved and her lips closed over the wound he'd made for her. As her pulse strengthened and her heartbeat grew stronger, he pulled his wrist from her and watched his blood trickle down her neck and chest. She fluttered her eyes open and looked at him in confusion.

He bowed his neck and kissed her forehead, leaving a bloody smear. He licked his lips, then swiped the back of his hand over his mouth. "I'm sorry, Shanna. I shouldn't have drunk from you. I knew the bloodlust was finished, but I didn't want to let it go. I promise I'll never—"

She touched a limp hand to his chest. "Don't … don't apologize, Aiden."

He sighed with a shudder and hugged her tight as tears rolled down his cheeks. How could he keep from becoming a monster? He loved her so much, and desired her so intensely, that he wasn't sure he could control himself in the throes of passion. Was that why he'd been selected to be a Protector — because the Elders always knew he was a Master prone to overindulgence, and complete abstinence was the only way to combat it?

He shook his head and stroked Shanna gently as she lay in his arms. He would not fail her. He would never harm her. He would not!

"Come," he said, gently easing her forward. "Let's shower and dress. I must teach you more techniques to control your mind."

Slowly Shanna moved to the edge of the bed. Before she could ask, he grabbed some tissues and handed them to her. When she got to her feet, he escorted her to the bathroom, cursing himself silently for pushing beyond the point of safe mating, hoping he hadn't done either of them any real harm.

CHAPTER 22

The torch flames illuminating the rock walls danced in the cold draft wafting through the cavern. Shanna shivered despite the jacket Aiden had advised her to wear.

Beside her, Jewel Ann whined in Marta's arms. She glanced over at Noel and Talya standing on the other side of Marta, but they didn't look her way. They seemed intent on watching the far wall of the cavern chamber.

Aiden squeezed his arm tighter around her shoulders, pulling her closer as they stood waiting for the Council to assemble. Shanna squinted in the dim light, just barely making out a theater of stone seats carved in the far wall. She guessed the rough-hewn doorways on either side served a purpose other than to cross-ventilate the chamber. Perhaps they were entrances leading from elsewhere aboveground.

Shanna glanced back at the way they'd come, down a long, winding corridor carved out of solid rock that delved deeper into the ground the further it went. She wanted to retrace her steps to the carved stone stairs leading back to the trapdoor in the church's wooden floor.

Hidden under a rug in the vestibule behind the altar, the secret entrance would never be discovered by anyone not looking for it. And who would search for it in an old country church located far down a serpentine lane shaded with overhanging tree branches? The church looked to be over a hundred years old with its wood clapboard siding painted many times over until the paint peeled over paint to reveal more paint underneath. Renamed with a modest little sign proclaiming it to be the Church of the Chosen, it stayed cozy and unharmed in its secluded rural area outside Hartford. Only those who ventured past the altar into the vestibule and below knew the true purpose of the Chosen and their secret underground meeting place.

Shanna lurched as the air stirred suddenly, almost blowing the torches out completely. By the time she regained her composure, she was surprised to see ten shadowy figures robed in black filing in through both doorways by the stone theater. She gulped and sucked in a shaky breath.

"Just stay calm," Aiden whispered, rubbing her upper arm as he continued to hug her shoulders. "Focus like I taught you."

Focus? On what? Everything was dark and smelled of the cool dampness of the underworld, steeped in the scent of the torches' burning oil. She imagined them all trapped in a catacomb, about to be descended upon by these cloaked specters of evil.

The figures stood in position approximately twenty feet away from them, lined up in front of the theater seating as if ready to draw guns and have a shoot-out. Unfortunately Aiden wouldn't let Shanna bring her gun because weapons were not allowed in the Council chambers. She felt it was time to change that rule.

An unreasoning fear gripped her as she eyed those creatures standing in silence, completely concealed in heavy black fabric. She worried they'd rush and attack. It didn't help to remind herself Aiden was the same kind of creature they were. She looked up and caught him frowning at her. He'd overheard that thought, obviously.

She followed Aiden's gaze as he looked back at the Council. One member moved forward and stopped at the stone dais at the front of the theater. When he pulled his hood back, the others of the Council did the same. The man at the dais stood tall with short, straight, white hair that sprang to attention all about his head. His long, narrow face sported an aristocratic glower. The distance and dim lighting made it difficult for Shanna to glean any other identifying details about him. He lifted a round rock with a flat bottom and hammered it on the dais three times, then said, "The Northeast Regional Enclave Council is now called to order."

The nine people behind him chanted in unison, "Here, here."

Shanna strained to see them all. Including the gent standing at the stone podium, she made out seven men and three women. She got a gut feeling they were all very old, although they didn't really look aged. She guessed that's why they were called *Elders*.

"Aiden Marschant, Protector of the Central Connecticut Enclave," the spike-haired Elder at the podium announced, "you have been charged with the following acts of betrayal against your sacred profession, constituting treason against the Enclave and all Shanrak peoples. The charges against you will be enumerated, and you will be asked how you plead to each — innocent or guilty."

Shanna lifted her brows and looked up at Aiden, who remained perfectly still. The Council sure didn't waste time getting down to business.

The Elder at the podium slammed his rock gavel down. Its hollow clack echoed through the chamber. "First charge. As a Protector you have sworn never to surrender to the bloodlust and take a mate, yet have committed that very act. How do you plead?"

Aiden swallowed carefully then said in a clear voice, "Guilty."

Shanna glared at Aiden in alarm, but he didn't bother to look down at her as the dude at the podium smacked his stone gavel again. "Second charge. You have mated with and turned a human, an act with grave repercussions, including possibly causing death or creating a rogue, and betraying the secrecy of the Shanrak peoples. How do you plead?"

This time Aiden glanced down briefly at Shanna, giving her a quick reassuring smile before looking ahead at his accusers. "Guilty."

The stone gavel hit the dais once again. "Third charge. You have abducted a human child, an act that could bring harm to the Enclave Protectorate's ability to preserve the secrecy of the Shanrak peoples. How do you plead?"

Aiden glanced over at Jewel Ann clutched in Marta's arms. The baby, gnawing on her fist in her mouth, eyed him with uncertainty. He sighed and turned back to face his accusers. "Guilty as charged."

The man in the black robe smacked his rock on the stone podium yet another time. "You have admitted guilt in every charge brought against you. Do you have any remarks to make in your own defense before this Council pronounces judgment in the matter?"

Shanna watched in stunned silence as Aiden shook his head slowly. His lovely dark auburn hair shimmered in the dim light of the torches, fluttering around his face and shoulders as if the breeze in the cavern caressed his tresses.

"Very well. As Council Chair, I—"

"Wait!" Shanna squawked, stepping forward.

264

Aiden grabbed her roughly by the arm and pulled her back. "Don't!"

"You dare bring this abomination into our sacred Council chamber," the man at the podium yelled, "and allow her to disrupt these proceedings?"

"I am not a frigging abomination!" Shanna shouted, jerking free of Aiden's grasp as she stomped forward. "I am an individual with as much right to—"

"Silence!" the Elder boomed.

Shanna closed her mouth as Aiden moved beside her and whispered, "There is nothing you can do for me, Shanna, except make things worse. Please, say no more."

"How could things get any worse?" she said, looking up at him. His face blurred as tears filled her eyes. She swiped the back of her hand over her cheeks and glared at the Council. She wasn't going to back down and let this cloaked bunch of hoity-toity Shanrak snobs have the satisfaction of railroading her and Aiden without first listening to what she had to say. "I want to speak in Aiden's defense."

The man at the podium glared at her like she was a snake that had slithered uninvited into his garden party. She refused to flinch. He finally turned aside and conversed in a low tone with the rest of the Council members behind him. After a moment a very tall black woman with short, almost shaved black hair, stepped forward and said, "Allow me the opportunity to question this human."

The Council Chair nodded and stepped away from the dais as the tall black woman glided forward to take his place. "I am Obsidia Rhea, Elder from the New York City Enclave. How are you addressed, human?"

Shanna cleared her throat. "Shanna Preston."

"Step closer, Shanna Preston," the tall woman urged with the regal air of an evil enchanted queen. "I will know your thoughts as you speak, so that I may judge the trustworthiness of your words."

Shanna glanced back in alarm when Aiden grabbed her arm and pulled hard. "She will not submit to mind-probing."

"She *will not*?" Obsidia Rhea objected imperiously. "She has no power to refuse me."

"But *I* have," Aiden growled. He stepped forward, shielding Shanna from the Elders now looking her over with new interest.

"You dare challenge me? I am an Enclave Elder and—"

"I know what you are," Aiden said, seeming to grow several inches taller as he straightened to face his accusers. "And I know what you're all trying to do. You can make whatever example you want to of me, but you will not harm Shanna. I accept full blame and punishment for her involvement in this matter, but I will not cower in fear while you flay her before me. Your summons demanded her presence, but she is here only by my grace."

"How dare you?" Obsidia Rhea growled, slinking down from the raised stone podium platform like a panther on the prowl. "With one flick of my wrist, I could torch your lovely in a pillar of flames!"

"You could try. But you wouldn't succeed."

Obsidia glared at Aiden with her black irises completely surrounded by white. Suddenly she laughed out loud, throwing her head back, showing a maw of long pearly whites complete with fully extended fangs. Shanna shuddered at the display.

Straightening, the towering black woman glared at Aiden with a prickling smile. "You fancy yourself powerful enough to defy ten of the most feared Elders of the High Council? You foolish, foolish man. Your folly will soon become apparent when we roast you alive with the mere concentration of our thoughts."

Aiden shrugged. "I am ready to face punishment, and I will not fight it. But again, I say to you — to all of you. Shanna and the child will not be harmed in any way. Once you have made your ruling on my case, she and the child will be free to go."

Obsidia snorted, then whirled away, her cloak unfurling behind her to reveal a shimmering golden gown more appropriate for a posh nightclub. Reaching the podium, she turned on Aiden. "You are in no position to make demands, Protector. The Council will rule as it sees fit, and you have no say in the matter."

Talya cleared her throat behind them and stepped forward. "Elder Rhea, may I speak on Protector Marschant's behalf?"

Shanna and Aiden both eyed Obsidia as she nodded her head. "Be heard, Protector."

Talya stood beside Aiden, on the opposite side from Shanna. She bowed low, then straightened. "Aiden Marschant's service to the Protectorate has been exemplary. His record of rogue kills is legendary among those of the Protectorate. He has served our people

266

with distinction and unwavering loyalty. Without question he is one of the most valuable citizens of the Shanrak peoples."

"Until now." Obsidia let her glittering black gaze skitter over Aiden to settle on Shanna. Shanna shuddered inwardly.

"Begging the grace of the Council," Talya interjected. She bowed quickly and then stood facing Aiden's accusers. "Many who join the Protectorate fail to complete the initial training program, due mainly to the lifestyle restrictions placed on Protectors."

"You find your position unsatisfying?" Obsidia purred, sounding like a lioness interrupted after a great feast.

"I find my life unsatisfying. And I think so did Aiden, until he met Shanna."

Shanna turned to look at Talya, who failed to return her glance as she stared steadfastly at Obsidia Rhea.

"How does your inability to find a private balance in your life affect these proceedings? We have no interest in hearing of your personal problems, Protector Zhakovika."

"You *should* be interested, Elder Rhea. Because my personal dissatisfaction is mirrored in the life of nearly every other Protector. Only those with the rare gift of needing no one can find the Protector lifestyle sufficient long-term. And they are few, judging by the great number of Protectors who are retired before their time."

Obsidia cocked her shorn head, her elongated bony face looking almost alien as the soft torch light glistened across the planes of her dark face. "I assume you have a point you wish to make."

"Yes, Elder Rhea. The restriction of celibacy may have seemed a good idea when it was first required of the Protectorate, but it is an unrealistic expectation to hold men and women to for the duration of their adult lives. It goes against their very nature." Talya took a step forward as she added, "And it is common knowledge many of the Protectorate, especially trainers, do not adhere to that restriction."

Obsidia Rhea glanced over her shoulder at the other Elders behind her, then stepped down from the podium to approach Talya. She stopped just three feet from her and said in a low voice, "And why should I take your last supposition as truth?"

"It is not a supposition," Talya challenged. "I know for a fact that at least two male Protectorate trainers from my Enclave chose female trainees specifically to use in pleasuring themselves sexually.

Those trainees were later expelled from the program for failure to meet Protector expectations."

Obsidia's face betrayed no surprise as she smiled. "And what are the names of these transgressors, so that I may verify your story?"

Talya said nothing, merely stood with her hands behind her back in severe opposition. Obsidia stared her down for a moment, then turned away with casual ease, as if the confrontation meant nothing. She returned to the podium and looked down on them all. "Your inference that Protector Marschant fell victim to his own biology may be true. But it still does not excuse him from breaking the oaths he made as a Protector."

As Obsidia lifted the stone gavel in the air, about strike the podium, Talya yelled, "Wait! There's more!"

Obsidia set the stone down and lifted her hand. "Continue."

"Shanna helped Aiden and me to vanquish the rogue, Cameron Ryben. His reign of terror in the human community ranks as one of the worst in recent history. He proved to be a more clever and dangerous adversary than Aiden had first thought. The rogue planned to join with Aiden and Shanna in an unholy threesome to continue his killing spree. But Shanna was able to terminate him — after he'd already brought me down and wounded Aiden. She saved our lives and aided our people by extinguishing the rogue threat."

Obsidia nodded thoughtfully. "That goes to her credit. But perhaps she was only acting in self-defense."

"No," Talya said, shaking her head. "She is a police officer. She was trying to bring down Ryben herself before she met Aiden. And once she realized our situation, she aided us, to the exclusion of her people's efforts. She helped protect the Shanrak secret."

Obsidia nodded again. "Further to her credit. But she is still an abomination we cannot abide. She will never be fully Shanrak, or—"

"But she already is Shanrak — as close as any human can hope to become. She and Aiden have both come through the bloodlust successfully. I sensed it while I was near them. Neither of them is a danger to others. And she is gaining Shanrak attributes. The longer she and Aiden remain together, the stronger her powers will become. And the human child — Aiden removed it from danger after its mother was killed by the rogue. The babe has no competent family to care for her. Surely, considering Aiden and Shanna's service to our people, they can be allowed to live their lives in peace, to raise the human child as their own."

Obsidia scowled like a black thundercloud. "They will never be fully accepted by our people. A turned human and a failed Protector raising a human child among us. What lunacy!"

Talya sighed then spoke softly, "I sincerely hope you change your mind. But ... there is something else."

Obsidia took notice of her tone and stiffened. "Go on..."

"A secret faction of the humans' government in this region has been conducting experiments."

Obsidia's nearly invisible brows rose. "Explain."

Talya glanced at Aiden and Shanna, then took another step closer to the podium, standing only a few feet away. "Apparently they have caught onto previous rogue activities, and have retrieved enough blood and other tissue samples to become suspicious about Shanrak attributes. Enough so, I believe, to identify and capture some Shanrak for intensive lab study."

Gripping the podium with both ebony hands, Obsidia reared back. "What basis do you have for making these disturbing claims?"

Talya's gaze slid back to Shanna and Aiden again, then she faced Obsidia. "Shanna reported that a human government team came to the investigation headquarters where a collection of police representatives had gathered to pool resources in locating Cameron Ryben. The government team consisted of scientists who were especially interested in the site of Ryben's execution, which the humans became aware of by pure happenstance. The—"

"Necessitating the premature departure of the cleaning crew sent to sterilize the area."

"Yes. But Aiden and I were able to cleanse the area before anyone returned to gather further evidence. The real problem lies in the fact that this human government agency appears to already possess intimate knowledge of our people. Especially since the wife of one of the researchers was attacked by Cameron Ryben a month ago."

"You say attacked. Not killed?"

"No. She survived, and has since turned rogue."

Obsidia backed from the podium and then turned to her compatriots, who immediately began conversing among themselves. Talya turned to Aiden and Shanna, her face appearing grim in the flickering torchlight.

Obsidia returned to the podium, and Talya whirled around to face her. "You," Obsidia said, pointing to Talya, "will research the situation further and make a report to the Council by the end of the week. Do you have any firm leads? Can you locate the researcher's rogue wife?"

Talya shook her head. "I know only the location of the lab where the researcher reported he'd last seen his wife. I may be able to stay in contact with him, but I doubt I will gain easy access to his wife to eliminate her. She will certainly be kept under heavy guard, in an area I may not be able to penetrate with the usual means. But ... there's something else."

Obsidia snorted with obvious disgust. "Of course. What is it?"

"The researcher, Peter Burkhart, believes he can devise a cure to help his wife recover from her rogue state."

Obsidia turned at the gasps of disbelief coming from her fellow Elders. Whirling back around, she nearly yanked the stone podium from its perch. "Have you seen evidence of his claim?"

"No."

"You must find his research documentation and destroy it!"

"What?" Shanna squawked, charging forward. Aiden hurried behind her and grabbed her arm, trying to silence her.

"Quiet, human!" Obsidia roared. "This is not your concern!"

"It damn well *is* my concern! If turning rogue is something that can be cured with medication instead of execution—"

"There is no cure! Now be silent!" Obsidia smoothed her elongated black fingers over the front of her robe, then eyed Talya. "Do your best to accomplish what you know must be done. We cannot have the threat of human interference further jeopardize the safety of our people. If necessary, eliminate everyone."

"No!" Shanna screamed, running toward the podium. "You have no right to kill my people to protect your own!"

"Your people," Obsidia growled. "So you still think of yourself as human."

Aiden grabbed Shanna by her shoulders and physically lifted her back from Obsidia Rhea. "If you want to live," he growled, "keep your mouth shut!"

Shanna felt herself trembling with the onset of angry tears. She couldn't let them kill Peter. They had no right.

"The Council will meet regarding this disturbing development. In the meantime, Talya Zhakovika, you will monitor the situation and make daily reports."

Talya nodded and bowed in acquiescence.

"Now we must deal with the situation at hand," Elder Rhea announced. "Step forward, Aiden Marschant and Shanna Preston."

Talya stepped back, giving both Shanna and Aiden a dour look as she moved behind them. Shanna held Aiden's hand and glared blindly into the eyes of the dark Elder, Obsidia Rhea. She would not be intimidated by that ... that woman. She would not be.

"Shanna Preston, we of the Enclave Council, on behalf of all Shanrak people, wish to express our sincere gratitude for your assistance in bringing down the rogue, Cameron Ryben, and aiding two Shanrak Protectors felled in the line of duty."

Aiden squeezed Shanna's hand, and she finally managed to nod in acknowledgement of Elder Rhea's pronouncement.

"Further, in gratitude for your assistance in protecting the secret of the Shanrak people, even though this may have been in opposition to your duty as a human police officer, the Council members have voted to grant you amnesty from execution."

Shanna paled. They'd considered executing her?

"Your condition warrants constant monitoring, and because of that, the Council recommends that you stay under Shanrak care. Because you are familiar with Noel and Marta Montgomery, they will monitor your progress during your change."

Shanna gulped, looking at Aiden fearfully. What about him?

"As for you, Aiden Marschant, the Council recognizes your long years of service to the Protectorate. However, due to your failure to keep your oath of celibacy, and your further transgression of turning a human female during mating, you are hereby stripped of all Protectorate privileges. Due to the extenuating circumstances of your last assignment, the Council has voted not to execute you or to banish you, but to provide a serviceable severance package so that you may continue with the human Shanna Preston, under the watchful monitoring of Noel and Marta Montgomery."

Shanna breathed a sigh of relief and glanced at Aiden, who showed no emotion.

"The human child will remain in your care until an appropriate human family can be located to take her."

"No."

Shanna glared up at Aiden. She couldn't believe he'd just defied Obsidia Rhea after she'd made those generous pronouncements about his fate.

"You may not object. The Council has spoken."

"I won't give up the baby."

Obsidia glared down from her podium, smiling like a snake about to strike. "It is not up to you, Aiden Marschant. The decision has been made."

"I may never have children of my own. I want a family," he said, not quite pleading.

"Many Shanrak never raise a family, because of the difficulty of producing offspring. You must accept your fate as others do."

"But the child and I have bonded. I am as close to a father as she is likely to ever have."

"You press your luck and the Council's charity, Marschant."

"Please. Let Shanna and me raise the baby as her parents."

"But the child is human! She'll never fit in."

Aiden sighed, looking defeated. "Please..."

Obsidia glanced over her shoulder at the others, with whom she seemed to be communicating silently. Finally she turned and faced Aiden. "Very well. But if difficulties arise..."

"Thank you. There won't be any difficulties, I promise."

Obsidia nodded. "Go then, and live in peace, Aiden Marschant. The Shanrak peoples everywhere are indebted to you for your many years of service. We wish you luck in your new life."

* * * * *

Aiden followed close behind Shanna. She couldn't seem to get out of the cavern fast enough and nearly ran to the car, pulling him behind her as Noel and Marta silently brought up the rear. "We won!" she whispered, sounding downright giddy as she unlocked her car. "Let's get the hell out of here before they change their minds!"

Aiden stroked Shanna's back and smiled. "They made the decree. They won't go back on their word." Still, the Council's leniency surprised him. Perhaps Talya's words had been more effective than he thought.

He looked over his shoulder at Talya walking to her rental car parked at the other side of the small gravel lot in front of the church. She drove rather than waste energy transporting herself here. That feat they reserved for emergencies or situations where speed was of the essence.

Talya gave him a single nod and held his gaze. And in that instant, she let him know. Somehow she'd figured out he and Shanna had done something more than they'd confessed to the Council. Somehow she knew they'd done something forbidden that involved Peter Burkhart. How much she knew, Aiden wasn't sure. But she knew something, and yet she had said nothing of it to the Council. Even if she'd mentally tattled, he would have noticed. She'd kept their secret, thereby protecting Peter Burkhart and situating herself as a cohort in their unspoken crime.

He nodded his thanks to her. She smiled briefly, then got into her car. He knew she would protect their secret and keep Peter Burkhart safe for as long as she could — her mating gift to them.

"Are you all right, Aiden?" Shanna asked, touching his arm.

He bent and kissed her softly on the mouth. "Yes, love. I'm all right. Everything is all right."

He turned and took Jewel Ann from Marta, ignoring his vassal's curious frown. Hugging the baby, he closed his eyes and breathed in the clean powdery scent of her tiny body. He never expected to come this far. He never dared dream he could have the family he didn't know he'd wanted. And yet, here he was, the impossible within his reach.

"We'll be okay, won't we?" Shanna whispered with a tinge of worry in her voice.

He opened his eyes and smiled. "Yes. We have much work to do to get everything settled, but we'll be just fine."

"But will we be safe? That Obsidia Rhea seemed to think we'd be pariahs among your people."

"Perhaps we will, but we don't have to associate with my people. The Enclave communities in each of the major human cities are loosely formed. Some offer private schooling for the children of those who choose to stay within the Enclave's protection. Close association is recommended but not enforced, as long as individuals maintain firm control over their youngsters, ensuring they do nothing to betray their heritage to the outside world."

He reached out to stroke her alabaster cheek. "It is not mandatory that we cleave to the Enclave environment. To do so might be stifling for you and unwieldy for Jewel Ann as she gets older. We can just as easily, perhaps more easily, blend with your people and live among them without fear. Considering our circumstances, I believe that is our best choice for now."

He swept his gaze to include Marta and Noel standing arm in arm, watching him with his new family. "Don't you agree?"

Noel elevated his bushy brows as if he'd just awakened from a deep trance. "Aye, it would seem to be the best choice." He looked to his wife. "Eh, Marta?"

She nodded and strode toward Aiden. Taking the baby from him, she said, "Yes, probably so."

"But you'll still make your reports to the Enclave, no doubt," Aiden remarked in a cynical tone.

Marta jostled the baby softly in her arms. "No doubt I will. That is part of my job."

Aiden frowned and turned to find Shanna gawking in fear. He wrapped an arm around her shoulders and drew her near. "May as well get used to it. Being monitored is a part of our sentence."

Shanna let out a shaky sigh, then managed a smile. "But at least we'll be free to live as we please. Together."

"Yes, my love" Aiden hugged her tight and kissed the top of her head. "Together, always."

~About the Author~

DANA WARRYCK

Dana Warryck enjoys writing dark and emotionally charged romance fiction in various subgenres, including contemporary, fantasy, paranormal, and science-fiction. Several of her other books are currently available, including two series first installments, with second installments scheduled for release soon.

Dana lives with her husband and temperamental cat, and is busy finishing her next novel. To find out more about her books, visit her web site at...

http://www.DanaWarryck.com

Dana enjoys hearing from readers and can be reached at...

DanaWarryck@aol.com

Breinigsville, PA USA
24 September 2009
224710BV00003B/17/P

9 781935 563013